CALEB'S JOURNEY

BY

SIDNEY P. LITTLE

Caleb's Journey

Printed in the United States of America
ISBN 978-1-64133-985-8 (hc)
ISBN 978-1-64133-986-5 (sc)
ISBN 978-1-64133-987-2 (e)

This book is printed on acid-free paper.

Because of the dynamic nature of the Internet, any web addresses or links contained in this book may have changed since publication and may no longer be valid. The views expressed in this work are solely those of the author and do not necessarily reflect the views of the publisher, and the publisher hereby disclaims any responsibility for them.

2025.01.20

Blue Ink Media Solutions
1111B S Governors Ave, Lakeside Park,
STE 7582 Dover, DE 19904
United States

Blue Ink Media Solutions

TABLE OF CONTENTS

PROLOGUE

My name is Caleb; I am the son of Isaac who was the son of Samuel. I have lived a long and what you'd probably think of as an eventful life for I was born during the forty-third year of the reign of the Roman Emperor, Caesar Augustus. During the many intervening years that I have been fortunate enough to spend on this earth I have seen many things—things that no other generation has ever before been privileged to witness—for I have seen the living God incarnate in the form of man, a man called Jesus.

As I grow weary and approach the end of my years I feel it is essential to tell my story so that you too may know of this man. He was a man full of wonder and wisdom—a wisdom that reaches beyond my knowledge to explain. He performed miracles and talked of God in ways that were so different from the way the teachers of the Law advocated. He taught with authority. He spoke of love and forgiveness, and all of his actions demonstrated not a God of wrath, but one who loves His people.

Not only did Jesus perform miraculous healings, but he was also a prophet speaking of things to come. This was especially evident when he predicted the destruction of Jerusalem and of its Temple long before these proceedings ever took place. The first time he spoke of these future events occurred one day as he was teaching his disciples:

And when you see Jerusalem surrounded by armies, then you will know that the time of its destruction has arrived. Then those in Judea must flee to the hills. Let those in Jerusalem escape, and those outside the city should not enter it for shelter. For those will be days of God's vengeance, and the prophetic words of the Scriptures will be fulfilled. How terrible it will be for pregnant women and for mothers nursing their babies. For there will be great distress in the land and wrath upon this people. They will be brutally killed by the sword or sent away as captives to all the nations of the world. And Jerusalem will be conquered and trampled down by the Gentiles until the age of the Gentiles comes to an end.

This Jesus said while Jerusalem still stood. It stood as a bastion against all that is wicked, a beacon to God, surrounded by beautiful grasslands and trees. This was at a time when it was inconceivable to the Jewish mind that this city built as a dwelling place for the living God could ever be destroyed.

In a similar manner, Jesus answered a question put to him by his followers as they were leaving the Temple on another day. One of his disciples turned, looked and gestured towards the structure and said, "Teacher, look at these tremendous buildings! Look at the massive stones in the walls! They will stand for all time so that all men will come to know the greatness of Yahweh."

His reply shocked this disciple and surprised his other listeners into silence. He answered: "These magnificent buildings will be so completely demolished that not one stone will be left on top of another."

These things as you know have come to pass, but when He spoke those words it was heard by many as blasphemy. It resulted in one of the more serious charges brought against him by the Jewish leaders for they heard his prophecy as sacrilege, a slander against the Lord God, for they failed to see that he was the Messiah, the anointed one for whom they had been waiting.

During the time that he was with us, I actually saw and heard him and I even witnessed more than just a few of his miraculous works. But it wasn't until after his death, resurrection and ascension that I learned of the many other things that I am now going to tell you. I was fortunate enough to watch as he fed a multitude of people with little more than a few loaves of bread and two fish. I saw firsthand as he restored sight to a blind man, and most importantly I watched the horror and dreadful destruction of Jerusalem, which actually occurred as a fulfillment of the prophecy Jesus spoke of so many years before the event took place. However there were other miracles that I only heard about for he performed many healings that were witnessed by a multitude of others, the curing of a crippled man, the restoration of good health to a leper, the raising of his friend Lazarus from his very grave and many additional events that proved to me that he was truly the Son of God.

So, let me begin at the beginning. During this last one hundred years divisions in Jewish society have widened and deepened. The politics of Israel have become broken and divided into many highly polarized factions. The Pharisees, the Sadducees, the Essenes, the scribes, the Herodians and the Hellenists each preach a different doctrine concerning the Lord God and His law. Evil lurked in the land. There were bandits, criminals and false prophets each with the intent of throwing off the yoke of Rome and seizing power over Israel, in particular Jerusalem, and ruling the land as they saw fit, not as God had prescribed. The only thing each of these groups had in common was their hatred for the Romans. They had no love for the Living God; their intentions were not honorable for they sought only personal power and wealth. Long before this time of internal strife had come to Israel, many Jews had forsaken the God of their fathers, the God of Abraham, the God of Isaac and the God of Jacob. Fortunately though, there were those that remained faithful to the law, and they were the ones that earnestly sought the true God, the one and only God of creation. My father Isaac was a living example of that remnant, for throughout his life he loved Jehovah and the scriptures and always sought the truth of God's love for his people.

During my lifetime, this first eighty years since the birth of this man Jesus, the Romans that ruled Israel held both our Jewish law and our God in contempt. However, as long as we were obedient to their rule and paid our taxes, we were allowed to go on with a somewhat normal life.

Things began to change less than ten years after the crucifixion of Jesus. This transformation came during the reign of Emperor Cauis Julius Caesar Germanicus, whom you may know better by the name of Caligula. This mere mortal desired to see himself as a god and so he ordered his general, Petronius, to place his statue, that of Caligula, in the Temple of the Lord in Jerusalem. And he further ordered that if Petronius encountered any opposition to this command, then all combatants were to be put to death and the rest of the city carried off into permanent captivity and made slaves of the Roman Empire.

Petronius in attempting to carry out his orders encountered stiff opposition from the Jews, so much so he soon discerned that they would prefer death than to see their Temple desecrated. Petronius, impressed by the courage of the people, ceased trying to place the statue in their holy of holies and temporarily avoided a conflict. However, when Caligula heard of the actions of his general, he was so enraged that he sent orders for Petronius' immediate execution. Before these orders arrived in Jerusalem—for they had been delayed en route—Caligula, the man who thought himself a god, was assassinated and thus Petronius was spared his life, as was the Temple spared from the desecration.

Following the death of the emperor the nation of Israel became more rebellious against their Roman oppressors. This opposition by the Jews to the Romans was met with quick and brutal repression of the various rebel groups throughout Judea. There were numerous other powerbrokers bent on seizing control of Israel who led these various rebel groups and bandits.

The Romans, seeing their authority and rule being challenged, began a campaign of brutality against all opposition in the land of Judea. Several insurrections cropped up during the years that followed the death of Caligula, and these so-called "messiahs" who led the rebels were eventually defeated and they and their followers put to the sword.

Not only did the Romans face a defiant though divided people, they themselves became equally guilty of grave injustices towards the Jews. Over the years the various emperors appointed assorted procurators to rule over the conquered lands. Those sent to Israel and Syria were corrupt, self-serving men bent on accumulating personal wealth from the Jewish people over whom they were sent to rule. As time went by different men—Pilate, Cumanus, Felix, Festus, Aquinas, and Florius— were appointed to these positions of authority over Judea, and their moral character seemed to degenerate with each succession. All were determined to enrich their own individual treasuries and through their authority they stole from the people's reserves on one pretext or another. It was Florius who not only stole from his subjects but also was determined on destroying the whole nation of Israel.

The Jews had not been just innocent and passive victims, for many who had possessed and lived in this the Promised Land that God gave to His people out of love had turned their hearts from Him and dedicated their lives to lawlessness and to worshiping pagan gods. This heresy led Israel down the path to its own destruction.

For it wasn't even twenty years after the death of Jesus of Nazareth that the Zealots, embolden by their numbers and a charismatic leader, attacked the Roman garrison in Jerusalem and forced them from the city leaving Judea in a state of chaos.

It was during this time of instability that the cruel procurator Gessius Florius increased the taxes on the people's treasury, primarily for his own benefit and greed. Finally, a short time later, Florius was forced to attack the Zealots in Jerusalem in order to reclaim the city in the name of Rome. This he did, and his army slaughtered over 3,500 Jews. As he and his troops sacked the upper marketplace the Zealots, with the Temple at their backs and in defense of their position, destroyed the northern portico of the Temple. This prevented Florius from raiding and taking the treasures stored there. Eventually, after a costly and bloody battle, the Zealots were able once again to drive the Romans from the city.

At this time the grandson of Herod the Great, Herod Agrippa II, king of all of Judea and a staunch ally of Rome, moved a large army into Jerusalem and regained control of the upper city situated atop Mount Zion. However, the high priest Eliezer in league with the Zealots retained control of the lower city and the Temple mount. The king then tried to negotiate a peace with the citizens of Jerusalem. The rebels would have nothing to do with his effort and set fire to his palace, the palace of his sister Bernice and the house of the high priest. Agrippa fled Jerusalem as the rebels captured the Antonia fortress as well as the palace of his grandfather, Herod the Great.

It was in the twelfth year of the reign of the madman Nero, or 66 CE, that total war broke out between Rome and Judea. Subsequent to an ever-growing escalation of serious outrages committed by one side against the other, a highly motivated group of youthful Jewish Zealots stealthily attacked the Roman garrison at Masada, quickly dislodged the troops stationed there and secured the fort for their own use. At the same time this clash was taking place at Masada, another event was developing in Jerusalem. The son of the high priest, a young man named Eleazar, swayed the Temple leadership to stop paying tribute to outsiders, in particular to the Emperor and to Rome itself, a practice that had been in place for nearly a century.

Though the older leaders of Jerusalem tried to cool the tempers of the passionate youth, their efforts were in vain.

Realizing that the rebellion was beyond their control, the most influential citizens of the city went to Agrippa and the procurator Florius, imploring them to put a stop to the insurrection.

This was not to be. Once again King Agrippa sent troops to quell the uprising and soon these troops were able to regain control of the upper city. After a few more days of heavy fighting, the king's army seized and occupied the Antonia fortress. These battles spilled a great deal of blood on both sides, and it wasn't long before the rebels counterattacked. Eleazar, aided by the rebels known only as the Sicarii, a name for the knives they used in their assassinations of those loyal to Rome, and other bandit gangs drove the king's troops back out of the upper city, which the rebels promptly tried to burn with limited success. A few days later the rebels reestablished control of the Antonia fortress by overwhelming and slaughtering the entire garrison before turning on the king and his royal guard.

Again Herod Agrippa and his followers withdrew from Jerusalem in favor of Caesarea, not to return again.

In the meantime a little known rabbi from Galilee took some followers to the fortress at Masada. With the help of the Zealots who still held that fortress city, he broke into the king's armory, which until this time had been left undisturbed, and distributed the weapons to his supporters. He promptly traveled to Jerusalem, where through subterfuge he took control of the rebels and continued the defiant resistance to Rome.

These events forced the Roman general Cestius to take another course of action since it was clear that the Jews were now in a total war with the Empire. Early in 66 CE, he set out from his headquarters situated in Antioch and with the Twelfth Legion, which incorporated a large infantry contingent and numerous cavalry troops. He started south into Judea.

This powerful legion on their way to Jerusalem burned the cities and slaughtered the inhabitants who were in their path. Cestius stopped for a time in Caesarea where over 8,000 Jews were massacred. From there Cestius split his forces and sent his commander Caesennius Gallus into Galilee to put down the uprising that was still under way there, as he and the main body of his army continued on towards Jerusalem. It was during this same year that many of us, Jews and those newly converted to our faith in Jesus as the Messiah, were fortunate enough to escape from Jerusalem and flee to sanctuaries outside of Judea and into other cities and towns of the surrounding countries. I, son of Isaac, was one of the fortunate few able to flee into the wilderness and seek safety as the war continued to rage. With my fifteen-year-old grandson, Abram and thirty-six others who foresaw the end of our great capitol of Jerusalem, we escaped through the dung gate late one night as Cestius's army was battering at the walls of the upper city.

Things in Jerusalem had become untenable for the citizens, as the city had fallen under the influence of evil men. Different rebel leaders would fight with other rebels in order to gain or regain control of the city. These constant battles left many of the noncombatants, innocent citizens, suffering from injury or even death for just having been in the wrong place at the wrong time.

This struggle for power over Jerusalem had little to do with religion. Rather, it was brought on by greed—greed for power and for wealth. The thought of God and this being His holy city or dwelling place made no difference in their thinking.

My father, who at this time was old and somewhat crippled, dedicated himself to bringing the Jews back to their faith and to glorifying God in all things. He was outspoken in his views and publicly rebuked those in power for the abandonment of their faith in God.

This did not sit well with those who sought to control Jerusalem, and eventually they arrested him on trumped up charges for blasphemy and threw him in prison. The Temple leadership, those who were the spiritual guides for the Jews, ignored my father's pleas and left him to languish in his confinement.

I sought out all of the leaders I knew, requesting that they look into my father's case. I begged that they release him, as he was an old man and he posed no real threat to their authority, but my pleas fell on deaf ears. My mother had died just two and a half years before, and I think I knew in my heart of hearts that my father not only felt strongly for his cause but that secretly he missed my mother desperately and had chosen this course of action to bring on his own end sooner than later.

My father had come to believe that Jesus was truly the Son of God, the Messiah, and this only strengthened his faith in God and in the ways of the Jewish faith. He was truly a messianic Jew. My father and I disagreed on how best to preach the Word for I felt God invited all to come to Him. This included the Gentiles as spoken by the prophet Isaiah, who declared nearly six hundred years earlier, "I will keep you and make you to be a covenant for the people and a light for the Gentiles." On this point my father disagreed, for he felt that Jesus' coming was meant for Jews and Jews alone. No matter, he ended up in prison and all of my efforts failed to set him free. As Cestius's legion moved from Antioch towards Caesarea, the Jewish authorities requested that the rebels in control of the city have my father scourged and executed for blasphemy. This they did. He died at the hands of the man who laid the whip to his back. I was devastated, for it hadn't been too long since I had lost my mother, and my wife had died ten years earlier from a plague that ravaged the countryside during the winter months. It wasn't long after my mother's death that my daughter and her husband had also died a violent death during an early insurrection in Jerusalem. My grandson and I were now alone in a city that had gone mad.

With my father gone on to his reward and with Cestius's army getting closer to the city, I determined it was time to leave. It appeared to me that God's wrath was being poured out and all of the citizens of Judea were going to suffer.

Our sect of the followers of The Way determined that it was time to abandon Jerusalem and seek sanctuary elsewhere.

As we made preparations to depart we received word that the Twelfth Legion was now within a three-day march and would soon arrive and surround the city. This proved to be a frightening development for us, for if we waited much longer we would not find a way to safety. Many Jews who got wind of our escape plans were soon clamoring to join us.

Conditions in Jerusalem had worsened as the rebel bands were in an all-out struggle for control of the city. Their continued fighting went day and night without respite. This caught many of the upright citizens in the center, between the differing factions, which resulted in untimely deaths for many of them. In the middle of this civil war we received word that the Twelfth Legion was within sight of the city and would be at Jerusalem's gates the very next evening. As this word spread like wild fire throughout the city, all of the infighting ceased as if by magic and the citizens came together to meet the threat of the Roman army, which would soon surround the outer walls of the city of God.

As the Twelfth Legion approached from the north and established their camp on Mount Scopus, located across and east of the Kidron Valley a short distance from the north-east corner of the city, the citizens quickly came together and rushed to arms in defense of their beloved Jerusalem. On the following day, this powerful Roman legion marched from Scopus around the north end of Jerusalem to the western side of the city. Here they established their camp just opposite Herod's towers, where they began to array their forces for the assault. As the Twelfth Legion was forming their battle alignment, the citizen soldiers of Jerusalem ran out of the gates in mob-like fashion to attack the

Romans, taking them by surprise. Though superior only in number, the undisciplined Jews attacked the regimented soldiers of Rome with a ferocity that caused gaps to open in the Roman lines. This charge by the Jewish mob against the seasoned troops nearly divided Cestius' infantry, which was already weary after completing the long march from Caesarea. This attack was totally unexpected and nearly brought the vaunted Twelfth Legion to destruction. Had it not been for the Twelfth Cavalry's commander seeing the desperate state the infantry was in and then ordering his mounted troops to detour to aid the infantry, the Romans might have been defeated right then and there. As it was, the losses were heavy on both sides as I saw many fall to the swords, darts and arrows each side let fly at the other. These things I tell you about, I personally saw from atop the outer west wall that guarded the city.

After this first encounter with the Jews, Cestius withdrew his army from the western outskirts of Jerusalem and returned to his original encampment on Mount Scopus. They remained there for three days and three nights without making a move other than sending out small bands of infantry to confiscate food and grain from the citizens living in the area surrounding the city. During this time the final elements of the entire Twelfth Legion arrived in camp bringing with them their dreaded machines of war.

Then on the fourth day after his initial attack Cestius moved his troops back to the western outskirts of the capitol where another tremendous battle ensued. Before mid-afternoon of that same day, the Romans soundly defeated the Jews that went out to meet the attacking army. The Jews slowly withdrew to the gates of the upper city and finally entered them and shut them tight against the Roman infantry. As the sun set in the west, Cestius ordered his soldiers to burn the bordering communities and to move their camp once again to the western walls of the upper city. The now demoralized citizens and rebels that held Jerusalem spent a restless night behind those walls awaiting the next assault. The old guard of Jerusalem, those who had spent a lifetime of building a prominent name for the city, came together late that evening and elected two emissaries who went forth with entreaties to Cestius to inform him that they would open the gates if he would only rid them of these Zealots and bandits who were in control.

Cestius refused to hear these elected officials and sent them back inside the gates without even listening to their pleas. When I heard from the council of the elders that the Romans would not hear the emissaries, I determined that I would then lead the group of men, women and children from the city the very next night. I didn't have much time to formulate a detailed plan. However, I felt that with the battle for control of Jerusalem in the balance, thirty-eight citizens would not be missed.

Early in the morning of that sixth day just before daybreak Cestius continued his attack, and the gates remained closed. While this battle raged throughout the morning, I walked the deserted streets along the south and east side of Jerusalem in hopes of finding a way to escape without notice. The sound of the battle was intense, and I could hear the clamor of the voices of the combatants above the loud din of the Roman battering ram that struck the gate and resounded throughout the city.

As I walked the city, I chanced upon the Dung Gate located at the very southeast corner of the wall. The gate was low and narrow and it had a most unpleasant odor about it. It would be the perfect place from which to escape. I determined that we would leave the city that very night. I found my way to the top of the wall just as the morning sun was peeking over the eastern horizon. There were some very young men keeping watch to see that the Romans didn't try to enter the city through the back way. Except for them, the wall was quiet. I sneaked carefully to a parapet, surveyed the countryside and saw little movement. The Roman cavalry had a few patrols out, and it appeared we could make good our escape without detection. After I spent a relatively short time at the wall I stealthily found my way back to the street. I did not want to be confronted by the young men guarding the wall, for that could lead to a lot of trouble. I found my way back to those who were to escape the city with me. I told them to gather just enough provisions to last them about a week and meet me at this gathering place for we would leave that very evening. I cautioned all to be guarded in what they said to anyone including their own family members, for if our plan was discovered the provisional government would execute us all.

As the sun set that evening, we gathered in the house of one of the believers and planned our route to the Dung Gate.

Once outside the city wall, we would descend into the Well of Joab, the junction of the Kidron and Hinnom valleys at the southeast corner of Jerusalem, before turning north to follow the stream at the bottom of the Kidron Valley that would lead us to the north end of the eastern wall. The route would take us past the Golden Gate, the eastern entrance to the Temple situated high above our route to our left, and then on below the Garden of Gethsemane on the eastern slope of the valley to the right of our path. From here our route would lead us on past Mount Scopus, another point high above the Kidron that overlooked Jerusalem. Scopus was situated on the broad plain just east of the Kidron Valley that afforded a view of the northeast corner of the city and was frequently used as a staging area for the Roman army. Once we were well beyond the heights of Mount Scopus, we would then climb out of the Kidron Valley and travel northwest to join with the road that led to Jotapata.

After the streets were dark, we left in groups of four and started for the gate. There were some patrols out that night, and it took a while for all of us to come together in a deserted house directly across from our exit. None of the groups encountered the patrols, and it wasn't long before a member of our band crossed the narrow street and unlatched the gate. This man was especially chosen for the task as he was familiar with the gate and knew how to open this seldom-used exit from Jerusalem. It was also through his expertise that we were able to latch and bar the gate once we departed. Though we were leaving for good, we felt it necessary to secure the gate so that the Romans would not have access to the city through a fault of ours.

The night was dark; no moon had yet come up and all was quiet since the Romans had ceased their attack just before the sun had set. We left the wall and went to the small streambed that traveled north along the bottom of the valley and parallel to the eastern wall of Jerusalem. We stayed in the shadows, keeping as quiet as we could. The Roman patrols and their small camps were spread out all along the wall.

Walking was difficult for us due to the stones and some standing water in the creek. More than once we had to lie on the ground and hush the children for fear we would be heard. It took us a much longer time than I had estimated before we reached a point that was opposite and to the east of the northeast corner wall of the city just below Mount Scopus on our right. Here we rested for a short time before continuing on. We were more out in the open now, so I placed some of the young men far to the front of the main group as lookouts and also some men to the rear; all of this to protect us from being discovered by the few men of the Twelfth Legion who remained in the camp atop Mount Scopus. It was a harrowing experience, for more than once we almost came upon some un-mounted troops and had to quickly and quietly circle around their small camps. Shortly before dawn we were nearly a half days walk north of Jerusalem. I recalled the lookouts and ordered a halt to our journey. Here we would sleep during the day and eat cold meals since a fire would attract too much attention. Before lying down and sleeping, I established a routine for posting guards that changed personnel every so often. This I did among the men only and let the women and children sleep throughout the day. This allowed all to have sufficient sleep while keeping the camp safe from intruders.

Just before I could drift off to sleep, I heard a great sound arise in the distance—a sound made by many men the sickening sounds of battle. The siege by Cestius's army had once again begun. All of those in our group climbed the bank of the streambed and peered off into the semi-darkness towards Jerusalem where a number of great fires could be seen burning. Each of us, I think, was giving thanks that we had at last escaped the bondage of the city and were able to look towards a more secure future.

We later learned that the siege of Jerusalem lasted nearly seven days. It was during the sixth day of the battle that the rebels, feeling betrayed, dealt harshly with those citizens they felt had tried to appease the Romans. It was also on the sixth day that Cestius began his assault on the Temple Mount itself. As the battle raged, many of the rebels, seeing only defeat, began deserting the city. Those citizens who remained in Jerusalem saw a glimmer of hope before them and finally gained the courage to try and open the gates in order to let the Romans into the Temple area and end the insurrection once and for all. Cestius, unaware of what was taking place inside the walls of the Temple Mount and for no apparent reason, called off his attack and withdrew from Jerusalem. As the fleeing mob of bandits and rebels realized that through some strange quirk of fate they had indeed won the day, they quickly reversed their retreat and returned to Jerusalem to resume their control. In addition, many of the Jewish rebels followed Cestius's army in its withdrawal, causing a great number of casualties among the Roman's rear-guard while taking many of their siege engines from them. Following this debacle, Cestius then left a large force encamped outside the western wall. The discouragement of those upright citizens who still remained in the city was devastating, and many made plans to escape the genocide that seemed to be coming. Jerusalem and the whole of Judea were now under the leadership of evil men who were at war with Rome.

Within a short time after our exodus from Jerusalem, the rebels cracked down and refused to let any additional citizens leave. Those that tried and were unfortunate enough to be captured were summarily executed by the rebel leadership. The Romans did little better, for women caught trying to escape the city had their hands slashed off and were sent back to the gates where they could go back into the city behind the walls. The men who were captured by the Romans were crucified in full view of those Jews who could see the executions from the top of the wall.

In the capital city itself the civil war between the various rebel groups resumed and continued to rage out of control. Not only were the Jews fighting among themselves but they were also involved in a total war with Rome. It was in this civil war that enormous quantities of the city's food supplies were burned by one side of the fighting or the other—a reality that later led to massive starvation.

As I have said, it was during the sixth morning of the siege by Cestius and his Twelfth Legion that my small band made good our escape to seek sanctuary somewhere safe from the war between Rome and those bandits and criminals who sought to rule all of Judea. All of us who escaped had foreseen the end of our capitol city. With great trepidation, we left Jerusalem late at night as Cestius's army was battering the walls of the upper city.

We who had escaped the rebels in the city and the Roman patrols outside the walls traveled only at night, sleeping during the day. Our goal was to journey north into Galilee.

Once we arrived in the vicinity of Jotapata, we were surprised to find that this city was also making preparations for war with the Romans. For it was rumored that Vespasian and his Fifteenth Legion were preparing to march into Judea to lay siege to that city as well. So our little band of wanderers turned east towards Philadelphia, where we hoped to find sanctuary and to escape the danger of capture by the

Romans or of being enslaved by the bandits who freely roamed the land—a thought that was constantly on our minds.

After five days and nights of arduous travel, we arrived at a small town to the east of the Jordan River. This town was little more than a grouping of two or three farms situated near the road. The owners of the land were good people and shared their meager supply of food and water with us as we tried to rest and regain our strength before continuing our journey. These people were isolated from the events taking place in Judea and were eager for the news of Jerusalem. Up to this time they had been unaware of the war with Rome. These farmers offered us a place to stay on the land near their small community. In return for this generosity, we helped the farmers in their fields and I, in particular, helped in repairing the buildings and fences that were in a sorry state of disrepair.

As I was the oldest in the group of the thirty-six men, women and children, I was looked to for guidance and leadership. All of these people, including the farmers, were Jews by birth and questioned what was happening in this land given to them by God. The farmers and their families listened intently to what I had to say.

I spoke to the group each night after our meal reciting much of what I knew about the scriptures of Moses and of the other prophets who had followed him. I tried to explain that many people had rebelled against God and that we all were suffering because of the action of the non-believing criminals that seized control of Jerusalem. These hard times had been predicted in the scriptures, and there was still greater suffering yet to come.

Then on the third night, after I told them all I knew of the history of the land of Israel, I told my own story—of my encounters with the true Messiah who had come to redeem all of God's people.

And so I began.

ENCOUNTER WITH JOHN THE BAPTIST

"I was born fifty-three years ago, during the forty-third year of the reign of Caesar Augustus or the thirteenth year after the birth of the man they called Jesus. The first seventeen years of my life were spent in Jerusalem, as my father was a teacher in a synagogue located within the walls of that great city. Like all youth of our time, I grew up under the tyranny of Rome, but on the whole these tyrants left us alone as long as we didn't break any of their laws and if we paid our taxes to Caesar.

"However, there were those Jews who stood up and fought these oppressors. These men were universally referred to as the Zealots. These so-called freedom fighters constantly harassed the Roman outposts and did as much injury to the enemy as possible. Of course, these people were not only fighting for Jewish liberty, but were also waiting for the coming Messiah—the anointed one chosen by God to save the land of Israel—to declare himself publicly and lead Israel in its drive to oust all foreign influence from the Promised Land. In the meantime, those Zealots who were captured by the Romans were dealt with in a very barbaric fashion. They were tortured and then usually crucified.

"Although the prophets of old had predicted the coming of a Messiah, no one was able to say when that would be. Many felt that it would be soon, and some even thought he'd already come but had not yet made himself known.

1

"My father was one of the latter. He often told me the story of a time before I was born when there was a spectacular star that shone for the longest time. It was so bright that it could even be seen in the eastern skies during daylight. He told me that he had witnessed its appearance over the town of Bethlehem, and for many, including my father, it was the answer to prayer and especially to the prophecies of old. There were even simple shepherds in the fields near Bethlehem that at the time claimed that angels had appeared to them announcing the birth of a new king. It was also said that men of great wealth and knowledge came from the east searching for the one heralded by the brilliant star.

"But enthusiasm soon died away as nothing seemed to come from this event. Soon after the star's appearance, it was rumored that Herod had sent his own palace guard into Bethlehem with orders to kill all of the male children who were two years of age or younger, for he feared that he might be replaced by a new and more powerful king. This was not going to happen under his leadership, and he determined to stop this challenge to his rule before it overwhelmed his sovereign authority. This barbaric act by Herod seemed to silence all feelings that a change was in the wind. By the time I was born, this thought was nothing but a distant memory in the minds of most Jews. Even my father came to doubt that the Savior of Israel had come, and he went on with his work teaching in the synagogue. My father in his role as a rabbi had put great faith in the coming of the Messiah. He'd spent many years studying the scrolls of the ancients searching for the answer as to when this king would appear. He wasn't able to determine an exact time, but he felt it would definitely happen and probably during his lifetime. He kept a close watch on the skies and of all the news in Israel, but he couldn't discern when Israel's Savior would appear.

"All Jews felt that this king would be the great deliverer of the nation of Israel, even greater than King David. He would come forth on a magnificent steed leading an unbeatable army of giants, and he would thoroughly thrash the Romans and all of our enemies and set up a permanent government devoted to praising the living God.

"Though my life revolved around the Jewish law, I was never a very good example of love and devotion. I felt that it was useless to try to keep the law in a strict sense of the word, for even a little stumble on my part would cause me to break all of the law. Then the Great Living God would have nothing to do with me, at least until another living sacrifice could be made on my behalf. If in the meantime I were to be cast into the fiery furnace at the end of my days, I thought I might as well live the most enjoyable life I could while I was alive and young.

"I was never satisfied with my faith, and there was something deep inside that compelled me to continue my search for a better answer. Then when I was seventeen, I heard of a man who lived in the desert near the Jordan River who was baptizing men and calling upon them to repent and turn from their wicked ways. When I heard this, I thought, maybe this is the one that I should follow—the one that might lead me to the most Holy One.

"Within a short time, I concocted a plan to search this man out. I went to my parents and told them that I was going to visit my good friend Ezra who lived in Jericho and that I would be gone three or four days. But my intent was not to see Ezra. The very next day I set out early in the morning for the Jordan Valley. My route took me on a rigorous walk northeast from my parent's house and on past Jericho, a long journey on foot. It took two days for me to travel to the Valley of the Jordan and then to locate this man—the man they called the Baptizer.

"I didn't have much difficulty finding him once I reached the Jordan as there were many other pilgrims on my route, both seeking him and returning from an encounter. These people quickly pointed the way to the one I was seeking. When I finally did come upon this strange fellow, in the late afternoon of the second day, I found him surrounded by a large crowd. His looks surprised me, as he was dressed in a cloak of woven camel's hair that was held to his waist with a thick leather belt. His hair and beard were unkempt, long and dirty. He was a striking figure only in that he was so different from the citizens of Israel, who were normally clean and well groomed.

"His name was John and those in the crowd there that day referred to him as John the Baptist. He was a tall, well built man, and his beard was long and braided. This I supposed was done to keep it out of the way as he went about his work. He was very dark and deeply tanned as a result of living out in the sun. When I first saw him he was standing at the river's edge poised to baptize the next person to step down off the bank and into the water. It was here that a fellow pilgrim told me he'd heard that John and his followers ate nothing but locusts and honey. "I stood at a distance and observed him. I was struck by his appearance, by his voice and most certainly by what he had to say.

"Repent and turn away from your sins. Prepare yourselves for the Lord!' He shouted. 'Come unto the water of the Jordan and be cleansed.'

"Those who stood along the bank seemed hesitant to venture into the water. It was during this lapse that some important looking men whom I presumed to be from Jerusalem pushed their way through the crowd and stood on the bank.

One of them shouted out to him, 'Are you the Messiah whose coming has been foretold by the prophets?'

"John looked intently at the man and then replied in a loud clear voice. 'I am not the Messiah!'

"Well then, who are you?' another asked. 'Are you Elijah? Are you the Prophet?'

"No,' he replied.

"Then who are you? Tell us, so we can give an answer to those who sent us. What do you have to say about yourself?'

"John replied in these words that I later learned were the words of the prophet Isaiah. 'I am a voice shouting in the wilderness; preparing a straight pathway for the Lord's coming!'

"One of these men then demanded, 'What right do you have to call these people to repentance and then to baptize them?'

"The others joined in yelling their questions to him, one right after the other. John became angry and, shouting in a loud voice, stopped one of them in mid-sentence, 'You brood of snakes!' he thundered. 'Who warned you to flee God's coming judgment? Prove by the way you live that you have really turned from your sins and turned to God. Don't just say, *we are safe because we're the descendants of Abraham.* That proves nothing. God can change these very stones upon which I am standing into children of Abraham.' His voice was easily heard by all, and he motioned vigorously with his arms and hands as he walked up and down the bank. 'Even now the sharp ax of God's judgment is poised, ready to sever your very roots.' He stopped in front of the contingent of men from Jerusalem and pointed his finger directly at them. 'Yes, every tree that does not bear good fruit will be cut down and thrown into the eternal fire.'

"Immediately another man in the crowd asked, 'What should we do?'

"John dropped his arm to his side and turned to face the man. He then replied in a compassionate voice, 'If you have two coats, give one to the poor. If you have food, share it with those who are hungry.'

"There was even a tax collector who came to be baptized. He asked, 'Teacher, what should I do?'

"Show your honesty,' John replied. 'Make sure you collect no more taxes than the Roman government requires.' How John knew that this man was a tax collector was beyond my understanding.

"What should we do?' shouted some soldiers standing on the opposite bank.

John turned to face them and replied, 'Don't extort money, and don't accuse people of things you know they didn't do. And be content with your pay.'

"Then he went on to speak to those who had questions about the coming Messiah, 'I baptize with water; but someone is coming soon who is greater than I—so much greater that I am not even worthy to be his servant. He will baptize you with the Holy Spirit and with fire. He is ready to separate the chaff from the grain with his winnowing fork. Then he will clean up the threshing area, storing the grain in his barn but burning the chaff with never-ending fire.'

"By this time the sun was getting low on the horizon. John sent the crowds away saying, 'Go in peace. Find a place to eat and to rest, and I will be here early on the morrow. Pray that you will turn from your sins, for truly I say to you the coming of our glorious Lord is closer than any of you think.'

"With that said he and his followers crossed the river, climbed the west bank and soon disappeared from my view as they entered the tall reeds just a short distance away.

"I was excited about what John said about the coming of a great one who would baptize with the Holy Spirit. I decided to stay the night at this very place, for I had much to think about. I unrolled my mat on a nearby dry spot and sat down to eat the biscuits and dried fish I had in my pack.

Others were doing the same, for many had prepared to stay for the night. There were numerous campfires dotting both banks of the Jordan and a young family nearby invited me to come and enjoy the warmth of their fire.

"We talked well into the night, about things of God and His creation. We talked at great length about what John had said about the soon—to-come Lord. I didn't understand what this meant and neither did my new friends, David and his wife Martha.

"Was he predicting the coming of the Messiah or was he talking about the Lord God reappearing to the Israelites again, as he had during the time of Moses?' I asked aloud, but received no answer. We pondered these things for long time and drew no conclusions, just shared a lot of speculation. Near midnight I bid farewell to my friends and went back to my mat. I rolled up in my blanket and fell fast asleep.

"As promised, John was back early in the morning at the river, preaching and baptizing. The things that he said enthralled me. But I wasn't able to discern an answer about the Lord's coming and who it would be. I finally became convinced that John didn't know this answer either, other than it would be soon.

"John, his followers and their lifestyle fascinated me. Before the day was over, I repented of my sins, and I, too, was baptized in the Jordan. I was convinced that I wanted to become one of his disciples. When the time was right I approached a young man whom I knew was a follower and asked what I needed to do. The man said to me that I would need to give up all that I had and turn it over to the poor, repent of my sins and join them as they proceeded up and down the Jordan calling on people to ask for forgiveness and follow the teachings of the Lord.

"I was thrilled about what he said and told the young man that I would do just that, but that I first had to go home and finish up my business there. Then I would return in a few days to follow John.

"I spent one more night at the rivers edge with David and Martha. I told them of my decision to follow John. To my surprise they were as excited about my choice as I was. In the morning I bid them a final farewell, and then spent a short time watching and listening to John. Before midmorning, I was on my way back to Jerusalem. The walk was long and arduous, and it was very late at night before I returned to my home. I was exhausted, and, as my parents were asleep, I went straight to my bed and slept late into the morning of the following day. In the early afternoon, I rushed to the synagogue to tell my father of the events that had taken place during my journey to the Jordan. I hadn't told my mother that I had lied to them and felt I'd better tell my father first.

"As I approached the synagogue I came to a small crowd of men, standing outside the main entrance, who were jubilant over some news that another man was telling them. This man was a little older than me. As I approached this group, I heard him say that he had been with John the Baptist just the day before. This immediately caught my attention for I had been there in the morning as well. He told them that he'd been at the Jordan listening to John. In the early afternoon as John was preaching, a man approached and indicated that he wanted to be baptized. John looked closely at him and then suddenly bowed before him. John said that it was he, John, who should be baptized by him. This man waved him off, and then John asked, 'So why then have you come to me?' The man answered him, 'It must be done, because we must do everything that is right.' So then John baptized him.

"When John brought the man up out of the water, he said to the crowd, 'I saw the Holy Spirit descending like a dove from heaven and resting upon him. I didn't know he was the one, but when God sent me to baptize with water, he told me, *When you see the Holy Spirit descending and resting upon someone, he is the one you are seeking. He is the one who baptizes with the Holy Spirit.* I saw this happen to this man called Jesus, so I testify that he is the Son of God.'

"This statement by the young man sent shivers up and down my back. Was this truly the Messiah who had come?

When the man had finished speaking with the crowd, I pulled him aside and asked that he repeat all that he had said. When he finished, I told him that I, too, had been to the Jordan just the day before but had left before this event he had just related. I, at last, asked him straight out if he believed that this was truly the Messiah.

"He said, 'I can only report to you what I saw and heard. When John brought this man they call Jesus up from the water, there was a loud roll of thunder that almost sounded to me like someone speaking. Others in the crowd said they'd heard a voice in the thunder that had said, *This is my son, with whom I am fully pleased*.' This man, called Andrew, then excused himself and went to join another group of men standing a short distance away.

"I immediately rushed into the synagogue to look for my father. When I found him, he was talking with a woman and motioned for me to wait. I tried to break in on their conversation a couple of times, and all my father did was to raise his hand indicating for me to wait. Patience has never been one of my virtues, but I held my tongue and waited until he was finished. I respected my father, for his tongue was sharp when I disobeyed and I didn't want to be subjected to one of his fits of temper. He was a private person and a strict disciplinarian, and it was very difficult for me, or anyone for that matter, to determine what he was thinking.

"As I waited, I paced back and forth with all sorts of thoughts racing through my mind. I could barely contain my excitement, and I felt as if my feet didn't touch the ground.

"It seemed to take forever for my father to finish but finally his conversation ended. I went over and stood in front of him. Before I could say a word, he asked me why I had tried to interrupt him. 'You never come to the synagogue anymore,' he admonished, 'and now that you have you are rude before me and before the Lord. Take a deep breath, slow down and count to ten and do it for me in the tongue of the Romans. Then tell me what it is that you want.'

"It took me a minute to calm myself after I finished counting, and then I started to relay my story. First, I told him that I hadn't gone to see my friend Ezra but instead had gone into the Jordan Valley in search of this man, John the Baptist.

"To my surprise my father seemed to be intrigued by my tale and didn't rebuke me for telling him a story about my trip. I told him all that had happened, even the part about being baptized and of my decision of following this man. At this my father raised his eyebrows, but before he could say a thing I told him that events that took place outside this synagogue had changed my thinking.

"And what could have happened since you arrived here that caused you to change your thinking?' he asked. I then went on to relate what the young man, Andrew, had said. My father questioned me at some length on this subject and then seemed to be lost in deep thought, even to the point of distraction.

"My confusion was great as I pondered the events of those few days. I had been convinced that I wanted to follow John, but the coming of this man that John had called greater than himself had left me filled with doubt as to what I should do. I think my father was confused also. He said very little about the event and was more reclusive than usual. He spent more time at the synagogue sequestered with his precious scrolls. I didn't know what I was to do and spent a long time in conversation about these things with my mother and my friends. We were unable to draw any definitive conclusion other than to sit and wait for events to develop."

At this time it was dark, nearing the middle of the night. As the fire dwindled down to glowing embers, I finished the first part of my story. After a short prayer, I dismissed the assemblage for the night, promising to continue my account after the evening meal the next day. I said goodnight to those who remained and went to my tent, which had been given to me by the men of the village. My grandson Abram was already asleep. So I sat outside on the ground near the entrance and surveyed the magnificence of the starry display overhead. Soon I said my prayers and thanked God for this opportunity to witness to these people. Then I crawled into my blankets for a peaceful sleep.

THE FIRST ENCOUNTER
AT CANA

After a hard day's work in the fields of our hosts, we pilgrims, along with the farmers, again gathered for the evening meal. As we finished eating, we watched the sun slowly descend behind the horizon. Once it disappeared and could no longer be seen, the air cooled rapidly. We all felt the chill of the evening air, and soon the children scattered to gather wood. It wasn't very long before we, along with our hosts, were sitting in a large circle around a roaring fire.

Once I saw that all were comfortable I stood between the people and the fire and continued my story.

"A short time after I had been with the Baptist, my father, mother and I were privileged to travel to the village of Cana, located in Galilee. We were going so that we could participate in the wedding of my cousin Timothy. My uncle, my mother's brother, was a well–to-do businessman in that district, and this wedding of his oldest son promised to be a big event. Timothy and I had played together in our youth.

Though we didn't know each other well, we were always very close whenever we were together. I looked forward to this time of travel and also to the time I would spend with Timothy before the wedding.

"Our preparations were quite extensive for we would have to travel a very long time, as Cana was an arduous six day walk north of Jerusalem. We traveled in a small caravan of other travelers and merchants who were headed in that direction. A few of these people we already knew since they too were going to the wedding. There were other young men of my age that joined the caravan whom I became acquainted with as we traveled north.

"The weather was wonderful, for the days were not too hot and the nights were cool. It had been many years since I had made this trip. I enjoyed the opportunity to be with family and friends and at the same time view the sights and listen to the sounds of the Jordan Valley. It also gave me time to reflect on the encounter I had a few months earlier with John the Baptist. This was also the last time that I would probably be traveling with the family, as my father had made arrangements for me to live with his brother in Emmaus and train under his tutelage to be a tent-maker. My apprenticeship was to start as soon as we returned from Cana.

"It had been difficult for my father to get away from his work but I think that he had secretly hoped that if he went on this trip that he too might see John the Baptist for himself, and maybe even discover other evidence of this man they called Jesus.

"Though the trip was arduous as we covered a great distance each day, I remember it as a most pleasant experience. A few of my new friends and I would roam far and wide of the caravan playing games as scouts and spies looking out for dangerous robbers and thieves that we would defeat in mock battles and thus save the people in the caravan.

"It was a memorable trip both going and returning.

We finally arrived in Cana late in the evening of the sixth day. This then gave us two days before the wedding to visit with my mother's family. Timothy, who was two years older than me, and I had a joyous reunion. Though we had not seen each other for many years, we talked and enjoyed ourselves as if only a few days had passed since our last meeting. His soon-to-be wife was a girl neither of us knew since this marriage had been arranged by Timothy's father and the father of the bride-to-be, as was the custom.

"My cousin was apprehensive about the marriage but he didn't dare go against his father's wishes. His betrothed was a very plain and shy young girl who was five years younger than he. Timothy, therefore, clung to me those two days before the wedding, trying to put aside any thoughts of the great changes that were going to take place in his life.

"The day of the wedding finally came and all of the proceedings passed quickly. They were little more than a blur to me. It was the wedding feast that stood out in my mind. It was an event that I will never forget! This young girl was from Nazareth and many of her family and friends were in attendance.

"There was an abundance of delectable foods and all ate and drank as if there were to be no tomorrow. I stuffed myself to the point that my discomfort was great. I felt that I needed to get up from the table and walk around to relieve my pain. I walked through the large courtyard where the feast was being held, and I then decided to go out through the gated entrance to the street.

"It was at this entrance that I observed a miraculous incident. Just as I stepped into the portico I overheard a woman speaking to a man, who I later learned was her son. I heard her whisper loudly to him, 'They have no more wine.'

"How does that concern you and me?' the man asked. 'My time has not yet come.'

"Then I heard his mother tell the servants, 'Do whatever he tells you.' She turned and looked at her son and then hurried off to rejoin the festivities in the courtyard. The man then turned his attention to the servants and pointed to the six large stone water basins standing at the entrance-way. He instructed the servants to fill them with water. 'When the jars are filled to the brim dip some out and take it to the master of ceremonies.' He left them alone.

"I watched as the servants ran to the well numerous times and filled the large stone jars. When they had finished, the head servant took his dipper and filled it from the first basin and rapidly entered the courtyard and headed towards the master of ceremonies seated at the head table. I followed a short distance behind, as I was curious as to what would happen.

"The servant quickly caught the man's attention and bent to whisper in his ear. The master of ceremonies took the silver dipper from the servant and sipped the wine, swirling it in his mouth and then swallowing it after which his eyes seemed to brighten with delight. He then drank what remained in the dipper. When he finished the wine he returned the dipper and motioned for him to go serve the drink to the guests.

"After the servant departed the master of ceremonies called to the bridegroom, seated a short distance away, and said in a loud voice to him. 'Usually a host serves the best wine first, then, when everyone is full and doesn't care, he brings out the less expensive wines. But you have kept the best until now!'

"Timothy thanked the man for his comment but looked puzzled at what was said "I was astounded to think that this water had been turned into wine. How could this be? I stood still for a time trying to figure out what had just taken place. How could that water I saw the servants bring in from the well have turned to wine? Being the skeptic that I am, and after gathering my thoughts, I rushed out to the portico and removed the cover on one of the jars and plunged a dipper into the fluid and took a swallow, first savoring it in my mouth for flavor. To my amazement it was a wonderful wine. I replaced the cover on that jar and went to the next and tasted it and so on down the line to each of the six jars. They all tasted the same, and they all had the same deep red color when I held the wine to the light. Who was this man? Was he a magician?

"I reentered the courtyard and searched the crowd for the man and for his mother. I had so many questions to ask. To my wonder I could not find the man or the woman for they had apparently gone.

"I then searched out and found the head servant and asked him if he knew who the man was who had ordered him to fill the six stone jars. All that he could tell me was that the man was the son of a woman named Mary whom he thought was from Nazareth and he was certain that he'd heard the woman call him Jesus.

"This news set my mind reeling. My first thought was back to what the man named Andrew had said in Jerusalem about his encounter with the Baptist. I quickly searched out and found my father. I breathlessly told him all that had transpired. My father looked at me in disbelief and shook his head. I think that he thought I'd had too much to drink, and after I had sampled all of the wine I probably had. But this didn't change the facts of what I'd told him. He said very little about this event. All whom I told seemed to think I'd lost my head and refused to discuss the matter, except for Timothy who I saw briefly two days after the wedding and just before we were ready to start on our way back to Jerusalem. He was fascinated by my tale and asked me many questions. However, before we were able to search out any clues I had to return home.

"All these proceedings, those with John and the wedding at Cana, left me somewhat bewildered as to what was happening in Israel. I couldn't come to any conclusions that made sense. I decided that I should go to Emmaus and learn a trade as I pondered these extraordinary events.

When I finished speaking of this event I knew that it was late. I said a short prayer of thanks to God for our safety and thanks to the local farmers who had taken us in, fed us and given us comfort.

"We are so thankful to you, Lord Jesus, for seeing us this far on our journey. Without your help, our hardships would be far greater, maybe even leading to our capture and enslavement. We are grateful for your guidance and to these people who have become our benefactors. Bless them and grant them wisdom, as they exemplify your love and devotion." With that said, the people slowly rose to their feet and walked away into the darkness to their beds.

CLEOPAS

The next day after the evening meal I once again stood before this group of travelers and farmers and continued telling them of my life and of my encounters with the man called Jesus. When all of my listeners were settled and quiet, I continued my story.

"My apprenticeship as a tent-maker went well. I stayed at a house owned by my uncle and worked long days learning to piece together all of the elements used in the trade. My hands became hard and calloused as I manipulated the needle and thread. The cutting and shaping of fabrics and skins into tents of all sizes and shapes became easier the more I worked at the craft.

"Within a short time after starting to work for my uncle, the demand for his wares grew as more and more caravans passed through Emmaus going to and from Jerusalem. So much in demand were the wares we produced that my uncle took on another apprentice. I was a little envious of this new man at first as he was a older than me and he had worked at the trade for a short time a few years earlier. My uncle hired him, paying him a little more than he paid me. His name was Cleopas, and he was all of two years my senior.

"I guess that I am a lot like my father and somewhat hard to get to know. Cleopas, on the other hand, was a wonderful and open person and quickly overlooked my sour disposition towards him. We both lived in a small house next door to my uncle and aunt's home located near the outskirts of Emmaus.

"After a while I became used to Cleopas, and it wasn't too long before we talked openly to one another. He had been orphaned early in life and had drifted from place to place over the past seven years or so. He had been in trouble with the authorities more than once, and before things got too bad he had come upon John the Baptist. John and his followers had taught him a great deal about how he should live, and this eventually led to his settling down a year or two before we met.

"Of course when I heard him talk of John, I had to tell him of my encounter with the Baptizer earlier that very year. This experience broke the ice between us and we soon became close friends.

"More importantly, Cleopas had been with John on that fateful day when Jesus appeared before him to be baptized. He, like me, was confused about whom he should follow and questioned whether he should choose John or should he change his allegiance and follow Jesus. Initially Cleopas continued to stay with John and his disciples; however, he kept a close eye on Jesus and his followers.

"Then one day Cleopas told me that he and some of John's other disciples got into a heated argument with a Jewish rabbi about ceremonial washing, which is the washing a devout Jew does of himself and of his dishes in order to appropriately prepare for worshipping God. This and many other questions came to them, all of which they weren't able to answer and which the rabbi, with whom they were arguing, was unable to settle properly. He even exhibited uncertainty in his beliefs. They then went to John and presented these questions to him. In conclusion, they asked him, 'Rabbi, you spoke of the man we were with when we were on the east side of the Jordan, a man who is also baptizing people, and now everyone is going to him. Tell us, what does all of this mean?'

"John looked at his disciples in a caring and tender way and said to them, 'No one can do anything unless our loving God in heaven ordains it. You surely remember how I told you that I am not the Messiah. I am only the one sent ahead of him. At a wedding, the groom is the one who gets married.

The best man is glad just to be there and to hear the groom's voice. That's why I am so glad. Jesus must become more important while I become less important. Our purpose is to glorify God and the one whom He has sent.'

"After hearing John's words and following a great deal of personal reflection on his part, Cleopas left John and his followers and sought out Jesus. After finding him in Galilee, he went wherever he and his disciples went, studying the man and the things he did and said. At first, he kept his distance because he felt unsure of himself. This eventually led him to come and work for my uncle.

"Cleopas was a free spirit and took many days off from his work to go and be with Jesus and his disciples. That was one of the conditions for his coming to work with us.

Uncle was truly a wonderful man, full of love for everyone and compassion as well as being gifted with a wonderful sense of humor. He, too, was interested in this man Jesus and had agreed to certain conditions such as he would not pay Cleopas when he was gone and that Cleopas was to report all things that he learned about Jesus upon his return. It was also the case that Uncle did not need him from time to time. For me it was different. I was needed full-time, and I did not get the opportunity to take off whenever the desire to do so struck me.

"Whenever Cleopas returned from one of his excursions with Jesus, Uncle and I would sit with him as he told us of everything that he did and of the things that Jesus taught. He told us of Jesus' teachings, which to me were so astonishing that I had difficulty believing these things. It was so different from what I had learned as a young Jewish boy, yet I soon discovered that they were not quite as dissimilar as I had first thought.

"As the time for Passover approached Cleopas learned that Jesus was going to be in Jerusalem. He told me that he was going to go there to be with him and his followers for the celebration. Because I too was going to the city to be with my parents for the festival, I quickly agreed to walk with him to Jerusalem.

"We talked the whole way discussing the teachings of Jesus and those teachings of the ancient Jewish scriptures. Our conclusions were interesting in that we did not find anything in what Jesus said that contradicted the scriptures; in fact, it seemed that they supported all that I had learned about them in my youth. Apparently, though, the Temple leaders were at odds with his ideas as they declared they were in contradiction of the law and of the scriptures. They even accused him of blasphemy and sent emissaries that posed questions to trick him and give them an opportunity to challenge what he said. But they failed miserably, for he answered all of their questions with a wisdom that was beyond my understanding.

"As we entered the city, I continued to walk with my friend to the Tabernacle where I would leave him before I continued on to my parents' home. When we at last reached Herod's great Temple and as I was preparing to continue on, we heard some shouting. We quickly climbed the stairs of the Temple Mount and rushed to the outer court to see what caused all of the pandemonium.

"There, in that crowded yard, were the merchants selling cattle, sheep, and doves for sacrifices, and also there were the money changers behind their counters. In their midst stood the man Jesus speaking to them in a loud voice I could easily hear over the din of the crowd.

"To my amazement he was asking them to pack up their things and leave the Temple. I couldn't remember a time when they weren't there selling and exchanging coins to the pilgrims who had come to Jerusalem for the annual celebration of Passover.

"I stood and watched, my mouth open, as Jesus made a whip from some ropes and drove these merchants out of the Temple, along with their cattle and sheep. He overturned tables and stools scattering coins all about. He snapped his whip, and at the loud crack the animals stampeded causing further uproar with everyone running, seeking a safe haven. Cleopas and I stood on the steps and watched in fascination as the animals and people scattered.

"Then, going over to the people who sold doves, he shouted at them, 'Get these things out of here. Don't turn my Father's house into a marketplace!' Again he snapped his whip, overturning the cages, some of which came open, freeing the birds to escape into the air. It was then that I began to understand what he was doing. When we first came upon him I thought that he was trying to draw attention to himself in order for the Sadducees and Pharisees to take note of him. But, then it dawned on me that he was trying to preserve the sanctity of the Temple, of God's House.

"It was later in my life that I learned that what he did was prophetically written in scripture, 'Passion for God's house burns within me.'

"Before we bade one another good-bye, Cleopas and I looked at each other in amazement, trying to understand what we'd just seen. Finally after an awkward pause, Cleopas said to me, 'I told you He was different, truly a man of God.'

"I nodded my agreement and mumbled that I would meet him here at noon two days hence. I quickly went to the home of my parents to tell them of what I'd just seen."

At this point, I paused my storytelling for a few moments; I paced back and forth before my audience trying to think of all that I needed to say. Then when the spirit moved within me, and I stopped pacing. I stepped in front of the people, looked at each individual before I continued with my narrative.

"There are too many examples of what Jesus did and said for me to tell you here, for nearly every word he uttered was a further illumination of God and of His love for the people. For Jesus not only performed miracles but he also used parables or stories to illustrate this relationship he wanted us to have with the Lord God.

"I did not see or hear everything that he said, but over the years I've heard of many of these things I did not personally observe from people who were there and witnessed them. Different people who were present during the time he performed the miracles have told me about the many events that took place during his short ministry. Keep in mind that he was with us as a teacher for less than three short years. However, during that time, the things that he did and said changed and blessed so many lives that his impact on the citizens of Israel is immeasurable. On the other hand, during that same time he turned the whole of the Temple leadership against him. They saw him as a threat to their positions of power and influence.

"Never forget that God wants us to be obedient to Him and not to seek riches here on earth. This is what Jesus taught, that God would take care of us if only we turn our lives over to Him. Everyone who saw and heard Jesus was amazed at his teaching. He taught with authority, as one who knew what he was saying and what his relationship with the Lord was all about, not like the teachers of the law of Moses who never seemed to grasp the importance of what they were saying. These Jewish leaders were more interested in maintaining their appearance as important men in the eyes of the people, not as true teachers of God's word. They sought the adoration of men rather than giving the glory to God."

Once again I, Caleb, paused and bowed my head in silent prayer before lifting my eyes to my audience; I took a minute to look at each person before saying. "I'll complete my story tomorrow evening after our meal. So as you go to your beds, keep your thoughts on the many blessings you have received from the Lord. Pray that as we continue our journey on the day after tomorrow that He will lead us to safety and guides us into His righteousness. And at the same time that He will richly bless you who have taken us in."

THE CRUCIFIXION

The next evening, the final night we pilgrims would spend with the farmers, our hosts went all out and prepared a large feast for their guests. All were sad to leave, but we felt that we needed to continue north and east out of Judea to insure our safety. I also felt that it was necessary for the protection of the farmers, for if it was found that they'd given safe harbor to these pilgrims they might suffer harsh retribution from both the Romans and the rebels.

Before I rose to give the final elements of my story, many words were said of the blessings both groups had poured on one another. As the sun began to sink behind the horizon the children brought armloads of wood that they had gathered. They placed them on the fire, as there was a definite chill in the air. The people sat in a circle around the fire, and I stood between it and the people and walked around the circle as I spoke to them.

"We all have been greatly blessed by your kindness and generosity," I began. "Without your help and compassion we would never be able to reach our goal. I praise God for you and ask that He continue to pour out a multitude of blessings upon you and your families. I also ask that you listen carefully to what I have to say and to take to heart the lesson of who Jesus was, both as a man and who he is as the Son of God, the true Messiah.

"Many people witnessed the miracles that he performed, so there is no question as to the fact that he physically healed the blind, the lame, and the sick. But most importantly, it was the things that he said about how we are to view our Maker that should be of greatest import to us here and now.

"Do not forget that Jesus was without sin!" At this there was a murmur from the audience. "He died upon the Cross, as a perfect sacrifice, a sacrificial lamb without blemish.

"Now let me tell you about his death so that you may see for yourselves what I mean.

"As always for the occasion of Passover, I traveled from my uncle's dwelling in Emmaus to my parent's home in Jerusalem. My friend Cleopas had left for Jerusalem earlier in the week and was not with me. Instead, I would meet with him on Sunday after the Passover celebration for the return to Emmaus. This particular day was a beautiful one, without even a hint of a cloud in the sky. I had started out early in the morning and the half day walk seemed like a short stroll. I remember feeling how great it was to be alive and to at last have some time off to enjoy spending time with my parents and my uncle and aunt from Cana, who were staying with my mother and father for the festival.

"As I approached the city on my journey, I heard a great clamor of people. Intrigued by the sounds of the large crowd, I rushed to the western gate and arrived in time to see a large multitude surrounding a troop of soldiers taking a man to Calvary. As the crowd was too large for me to see who the hapless soul was, I rushed up the hill to await the arrival of the throng. Once there I noticed for the first time that there were two crosses already standing, each with a victim nailed in place and groaning loudly from the excruciating pain they were enduring. I was transfixed by the sight and didn't look back at the crowd until their shouting refocused me on the reason I had climbed to the top of Calvary in the first place.

"The noise of the mob grew louder as they approached the top of the hill. Those in front of the procession moved to the side to let the soldiers and the victim approach the crosses. There was a man carrying a large timber and behind him was the victim who stumbled but was firmly brought back to his feet by the soldier who walked beside him. As the condemned man approached where I stood, I could see that he had been severely beaten. Blood flowed down his head from where a ring of thorns had been placed and then viciously pushed down. As he regained his feet after stumbling I could see that he had been brutally beaten with a cat o' nine tails, for his back was raw, bruised and bleeding. He was dirty from having fallen many times as he struggled to walk the distance from the praetorian to this hill outside the city, Golgotha. His face was also bruised and bleeding and I winced when he again lost his footing. He didn't fall this time and soon continued on up the hill. I cowered back into the crowd for I could feel his pain. *No one should be treated this way,* I thought to myself.

"As I stood and watched, the Roman soldiers pushed the man who had carried the crosspiece back into the crowd. Next they took their victim and threw him to the ground, and then lifted him onto the horizontal crosspiece that was now lying flat next to him. It was then I realized that this was the same man I had seen on other occasions, the man they called Jesus the Christ. I had even seen him perform miracles and heard him speak. He hadn't talked of insurrection or of war, but always spoke about love and understanding. I asked myself, *How was it that they were crucifying him? What had he done?*

"As this man lay on his back with the crosspiece under his shoulders, a soldier on either side placed his arms out on that crosspiece and tied them tightly with a rope. It was then that our eyes met, and his gaze dug deep into my soul. I couldn't look away for his dark gray eyes penetrated my very being. I saw a calmness there that surprised me. Out of the corner of my eye, I saw the soldier on his right side, a large powerfully built man, place a long iron spike on the victim's arm with his right hand while with his left he lifted a heavy wooden mallet. Then he slammed it down on the nail driving it through the wrist and deep into the wood of the cross. The man writhed in pain but his eyes did not look away. I saw the perspiration on his brow mixed with the blood that had been caused by the coil of thorn branches forced down upon his head. I could see the pain in his face as another soldier drove home the spike on his left arm. Even though his face was contorted with pain, his piercing gaze showed a peace and quiet that defied my understanding. The only sound he made was a low moan as the soldiers drove home the nails.

"I winced and trembled as the soldiers lifted the man to his feet and then with ropes hoisted the crosspiece and the man to the tall stake that had previously been stood vertical into the ground between the other two men who had been crucified a short time before. Once he was positioned and the crosspiece affixed to the stake, a nail was driven through his feet deep into the wood of the vertical stake. Again he moaned from the horrible transgression made against his body.

"I felt his pain and I couldn't look into his eyes any longer, so I looked away at the people who were standing around. It was at this time I realized how large of a crowd had come out to witness the event. Many of them were the Jewish leaders that had made jokes of him. A Pharisee yelled so all could hear, 'If you are truly the Messiah, then come down off the cross and drive the Romans away.' This was followed by laughter. Others were pointing at him making jokes of his anguish. But, it wasn't too long before these people began to leave, for clouds were beginning to cover the sun and I could hear thunder in the distance.

"I stayed and watched as the crowd began to thin. A group of women stood at the foot of his cross, and I thought that they must be part of his family; one I know was his mother. I recognized only one of his followers, a man named John, who stood with the family. I didn't know why the other disciples weren't there. It appeared to me that they had deserted him.

"I stood there for a long time, for how long I haven't a clue. The sky continued to darken and the roll of thunder became more frequent and louder as time passed.

"Most of the Jewish leaders had gone, probably to their homes to prepare for the Passover. There were just a few people left along with the Roman guards who were sitting on the ground near the middle cross, the cross on which Jesus hung, playing with their dice.

"In the middle of the afternoon it became very dark almost as if night had fallen. I was startled to hear a man cry out, 'Eloi, Eloi, lema sabachthani?' I looked up at first wondering where the voice came from and then realized that the cry came from Jesus.

"One of the few Jewish leaders who had stayed throughout the day thought that he had called to the prophet Elijah. He said in a loud voice to another man who had run to get a long stick that had a sponge on it to give to Jesus to help relieve his thirst, 'Leave him alone. Let's see whether Elijah will come and take him down!' After another pause Jesus said in a harsh whisper, 'Father, I entrust my spirit into your hands!' His breathing was labored, and soon there was a last gasp and then he died.

"Shortly after, I saw a Roman soldier come up out of the city to Golgotha. When he arrived, he whispered into the ear of the large executioner, who then picked up his mallet and went to the first cross and swung it hard breaking both legs of the first criminal—this to hasten his death. He then walked over to Jesus and saw that he was already dead. In order to confirm this, he grabbed a spear from the smaller soldier who accompanied him and thrust it into Jesus' side. Out flowed water and blood from the wound and there was no reaction from the body. Satisfied, he walked to the last cross and swung his heavy mallet and broke the legs of the last victim.

"By this time the sky had turned black as night, and the thunder and lighting was intense. The very earth shook beneath my feet, and I fell to my knees and cried.

"I don't know how long I was there with my face buried in my hands crying and then praying to the Lord. Suddenly voices carried by the wind jerked me back to reality. When I looked up I saw two men, both dressed as Pharisees, standing and talking with the women. Though they spoke in hushed tones I could tell that they too were saddened by the events of the day.

"Shortly after their words with the women, the men went to the cross and prepared to take the body down. One climbed a ladder and tied a rope around the body and over the cross piece so that Jesus would not fall. Then he carefully dislodged Jesus' right wrist from the nail and put his arm gently to his side. Next he did the same with the left arm. The other man stabilized the legs and feet and then gently dislodged the feet from the spike. The man on the ladder then tenderly lowered the body into the other man's arms with the rope he'd tied over the crosspiece.

"The man that held Jesus gently laid him on the ground at the feet of Mary who knelt down and put her arms around him and held him as she gently stroked the hair from his face. She rocked slowly back and forth as she held her son, and the tears streamed down her face onto his. It began to sprinkle lightly, and I could only think that God too was shedding tears for this loss of truly a godly soul.

"The man who had held Jesus bent down and gently lifted the body into his arms after the other one had climbed down the ladder and quickly gone to pick up a large bundle. They both proceeded a short distance to a tomb that had been hewn out of the rock. The one who carried Jesus went into the sepulcher, and from what I could see laid the body out on an elevated rock bed inside. The women followed and waited outside as the two Pharisees prepared the body. I, too, followed at a distance. That is why I'm able to tell you of these things.

"When they were finished, the men stepped out of the tomb and summoned three of the Roman guards to help them roll a huge stone in front of the burial chamber. It took the labors of the soldiers and the two men to roll it into place.

"When they were finished the Pharisees said some reassuring words to the women and then departed.

"The women continued to cry and my heart went out to them, but I didn't dare approach them in their grief. Soon they too, left.

"I sat there staring at the rock that covered the entrance of the burial place. So many questions raced through my mind. I nearly lost any faith I had in God. Why would He send the Messiah only to have him crucified before any of the wrongs done by our oppressors had been set right? All seemed useless and wasteful of any divinity that Jesus may have possessed. My only conclusion was that there must not be a God.

"After what seemed like a long time I started my walk to my parent's house located in the city. It was then that I realized that the sun was disappearing behind the horizon. By this time, the rain had ceased and the sky was clearing. I knew that my mother would be cross with me for staying out after sunset on this most holy of nights. She would be angry at me for not going straight to my home when first arriving from Emmaus, but I thought she would understand when I explained to her what I had just witnessed.

"When I finally arrived, both my father and mother had a few choice words with me when I entered the house. But when I explained what I had seen, they relented and dropped the subject. I know that my father had hopes that Jesus was the Messiah, but he never let his true feelings be known.

My mother's brother and his wife were there and they let it be known that this man called Jesus was truly a criminal and deserved to die on the cross for his blasphemy.

"After this we talked no more on the subject and celebrated the Seder. I then went to my bed that was on the roof of my parent's house. I didn't sleep much and tossed and turned all night, wrestling with my conscience about what had happened this day. Not only was I disturbed over Jesus' death, but also I was particularly repelled by the way in which he'd died. I had heard of crucifixion before but I had never witnessed its cruelty until that day. Finally, long after midnight, I drifted off into a fitful sleep.

"The next day was the Sabbath, and we spent a good deal of time at the Synagogue. While there I learned of a strange event that had taken place in the Temple the day before at about the time Jesus had died. It seems that the great curtain that covered and separated the Holy of Holies had been torn from top to bottom. When I was a boy I had seen this curtain, and I knew how thick and heavy it actually was. There was no way a man could tear it. Even two teams of the finest Roman horses would be unable to do this. This fact rekindled a spark in me that didn't answer any questions mind you, but left me wondering about the divinity of Jesus. It was also reported by some that they had seen people walking the streets of Jerusalem that were known to have passed on long ago. This, too, was a curious thing, and I discounted these reports as mistaken identities. The Sabbath dragged on. At long last the day ended and I was able to go to my bed and sleep.

"I didn't arise till late the next morning after a long, sound sleep. My parents and I talked much of things happening in my life and of my work as an apprentice tentmaker with my father's brother in Emmaus.

Nothing was said about the crucifixions I had witnessed just three days before.

"Cleopas had been a follower of Jesus for some time and was always trying to convince me that Jesus was the true son of David and the Messiah. As we walked we discussed the events that had taken place on Friday. I told him how crushed I was when I saw him hung upon that cross and how I even came to doubt that there was a God. But I told him that the torn curtain in the Temple and the reports of sightings of people who had died walking the streets of Jerusalem restored some faith in my heart.

"My friend, too, was anguished over the events, and related that, as he watched Jesus being nailed to the crosspiece, he had made eye contact with him and was impressed by the calmness he saw in his eyes.

"When I heard this I almost stumbled and fell and I quickly related that I, too, had made eye contact and was amazed at the calmness. We then discovered that we both had witnessed the event from two different locations and had not seen one another.

"Then Cleopas told me of the things that had happened at the tomb this very morning; how the women had found it opened and Jesus was gone, and that there were angels there telling them that he had arisen.

"It was at this point another man, who was walking our direction, overtook us on the road and just as suddenly joined us. As he came abreast of us he slowed and greeted us. After a few words of greetings in return, he said, 'You seem to be in a deep discussion about something. What are you so concerned about?'

"We stopped short; my friend had a pained expression on his face and replied. 'You must be the only person in Jerusalem who hasn't heard about all the things that have happened there the last few days.'

"What things?' the stranger asked.

"The things that happened to Jesus, the man from Nazareth,' Cleopas said. 'He was a prophet who did wonderful miracles. He was a mighty teacher, highly regarded by both God and all the people. But our leading priests and other religious leaders arrested him. They handed him over to be condemned to death, and they crucified him. We had thought he was the Messiah who had come to rescue Israel. That all happened just three days ago; then some women from our group of his followers were at his tomb early this morning, and they came back with an amazing report. They said his body was missing, and they had seen angels who told them Jesus is alive! Some of our men ran out to see, and sure enough, Jesus' body was gone, just as the women had said.'

"Then the man said to us, 'You are such foolish people! You find it so hard to believe all that the prophets wrote in the Scriptures. Wasn't it clearly predicted by the prophets that the Messiah would have to suffer all these things before entering his time of glory?' He then went on to quote passages from the writings of Moses and all the prophets, explaining what all the Scriptures said about the Messiah.

"By this time we were nearing Emmaus and the end of our journey. The man prepared to go on, but we insisted that he stay the night with us, since it was getting late. So he came into our home with us. As we sat down to eat, he took a small loaf of bread, asked God's blessing on it, broke it, then gave it to us. It was then that I noticed the wounds on his wrists and suddenly both Cleopas and I recognized him as being Jesus the Christ. And it was at that moment he disappeared! We both sat still for the longest time our mouths open in wonder. It was at that very moment I knew that Jesus was truly the Son of the Living God.

"Cleopas and I hurriedly gathered our things and started back to Jerusalem. 'The others need to hear the great news,' Cleopas shouted as we ran to the door and rushed out into the cool evening air. We walked as fast as we could and said little to one another as we focused on our quick pace back to the city.

At this point I paused a moment to let the audience absorb the words I'd just spoken. I bowed my head lost in thought and said a short prayer to myself. When I looked up my audience too, seemed lost in their own reflections of my story, as if trying to sort out the reality of the personal account they'd just heard. Sensing their confusion, I continued speaking.

"After Jesus' resurrection he remained with us on earth for forty days. He didn't appear only to Cleopas and me but to a great multitude of other people before he ascended into heaven on that fortieth day. This ascension happened before the very eyes of his closest followers, and many others were also present."

I looked at the group of farmers and pilgrims and then spoke in a loud voice, almost a shout. "Believe what I have said. I personally witnessed his death and then spoke with him three days later as Cleopas and I returned to Emmaus. This man is truly the one sent by God to save us from our sins. That night in Emmaus I came to believe; I finally accepted all that I'd been afraid to accept up to that time, but when I saw him I knew that he was the one. I ask that you, too, accept my words and believe in Jesus as the Messiah. If you do, you will be saved from your sins and receive God's free gift of eternal life, to be spent with Jesus and with God our creator.

"The time will come when those of us who witnessed his life will be gone. Then the people must come to accept these things based on their faith. But for now you can accept my word, for I did witness these truly miraculous happenings. There is no doubt that he did live. Even the Jewish leaders know that. No one has said or can say that he ever committed any sins. Multitudes were present to see him crucified, and great numbers saw and heard him after his resurrection.

"If any of you here want to accept him as your Lord and Savior, then stay here with me. I'll pray for you and with you as you accept him into your lives. As for the rest of you, I pray that when you go to your beds tonight that you ponder these things in your minds and hearts and draw your own conclusions that what I have told you are true. There is only this lifetime during which you may accept Jesus as the Son of God. After our passing from this life, we will no longer be able to make the choice and will remain eternally separated from God if we refuse to accept Jesus as our Lord."

As the group slowly got to their feet I, Caleb, said, "We will leave tomorrow in the late afternoon and travel only at night. Sleep well and pray for our safety." About half of those present left the circle to go to their beds. The others crowded closer to me. I prayed over them as they confessed their sins and accepted Jesus into their lives.

PHILADELPHIA

The next day, we pilgrims prepared for our trip, which would take us further to the east-northeast, towards the city of Philadelphia. The farmers were sad to see us go but they understood the dangers both groups would face if the Romans found us there. They therefore took from their own stores quantities of preserved food and gave it to us so that we would not want during the weeklong journey.

As the sun began to sink low on the horizon, we pilgrims assembled on the outskirts of the village. Amidst tearful goodbyes, we began our journey. One of our families stayed behind with the farmers, as the woman was pregnant and unable to travel. She, her husband and two other children were quickly taken in by one family and there they would stay and become a part of the community.

I had made many similar trips over the years as I traveled with the many evangelists who had gone out spreading the word of Jesus. I took the lead and assigned reliable believers to be in charge of the food and supplies. In their generosity, the farmers had given us two donkeys in order to help us with our load.

The temperature was high and the sky was clear. There was very little water to be had over our proposed route. We journeyed by night and tried to sleep during the day, which was difficult due to the brutal heat and lack of shade. The many young children and two elderly women in the group slowed our progress, and we considered about one half the distance an average adult walks, from sun up to late afternoon, a good night's travel.

At this time in my life I felt much like the prophet Moses who had brought the children out of Israel. I not only led the way but also played the role of mediator, leader and spiritual guide. After three days of travel, I was persistently confronted by many of the younger men who felt that we should be proceeding at a quicker pace. Through prayer and diligence I was able to maintain peace and unity in the group. Many of these younger men wanted to take their portion of the supplies and proceed on ahead. I counseled that to do so would leave both groups open to assault from the desert people, who were not known for their generosity to foreign and unprotected travelers. I, therefore, devised a plan where each evening I sent three or four of these young men out as scouts to look and warn the pilgrims of problems ahead. This proved to be a providential move on my part as no fewer than four times we were able to skirt bandits and at least one troop of Roman soldiers without discovery. It also satisfied the younger men as they felt a greater responsibility towards the group.

At the end of the sixth night of our travels we pilgrims pitched our last camp as we were within a half days walk of the city of Philadelphia. As the sun disappeared below the horizon and my fellow travelers prepared to leave, I addressed the group.

"I think it best that we continue to rest until a short time before sunrise. Following our early morning meal we will travel to the city and proceed to the house of friends of mine in Christ. A short while ago I sent two of our scouts on ahead with instructions to these friends concerning our needs. As God blessed us when we were with the farmers I know that he will bless us again with provision for our new life here in this land.

"I pray that those of you who have not accepted Jesus into your lives that at this time you reconsider and do it now. Sleep in peace and pray for our opportunity to start anew. I wish you all well and pray that you get a peaceful night's rest. Those who want to stay and pray with me, you're welcome to stay."

The gathering quietly left for their blankets as four others remained and stepped forward in order to accept Christ.

Early in the afternoon we who had escaped from the terror of Jerusalem entered the city of Philadelphia and proceeded to the home of my friend. There we were received with love and open arms and quickly settled into our new way of life.

After shepherding the pilgrims and seeing that they were settled comfortably into their new life, my grandson Abram and I set up our business as tentmakers. This gave me the capability of earning enough for us to live while at the same time I had the freedom to work for the Lord. In this endeavor, I was able to convince all but three of the pilgrims who had fled Jerusalem with me that they should accept Jesus into their lives. I was unable to convince these last three that it was more than mere happenstance that we were able to escape and settle peacefully in our new environment. In addition to my work with the pilgrims, I toiled tirelessly in my efforts to bring other new converts to the church at Philadelphia.

The next three years seemed to fly by. I had very little time to myself. My main concerns were working for the Lord and bringing up my grandson. Abram had been orphaned early in the year 66 CE when both of his parents, my daughter and son-in-law, had been killed during the initial stages of the Jewish rebellion. The violence of the rebels who controlled the city and that of the Roman army led me to plan our escape.

Now, after three years of peace and comfort in the city of Philadelphia, I received word of yet another great Roman army forming in the north and beginning to move through Judea in order to put the issue of the rebellious Jews to rest. Many Christians still resided in Jerusalem, and it was my plan to reenter the city and lead as many to safety as I could. Abram was now eighteen and able to work the trade and continue his support of the followers of Christ in Philadelphia.

There was other disturbing news that we received. Since the death of Nero during this last year, the whole of the Roman Empire seemed to be in turmoil. A civil war had broken out in Rome as various men jockeyed for control. One of these men was the Roman general, Vespasian.

ESCAPE FROM
JERUSALEM

Though by outward appearances, Jerusalem had been cut off from the outside world, there were those who were still willing to risk life and limb to go to and from the city. They were able to move at night without being detected by either the rebels who controlled the city from the inside or by the Roman soldiers who patrolled the outside walls as they awaited the arrival of their commander Vespasian and the Twelfth Legion that was moving south through Galilee. These bandits that smuggled goods into and out of Jerusalem had no interest in the human suffering taking place inside the walls; they were only focused on how much wealth they could garner through their risky undertakings, that of smuggling food and supplies in and people and their wealth out.

One of these men I had known in my youth, and had run into quite by accident one day during our third year in Philadelphia. He had come to our place of business to have us do some work on the harness and saddlebags he used on his camels. It was through him that I learned of the dire straits that the good citizens of Jerusalem were in. This news grew grimmer after each trip that this man, Josephus, made to the great capitol of Judea. It was after his fourth visit to our business that I formulated a plan to return to Jerusalem with his help in order to affect the escape of some of my believer friends and bring them to Philadelphia. Though Josephus was an informant and, true, even a confidant, he was not a valued friend. To have him sneak me into the city was to cost me dearly, and to smuggle out some of the Christian friends trapped inside the walls was going to be a small fortune.

Josephus was a man of my age, an Idumean by birth, a man I had known when we both were very young. Even then he was a bully and enjoyed pushing people around. In his teens, he was constantly in trouble for stealing and other forms of larceny. From there he slipped ever lower into the wicked and sinful life he now enjoyed. He was a large, heavyset man with thick black curly hair with streaks of gray and a long scraggly beard. He had a dark complexion with deep-set eyes that were black as charcoal. His demeanor matched his appearance and he could be very mean-spirited to those he did not like. On the other hand, he did have a strong sense of fairness with those who hired him to take them to and from Jerusalem.

My plan was to use resources from my own industry and from the followers of The Way in Philadelphia in order to pay Josephus to take me to Jerusalem and then slip me inside the city itself. According to him, we would not be able to smuggle more than three or four people at a time out of Jerusalem. No matter how few we could save, the risk seemed to be worth the effort.

Early on in the year, nearly thirty-five years since the crucifixion of Jesus, we set out from Philadelphia for our return to the great walled city of God. Before leaving, we received word that Vespasian's Twelfth Legion was in Galilee where, after laying siege to the city of Jotapata, they had defeated it.

Once this city was conquered, they would move first towards Caesarea where the Tenth and Fifteenth Legions under his son Titus would join them. From Caesarea the entire army would proceed east to Jerusalem. We also heard that inside the city, after a great deal of fighting between the various groups, the more upright citizens, those who favored the return of law and order to Jerusalem, under the priest

Eleazar had entrapped the Zealots within the Temple area. However, another rebel by the name of John had escaped out of the clutches of the Romans in Galilee. He entered Jerusalem with a sizable following, and had through subterfuge, taken control out of the hands of the upright citizens and became a tyrant over a large portion of the lower city. To add to the distress of the citizens, an Idumean army had come to Jerusalem and was camped outside the gates. This army had been summoned by the entrapped Zealots in order to help them retake control of all of Jerusalem. As the Roman force outside the walls of the city was but a small garrison awaiting the arrival of Vespasian's army, the Idumeans were able to approach the ramparts of Jerusalem without interference.

Our trip west went without serious incident to within a short distance of that great city. We traveled only at night, and we gave wide berth to any caravans or groups of people we saw along our route. We traveled on camels, and our journey took a little less than a week. More than once we had to skirt around Roman patrols, one outside Jericho and another near Bethany, but Josephus and I were able to find sufficient hiding places in order to avoid detection. The real trial for us would come when we entered the city and had to remain clear of the civil war that was raging inside the walls.

We learned after our arrival that during the time that it had taken us to travel from Philadelphia to Jerusalem, the Idumean army had been denied entry into the city by the upright citizens. The Idumeans camped outside the western gate for three nights. Then during a tremendous storm late one night, the citizens let their guard down as they sought shelter from the driving rain and hail that showered down on them.

As the storm raged, some of the Zealots escaped from the Temple area, opened the gates and let the Idumeans in. The ensuing slaughter of the innocents of Jerusalem was without equal. When they'd finished, more than eight thousand citizens lay dead in the streets. One Idumean commander, recognizing the excess of their dastardly deeds, withdrew about half of the troops and returned home. With the exodus of a large number Idumean troops, control of the upper city defaulted into the hands of the Zealots. They immediately continued the rampage and dispatched much of their opposition that remained in Jerusalem by slaughtering another large number of citizens through rigged tribunals overseen by judges they had paid off in order to hand down the death sentences.

As we drew close to Jerusalem, we came to a small farm where we left our camels at the stable of an associate of Josephus. This land was a little less than a one half days walk east of the city's walls. We arrived late in the morning, and I spent some time feeding and bedding down the animals in the small corral just to the rear of the stable. As I did this, Josephus went into the house with the farmer.

After spending daylight in the stable of this business partner and being briefed on the recent events taking place in the city, we proceeded on foot to the southeast gate of Jerusalem. Our path led us down through the valley of the Kidron and then up to a gate near the southeast corner. Over the last one hundred paces to the wall, we encountered stacks of human remains on both sides of our path. These poor souls, the slaughtered citizens of Jerusalem, had been placed there by the Zealots. They, the now victorious rulers of the city, had refused proper burial to these residents they had murdered out of contempt for what was considered their acts of treason.

My immediate plan, on returning to Jerusalem, was to find the family of David and Mary, the couple that I had met so many years before on the banks of the Jordan River during our encounter with John the Baptist. They too, had searched a long time for conviction and then they as well had found Jesus and accepted him on faith. I had become reacquainted with them, and we had been together in ministry for a number of years. I knew that they had suffered, as I had, under the rule of the Zealots and bandits that controlled the city before I left early on in the insurrection. My hope was to help them escape to safety. They had elected not to flee with the pilgrims and me three years earlier as they didn't feel that they could leave their son and grandchildren. I had since learned that the son and his family had been slaughtered during the civil war.

During our trip from Philadelphia, Josephus and I had talked at great length. He told me how much had changed since I was last in Jerusalem and gave me directions on how best to find my friends who had lived in the upper city, much of which had been burned and looted. I, in turn, told him of my encounters with the man Jesus and how he had entered my life through faith. Josephus refused to believe me and called me foolish to even believe in God. He said that the man that I met on the road to Emmaus had deluded my friend Cleopas and me. I was unable to convince him of the fact that Jesus was truly of God.

We approached Jerusalem at night. Soon we could see the southeastern wall in the distance, and the closer we came, the higher it loomed before us. There was a half moon rising over the eastern horizon that cast just enough light so that we could see our way along the road and discern the bodies of the slain citizens. At the end of the road there was a large gate that was closed tight, and we could barely make out the two guards that stood on the wall high above the entrance. It was their duty to challenge anyone approaching to determine if the gate should be opened or remain closed. However, before we got close enough to be detected by the guards, Josephus pulled me off the road and behind some bushes and trees where we would remain unseen.

"We'll leave the road here," he said. "Over to our right is a path that leads to a small and infrequently used gate. Next to that gate is a tunnel that we will crawl through and thus enter the city undetected."

"A tunnel?" I stammered. "We're not going to enter through a gate?"

"That's right," he replied, "If we go through the gate then we'll be captured and sent to prison. You have to remember we're not wanted here."

I thought it was probably he that was not wanted, being the thief that he was; as a result of his unsavory past I would have to crawl through that tunnel just so he wouldn't be recognized. Then my thoughts became more rational as I realized that the only way to smuggle my friends out of the city would be through this tunnel. This brought a new fear to mind, for I hated tight places and tended to panic in enclosed dark spaces. My confidence quickly dropped to a new low.

Why did I ever think that I could do this operation so easily? There was always risk and I could deal with that, but crawling under the wall in a small tunnel was something else entirely.

Soon we were at the wall approaching the small gate of which Josephus spoke. Near it several cubits to our right was some shrubbery behind which was a round, flat rock that covered the entrance. Josephus easily rolled this aside. Even though the night breeze carried a chill, I could feel beads of perspiration breaking out on my brow and my hands were damp and clammy. I didn't want Josephus to know of my fears, so I clenched my teeth and followed his lead into the tunnel.

Once inside the entrance, he rolled the stone back and we were engulfed in total darkness.

"Caleb," he said. "Grab hold of this rope and just follow me through the tunnel. You'll have to crawl on your hands and knees for about one hundred fifty cubits and the air is thin, but don't worry we'll be through it in no time."

I didn't say a thing for fear he would hear my chattering teeth. I just grabbed the rope and tugged it lightly to let him know I was ready and then followed him, praying all the way that I wouldn't die in this dark and scary place.

It seemed to take forever and I had trouble breathing, but I continued on in silence. After what seemed to me to be a lifetime, Josephus stopped and whispered that we were approaching the other end.

"Let go of the rope," he commanded, "and I'll roll away the rock and check to be certain there isn't anyone nearby who could see us as we come out of the tunnel."

I mumbled an all right and let go of the rope. He moved away from me but it was so dark I couldn't see how far he went. I heard the stone move, followed by a rush of fresh air. I filled my lungs and gave thanks to God that this ordeal was finally over.

We entered the city through a small hole under the wall in an alley off of a residential street in the lower city near the lower portion of the Tyropoeon Valley. Josephus told me that he and several associates had dug the tunnel the year before. The city, now under the weighty hand of the Zealots, was heavily patrolled. Even Josephus was appalled at the destruction that had taken place since he was last there, just one month earlier. We had planned to separate to do our business and then meet at our entry point the very next night at this time. Josephus was meeting some people in order to smuggle a great deal of loot and other valuables out of Jerusalem. As it was close to dawn, we changed our plans and decided that we'd meet well after dark in the evening of the next day. Following our agreement, Josephus left me, and I was alone and very much afraid.

I quickly gathered my wits by first of all memorizing the location of the tunnel in relation to the rest of the city. With that position well settled in my mind, I started walking up one of the side streets towards the upper city. This part of Jerusalem had not been damaged and soon looked somewhat familiar to me. As I moved ever closer to my goal, I came upon that part of the city that had been severely burned. I had to walk around and over numerous piles of rubble that littered the streets. The sky continued to get lighter. It wouldn't be too long before the sun would rise. As I stumbled along, I heard a man's voice challenge me, telling me to stand still. I looked behind me and saw three men about a block away start running towards me. I knew I didn't want to be confronted by them so I started running up a nearby alley. One of the men shouted again telling me stop and wait.

My heart was banging inside my chest. I had never felt such great fear as I felt at that moment. I just knew that they were some of the Zealots who were up to no good. I ran as fast as I could, from alley to alley and street to street. I don't know how long I ran or where I was going. Soon I realized that it was dawn and that I could be seen easily by anyone who happened out on the street. I turned right at the next corner and ran into a burned-out house near the intersection. I crawled under some rubble and tried to catch my breath. I listened for the men who had been chasing me and soon concluded that I had lost them and needn't fear them any longer. After a while, I was able to calm down and began to think that maybe this would be a good place to sleep during the day as I was well hidden from view. Then another thought struck me as I peered through the rubble in which I was hidden; I was on the street where I had lived as a child, a place just below the wall that separated the upper city from the lower one. We had never been wealthy enough to live in the upper city but we had lived in a fairly well to do section of the lower city.

The thought of being in this place of my youth flooded my mind with a thousand memories. I thought of my mother and father who were both now dead and of all my childhood friends. In my mind's eye I could clearly see the faces of these people who were part of my past. It was at this time that I realized that I was hiding in the house of my very good friend, Ruth. The two of us, both all of eight years, would play together and she would occasionally walk me to my synagogue classes. I had lost track of her shortly thereafter and frequently wondered what had happened to her. There were others who had long since come to untimely ends. Many others had died just recently in the rebellion. I was proud of my heritage and of the nation of Israel and my heart ached over the events of the past few years. There were so many good Jewish people dying because of the greed of a few brutal men. This disaster that had fallen on Jerusalem was totally repugnant to me as it took so many righteous people from our midst.

I carefully checked for signs of other people in and around the streets before I left my hiding place, and then I cautiously crept up the street to the house where I had grown up so many years before. This building hadn't been so badly burned and the rooms were still intact, though the roof was gone and the inside walls had been blackened from the fires.

I thought of the many good times I had had with my mother as we talked as she prepared diner and waited for my father to come home from his work. As these thoughts flowed through my mind I sat down on the floor near the fireplace where our meals had been prepared, and before I knew it I fell fast asleep.

A sudden noise awakened me, and instantly I was alert. I soon determined that the noise was nothing other than some rats that had brushed under some fallen debris causing it to crash to the floor. As my heartbeat returned to normal, I noticed that it was beginning to get dark. I guess I hadn't realized how tired I was in the morning before I fell asleep, for I had slept soundly all day long. I decided to stay in my hiding place until after dark. As there was to be no moon until just before dawn, I carefully thought out the route I would take to David and Mary's home, which I thought was way more than twelve hundred cubits from where I now was. I didn't know how badly the area in which they lived had been devastated as a result of the recent rebellion.

I didn't even know if they were still alive. Things had changed so radically. If I were unable to find them then I would look for some other friends who had lived nearby.

It wasn't long before it was black as pitch. It was so dark I could hardly see my hand in front of my face. When I was certain that no other being was near, I carefully extracted my pack and myself from under the fallen timbers covering my hiding place. I moved slowly in order not to make any unnecessary noise. For most of the trip, my heart was in my mouth. I had a strong faith in God and knew He was with me, but I wasn't used to this type of work and it truly frightened me. Once free from the house of old memories, I moved slowly, careful not to trip over any of the piles of debris that littered the way to David's house.

I heard some of the patrols of the Zealots as they moved boisterously through the streets. They were easy to skirt around since they traveled in large groups of three or four and talked loudly in confident tones. I found that the gate that led from the lower city into the upper city had been damaged by one of the fires and was open and unguarded; however, I approached it with great caution and slowly made my way through. I was rewarded for this vigilance, for on the other side another gang of Zealots marched noisily down the street knocking on doors and in general terrorizing the citizens. I quickly ducked into an open doorway and entered a courtyard of a burned-out house. I hid under some debris and waited until the danger passed.

When it was safe I crawled out of my hiding place and continued my search. Within a short time, I finally reached the street on which David and Mary lived. Some of the houses had been burned, but others were left standing. All seemed to share some scars from the ongoing civil war. When I at last reached the place I had been hunting for, I was grieved to see that it had been burned, at least in part. David's father had been a Pharisee and enjoyed an elevated status in earlier

Jerusalem society. Because of his position and eminence, he lived in a large house located in a well-to-do neighborhood. After his death some years prior, the house fell into David's possession. On further inspection and as best I could determine on this dark night, a portion of the house remained intact.

Before trying to knock on the door and cause a certain amount of commotion, I pushed it and found that it easily swung open. I stepped inside and found myself in a burned section that had once been the main entrance. This had at one time been a large room always warm and welcoming. Since David and Mary had come to live here, this had been a meeting place for the early believers in Jesus. This house was a place of sanctuary for the believers and particularly for those new to the faith.

I felt empty and a little bewildered, as it appeared as if no one were here. This had been the goal of my whole trip, to bring Mary and David out of this war zone and take them to safety. Dejected, I sat down on a bench and put my elbows on my knees and chin in my hands as I contemplated my next move.

I hadn't sat there for long when I heard a women's voice, from far away. I couldn't make out the words as they were muffled. I wasn't frightened as it was distinctly feminine, and as far as I knew, there were no women involved in the rebellion. I stood and listened intently, trying to follow the sound. It definitely came from deep within the interior of the house. I walked toward the voice and came to a wall. I put my hands on it and felt along until I came to what appeared to be a door that was shut tight and locked. The voice came from the other side.

I knocked lightly and called in a loud whisper, "Mary, David, it is Caleb." All fell deathly quiet. There was no sound and no light for the longest time. Again I knocked lightly, and said, "It is I, Caleb son of Isaac."

Again there was a long silence then I heard some scratching on the door. It slowly opened, just enough for me to see the outline of a woman's head. I said, "Is that you Mary? I have returned to Jerusalem to take you and David back with me to Philadelphia."

"Praise God, it is you Caleb!" And with that she swung the door wide open and threw both of her arms around my neck. She held tight for the longest time, and I could feel her tears on my face.

Before she released her grip two other arms were flung around the both of us, and I heard David's voice say, "You are truly the answer to our prayers, Caleb."

As we were in David's embrace, a small bright flame drew my attention as someone on the other side of the room blew on a smoldering wick and reignited the flame of a lamp.

David released his arms from around us and Mary then withdrew her arms from around my neck and quickly closed and latched the door. David put his left hand on my shoulder and guided me across the small room to the man and woman who were sitting on the floor on the opposite side of the room. "These are our friends and brother and sister in Christ, Rachael and Saul."

I greeted them in the name of the Lord and sat on the floor opposite them in cross-legged fashion as Mary and David sat on either side of me to complete our circle. We were sitting on a heavy blanket or rug and I couldn't distinguish its color or pattern, but it was comfortable to me after I had spent so many days in the saddle, and nights sitting on the ground.

David then spoke of the conditions in Jerusalem. "Caleb, things are terrible here. We have run out of food, and there's precious little water. Fortunately, it rained a week ago and we were able to collect some, but it won't last long. The bandits under Simon and those Zealots foray out against each other every day, throwing their darts and shooting their arrows killing and wounding many. They drag innocent citizens from their houses and kill them in an indiscriminate manner. It's a horrid situation. The son of the Chief Priest, Eleazar by name, has his own gang through whom he tries to regain control of the city.

"We are fortunate in that we live in the upper city and have this house, which affords us some protection from the bloodthirsty rabble that roams the streets. This room was my father's treasure room that is well hidden from the casual observer. If it is ever discovered we would all soon be dead."

David stopped here and stared down at the blanket as the two women quietly wept. As Saul stared straight ahead, he added, "I believe that Jesus is truly the Son of God, but does he mean for us to just sit here and be slaughtered?"

I nodded and said nothing for a short time. Then I responded as best as I could. "What God wants most of all is a confession of our sins and an acceptance on faith that Jesus is the son of the living God. Once you place that trust then He will govern and direct your life. You have done that, Saul, so now all you need to do is turn yourself over to Him and He will lead you. We are all on the road to death for that's where all life leads, but the important thing is, do we spend eternity separated from Him? Or do we spend that eternity in His house?

"No one, or maybe I should say most people, don't want to die, even I am one of those. I do know though, that if He chooses to take me now, I am prepared, are you?" I left that question opened, and I could see that each one answered it in their own way to themselves.

From here I quickly changed the subject, for now we had more urgent business at hand. I told of the purpose of my visit and that I would only be able to take the four of them with me. I explained all about the new life in Philadelphia that the pilgrims and I enjoyed since our escape some three years before and the growth of our church of The Way and of the wide acceptance of Jesus as the Son of God.

Mary interrupted briefly to tell me that they hadn't known whether we had escaped or been captured and that this news brought new joy to her heart. I told her that it had been a difficult journey but that we had, through the grace of God, been truly rescued from the terrible tribulations that were taking place in all of Judea, and that I had returned to take them out of the city.

I then told them of Josephus and how he had brought me into Jerusalem and eventually to the house of David and Mary. As I talked I noticed that it was getting lighter in the room and surmised that the sun must be coming up. Though the room had no windows, the light was entering the room from the partially destroyed roof that had been incompletely burned in the fires which had engulfed the upper city. I then went on to explain that we could not move until after dark—a fact that they well knew.

Next I asked if they were willing to take the risk and go with me that evening to make our escape from the city. The four looked at one another and then fell silent as each stared at the floor directly in front of them. A short time latter David responded."Caleb, we've been hiding here for more than a month, fearing to venture out even during the night. Our family has all been killed, as have Saul and Ruth's family. We reached the end of our food supplies more than a week ago. We have been living on a few loaves of bread that we finished just last night, and as I told you, our water is about gone. Other than a small skin of wine to drink, we will all probably be dead in a week or two. Your proposal is sent from God. I think I speak for the four of us when I say we are ready and willing to go with you." The others nodded their approval.

I acknowledged their enthusiasm by saying, "It is settled. We will stay here until it is dark and then make our way to the Water Gate, for that is near the point of our escape through another exit." I didn't tell them of the tunnel for fear they would inadvertently let the Zealots in on the secret if they were indeed captured. "There we will wait for my friend and then leave the city and proceed to Philadelphia."

The others grinned as I said this and I could see some signs of relief on their faces. But I cautioned them by adding, "It sounds easy but this is a deadly business if we are captured." Each quietly contemplated this in stillness. I told them that we should stay hidden here until dark and then added a significant provision, "We'll have no room to take any possessions, just what you're wearing." They looked at one another and then back at me before they again nodded their agreement.

FEEDING THE MULTITUDE

After a long silence Saul directed a question at me. "David and Mary have told us much about you, and they have said that you actually talked to the risen Jesus. Is that true?"

"Yes." I answered, and I told them about my encounter with him during Cleopas's and my return from Jerusalem to Emmaus. Saul then asked if there were any other encounters I may have had with the Lord Jesus.

"There were others," I replied. "I believe the most significant of those encounters occurred during the time I traveled to Galilee. This happened before Jesus' crucifixion, maybe the year before. My uncle's business in Emmaus had slowed down considerably, and there was little for Cleopas or me to do. As a result, my friend urged me to ask Uncle if I could have some time off so that we could travel north together, find Jesus and then follow him for a week before returning. Cleopas knew that Jesus and his followers were near the Sea of Galilee and would not be in Jerusalem for The Passover. I, of course, thought that this would be a grand idea and quickly went to my uncle to ask his permission. Uncle was reluctant as this would take place during the time of Passover. He questioned me at length, trying, I think, to see if maybe there were some hidden motives in my request. When he was convinced that I truly wanted to go follow the man Jesus, he relinquished his doubt and sent us on our way with his blessing. I do think that he had some misgivings, however, since I had not talked with my parents about the trip and I would not be home during the festival. No matter—we left the next day.

"Our trip was pleasant. As there were only the two of us, we made good time. We traveled light with only a change of clothes, our blankets and food. We covered nearly a quarter of the distance each day. By the end of our fourth day we had reached our destination, the shores of the Sea of Galilee.

"I was anxious to look upon this man Jesus again. It had been nearly two years since I had seen him at the wedding in Cana. All that I had heard about him seemed to point to a man that had a strong sense of compassion for his fellow countrymen. I knew he was something special. All that the people we encountered could talk about was the miraculous healings that had taken place in his presence. His words always seemed to be about God, love for one another and how we should conduct our lives in trying to please God. I felt that he was a prophet like the ones who had come in the days long past—a Jeremiah, Isaiah or Ezekiel. I had determined in my own mind that he couldn't be the Messiah since he did not come to be a king, like David had been, and drive the Romans from Judea. There was no army and no attempt to take power from Herod. So in my mind he was a prophet, one I wanted to hear. It was also on this trip when we heard that early on in the year Herod had beheaded John the Baptist. We did not learn the reason or circumstances that brought Herod to do this but we surmised that it probably happened during one of his drunken orgies.

This was truly a tragedy, and it took me a long while to get this image out of my mind.

"We had heard that Jesus and all of his disciples and other believers were walking south along the shore of the Sea of Galilee somewhere near Gennesaret. Cleopas and I decided to continue our northward journey following that same Galilean shoreline in order to join up with them at some point along the way. It was in the late morning of the fifth day that we saw them moving towards us along the beach. There was a great clamor of people. Many were crippled or infirm in one manner or another. Cleopas told me that that was the way it always was when Jesus traveled. People would come from great distances seeking the healing hand of the master. Friends and relatives would also carry their loved ones just so that Jesus could touch and heal them. I was anxious to see these miraculous healings for myself. I'd heard much about them and some of the things were truly incredible, so my excitement increased as we approached the large multitude.

"Before we could reach the crowd, we saw what appeared to be Jesus and his disciples turn away from the shore and climb a small hill just to the west. A short way up that incline about two hundred cubits or so, Jesus stopped and sat down on an outcropping of rock that faced the sea and overlooked the throng of people below it all along the shore. These people who were following crowded around, and they, too, sat looking up at the master. We continued to walk until we reached the edge of the multitude near the beach. We could look up and see Jesus as he was sitting on a large flat rock, making him plainly visible to all around, both to those above as those of us below on the shore. It appeared to me that the disciples were leading the lame, blind, crippled, mute and those who were ill for Jesus to lay his hands on them. I was truly intrigued by the event and barely heard Cleopas say that he saw some of his friends near Jesus and was going to join them. I'm sure he asked me to come but for some reason I wanted to be alone to savor this moment as I tried to determine what all of this was about. Cleopas told me he would rejoin me here later in the day, and before I knew it he disappeared into the crowd. Though I was nearly forty to fifty cubits away from Jesus, I could see what he was doing. When a person was healed, there would be a joyous sound from the one healed and from the crowd. It was not solemn at all but reminiscent of a festival. Jesus talked to each of those he healed. I couldn't hear what he said in all cases, but he talked about faith and how through faith we are healed. Those that were healed walked away praising God for their new life. For me it was truly a glorious event. I don't know how long I sat and listened and watched all of the proceedings, but I soon realized that the sun was sinking in the west.

"At this time Cleopas rejoined me and said, 'My friends have asked that you come and join us up closer to the master. There you will see and hear everything.' I quickly jumped to my feet and followed Cleopas. When we were much closer to where he was, we found a place and we sat. I could easily hear what he had to say to those he healed. His voice was strong and convincing, but filled with love and compassion. The size of the crowd had continued to grow throughout the afternoon and evening, and those who were infirm in one way or another were brought to him and he healed them. I was spellbound by the whole event and amazed by the healing that was taking place. Still I was unable to say that he was of God. Something in me kept urging me not to believe what I was seeing. I had heard of people being healed of certain afflictions when they felt in their heart that the physician they'd sought out was able to relieve their pain. Was not healing of the individual's own doing? This then was the issue with which I wrestled—my own lack of faith.

"As I contemplated this whole situation, I was brought out of my reverie when I heard Jesus say to those disciples nearest him, 'I feel sorry for these people. They have been here with me for three days, and they have nothing left to eat. I don't want to send them away hungry, or they will faint along the road.'

"The disciples replied, 'And where would we get enough food out here in the wilderness for all of them to eat?'

"Jesus asked, 'How many loaves of bread do you have?'

"They replied, 'Seven, and a few small fish.' So Jesus told all the people to sit down on the ground. Then he took the seven loaves and the fish, thanked God for them, broke them into pieces, and gave them to the disciples, who distributed the food to the crowd.

"We all ate until we were full, and then the disciples picked up the scraps. That which was left over filled seven large baskets! By my estimate there had to have been over four thousand men who were fed that day—this in addition to all the women and children. When all of the people had eaten and the leftover food was picked up, Jesus sent the people home. He and some of his followers quickly got into a boat and crossed over to the region of Magadan.

"We spread our blankets for the night along the shore, and, after building a fire, Cleopas and I discussed the event we'd just witnessed. I was totally mystified by what I'd seen and told him that. He said that other followers had told him that the very same thing had taken place a short time before, but that he had fed a crowd of five thousand men plus all of the women and children that were with them. He went on to ask, 'Don't you now believe that he is the Messiah?' For some unknown reason, I couldn't bring myself to accept that thought, but in my heart I knew that he was someone special.

"The next few days we walked around the lake to Magadan and searched for Jesus and his followers, but we were not able to catch up with him before we had to return to our home."

I finished my story and fell silent as the others, deep in thought, considered what I had said. Within a short time we heard a great number of voices out somewhere in the city. The clamor created by a vast number of men yelling filled the once silent room. The quizzical look on my face elicited a response from David without my even having to ask.

"Those are the rebels and Eliazar's men fighting again.

Each group forays out two or three times a week trying to control the whole city for themselves. They each think they are destined by God to take control of Jerusalem."

I told my friends that there was a large force of Roman troops battering at the walls of Jotapata and that soon they would be in Caesarea before turning towards Jerusalem. So whoever took control of the city would not own it very long, for the Roman legions were determined to retake Jerusalem or to destroy it.

At this point Saul suggested that we start getting ready to leave. It would soon be twilight, and with the rebels and Eliazar occupied in their battle it would be a great opportunity to slip out of the house and head for our rendezvous with Josephus without being seen.

It wasn't long before we found ourselves in the street. David stopped a minute, turned and looked at his house. With tears in his eyes, he said his last goodbye to the place where he had lived his entire life. Then he turned his back to what had once been his home, and we quickly started on our way.

We found our route deserted, though the noise of the battle, over near the Temple area, resounded up and down the streets of the city. We hurried along without saying much to one another. Before turning on a new street, I would stop with the others behind me and peek around the corner to ensure no one was around. We stayed as close to the buildings and in the shadows as much as we could.

As we approached one corner the noise of the battle grew louder. I stopped my friends, and then I peered around the corner and saw a short distance down the street a large number of men yelling and flailing their arms in the air. Their backs were turned towards me, and some threw rocks and stones at another group of men still further on down the road that faced our way and seemed as determined to assault that group closest to us. These men with their backs to us were the rearguard of a force that was trying to attack the other group. They all were yelling, and many were not only throwing rocks and stones but also their deadly darts and arrows at the opposition. I could see the bodies of many who had fallen in the battle, lying askew and in a helter skelter manner over the street. Some I know were dead; others were wounded. It was a terrible sight, and it sickened me to think that countrymen were fighting countrymen. This would make it all the easier for the Romans to enter the city and re-conquer Jerusalem.

My attention quickly returned to our current situation when David grabbed my sleeve and pointed to an alley across the boulevard that seemed to be unoccupied. I nodded in agreement and sent Rachel and Saul across the street, followed by Mary and David. When they were safe I, too, followed and joined them in the alley.

The remainder of our mission was without incident and we were soon at the meeting place near the tunnel that would lead us from the city. By this time the sun had set and darkness had enshrouded the city.

I still hadn't let the others in on the secret as to how we were to escape the walls of Jerusalem. This I felt was better left unsaid until Josephus came to show them the way. We sat for a very long time without any sign of Josephus, and I was beginning to get nervous. What if he'd been captured or worse had been tortured into telling where the escape tunnel was?

I jumped at every little sound and soon began to fear for our lives. At one point, we heard what sounded like a gang of men headed our way, and we crawled ever deeper under the rubble in which we'd been hiding. Soon this gang of men began to move further away, and I was able to breathe a little easier. This did not quell my anxiety, though, so shortly after midnight I determined we should leave. Actually I kept hearing a voice in my head saying over and over, *Caleb, get up and moving. It's time for you to leave the city.*

I told my friends that I didn't think that Josephus was coming and that we'd better make the escape on our own. I then explained about the tunnel and where it was, just seventy-five cubits from our current position. I stood and walked with them to the hidden entrance. I told them that it was small and that we'd have to crawl on our hands and knees for over one hundred and thirty-five cubits.

"It will be black as pitch; you'll think that you've gone blind," I explained as I unraveled a rope that was hidden near the entrance. "Grab hold of this and don't let go. I will enter the tunnel first to lead the way; Mary and Ruth will come next followed by Saul and then David. Don't fear the dark for it is our friend. Grasp the rope tightly and follow its leading."

My old apprehension returned but it was too late in the game to tell them of my own fears. So I gritted my teeth and completed my directions. I instructed David on how to pull the covering over the opening after he was in the entrance. Next I whispered a prayer for our safety, and without another word I dropped to my hands and knees and entered the tunnel. We all crawled slowly in the stifling darkness. The air was thin and all four of us were panting from the exertion and from the lack of air. The trip seemed interminable, and I could hear the groans of the four behind me. When we reached what I thought to be the midpoint of our trip, I called a halt and told the others to sit still for a moment and rest. No one said a word, and all of us were breathing heavily.

After a moment to catch our collective breaths and for me to gather sufficient courage, I started forward, again instructing my friends to hold tight to the rope. We inched our way along for what seemed to be an eternity and suddenly the air started to freshen. I knew we were nearing our goal.

I pushed forward for another fifteen or twenty cubits and my head hit the covering of the tunnel's exit.

"Praise God," I said. "We've reached the end." I heard the others repeat the phrase as they sighed heavily over the good news.

"Sit and rest," I told them as I rolled the stone away from the opening. "I'm going out to reconnoiter the area to be sure its safe for us to be out in the open."

Once out of the tunnel I took a deep breath and savored the cool, fresh air as it filled my lungs. I thanked the Lord for our safe journey as I listened and looked for any signs of life. All was well as there didn't seem to be another living soul nearby. The sky was clear, and the stars stood out like brilliant jewels in the black velvet of the heavens. I stood staring and savoring the stillness for a moment and then went to the tunnel entrance and helped my friends out and to their feet. We all stood in silence staring at the brilliance of the stars. Soon David said a short prayer of thanksgiving as we bowed to the wonder and the might of the Lord.

After a few more moments of silence I carefully returned the stone in order to cover the tunnel entrance. I then commanded the group to follow me, and we started our walk to the small farm a good distance away from the great wall of Jerusalem, the place where Josephus and I had left the camels. I took a more circuitous route so that we did not walk by the bodies of the victims of the Idumean slaughter. As we walked, I conjectured that it was getting very late, somewhere after the fourth watch. I felt that it would be some time before sunrise when we finally reached the farm. As we walked I told my friends that we would quietly go to the stable and not bother the owner until after dawn, the point being that we would need to be very quiet. Secretly I was afraid of being confronted by Josephus's compatriot in the dark; there was no telling how he would treat us, or even if he would let us have the four camels.

The very early morning was quiet, and the only noise I heard was the sound of our own feet as we tramped along the dirt road. David was the first to break the silence, "The fighting must be over because I can't hear the men yelling any more. Even the city is dark for I see no light from over the wall."

I looked back and just as he had said Jerusalem was dark, as if the city had been abandoned. It truly saddened me to think of all the terrible things that had been taking place behind those dark walls. The once proud and vibrant city, God's city, was now dark no longer a dwelling place for the Lord. It had fallen into the hands of evil men, and I felt sure that what Jesus Christ had said many years ago was going to happen—Jerusalem and its Temple were doomed.

Our journey seemed longer than I had thought but finally I could begin to see the outline of the buildings of the farm where Josephus and I had left the animals, just two days before. It seemed much longer than that since so much had happened in the last two full days and nights. I suddenly felt weary; my feet felt so heavy I could hardly walk another step.

I called a halt to our journey and decided we should lie down under some trees along our path and wait until dawn before we continued to the farmhouse.

My companions were also exhausted and didn't say a thing other than to find a soft spot in the grass and quickly fall asleep.

The crowing of a nearby rooster brought me out of a deep sleep. I sat up and rubbed my eyes and then took in my surroundings. We were located in a small tree-filled depression of the ground just north of the road. The sky to the east was beginning to brighten, for the sun would be up soon. I judged that it was during the sixth watch in the morning. I sat with my back to a tree and tried to think about our next move. I wondered if Josephus had been caught and if I'd ever see him again. My next thought was about his compatriot, the farmer, and if he would release the camels to us for our trip back to my home. There were so many questions. What about the farmer? Would he turn us over to the Romans or worse to the zealots? I didn't know what to do. I did know that we needed a supply of food and water before we began our trek to Philadelphia.

That thought determined my next move. I would go alone to the farmer's house and see that everything was all right. From there, if all were well, we would continue on. If the opposite happened, then David, Mary, Saul and Ruth would have to fend for themselves.

I went to each of the slumbering figures and awakened them with a gentle shake of their shoulders. As they sat up and fought for consciousness, I told them of my plan. Mary asked, "What will we do if you're captured, we have no place to go?"

"Mary," I replied. "You will travel on to Philadelphia and go to my grandson, Abram; he and the followers of Christ will care for you. Do not fear—I won't be captured."

I know I sounded more confident than I felt. Before anyone could protest, I hurriedly left them and started towards the house. As I approached the small buildings, I could see a small light in the stable behind the house. Rather than knock on the door to the house, I walked straight to the open stable door. I stood there for a moment to let my eyes adjust to the light. The farmer was feeding his animals with his back to me. He was a short, stout man about my age or a little older. What was left of his dark hair was graying and his beard was tangled and hung limply from his chin. He was wearing an old robe filled with holes that appeared dingy and dirty. He was not what I would call a very pleasant looking fellow at all.

I took a deep breath and approached him with the greeting of, "Shalom." He nearly jumped out of his skin at the sound of my voice and turned holding his pitchfork at my chest.

"I'm the one who came with Josephus the other day." I stammered. "I've come to retrieve my camels for our return trip to Philadelphia."

"Where is Josephus?" he growled back at me. "He hasn't paid me my money for harboring and feeding the animals."

I knew this was a lie. I straightened to my full height of over 4 cubits and squared my shoulders as I replied in my gruffest voice, "I know he paid you for you told him you would not take the animals in unless you received payment in full first." I glowered at him as I conjured up the meanest look I could.

The farmer started to back away from me. Before he was able to take a step, I quickly grabbed a tine of the fork and yanked it from his hands. He was now defenseless, and quickly held up his hands and said. "Oh, yes, I remember now he did pay me."

I turned the fork in my hands and held the tines toward him but not in a threatening fashion. He put his hands down and asked if anyone was with me. I told him there were four others and that we would stay the day there waiting for Josephus and then leave at dusk.

His demeanor softened, and I returned the pitchfork to him as a show of my good will, hoping that this jester would ease his mind and allow us to spend the day in the comfort of the stable. He took the fork and held it for a few seconds before returning to his work of pitching hay to the animals.

"I will now go and get my friends and bring them to the stable," I said.

The man nodded and without another word being said I left through the door I had entered just a short time before. Once outside I stood and watched that door for four or five minutes. I wanted assurance he wouldn't run out on me and in some way summon help. When I was somewhat satisfied that I could trust the man, I turned and went to fetch my friends.

I left the stable and started towards the hiding place where we had spent the night. As I walked, I looked to the east and saw the top of the sun beginning to show over the horizon. I felt good as I thought that God had delivered us to a safe haven, at least for a short while. When I was within a short distance of my friends, I saw David come up from the depression and walk towards me. Before he could ask his question as to our safety, I told him to get the others and gather their things. We would spend the day in the stable.

They all looked relieved as I joined them and told them what had happened. None of us had much to carry and soon we were nearing our destination. The owner met us at the door, and I introduced each member to him. He nodded and stepped to the side so we could enter. However, before we went in, I asked his name.

He seemed hesitant to answer but then said in a low voice, "I am Silas."

After my friends were settled in the hay in the stable and the women already asleep, I stepped outside and went to farmer who was repairing the fence next to the shed.

"Silas," I said, "may I help you with the repair? I'm pretty good with my hands."

The man nodded and handed me small piece of rope, which I bound around one of the gateposts and a horizontal slat that had come loose. As I worked I asked Silas, "Are you currently practicing your faith as a Jew?"

Silas paused as if in thought. He then gestured towards Jerusalem whose walls could be seen off in the distance. After a short time he said, "How could I practice my faith with all of that carnage going on inside those walls? How could I believe in a God who would allow His chosen people to reduce themselves to nothing more than murderers? If there were a God, then this would not happen." He then fell silent as he went back to his work.

"It is terrible isn't it?" I said. "But you must remember that one of the gifts God has given us is our right to choose. A great number of Jewish people have chosen the wrong path to follow. It is through this choice that many have forsaken their God and are therefore suffering from His retribution, from His wrath. What I see happening in Jerusalem and in the whole of Judea are too many people who have strayed from their faith. By denying God and His love, they are paying a dear price."

"That's nonsense," Silas replied. "There isn't, nor was there ever a God. Everything that develops is mere happenstance. Man determines his own fate. So while we live, we must take everything we can or else someone else will come along and take it."

"Have you ever heard of the man called Jesus of Nazareth?" I asked.

"Do you mean that Zealot that the Jewish leaders crucified a number years ago? I know that he was a false prophet—that he misled many to believe that he was truly the son of God."

"That's the man," I said, "but he was neither a Zealot nor a false prophet. I saw him hung on that cross. I watched him die, and I watched as they laid him in the tomb." I studied Silas as he listened, and I paused long enough to let my words sink in before continuing. "Three days later my friend and I were walking from Jerusalem to our home in Emmaus, and we met a man on the road who walked a short distance with us. That man was Jesus, the very one I watched die on the cross. Not only did he appear to my friend and me but to many others. I saw with my own eyes the wounds in his arms from where he was nailed to the cross. He spoke and even ate with us. He was seen by his disciples and a multitude of other people, and he stayed here in Judea for forty days before he ascended into heaven.

"I saw him before his crucifixion and I witnessed him perform miracles and other wonderful healings. He spoke of love and respect for our fellow man, and it is his life we are to emulate. However, a greater number of our Jewish leaders have rejected him as our savior, and I believe that is why we see our nation crumbling around us."

"You mean you actually saw this man die? Next, you say you talked to him?"

I nodded and continued to study his face. He seemed to be thinking hard as if his mind were in turmoil, so I continued my silence. Finally he said, "I have heard similar things before but I have tried not to believe them, and especially now that all of Judea is at war. I could not understand how this land given to us by God could fall so low as to be destroyed by the very one who created us. I therefore have rejected the thought that there is a God. I've come to believe that we are just here; we just developed at the whim of nature. So you're saying that if I believe in this Jesus as being of God, then all of this will just go away?"

"I wish it were that easy," I said. "But it is that simple for you to receive your own salvation. By accepting Jesus who died for our sins on faith, that he is who he says he is, you will dwell in the house of the Lord forever."

Silas was quiet a long time and then said to me, "I have to think this over. I've spent a long part of my life rejecting God and convincing myself that there was no outside help and that I just had to take what I could get. These things that you have said change everything. But, what if you're wrong?

"Remember what the prophet Isaiah said, 'And we thought his troubles were a punishment from God for his own sins! But he was wounded and crushed for our sins. He was beaten that we might have peace. He was whipped, and we were healed! All of us have strayed away like sheep. We have left God's paths to follow our own. Yet the Lord laid on him the guilt and sins of us all.' This was the reason that Jesus died.

He died to absolve us from our own sins if only we just turn them over to him. Don't make it so difficult for yourself, Silas. I know I am right for I have seen these things I speak about.

There are those who have not seen them but accept them on faith and thus are saved. If I am wrong, then I die a better person for I have treated others well. You will die and leave nothing but distrust and hatred behind you. Now assume that I am right, then I will die and go to dwell in the house of the Lord forever. You? You will die eternally separated from the Lord. Your lone chance at redemption is only while you live. Once you cross over the line between life and death, you won't be given a second chance to change your mind."

Silas nodded and without a word returned to his work. I told him that I needed some sleep and that I was going to the stable. I turned and walked away.

When I entered the stable and climbed up to the hayloft, I found David awake as the others slept on. He asked me what I'd been doing. I told him that I had just witnessed my faith to Silas and implored him to pray for Silas's soul.

In the late afternoon Silas awakened me as he yelled up the ladder to the low loft in which we were sleeping. He said that someone was approaching the farm from the road to the west. I quickly went outside and stood next to him.

"I think that is Josephus coming," he said, "and it appears that he's hurt."

I ran up the road without a word, as I too saw that it was my companion. When I reached him, I saw that he had an arrow in his back near his right shoulder. I was surprised that he had been able to make it this far.

"When were you shot?" I demanded.

"Late last night or early this morning," he mumbled as he started to fall. I grabbed his left arm, put it across my shoulders and literally carried him to the stable. His weight was so great that I wasn't able to talk, and I struggled just to reach the door. David and Saul met me there and helped me carry the man to a soft pile of hay. There we laid him down on his side and realized that he'd lost consciousness. Mary and Rachael came and ordered Silas to bring some hot water. Together they began to attend to Josephus' wound.

Silas soon arrived with some water, and Mary extracted the arrow from the wound. The man had lost a lot of blood, but once the arrow was removed, she was able to stem the flow of blood. She bandaged him, and then left him unconscious on the hay.

Silas was back at his work as Josephus slept. The four of us stood near the entrance to the stable as we discussed our next move. My plan had been to leave that evening; however, Mary informed us that she didn't think we could start out with Josephus, since he was too weak from the loss of blood. Our dilemma grew even greater when Silas came and told us that we must leave right away for he feared that a Roman patrol would stop by late that afternoon or early evening. I felt that Silas wanted us off his land, and therefore he was doing all he could to get us to leave. I found it hard to believe that he suddenly remembered the Roman patrol and was trying to give us adequate warning to escape.

There was little we could do but to start towards Philadelphia right away. I then bartered with Silas, and he agreed to give us a donkey and a two-wheeled cart in which to carry Josephus in exchange for two of our camels. I agreed, though I knew we had come out on the short end of the deal. I also knew that Josephus would be furious over the exchange, but I could see no other way out.

Before we left I pulled Silas aside and asked if he had thought over what I had told him about Jesus and about the salvation he could gain through acceptance of him as Savior. He shook his head. I feared that he had rejected Jesus, but instead he said that he was still trying to figure it all out. I told him not to put it off and that I would pray for him.

He took my hand, shook it and thanked me. "I've never met anyone like you before, Caleb," he said. "No one has ever gone out of their way to treat me with such courtesy. You have renewed some feeling in me that I have not known since my youth. I will think seriously about what you have said."

With that we said our goodbyes, and I went to the stable to get everything ready for our journey. Before I was finished harnessing the donkey, Silas appeared at the door. Without a word, he handed me a large bundle and immediately turned and left. I looked inside and found enough food and supplies to last the four of us for our journey. After hitching the donkey to the cart, David and Saul brought four skins filled with water and then helped the two women climb aboard the cart.

It was just before sunset that we laid Josephus next to where the women were sitting with plenty of straw under him to ease the jolts as we traveled over the rough roads that lay head of us. As it was, he moaned each time we turned or went over a bump. Just as the sun was disappearing below the horizon, I turned and took one last look at the farm where we had stayed. I was able to discern a small troop approaching the house on horseback. I assumed these were the Romans that Silas had warned us about, and I had to admit that my distrust of him had changed to one of trust. Again God's grace had been with us.

David asked about hiding, and I told him that we were east of the farm and in darkness, so we would not be seen.

"We see them," I added, "because the setting sun is at their backs."

So we turned our faces to the east and continued our journey on into the night.

During that first night of travel, Josephus was delusional and little that he said made sense. His wound reopened, and he continued to lose blood. He slept all the next day, and finally by midday the bleeding stopped. During the second night on the road, he regained consciousness. He told us that he had been trapped during the street fighting and had been hit by a stray arrow. He said that it took a great deal of energy to get to the escape tunnel, through it and on to the farm.

During the middle of the following day he became feverish, and again he lapsed in and out of consciousness. I became fearful that he might not make it. We were camped near a small streambed that had a little water in it, and I decided we should stay an extra day to give Josephus time to regain his strength.

Rachel nursed him for a short while as he lay reclined under the cart. In mid-afternoon she came to me and said, "I don't think he's going to live much longer. He seems to have a high fever, and the bleeding has started again. He wants to see you."

I went to him and sat near. "I'm going to stay here for a few days," I said, "I want to give you time to heal before we continue on to Philadelphia."

"Caleb," he sputtered out after a while, "I know I'm done for. I wanted you to come here so I could say goodbye. You've been a good friend other than all that gibberish about the Messiah."

"Don't discount it out of hand, Josephus. For if you don't accept the truth now you'll never have another chance." I was anxious as I could see that he was on the verge of death. I prayed that God would change his mind and then fell silent.

"You never give up, do you?" He gurgled and then choked and coughed, spitting out his blood through his mouth. "Let me be precise, I reject God, and if He ever existed, He hated me. So leave it alone, Caleb."

"But Josephus," I cried. "This is your last chance for salvation."

He looked at me opened his mouth as if to say something and then he died. I sat at his side for a long time, just staring at him, knowing that he was lost for eternity.

After awhile I called my friends over and told them what had transpired before he breathed his last. We each said a short prayer over his body before using sticks and boards and whatever else was at hand to dig a grave and bury him.

When we were finished, I turned to Mary, Rachael, David and Saul and told them we might as well sleep a short time and then continue our journey after the sun had set.

In the following three uneventful days, we arrived and entered Philadelphia, where we were greeted warmly by the members of the Christian community. It didn't take long for my friends to find work and to continue spreading the good news about Jesus.

THE MARCH ON
JERUSALEM

I continued my work with my grandson, but I was worried about the friends who believed in Jesus as the messiah that still remained in Jerusalem. It didn't take long before I determined I would have to return and help lead them out to safety.

This timing became critical as news reached us in Philadelphia that the Roman Twelfth Legion along with the Fifteenth was reportedly making ready to leave Caesarea and march on Jerusalem. Much had taken place since the suicide of Emperor Nero. There had been a swift grab for power by different men that led to a rapid succession of emperors in Rome; first there was Galba, then Otho and then Vitellius. The whole of the empire became embroiled in a civil war, and if things didn't settle down quickly, chaos would rein. The troops under the command of General Vespasian urged him to seize the throne and bring peace to the empire. This he did in the year 69 CE. He turned his military command over to his son, Titus, who continued to lead the legions on their march towards Jerusalem. Vespasian then embarked with another portion of his army, triumphantly entered Rome and assumed power as Caesar.

I therefore found that I didn't have much time left before the city of Jerusalem would be surrounded by the legions under Titus's command. It was early in the year of our Lord 70 CE that I set out from Philadelphia to Jerusalem. This time I set out on my own on one of the camels that had belonged to Josephus with two others in tow. It had been my intent to go to the little farm owned by Silas and leave my camels there before continuing on to the city and the secret tunnel that would put me inside the walls of the City of God.

As I was leaving Philadelphia, I received the news that not only Titus and the Twelfth and Fifteenth Legions were en route from Caesarea, but that the Tenth Legion was coming south out of Syria as reinforcement in laying siege to Jerusalem. I didn't have much time, as it was not my aim to be caught there when the Roman army surrounded the walls.

I left my grandson to run the business. With the prayer of the other members of our church still ringing in my ears, I set off early in the morning of the 12th day of February. I had decided that since I was traveling alone, I would make this journey during daylight. This, I thought, would allow me to cover the distance in less time. Because it was early in the year, the daytime temperatures were moderate and comfortable.

For my first two days on the road, I did not see another soul. The farms I passed seemed to be deserted, and the land was deathly quiet. An unusual phenomenon was with me for those two days—a heavy fog. This was something not seen often in this part of the world. My visibility was normally less than a mornings walk. I felt encouraged by this, for even as I was not able to see others, those who were out there were unable to see me.

On the third day I awoke to a thick overcast sky with showers that at times were quite heavy, soaking me to the skin, yet I plodded on. I didn't dare stop, for I needed to get into and out of Jerusalem as quickly as possible. During this third day, I saw evidence of others in the vicinity. I stayed clear of all people and tried as hard as I could to remain invisible to them. There were some I saw on horseback, and those I believed to be Roman soldiers—probably scouts who were trying to keep track of the movements of all Jews near Jerusalem. When I saw these men, I quickly left the road and went into hiding until I was sure they were gone. As far as I know no one saw me, or if they did, they paid no attention to my presence.

The fourth day brought with it warm and dry weather. The skies were clear, and the visibility was unlimited. I pushed the camels hard, and we covered nearly twice the distance as I had during the previous day. I encountered a few refugees on the road. They too had heard of the movement of the Roman army and decided to abandon their land near Jerusalem and seek refuge to the east. This day I didn't see any of the Roman mounted patrols I had seen just the day before.

That night I slept soundly. Before lying down, I ate most of the remaining portion of my rations, then I took off my wet robe and hung it out to dry. I needed as much energy as I could muster, for on the morrow I would arrive at the farm owned by Silas. Then the next night I would go into the city.

I awoke before the sun was up and quickly crawled out from under my blankets and put on my now dry robe. The night had been cold, and I built a small fire with which I cooked the remaining rations and by which I was able to keep warm. After eating and packing away my equipment, I said my prayers. I implored the Lord to keep me safe and that above all, His will be done. I asked that He speak to me and to give me guidance. My purpose was to glorify Him in all that I did.

With those things done I went on my way, for it was just another half-day journey to Silas's farm. I encountered more refugees on the road, carrying as many of their prized possessions with them that they could on their carts for the prospect was that they may never return. It seemed that I was the only one who was traveling west; all others were eastbound trying to avoid the disaster that seemed to be headed for Jerusalem.

Shortly before noon, I could see Silas's farm buildings off in the distance. I dismounted the camel and walked the remaining distance. I saw Silas working in his corral and hailed him as I approached.

"Hello Silas!" I shouted. "It is I, Caleb."

Silas looked up from his work and studied me as I approached him. When I was close enough for him to recognize me, he lifted his left hand in greeting and stood to shake my extended hand.

"Shalom, Caleb. I didn't ever think I would see you again. Did you and your friends make it safely to Philadelphia?"

"Yes!" I said as I grabbed his right forearm and he mine in the traditional Roman greeting. "How have things gone with you since I was last here a little over a month ago?"

"All right," he said somewhat hesitantly, "but with the approach of the Roman legions from the southwest and from the north, I'm preparing to leave this place and seek sanctuary in Philadelphia."

"Good idea." I replied. I then explained my presence and told him, "I have come to assist some other believing friends to escape the city before catastrophe strikes. How are things going in Jerusalem? Have you heard any news?"

"The news is not good. The people are starving, and the various factions are still warring against each other. When is it that they will come to realize that they must stop fighting one another and prepare their defenses to stop the whole Roman army from overrunning the city?

"By the way," he added, "aren't those Josephus's camels?

How is he doing anyway?"

I didn't answer right away and looked at the ground as I shuffled my feet.

"He didn't make!" I finally blurted out. "He lost too much blood and died the third morning out. We buried him about midway between here and Philadelphia."

"He was a good man." Silas said in a somewhat unconvincing manner.

Again I hesitated before I answered but finally said in a firm voice. "He was a rogue, a renegade who would steal the last piece of bread from a starving widow and her infant child."

Silas burst out laughing, the first time I had ever seen him even smile, let alone laugh. "You sure had him pegged for what he was. Well, for some reason I liked him, and he was the only one of his crowd that I could trust."

"I liked him too. I'd known him during my childhood. Though he was a bully, he had a strange way of keeping his word to those to whom he had given it. Alas, I couldn't get him to turn to God and admit his sins, even at the moment of his death. He is and always will be separated from God."

I turned and faced Silas at this moment and asked, "How is it with your faith? Have you thought over those things we'd talked about when I was last here? Have you accepted Jesus as your Lord and Savior?"

Silas looked at me intently before responding. "I find your arguments very convincing. My parents were religious and faithful to the Lord. Early on, I rejected them and their beliefs. I ran away and never came back until after they'd died. That's how I ended up with this farm. It was theirs, and as the only child it naturally fell into my hands. I have worked hard and gained little by staying here. I had come to the conclusion that there was no God. That's how I got in with the likes of Josephus and his kind, all rogues and robbers. You, Caleb, yes, you, were the first person since my childhood that ever forced me to think about my beliefs.

"Ever since you left I have wrestled with all that you had said. Just a little over a week ago, I heard a voice from within me telling me to believe. I got on my knees and confessed my sins and invited the Christ into my life. And, though things have not gotten any better, I have felt a calm within that I've never felt before. I'm at peace with myself and with the Lord.

"This was another reason that I was on my way to Philadelphia for it was my purpose to search out you and your gathering of believers so that I could learn more of the Christ."

"Praise God," I replied. "I'd hoped that you would come to that conclusion. I have been praying for you for a long time.

"I want you to go to Philadelphia and look up my grandson Abram, who will introduce you to the other believers of The Way. They will lead you in your search for a strong spiritual life. If things go well, I will be there with you in a short time."

"Do you want me to wait for you, Caleb?" Silas looked very uncertain as to what he should do. "I was planning to leave early in the morning day after tomorrow, but I guess I could hold off for another day."

I shook my head. "I'm not sure that I will be able to accomplish what I have in mind to do, but I sense that the Lord has led me here for one reason or another. I feel compelled to follow His lead. If, indeed, I am captured, I feel that it will serve His will in some other way."

Silas looked relieved that I would not be the one to hold him back, and he abruptly turned to complete his work in preparation for his departure.

I called out to him as he walked away towards the house. "I will put the camels in the corral and sleep until twilight before I go into Jerusalem. If I'm not back by tomorrow evening take the camels with you. If you have sufficient rations, I'd be obliged to you if you would leave them for me and two others so we will have something to eat for our return to Philadelphia."

He waved his arm at me and shouted, "God be with you." He then disappeared into the house. I led the camels to the corral and went into the stable, lay down on some hay and was soon fast asleep.

At sunset I felt someone shaking my shoulder. As I sat up rubbing my eyes, I could make out Silas sitting across from me. The light was dim, and I determined that the sun must have been setting.

"What is it Silas?" I said.

"It's getting dark," he replied. "I thought that I'd better wake you and get you on your way. I've just heard some news from a refugee who passed by the farm that the lead elements of the Twelfth Legion are about a day's march away. You'd better get up and get your business done before they surround the city. I am leaving tomorrow morning instead of the day after.

I've left rations for you by the well. There's a little shed on the south side, and I've left a sack for you in there under a loose floor board."

"Yes, you were right to get me up. I thank you for the provisions. For the sake of the animals, take the camels with you if I'm not back by the time you leave. I had a dream, and in it I was captured. I think the Lord is telling me something, but in that same dream I was also spared.

I believe this is a premonition from God. Just tell every one that I will be safe and eventually return."

As I stood to ready myself for the events to come, Silas put his arm around my shoulder and said, "May the great and almighty God be with you now and forever." As he released me, he handed me some bread and some wine. "This will sustain you throughout the night. Goodbye, Caleb, I hope we meet again." With that he left the stable. I had so misjudged this man, and my heart went out to him. I prayed that God protect him as he traveled from here to Philadelphia.

I gathered my little belongs, stuffed them into my shoulder pack, and walked out of the barn and up to the road that would take me to Jerusalem. Silas was nowhere to be seen. I had no idea where this road would take me, in the metaphorical sense. Though it led to the city, I didn't know whether it would lead me there or into imprisonment of some sort or other. I felt sure that my life would be spared at least for a while. I hoped that my dream of capture was wrong, but I couldn't shake the thought that that prospect was definitely in my future.

As I walked to the great wall of Jerusalem, I was struck by the darkness. There were clouds that covered the stars, and there was no light coming from the city. Even though it was approaching Passover, which was normally a joyous time in the life of the Jews, everything was deathly quiet. My sense of foreboding grew ever stronger. I had to feel my way along the road with my feet as I walked in some wagon wheel ruts. There was neither a sound to be heard nor a light to be seen.

I quickened my pace, for the quiet of the night only heightened my fears. It was strange that I could not hear any birds or other animals that normally chirped away in the evening as they prepared for a night's rest.

Before too much time had past, I could see that I was nearing the city walls. They loomed well above me and on out of sight. Before I reached the gate that led into the city, I left the road and walked north until I reached the huge stones that made up the base of the massive wall. Once there I groped my way along the smooth stone for another four hundred cubits to the east. Here I came to a corner that would lead me another two hundred cubits north and to the tunnel that would take me into the city. I started to feel more exhilarated as I now was within my goal of getting into the city. I turned the corner and to my shock and horror came face to face with three Roman soldiers.

CAPTURE

When I was a youth, my father instructed me in many things. The one thing that he stressed was instruction in foreign languages. At home and in Jerusalem we spoke Aramaic, the language of the people of Judea. However, my father put great emphasis on the Greek and Roman languages. Over the years, each of these languages had been a great benefit to me and had served me well during the years I was a missionary in Greece and in the captured provinces of Rome.

When I came face to face with the Roman soldiers one, their leader, challenged me in his native tongue, Latin. "Who are you and what are you doing here?" He demanded.

Recognizing his tongue I responded in his language. "I am a follower of The Way," I replied. "I was lost in the dark and was trying to get away from the city. I did not know that it had been closed. I had just heard that the people behind these walls were at war, and the gates had been closed and locked.

I arrived from Philadelphia earlier today and I had no idea that there was a war. I came to celebrate the risen Lord Jesus Christ." Before I realized it I had lied to this man, and as I waited for an answer I prayed to God that He would understand my reason for not being truthful and forgive me.

One of the men pulled a lantern from under his cloak and opened the light shield and held it to my face. The second man twisted my arm behind my back and held me so that I faced the first man their leader. My arm was so twisted and bent that the pain was excruciating. I let out a screech, and the man only twisted it harder and growled for me to shut up.

"Tie and bind him," the leader said, "and we'll take him back to the centurion so that he can cross-examine him."

The one holding my arms tied my hands together behind my back with some rawhide strings as the gruff leader stuck his face into mine and growled. "How is it that you, who looks like a Jew, know the language of Rome?"

Again, I lied out of fear for my life and said, "I am a Roman citizen, though brought up in Jerusalem." I hoped this would appease them enough so that they would not finish me off right then and there.

The leader mulled this over for a minute and said nothing. The one who had tied my hands asked, "Why don't I run him through right here and be done with it?" With that said he drew out his sword and pressed to my throat.

"No," the leader replied, "he may be useful to our purposes. If he truly is a Roman citizen, we need to be careful that we don't take an innocent life."

"No one would know the difference," the other soldier pleaded. "He's just another Jew."

"We'll take him to the centurion! Now shield that light and let's get back to camp." When the leader said that, I knew that I had at least a little more time to live and breathed a bit more freely.

The soldier with the drawn sword released my arms, withdrew the sword from my throat, put its sharp point in my back and pushed just enough to let me know that I'd better do as I was told or I would end up skewered through and through. I immediately started walking, following the leader as we headed for their camp.

It was dark, and I stumbled over the path. More than once I felt the sharp tip of the sword dig into my back. The camp was some distance away, and it took us a long time to wend our way back.

The sun was a little above the horizon when we arrived at the Roman camp. The other soldiers stared at me as if I were some strange being not of this world. No words were said as we walked to a place that must have been near the center of the camp, to a tent that was large and seemed to be the quarters of the commander of this unit of soldiers. The leader left me and the two other soldiers outside as he went to the flap of the tent and entered.

I didn't know what to think. I began regretting the fact that I had lied about my nationality as this might hurt my standing once the truth became known. I'd come this far, and I had a feeling that I should tell the truth and then stick with it.

I think for a lack of anything better to do the soldier who had tied my hands told me to get down on my knees. I turned to look at him wondering what in the world for when he struck me hard between my neck and shoulder with the hilt of his sword that he held in his right hand. The force of the blow stunned me in such a way that I fell to my knees gasping for air. He then put his foot on my shoulder and shoved me to the ground. Next he placed his right foot on the back of my neck holding me in place. I could barely breathe and nearly passed out. The other soldier laughed, and they both made fun of my plight. I was beginning to wonder what it was that God had in mind for me. As it was useless for me to struggle, I just lay there under his foot as they taunted me. Fortunately this soldier released some of the pressure he had on my neck, and I began to regain my breath.

Soon the leader came out of the tent and told the other two to pick me up off of the ground and take me to the whipping post in the center of camp. The other two literally lifted me up to my feet and dragged me to a post that stood in the middle of the clearing surrounded by numerous shelters and tents. One of these men then untied my hands from behind my back and turned me so that I faced the pole and quickly retied them to the rings of iron attached to the post near to the top. The other soldier kicked my feet out from under me, and I fell to the post hanging by my hands tied to the rings. Someone then tore the clothes off of my back and stepped away. In just a few seconds, I felt the sting of the whip, a cat o' nine tails, dig into the flesh of my back. I'd never before felt such pain in my life. I gasped, and before I could take another breath, the ends of the whip dug deep into my back again.

I don't know how many times they hit me for I soon passed out from the intense pain. When it was over, I was conscious enough to feel rough hands untie me and then drag my limp body from the post and after a short time drop me to the ground. I gasped for air and moaned from the pain that filled my whole body and said a short prayer that this ordeal be finished.

Next I felt a sharp pain in my ribs where someone kicked me and then two hands grabbed my shoulder and rolled me over on my back. I looked up into the face of another soldier I had not seen before. He wore the uniform of a centurion.

He knelt down on one knee and stuck his face into mine. "You're not a Roman citizen, you're just another Jew," he spat out at me. "Where did you learn to speak our language. Jews don't speak to us in our own tongue."

I continued to gasp for air and then said, "You're right, I'm not a citizen of Rome, but I once was a Jew, now I'm a believer of The Way. I was brought up in Jerusalem and my father who was put to death by the Jews now in control of the city, taught me to speak Aramaic, Greek and Latin."

"You also speak Greek?" he asked. "The general might have a need for your language skills."

The first soldier who had originally tied my hands at my capture then dug the point of his sword into my chest and asked, "Shall I run him through for lying to us?"

The centurion looked up at the soldier considering the question and after a short time said, "No, he may be useful to us as a translator. We have prisoners that we must interrogate who speak only Aramaic, and we need to know what they're saying. Take him to the prisoner compound and hold him there with the other prisoners. We'll then take him to the tribune or to Titus himself to see if they can use him."

I was then lifted to my feet with my hands tied in front of me, led to the prisoner compound, and put behind a roped barrier that had numerous guards stationed around with orders to kill any who tried to escape.

The pain I felt on my back was excruciating. I was miserable, and the bleeding didn't seem to be stopping. I staggered over to a shelter made up of some branches and fell face down and passed out.

I don't know how long I was unconscious, but when I came too I felt the soothing coolness of some water being put on the wounds on my back. I raised my head, and, looking to my right, saw a woman kneeling next to me using a sponge that was laden with water and mopping my wounds ever so gently.

I gasped, and then said in a harsh whisper, "Thank you for cleaning my wounds. I don't know whether I'll ever feel right again."

"They whip all of the men they bring in here," she responded as she continued her work on my back. She then went on, "I have some salt water that I'll use next. It will sting like anything, but it will help in the healing. Here, take this stick and bite down on it as I finish with the nursing."

She handed me a short stick that I put between my teeth. As soon as the saltwater touched my open wounds I knew why she had given me the stick. I did all that I could not to scream out in my pain.

After a few more swabs of the water on my back, my agony eased considerably. I said my thanks to her and she then encouraged me to sleep. I added, "After I've rested, we can talk later."

It had been a difficult night, and it didn't take long for me to fall fast asleep.

I must've slept for quite a long time, for when I awoke the sun was directly overhead. My back felt better, but still hurt and stung as I rose to my knees. I slowly got to my feet and felt sick to my stomach, but the nausea soon left me as I took a deep breath of air. The woman who had nursed my wounds was quickly at my side. She was tall and beautiful with long dark hair and light brown eyes. I felt that she was probably five or six years younger than me and apparently well educated.

"Are you feeling better?" she asked. "You slept through the morning."

"Yes, I feel much better, and thank you for cleaning my back. I think I will survive though I have never been under such pain before in my life. Even when I had traveled with Barnabas and saw him scourged with the whip, I couldn't imagine how terrible it was for him at the time. Now I know."

"Oh, you are a believer of The Way then? I know of Barnabas, a great missionary well known throughout the world. I saw him once when he came to Jerusalem many years ago. He was a kind and gracious man who believed that Jesus of Nazareth was the Messiah."

"The very one. Are you a follower of Jesus? Do you believe in him as the true Christ who came to redeem the Jews and all of mankind?"

"No," she said hesitantly. "I am a Jew, and I don't believe the Messiah has yet come. For if he had, then our people wouldn't have fallen on such terrible times."

"There are many things that you and I need to discuss," I replied, "but first we need to talk of our situation. What can you tell me about where we are and what is going on around us?"

"I cannot help you, sir," she answered. "The people I was traveling with, five in all, were captured two days ago as we were making our way from Galilee to Jerusalem for the Passover. We knew the Romans were in Judea, but we didn't know that they were planning to lay siege to the city. These soldiers who hold us captive are scouts for the main army that is to arrive from the west today or tomorrow. These men are Roman and Greek, and they do not understand our language. But they have been capturing Jews that have come to the city, I suppose to discover what they should do in order to defeat it."

"I think that is why they spared me, as I will be able to interpret for them," I said. "Have they told you what they want of you and your friends?"

"No," she answered and hung her head. "I'm afraid that they'll kill us."

"Where are your friends?" I asked. "Maybe in some small way I can intercede for you."

"Over there." She pointed out a group of three women and a young child of about eight or nine years. "They are my cousins, and the young boy belongs to the one on the left. Her husband died on our trip down from Galilee. He was bitten by a venomous viper. It's truly been a sad and hard trip, and then to be caught up in a war..." As she finished her voice trailed off, and I could see tears in her eyes.

"My name is Caleb," I said, "and what is yours?"

"Naomi," she answered as she looked up into my eyes. "Do you think that there is any hope for us?"

"We all are at the disposal of God's will," I responded, probably more confidently than I felt. "We must place ourselves in His hands and pray to Him for our deliverance. Now tell me, Naomi, how long has this troop of soldiers been camped in this place?"

"They brought us here right after we were captured. I assume they have been here for at least four or five days."

I stepped out from under the shelter and surveyed the area. We were on the east side of Jerusalem, a short walk from the wall, east of the Kidron Valley and southeast of the Mount of Olives. I guessed that the camp was about half an afternoons walk north of Silas's farm. We were camped near a small stream that had some water running in it even though it was still early in the year. There were trees and bushes that grew along the banks of the stream and provided shade from the sun, and I surmised that it protected us from view of those who were in the city. I further assumed that this troop of soldiers was used to reconnoiter the area in order for the army to determine the best place from which to launch an attack on the city. Why they sent soldiers who were unable to talk to the local people was beyond my knowledge.

"Naomi," I whispered as I turned to face her, "I know of a farm that is just an afternoon's walk or so south of here in which there are hidden some provisions, food and water, a supply sufficient for four or five people to travel for a week, which would allow them to escape from Judea. I would like for you and your cousins to flee with me out of this camp and go there, gather the supplies and then travel on to Philadelphia and to safety."

"Oh, Caleb, that would be too good to be true. But how are we to escape from camp? There are guards everywhere."

"Leave that to me," I replied. "I need to study the routine of the camp and that of the guards. I just need time to think. It'll be dark when our dinner arrives later today, and perhaps then I'll be able to come up with an escape route." I know I sounded confident, but there was a great deal of doubt in my mind. I turned from Naomi and offered a short prayer that God give me His guidance through our Lord and allow me to get Naomi and her family to safety.

I no more than finished my petition when the centurion called to one of the guards. "Bring the one they call Caleb to me."

The guard quickly snapped to attention and nodded. He then faced me and told me in his own tongue to follow him as he lifted the rope with his lance in order for me to duck under it. I took a quick glance at Naomi, nodded to her and said that when I returned we would finish our talk. Then I looked at the guard as I ducked under the rope of the holding pen and started walking beside him. He held the spear towards me in a menacing way as we proceeded across the open compound of the camp.

We walked about fifty cubits to the centurion, who was standing near the outer perimeter of the encampment. While walking, I was able to take in the layout of this camp. One thing surprised me. The holding area for the prisoners was near the southern edge. I was able to see that the troop of soldiers made up a small *centuria*, a unit that is a part of minipuli, which in turn is a subdivision of a cohort. This particular centuria consisted of foot soldiers and some mounted cavalry. As far as I could see there were not enough horses for the whole troop in the corral. There were probably just enough for the centurion and a small number of men. I smiled a little to myself as I realized that God began to answer my prayer no sooner than it was out of my mouth.

The guard asked his commander if he needed to tie my hands behind my back. He shook his head and motioned for the guard to return to his post. The centurion was a big, powerfully built man who stood just a little short of me. He wore a metal breastplate and metal helmet with a bright red fringe on the top. He had a sword at his side and long powerful legs that extended below the plates of brass that formed the skirt of his dress uniform.

"You're not going to give me any trouble are you?" he said with a menacing snarl from lips that were curved upward at the corners around yellow teeth. His face was strong and revealed steely blue eyes that showed a total lack of compassion. His face also showed evidence of scars from what I presumed to be past battles.

"No sir," I answered. "What is it you want from me now?"

"We have some new prisoners that we just captured trying to escape from the city, and I need you to interpret for me."

I nodded my agreement for I, too, was curious as to what was going on behind the walls of the great city of Jerusalem. The centurion then turned his back to me and walked through the camp. I followed and had trouble keeping up as he took a very quick pace. As I walked, I could still feel the pain in my back from the severe whipping I had suffered just a little earlier. I also used this opportunity to look the camp over and start my planning for our escape. The camp was not very big. It was laid out in a square of about fifty paces per side. The holding pen for the prisoners was located along the southeast border, and the troops were camped along the west side. It appeared to me that the officers were all located along the eastern boundary, while the animals were corralled on the north side along with their handlers.

It was hard for me to guess at the number of men who were in the troop, but I felt that it numbered well under one hundred and maybe as few as seventy. As with everything in the Roman military this centuria was well organized and strictly disciplined. Escape was not going to be easy.

I followed the centurion to a group of four men sitting on the ground, guarded by three well-armed soldiers standing over them with their long lances in hand. These men appeared to be badly frightened. I didn't blame them, for I, too, was afraid of the soldiers. The prisoners appeared to be well-to-do Jews with expensive clothes. On the whole, they were well groomed considering that their captors had just roughly treated them. I secretly hoped that they did not have to undergo a whipping like I had endured.

"Ask them who they are, where they came from and where they were going," the centurion demanded.

I said to the oldest and the apparent leader in Aramaic, "Please tell me about yourselves where you're from and where you were planning to go. If you don't tell the truth they will deal with you harshly as they did with me earlier. My back still aches from the beating I suffered earlier today.

"Are you Jews and were you escaping from the persecution of the gangs and thugs who have control of Jerusalem?"

This older man, a man about my age, looked up into my eyes and studied my face for a moment and answered, "Yes, we are Jews, and we had been under the hope that this madness would come to an end, that we could negotiate with the Romans and open the city to them in the hopes that they would enter and put an end to the insurrection and civil unrest going on behind the walls.

"Then the men under Simon ben Gioras and those under the leadership of John son of Levi went on a rampage through the city massacring all who got in their way. They burned our food stored in our homes and in the common granaries throughout the city. It has been pure madness, the work of evil men. They have looted the houses, dragged the owners out in the streets and slit their throats. It's intolerable, and all law-abiding citizens have been subjected to a terrible persecution. We, these other three and I, had decided to escape and throw ourselves upon the mercy of the Romans."

With that said the man hung his head and fell silent. I turned to the centurion and repeated word for word what the man had said. The centurion thought for a short time and said to me in an off-handed comment, "I, too, have heard of these things. I do not believe that it is Titus's purpose to destroy the city, but only those who are in control inside those walls." He gestured towards Jerusalem. "These anarchists must soon come to terms with us or face annihilation." He studied the prisoners for a minute as if trying to determine whether to hold them or kill them on the spot.

I saw coldness in this man's eyes that frightened me even more than when I was captured. "I don't have the men or the time to deal with prisoners," he continued, "but tell them that we will hold them for now in our stockade."

I quickly relayed this message to the prisoners and told them to abide peacefully to the orders of their captors or that this centurion could change his mind and the results would be devastating. Each of the men nodded in agreement. The centurion ordered the guard to take us all back to the holding pen.

As we were on our way, back to the holding area, the centurion called to me, "You, Caleb, wait; I want to talk with you."

I stopped and turned around and went and stood in front of him. My heart pounded in my chest, and I felt cold. I couldn't take another beating and I was fearful of what this man would do with me.

"You have been helpful and I think we can use your talents in language, so thank you. I'm going to take you to the Tribune Festus tomorrow, for we need to find out as much as we can about those who hold the city."

I nodded in the affirmative before he continued. "I'm not the rogue that you may think I am. However, I do not tolerate lies as you already know. So be straight with me, and I'll be straight with you."

"Thank you," I replied, "but I didn't know what your men were going to do to me when I was captured. My faith in Jesus Christ requires me to be truthful, and I deserved the beating for lying to you. It won't happen again." I swallowed hard, for I feared that he would ask me not to try to escape. Then what would I do?

"All right then, we have an understanding. Guard, take this man back to the holding pen."

With that said I found myself walking back with the guard at my side to the prisoner holding area. There I saw Naomi waiting for my return.

As soon as I entered the holding compound Naomi was at my side bombarding me with questions.

"Who were those men? What did they tell you? Did the Romans use you as an interpreter? Did you find an avenue for our escape?"

"Hold on a moment," I replied, "too many questions.

Let me start from the beginning."

I told of the men and what they had to say and how I translated that information for the centurion. I then explained to her that we would be able to escape that night after dark and that the best time would be very late into the second watch.

When we were out of hearing range of any other individual, I carefully explained to her how she should take her cousins and nephew to the farm owned by Silas. I further explained where the food and water were hidden and then how she should travel to Philadelphia and find my grandson, Abram.

"Why are you telling me these things? You will be there to guide us. We will just follow you."

"Naomi," I replied, "I feel God is calling me to do something else. I can't explain it, but ever since I left from Silas's place early this morning I felt the Lord was calling me for some reason. Don't question what happens, nor should you hesitate if I am not with you.

"Ever since I've accepted the Lord Jesus Christ into my life I feel his leading, and I therefore must follow. How do I explain these things to you?" I then went on to tell her of my encounters with Jesus and my belief that he was truly the Son of God. I was not sure that she believed all of the things that I told her. It was when I talked of seeing the crucifixion and later of our encounter with the risen Lord on our way home to Emmaus that her eyes got big in disbelief.

"This cannot be!" she exclaimed. "Men don't die and then come back to life. That is impossible."

"It is with ordinary men," I agreed, "but Jesus was not ordinary in any respect. He was truly the Son of God conceived by Him and born of a woman. He was the true Messiah and came to dwell with us in order to save us from our sins. His teachings were beyond mere human thought and understanding. He spoke of love in a way no man has ever spoken before. He taught of a life after death that we all could have if only we accept Him by faith. He was truly remarkable. I had seen Him on a number of different occasions, and even though I had seen Him with my own eyes, I still found it difficult to commit my life to Him. Seeing Him die upon that cross, then taken down and buried made me lose all faith I had in God. But on the third day after His death I talked to Him and saw the wounds of the nails. That made me believe, and I have ever since committed my life to telling others of this man. My faith is unshakable for I have personally witnessed these things. I try to tell everyone I can in order to bring them to believe what I know is the truth."

"I have heard of this man," Naomi replied, "but I did not know that he had come back from the dead. I had heard of his teachings and had thought of him as a great prophet, but to call him the Son of God is hard for me accept. Listening to you has added a bit of confusion to my beliefs. You say that he was a Jew but you talk of him as if he came to save everybody. Even the Romans?"

"Yes," I replied, "even the Romans. All who will accept him on faith will be saved, not only the Jews."

"I must think this over."

"Don't take too long, Naomi. For this acceptance must come of your free will and while you still live. Our time on this earth is short. Who knows what lies around the corner? The Romans are preparing to invade the City of God at this very moment. You and I are in their clutches, and we don't know what will happen to us even in the next few days. If we are caught in our attempt to escape, we in all likelihood will be sentenced to death.

"I will answer any questions you may have and once again I give you my assurance that what I have told you is true. Most importantly, believe me when I tell you that the prophets have foretold his coming for many centuries. Isaiah and other prophets wrote of the Messiah's coming—that he'd come to save us from our sinful ways. I'm here to tell you that as predicted he did come. Our religious leaders at the time saw him and refused to accept him for who he said he was. They turned their wrath on him and caused him to be crucified. Then he was buried. Their work complete, they returned to their old ways and dismissed him. But on the third day, he arose from the grave. After being with us for forty days, he ascended into heaven. He is still alive and sits at the right hand of the Lord God!

"It began at his miraculous birth over seventy years ago."

THE FIRST CHRISTMAS

"My father had told me of a time, long before I was born, about a strange occurrence that took place near the town of Bethlehem.

"Shortly after marrying my mother and because they both were of the linage of the great King David, they were called, as were all people of Judea, to return to their own town in order to take part in a census that had been ordered by the emperor, Caesar Augustus. This census was called for the whole of the Roman Empire, which at the time included Judea. It therefore came to pass that during this period in our history there was a great movement of our people as they traveled throughout the empire in order that all of the citizens could journey to the place of their forefathers to be counted.

"As my father and my mother were both of the House of David it was necessary for them to travel the short distance from Jerusalem to Bethlehem so that they too would take part in the census. My father and mother had not been married for very long and did not know one another well because it was the custom of the time that marriages are arranged by the fathers of the bride and groom. My parents met for the first time on their wedding day. At the time of the census, they, along with my father's parents, went to the small farm of my grandfather's brother located on the outskirts of Bethlehem, where they stayed for the few days required of them in order to be counted.

"My father was unsettled in the new way of life and was restless about taking on the responsibilities of a wife and eventually the added burden of a family.

"After traveling to Bethlehem they stayed at the small farm and, as the house was very crowded, my mother and father were relegated to sleeping in the hayloft of the stable. My father was restless on the third night of their stay. Since he was unable to sleep, he arose and quietly left the stable to go for a long walk in the nearby fields. The time, as best he could gauge, was near the middle of the night. Once outside the stable, he saw that the sky was crystal clear. He told me that he had never seen such an evening and that the stars were brilliant against the blackness of the heavens. There was no moon, nor was there any other light. He even said that the brilliance of the starry sky was so intense that he could easily see the path he followed as he meandered about the fields.

"He had told me that he had many concerns and that he at the time had been newly ordained as a rabbi in Jerusalem. He was concerned over the direction the religious leaders were taking as they led the nation in faith. He also said that he felt that the leaders were more concerned over their own wellbeing than over the relationship they and the people had with the Lord God.

"My father, even as a young man, had a vast interest in the historical aspects of the Jewish nation. In his years as a student of the law, he had studied the ancient scrolls of the prophets and of all things that had been prophesied. He told me that even then he was convinced from his studies that there was to be a great savior to come from the House of David, and he further concluded that this coming Messiah would make himself known soon, probably during his lifetime.

"The Jews had been under the domination of the Romans for over one hundred years, and this census demanded by Augustus was only another reminder that the Jews were not free to follow their beliefs and glorify God. Rather, they were to pay homage to Rome. It therefore seemed only right that a great leader would come and guide the nation to independence, thus giving them the freedom to celebrate the glory of God without outside interference.

"As my father walked along contemplating all of these things on that starry night, he was struck by the feeling that the sky was getting brighter and that he could see further off into the distance. He continued his walk consumed in deep thought barely conscious of the ever brightening sky as he continued to consider all of the different religious aspects of Jewish life. As he walked along lost in deep thought, he looked down at the ground and wasn't conscious of anything around him. When he finally did look up, he saw, ahead on his path, some shepherds about two hundred or more cubits in the distance and realized that they were staring at the sky.

"It was at this time that he stopped and also looked up to see at what these men were staring. To his shock and amazement, he saw a brilliant star which shone directly above him. He immediately fell to his knees and stayed perfectly still, paralyzed by both wonder and awe, almost in a trance.

"As he continued to watch, the sky seemed to change directly in front of him. He saw what appeared to be a large bank of clouds forming out of nowhere almost as if it were streaming from that brilliant star overhead. He thought he could hear strains of beautiful music emanating from off in the distance. There appeared before him, near where the shepherds and their sheep stood, what he said was a heavenly host of angels singing glory to God in the highest.

"He couldn't discern voices or words but he knew instinctively that something was being said to the shepherds. Then, as suddenly as the clouds and the host of angels appeared, they vanished from view. However, the star remained.

"My father said for the following few moments, he tried to re-gather his wits about him as he struggled to his feet and then ran to where the shepherds were.

"As he ran he shouted at the top of his voice, 'Did you see that? Did you hear the music? Did they say anything to you?' The shepherds too, were still stunned by the event and practically ignored my father and his questions as they excitedly discussed all that had just taken place.

"One of them finally looked up at my father as he drew close and said in a still dazed manner, 'An angel spoke to us and told us that the savior of all of Israel has been born this very night in Bethlehem.'

"Father, by then, had come to the men and stood speechless before this small group that was still staring at the brilliant star overhead. Finally another shepherd said, 'I'm going to find this stable and this child so that I can see and give him my praise.' Without another word, he turned and started towards town. The others looked at one another and without saying another thing, they all started after the other man leaving their sheep to graze unattended.

"My father hesitated for a few moments and then decided that he, too, would follow them. He walked a distance behind the men who were headed towards the outskirts of Bethlehem. In what seemed to my father to be little more than a few short minutes, they were approaching a dingy stable that appeared to be little more than a cave, dug out of an outcropping of rock located at the edge of Bethlehem. The shepherds quickly entered into the dark interior and disappeared from my father's view. He stopped a short distance from the entrance.

He told me that his heart was pounding from excitement, but that he held back as he didn't want to intrude on something not meant for him. He looked up and it appeared as if the star was directly overhead. Its light illuminated the stable's entrance, but not the interior.

"After some hesitation, he walked slowly to the entrance and peered inside. He said that he couldn't see a thing at first because of the dim light within. Soon his eyes adjusted to the surroundings, and he was able to make out the shepherds who were all kneeling in front of a manger at the far end of the cave, all illuminated by one small oil lamp that hung from an overhead beam. In that manger lay a tiny baby. The mother and father were there also on the other side of the manger admiring their newborn child.

"Father said that he stood at the entrance for a long time taking in the whole scene and not knowing what to do. He was struck by the fact that a significant event was taking place before his very eyes. At first, he couldn't discern what the event was all about until suddenly he remembered some scripture he had recently studied. It was in the prophetic words of Isaiah. In that scripture somewhere near the beginning Isaiah had said, 'For to us a child is born, to us a son is given and the government will be on his shoulders. And he will be called Wonderful Counselor, Mighty God, Everlasting Father, and Prince of Peace. Of the increase of his government and peace there will be no end. He will reign on David's throne and over his kingdom establishing and upholding it with justice and righteousness from that time on and forever.'

"Father told me that he couldn't get those words out of his mind. As he stood and gazed at the mother and child, the words, 'For unto us a child is born, to us a child is given,' kept repeating themselves over and over. Was this the true Messiah?

"All was very peaceful and quiet. Nary a person nor animal made a sound or moved much at all. As he watched, the shepherds finally began to leave, each rising slowly one at a time and leaving the stable through the one and only exit. Each one passed by my father without saying a word and walked out into the cool night air. Father remained riveted in place and watched in fascination.

"Soon after the first shepherd left, other people from nearby homes started to come by the stable and look in on the scene. Father was intrigued by all that had taken place and stood at the entrance for a long time, still reluctant to enter and take a closer look at the child and his family. Finally he left and walked slowly back to the farm. He went into the stable and awakened my mother from her sound sleep and told her of the things he had done and of the miracle he'd witnessed. She was intrigued by what he had told her and of the things he had seen. They both went outside to view the magnificent star. After contemplating this wondrous sight, my mother told Father that he should go and tell his own father and mother of what had transpired, especially about the angels who had spoken to the shepherds.

"This they did. In the days that followed, they and many other visitors, some from far away places, came to admire the newborn child. Both my father and mother were overjoyed and deeply touched by this event. Within two days they traveled back to Jerusalem.

"Father felt a miracle had happened and waited for something wonderful to come of this special event he had witnessed, but it seemed that nothing happened. Soon word was spread that King Herod had sent his own palace guard into Bethlehem, and it was further rumored that all the local infant boys aged two and under were slain in a most gruesome attack. It was apparent that Herod the Great wasn't going to take a chance that a new king would replace him. In the years that followed, word spread that the young baby had been spared as the parents of this special child had taken him out of Bethlehem and on into Egypt.

"This was the last that my father had heard of this incident. He often lamented that nothing ever seemed to come from the event, especially any action that would save the nation of Israel from her enemies.

"He later realized that nothing or no person was able to save Israel, not from her enemies but more importantly not from herself.

"Jesus' birth was a miraculous occurrence. For it is true that his mother, Mary, was a virgin and that her child was conceived by the Holy Spirit. He can therefore be called the Son of God. All of these other things I have told you about him and about his life only further support that truth.

"I must get some sleep," I concluded, "for my back is sore and I feel weary. We'll talk later. Think over what I told you and most importantly realize that I have no reason to lie to you; these things I have said actually happened."

"I will," Naomi replied. "I'm going to get my cousins and the boy Jeremiah and we will rest here near you."

I nodded and quickly lay down on the blanket and fell fast asleep. When I awakened I knew that even without opening my eyes that Naomi and her family were nearby. Even though I had not known her for long I had grown fond of her and was concerned over her wellbeing. In my mind's eye, I tried to work out the best escape route with the least danger to us all. I concluded that we should sneak under the rope shortly after midnight when the guards would be drowsy and not so watchful. I thought that we could then follow the little stream that was just east of the camp down to the road that led from Jerusalem and then go on to Silas's farm. With my mind made up, I opened my eyes and looked around. It was getting close to twilight and the overcast sky made it seem later than it actually was. The good news was that it appeared as if it might rain.

I sat up and rubbed my eyes and it was then that Naomi noticed I was awake and quickly came to my side. "They are bringing us something to eat," she said. "I hope you slept well and are still planning on our escape."

"Yes and yes," I joked. "I have a plan worked out in my mind that I think will work. We'll leave around midnight." I then went on to explain the plan in detail; I especially wanted her to be able to carry it out alone if for some reason I wasn't with them. I still had an overwhelming sense that the escape for me wasn't part of God's plan and that I wouldn't be going with them. I also admonished that they should travel only at night throughout the journey to Philadelphia. I explained where she could find my grandson and how he and the fellow believers would help her and her cousins.

"You still talk as if you will not be there to lead us," she said. "Why would God let us escape through your work and keep you a captive of the Romans?"

"I believe part of His plan is for me to help you. Place your trust in Him, and you will be free."

"I've thought these things over very carefully, Caleb, and because of you I have prayed for faith and turned myself over to this Messiah, Jesus. I pray that we will be safe."

"You have done the right thing," I answered. "We'll see one another again so don't worry. Just keep believing."

It was then that the guards showed up with some bread and water for us to eat. We each accepted our portion in silence, and then I said a short prayer of thanksgiving praising God for His grace and love. We all then ate in silence, our group of Naomi, her cousins and nephew sitting in a circle.

The other prisoners were just a short distance away and looked very frightened and whispered with one another.

After eating, we all lay down to sleep. It wasn't long before I was awakened by thunder and lighting that crashed all around us. I judged that it was during the third watch. Soon I felt drops of rain on my face and it wasn't long before it fell at a constant pace. Naomi was awake and grabbed my hand. "I'm afraid," she blurted out through clenched teeth.

"Don't worry Naomi," I answered. "Awaken the others as this is the best time to go. The guards will have difficulty seeing us in this downpour."

I whispered to each of the cousins telling them to follow Naomi and that I would follow the group. I told them to be quiet as they left the camp. I led them to the rope that bordered our compound and to a point that was furthest from the guards and then showed them the way they should take to the streambed and the safety they would find in the bushes on the other side. They left one by one, first the mother of the boy, then he followed her, next the other two cousins one by one and finally, as Naomi was ready to duck under the rope I heard my name called.

"Guard, bring the one called Caleb to me."

Naomi clutched my arm and whispered harshly, "What are we to do?"

"Continue on," I replied. "I have to show myself now or they will hunt us all down and kill us. If I go to them you'll be able to get away, so hurry! You know where the supplies are and how to travel on to Philadelphia. Keep away from the Roman soldiers, and you'll be all right. Now hurry and go. Tell my grandson that I'm all right and that I'll return to him soon.

I know that I'll see you again, Naomi, don't lose heart and be courageous. God be with you." I squeezed her hand then released her, and she quickly disappeared into the underbrush.

I said a quick prayer, imploring the Lord to guide and protect Naomi and her cousins on their journey. I then turned and walked to the center of the prisoner compound and called out to the sentry saying, "Here I am, guard. What is it you want of me?" The rain began to let up and then it stopped for a short time as I walked towards the guard who was holding a lantern. The stoppage only amplified my concern that the Romans would more readily notice that some of their prisoners were missing.

"The centurion is looking for you. He has some more captives who need to be interrogated." I followed the guard to the tent of his commander as the rain started again thus relieving my heightened concern for Naomi. When we arrived, I entered through the flap. I was soaked to the skin, and my garments were in tatters, but it felt good to be in a dry place. Standing just inside the flap of the entrance were two fairly well dressed Jewish men.

My session with these new prisoners went pretty much the same as it had with those whom I'd talked to earlier in the day. They were more of the upright citizens escaping the brutality of the bandits in control of Jerusalem and throwing themselves to the mercy of the Romans. Both of the men had been sentenced to death by a tribunal of bandits for voicing their opinions that the city should surrender to the Roman forces approaching the gates.

All during the interrogation I was worried that word would come of the escape of Naomi and her cousins, but nothing was said. When the centurion was satisfied that the prisoners were of no threat and that they could be put with the other prisoners it was nearly the beginning of the sixth watch. It had been nearly half of the night since the women and young boy had left. They should have been at Silas's farm by now and have continued on their way to Philadelphia. I knew that their escape would be reported very soon, and I continued my prayers for their safety. As the guard led me back to the compound, I saw that the storm had passed and the sky was clearing. I was extremely tired as I entered my little shelter and lay down on the wet mat and tried to sleep.

However, I was too restless and unable to keep my eyes shut. I soon was up pacing back and forth along one end of the compound, my mind focused on Naomi and her little group. Even though I had known her for only a short time, I longed for her company.

It was after the sun had risen and the guards entered the compound carrying the gruel they called food that it was discovered that the prisoners were missing. There was much discussion between the four men for they feared what would become of them for letting the prisoners escape. In many instances, in the Roman tradition, guards were doomed to the death sentence for allowing this to happen. From my mat, where I was sitting, I could see and hear them discuss how they should approach their centurion.

Finally they called their optio or noncommissioned officer over and explained what had taken place. He was extremely angry and verbally berated them in terms I would rather not repeat. He then turned on his heel and marched off to the commander's tent to inform him of the news.

It wasn't more than a short time later that the optio and the centurion returned and without saying a word to his men he came straight to me.

"You were seen talking to the woman, and I have a feeling that you helped them in their escape."

"I was with you last night as you interrogated the new prisoners. How could I have helped in their escape?" I replied. "I am glad they got away, what good is it for you to keep them? They could not give you any helpful information, and they would only slow you down when you have to move your camp. There is nothing they could do to hurt your mission. I feel it works only to your benefit not to have to expend energy and men to guard them."

The centurion considered these things for a moment before answering. "Well, maybe you're right," he growled. "I don't have the men or food for keeping a lot of prisoners. But my men did let them escape," as he said this he glanced angrily at the four guards who stood a short distance away taking in everything that was being said.

"I don't know what you would normally do to guards, but your men are soldiers ready to fight, not spend their time guarding women, children and old men. I would suggest you do nothing other than interrogate these remaining prisoners and then send them on their way, too. What does it gain you to imprison them or to even kill them? I understand why you hold me because I can use my skills as an interpreter to further your cause, but these other people can only slow you down. And what good is it to wash your hands in their blood? Or for that matter, decrease your own strength by punishing the guards?"

Again he thought this over and said in a hushed voice so as not to be overheard by the soldiers, "Your wisdom is great, Caleb. I will do as you say, though I believe that I'll give some extra duty to my guards so they will not think I am soft and that they can get away with dereliction of duty. I will continue to hold you, for the tribune will have need of your skills. I will let the older prisoners go, but the younger ones we took day before yesterday we will retain as I think they're up to no good. The flogging they received didn't seem to dampen their hatred for us."

He then looked to his optio and commanded, "Take these men who are responsible for the escape and put them to work with the horses. They will have only bread and water for the next two days. Any further failures on their part and they will be executed on the spot. Be sure that they understand that I'm in a particularly good mood today, and I'm letting them off with an easy sentence."

The optio saluted his commander and turned on his heel, growling at the offending soldiers as he ushered them away.

After they left the centurion looked me up and down and considered my attire. "You are not dressed properly for meeting with the tribune. I will have my men get you some suitable clothing, and then we will proceed to his headquarters at mid-morning."

He walked a short way with me to the compound, and turned and walked back to his tent. I went and sat on my mat confident that Naomi and her relatives were safely underway to Philadelphia. I offered a short prayer of thanksgiving and then stood up and gazed over the confining rope of the prisoner compound and tried to visualize where Naomi and her cousins might be in their journey towards a new life.

It was during the mid-morning that the centurion's second in command came to my shelter. He announced that he had brought some new clothes for me to wear. Where in the world he had found them was beyond my imagination.

This deputy commander hesitated and finally asked, "Why did you stand up for the others before the centurion?

You seem to know that we, as Romans, could receive the death sentence for letting those prisoners escape."

"I didn't think it important enough for someone to lose his life over. You are soldiers, not guards. I felt it was wrong for men to be punished so severely for not doing a job for which they had no training. Furthermore, my beliefs teach me to preserve life, not take it."

"You and your beliefs are strange, Caleb. I would not hesitate a moment to take your life, for you and all of the Jews are my sworn enemies. The Jews look down on us and hate us, yet they are no match for our strength or for our knowledge and skills as a people, as an empire."

"From a human standpoint, you are right when you say that you are strong and knowledgeable as a people. But you know nothing of God. You call me a Jew, but in reality I am a believer of The Way. I believe that God has come to earth in the form of a man to save mankind from its own folly and sins. This man, Jesus, lived and died to set all men free."

"I am a free man," the soldier answered confidently. "As a citizen of Rome, I can do pretty well as I please."

"I know that you have control of your life, but do you do sinful things such as steal and even kill others? Do you disobey your orders in hopes of not being found out? Do you cheat on your wife? These are the kind of things that Jesus teaches us to avoid, and instead to love one another, to honor our wives and children, to not kill or steal. By placing our faith in Him and believing that He is the Son of God, He will in fact set us free of our sinful ways. Because of that faith, He promises to give us eternal life."

"You are saying crazy things. There are many gods. They are the ones that give us strength. We obey them. They give us victory over our enemies. They give us the strength to go forth and kill those who oppose us, and if we fail in our courage we will die and fully deserve that death."

"I disagree with you," I replied. "There is but one God, the creator of all things. He first showed himself to the Jews, and many rejected Him. Then He sent His son conceived by God, born of woman, who lived his life right here in Judea and died upon the cross bearing both your and my sins upon his shoulders. Jesus was then resurrected and lived among us for forty days before ascending into heaven. His death represents God's forgiveness and grace so that we may believe in Him and live eternally in heaven."

"You are a foolish man, Caleb. I will let you continue to live a life of delusion. In the meantime, I thank you for interceding for the lives of my friends."

With that said, he turned and marched out of the holding pen and out of my sight. I said a short prayer for this soldier whose name was Longius, praying that my words would eventually sink in and turn his life around. I then, with a nearby bucket of water, washed myself and put on the clothes that had been given to me.

THE GATHERING OF THE ARMIES

Shortly after, I was summoned by the centurion and escorted to his tent.

"We will be leaving in just a few moments, are you able to sit a horse?" he asked.

I told him that I had ridden some, and as long as the animal was well behaved I would be all right.

"We'll ride to the tribune's camp on the west side of the city. There you'll interpret for Festus what some captured rebels have to say about Jerusalem's defenses. In the afternoon, we'll return here. Tomorrow, my men will break camp, and we will move to the northeast corner of the city. It wouldn't surprise me if the attack begins within the week."

With that said, a handler brought forth two enormous steeds, both larger than any horses I'd ever seen before—more than eighteen hands high. I wasn't sure how I was to mount my animal, let alone staying on without falling off. The saddle was typically Roman, and the stirrups seemed to have already been adjusted for my height. I watched the centurion as he jumped up on the stirrup and swung easily into place.

I was wearing a robe, and to do as he had done seemed impossible. It was then that I felt two large hands grab me under the arms and literally lift me high into the air and place me in the saddle.

After I was seated and had put both of my feet in the stirrups, I looked down to my left. There stood the largest, most powerfully built man I had ever seen. This soldier was the one that had picked me up and thrown me on the stallion. I was no lightweight, and this man's strength was phenomenal. If all of the Roman army were made up of men like this one, then the Jews had no chance of winning the coming fight.

"Are you going to be able to ride?" the centurion asked.

I suppose that he was concerned as I probably seemed very unsure of myself. I nodded in the affirmative, and with a short movement of his arm we were off.

My horse pulled alongside the centurion's, and I noticed that five other soldiers had joined in the entourage. All of them were dressed in their finest uniforms. All had long spears, except the two in front of us who carried their guide-ons with the unit designation emblazoned on the triangular flags at the top of the staffs. What a magnificent and powerful force we must have presented to those Jews who stood on the top of the city's walls observing our progress as we traveled south out of camp to the southern wall of the city. Once there, we turned west and paralleled that southernmost wall. We stayed a good distance from the fortification down in the Hinnom Valley, out of range of their darts and arrows.

We moved along two abreast, and the time slipped by quickly. I kept my eyes on the upper wall of Jerusalem. All of the gates were closed, and many men stood at the top watching us and other Roman units as they approached the city. I never before this time realized how large and massive the walls were. The centurion said little as we proceeded along the wall for he too was examining it closely. As we approached the southwest corner, he became more talkative.

"As you already know, General Titus and his army have been on the march for many days now. Last night the army was just a short days ride from Jerusalem, for they camped at Gabaothsaul."

"The Hill of Saul," I interpreted.

"Yes," he replied. "From there he and six hundred horsemen left early this morning to come to the city in order to survey the Jew's defenses. We are on our way to meet with Tribune Festus, who arrived ahead of the army to establish and prepare the road to and from the various campsites the army will use, as well as review the strategy needed to breach the walls at their weakest point. Tribune Festus is my commander and the one to whom I report. The work of my troop has been to work our way around the city and prepare various reports as to its strengths and weaknesses.

"That is why we are going to meet with the tribune now. You are here because we have need of your language skills in order to interrogate some of the rabble that were captured in a skirmish outside the walls yesterday."

I nodded my reply and continued studying the city. My heart went out to the vast number of faithful Jews who were trapped within the walls of Jerusalem. The Feast of Passover was drawing near, and I knew that many pilgrims from all over the civilized world had made their way to the Holy City of God to offer their sacrifices and to be cleansed of their sins. I asked myself over and over why more of them had not accepted the true Messiah when he came and made himself known over thirty years ago. Then maybe this catastrophic event would not need to take place. As these thoughts washed over me, I looked to the front of our path and saw that we were approaching an encampment that was at least four or more times the size of the one we had left not long ago.

We entered the camp, and the centurion dismounted and went to the quarters of his commander. One of the men in our troop took the reins of his horse and led the animal towards the corral. Another soldier roughly grabbed the reins of my animal and fell in behind the one who had taken the centurion's horse.

In just a short time, the rest of us arrived at the corral. We all dismounted. I had some difficulty and nearly fell flat on my face but was able to catch myself in time. As soon as I was squared away, another soldier grabbed my arms and bound me with rope at the wrists, behind my back. I was a prisoner, and I wasn't allowed to forget that fact. I was led to an open space near the stables and forced to sit on the ground in cross-legged fashion with two guards standing over me. No words were spoken, and I sat silently praising God for keeping me safe from further injury and harm. I don't know how long I was there, and I took in as much of the camp as I could from my position on the ground.

I didn't see anyone who was not involved in one activity or another. Some soldiers were marching from one place to another. I saw a group of officers, not far from me, pouring over some maps spread out on a rough hewn wooden table.

I caught a glimpse of some soldiers taking some prisoners to the tribune's quarters. It wasn't long after this that I spied the centurion coming towards me.

"The prisoners have been taken to the tribune, and none can speak anything but Aramaic. I need for you to come with me so that you can tell us what they are saying." He nodded to one of my guards who then lifted me to my feet.

I nodded, and then to the best of my ability held my hands out from behind my back to indicate that I wanted to be untied. He looked at the ropes and then at the guard and told him to remove the bindings.

"I want your word that you'll do nothing foolish after I release you," he said as the guard cut the bindings.

"And what am I going to do here in the middle of this large garrison—run?" I answered as I rubbed my wrists after the ropes fell to the ground. "I'm old and unable to fight a thousand Roman soldiers all alone. Besides, where would I go—into Jerusalem?" I chuckled, trying to make light of my situation.

The centurion didn't see the humor in my remark and glared at me as he said, "Follow me. This is serious business."

I kept quiet and fell into step at his right side while we walked to the middle of the camp to a large tent with two guards on either side of the entrance. They both snapped to attention, and one pulled open a flap where I entered first followed by the centurion.

Inside I was confronted by a group of officers standing around three young men who were bound with their hands tied behind their backs and were on their knees in the center of the tent. They had been badly beaten, and their clothes were in tatters. All three showed signs of a savage whipping similar to the one I had endured the day before. I winced as I saw them, for I knew what they had gone through. I felt a twinge of pain on my own back.

"Tell us what the plans of defense are and how the Jews are planning to greet us as our army approaches," the officer in charge of the interrogation demanded.

One of the men, most probably the leader said in Aramaic, "I don't understand what it is you want from us. We are just poor farmers who have come in from Galilee to celebrate the Passover."

I whispered this information to the centurion and then remained quiet. He looked at me and shook his head and said in a low voice that they had been captured as they left the city late the night before. Then

125

he spoke up to the group of officers, "This is the man I told you about. He claims he is not a Jew, rather a believer of The Way. He speaks Aramaic, Greek and our own language. He just told me that these men claim to be poor farmers from Galilee and know nothing of the city's defenses."

The officer who was conducting the interrogation shouted, "Liar, you were caught leaving the city, not entering it." He then beckoned me to interpret for him.

I looked at the three prisoners and said to them in Aramaic, "They know that you were caught leaving the city, not trying to enter as you claim."

The apparent leader of the three glared at me and spat through clenched teeth, "You are a traitor to the Jews. You are helping our sworn enemies."

"I am not a traitor, I too have suffered at their hands," I replied. "My back bears the stripe of their whip. However, I find my life worth more than to die just because I won't interpret what it is you have to say. Their interests in you are about the defenses of the city."

"I would rather die than to betray those things to the Romans," the leader answered.

The third man looked at me with large fearful eyes and whimpered, "I'll tell you what they want to know. I don't want to die."

The leader growled at this man, "Keep quiet you coward!" Then he looked at me and said. "We can tell you nothing of which you aren't already aware."

I looked at the centurion who stood next to me and told him that the leader said he'd rather die than to tell them anything. However, the third man would be willing to divulge all that he knows.

"Maybe," I continued, "it would be wise to interrogate them one at a time to see if they may feel a little freer in telling you of the things that you desire to know."

The centurion suggested this to the officer leading the interrogation, as if the thought were his, and the officer agreed. With that he motioned to the guards to take two of the prisoners outside the tent and leave the third man with those of us who were still inside. Once they were gone, the man was questioned at length.

"If you value your life, as you claim, then tell us the truth. Were you and your friends leaving the city?" The officer then motioned to me to interpret the question to the prisoner, which I did.

I then told this prisoner that he'd better tell all of the truth as he saw it or that the Romans would show him no mercy. With this, the man began telling us everything that he knew about the city and its defenses. He was a Zealot and had come out of the city with the others to gather information about the Romans by trying to spy on their movements. He was unaware of the coming of the great army under Titus that was approaching the city from the west, from Caesarea.

This prisoner and his compatriots had hoped to spy on Festus's camp and then later in the night with men from the city surround the small garrison and defeat it, as a lesson to them that any further attempt to take the city would result in their destruction. I relayed this information to the officer. As the Romans talked this over amongst themselves, I asked the prisoner, rather incredulously, if he or those in charge of the city believed that they could defeat the Roman army.

He replied, "We feel that the city's walls are too great to be breached."

"Are they such fools to believe that they can stand against an army made up of four legions? I know that the civil war going on inside the walls has decimated your food supplies. Further there are a great number inside the city who are willing to turn control over to the Romans so this madness will be brought to an end."

The prisoner just hung his head and remained silent.

After speaking with the hostage, I whispered all that we'd said to the centurion who relayed this to the others. He then growled at me. "How do you know about the civil war and food supplies?"

I told him the truth that I had been in the city two months earlier and had seen these things for myself.

"You have lied to me, Caleb," he said with disgust.

"No," I replied. "I didn't lie, for you never asked me of those things that took place before my capture. If you had, I would have told you. I didn't think that what happened over a month ago would have been of interest to you."

"Everything that has happened in Jerusalem interests us," he replied. "So when we are finished here, I want you to tell me all that you know."

The interrogation continued for I don't know how long. The other prisoners were brought in one at a time, and they weren't able to add anything new to what had already been said. They were then taken from the tent and led away. I have no idea what became of them, though I do fear they were sentenced to death.

The centurion and I left the tent. As we walked back to our mounts, he told me in no uncertain terms that I was to tell him all I knew about Jerusalem while we journeyed back to his camp. This I did, as I didn't want to see the city destroyed and I secretly hoped that he would hear something in my words that might change the course of the events. I talked of my first trip and of what I learned of the terrible conditions that existed behind the walls. I talked of the three different factions that sought to control the city and particularly how they had abandoned their beliefs in God and only desired power and control over the city and its people. I also talked of the large number of innocent citizens who lived in the city and those pilgrims who had come from all over in order to celebrate the Passover, and that their desire was as mine that Jerusalem would be preserved forever and not destroyed in a war.

As we approached our camp, I finished by telling him of my desire to see a peaceful resolution to this conflict and the overthrowing of the Zealots and bandits who were trying to control the people.

"How can we conquer these Zealots without going to war? Do you think if we show up and ask them politely to leave, that they would willingly depart?" the centurion asked in an incredulous tone. He then went on to answer his own question without waiting for me to respond. "They can only be deposed of by the force of arms. Do not be so naïve as to think that these men are going to give up without a fight. I also know of those who would welcome us in and allow us to continue to rule Judea, for two of those men are in my prisoner compound as we speak. You talked to them yesterday. These men are old and weak and will not be able to overthrow the rabble who are causing all of the grief and misery you have told me about. The city will be ours, but it will extract a tremendous price in the lives of those who reside therein."

I said nothing in response to this, as I knew in my heart of hearts that he was right. We then finished our trip back to camp in silence for I had nothing more to say. I knew then that the city was doomed.

When we arrived at camp, I was immediately taken to the prisoner compound. I noticed that there were only two other prisoners, and the guard informed me that the others had been set free and told to leave and leave quickly or else be sentenced to death. This they did.

No doubt they were still running as fast as their legs would take them away from the city. The two remaining prisoners had been sentenced to die by crucifixion that afternoon. My heart went out to them for they seemed innocent to me, but the centurion's second in command had caught them in an attempt to escape and sentenced them on the spot, before we returned from Tribune Festus' camp. My thoughts went out to Naomi and her family whom I thought should be well on their way to Philadelphia. I quickly said a prayer asking God to keep them safe in their travels.

The noon meal arrived, and the guard told me that they were breaking camp and that we would be traveling in force to join with Tribune Festus and his cohort at Scopus by mid-afternoon. There was a great amount of activity as the soldiers disassembled the tents and loaded them on the carts and mules. I also noticed four men making crosses from some lumber. I supposed this was to be used to crucify the two remaining prisoners.

It was the Roman way to perform these executions in full view of those who were still in the city. I felt for the men but I did learn that they were definitely part of the murderous brigands under the leadership of Simon. I just didn't feel that I could go to the centurion and intercede for them without endangering my own life.

In the early afternoon, the centurion summoned me. Again I was helped to my mount, and we left for General Festus's camp following the same route we'd taken earlier in the day. The remaining soldiers would leave later in the day and travel north by northeast direct to Scopus where we would join them sometime during the night. Our mission was to retrace our morning's steps and join with Festus and his cohort on the western side of the city before traveling around the northern end of Jerusalem and then to Mount Scopus.

As we approached the southwest corner of the wall, we could see a large troop of cavalry approaching the city from the west. The centurion pointed these men out to me and said that at the head of the troop was none other than General Titus, son of the Emperor of all of Rome, Vespasian. This troop numbered in the hundreds and was truly a formidable force, one I thought that the Jewish leaders would respect and fear.

Our little procession stopped and observed from the distance, outside the western wall and just north of Sultan's Pool, as we tried to discern what the defenders of the city would do, if anything. My hope was that they would lay down their arms, open the gates and sue for peace, for it was inconceivable to me that they could think or believe that they would defeat or even hold off this Roman force. Titus and his horsemen were only a small portion of the greater force yet to come. I estimated that he had with him about five or six hundred mounted soldiers and that his total army, once gathered and put into place, would number in excess of 60,000. How could the Jews expect to hold this vast army outside the city walls?

The troop of horsemen continued straight for the city's west wall, towards the tower of Psephinus. Before reaching the tower, the troop in columns of three abreast, led by Titus, turned south towards us paralleling the wall. The troop followed Titus as he led the way along the wall, each turning where their leader had turned. The troop began to string out, and the General and his fellow officers proceeded, leaving the majority of the horsemen some distance behind. Instead of waiting for the rest of the cavalry to catch up with him, Titus and these few others were some distance ahead of the main force. It was near the Women's Towers that a near disaster struck, at a place that was little more than one thousand paces from where we were. A large force of Jewish soldiers leaped through a nearby gate in a coordinated attack to intercept Titus and the few men with him. At the same time, another group stepped between Titus and the remaining troop still in the process of turning the corner trying to follow their leader.

It soon became apparent that the attack was well planned, for Titus and the few horsemen with him were unable to maneuver and thus escape. There were numerous hedges and trenches, those used to water and protect the many gardens in the area, which blocked their way of escape to the south or west.

Titus and the men with him, maybe ten or twelve, drew their swords and started slashing at the Jews who were rushing them. Other Jews were throwing darts at the entrapped men, but none hit the general though some of those with him were wounded. Titus then yelled to his men to follow him, and he turned his horse and charged back in the direction from which he had come—into the Jews who blocked him from the rest of his troop. The Jews who were attacking Titus were not mounted, and they were soon run over, if they weren't able to move out of his way, and driven into the ground where they stood, for his mighty steed was too large for them to bring down. They were unable to pull him or the others with him from their horses.

My centurion was enraged by this action and without a thought for his own safety spurred his horse to full gallop towards the place where the Jews were attacking his general.

The centurion's great horse was at full gallop in just one or two powerful leaps and within a few more moments was jumping the trenches and hedges that separated him from the Jews trying to encircle Titus. He soon fell in behind the Jewish force that was now following Titus, and he quickly overtook those men, running over those who did not get out of his way. He drew his mighty sword and slashed it from side to side, cutting a swath through the men on foot. The last two officers following Titus as they rushed through Jewish foot soldiers were struck by darts, and one slumped in his saddle just as the centurion reached him. The centurion grabbed the reins of the horse with his right hand as he held his sword high with his left, slashing at any man who dared to step in his way. Then another dart or arrow struck the wounded officer's horse, dealing it a fatal blow. The horse went down on its fore legs and then tumbled forward in a somersault throwing the wounded rider to the ground. These actions jerked the reins from the centurion's hands, and before he could respond the Jewish foot soldiers were upon the helpless Roman officer.

I don't know whether I took a breath or not during this action, for I was so shocked by what had transpired. The action, although it seemed to be in slow motion, happened so fast. The centurion was soon at the rear of those Jews that were attacking Titus. He swung his sword as he galloped through the Jewish foot soldiers, thus clearing a path through the men who were trying to overwhelm the general and the small number of Roman soldiers who were with him. The Jews finally became aware that they were being attacked from the rear and started to move out of the centurion's way. The ferociousness of their attack on Titus waned. The second officer who was in the rear was hit a fatal blow by an arrow, and he too slumped in his saddle. The Jews surrounded his mount. One grabbed the reins while others dragged the Roman officer out of the saddle and slew him. The man who had grabbed the reins of the horse then led it away.

By this time the general and his men broke through the remaining Jews and quickly rejoined the rest of the troop. The Jews also withdrew, and as quickly as they had appeared they fled into the city through the hidden gate they had originally used for their attack.

With the action ended, the decurion of my little band ordered us to move on to the camp of Tribune Festus. When we arrived, General Titus had dismounted and was surrounded by a large number of officers and men, all congratulating him on his heroic escape from the Jewish bandits. But Titus shook off those accolades and asked who it was that charged up through the Jews thus blunting their attack.

One man then spoke up and said that that man was none other than the centurion that was holding me prisoner, whose name he did not know. Another then spoke up and said that it was Aerius, the one under Festus's command. Now I, too, knew the name of the one who had been using me as his interpreter.

Titus called the man forward and thanked him for his bravery. "It is because of men like you," he said to Aerius and so all could hear, "that the empire remains strong and is able to continue to rule the world. Your gallantry and bravery in the face of overwhelming odds will be amply rewarded."

Aerius kneeled before his general and bowed his head in thanks. He then rose and stood before Titus and quietly thanked him for being a truly courageous leader who demonstrates to the troops a model of what they as soldiers of Rome should strive to be. Titus then gripped his forearm, and Aerius stood back and saluted his commander by crossing his right hand over his heart. He then stepped away and returned to the soldiers of his command as Titus called his generals together in order to formulate plans for the siege of Jerusalem.

These things I tell you so that you can understand that it was this little offensive action by the Jews against Titus, the son of Caesar Vespasian, that instilled in the hearts of the Romans and their allies a hatred of the Jews. It also instilled in their hearts a determination that the city would be surrendered or destroyed.

The remaining part of the day was spent in planning a move of Tribune Festus's cohort and the Twelfth Legion to a place north of the Temple Mount, a place named Scopus or The Prospect overlooking the northeast corner of the new city. While all of this was taking place, I heard the news that the Tenth Legion was making its way from Jericho, was due to arrive early the next morning and would set their camp on the Mount of Olives. As these preparations were being completed, I sat on the ground under the watchful eye of a guard and pondered the future and what was to take place in the coming days and weeks. I couldn't get over the feeling that the great city of God would soon be destroyed and lay in ashes at the feet of the Romans. The Jews were about to be defeated and then carried off in exile throughout the world. This had happened once before to the people of Israel when Nebuchadnezzar had defeated and sacked Jerusalem over six hundred years earlier.

I thought, *Oh, why hadn't they accepted the Christ when he appeared to them just a short time ago?*

Late in the afternoon, the centurion gave the order, and our group began moving to Scopus where we would prepare for the arrival of the forces of Tribune Festus and then later the Fifth, the Twelfth and the Fifteenth Legions, which would set up camp the next day.

Another great camp was to be set up across the Kidron Valley opposite the walls of Jerusalem. This was for the Tenth Legion coming from Jericho due to arrive after dark. There could be no question in the minds of the rabble who controlled the city that war was upon them.

We arrived at Scopus late in the afternoon, and the men of Aerius' centuria began the task of laying out the camp.

It was during twilight that the tribune and his cohort arrived at Scopus. I was told by one of the guards that General Titus was awaiting the arrival of the Fifth Legion from Emmaus, which was due to arrive after dark, and then all three legions would start out for Scopus early the next morning.

The purpose of Tribune Festus's cohort was to prepare the way for the regular army troops that were coming from the west. They had prepared the road from the western camp to our position on the northeast corner of Jerusalem at Scopus.

Once they arrived, the men began laying out the camp for the Twelfth and Fifteenth Legions due in the morning. When they had completed these chores, they would proceed further to the northeast to prepare a site for the Fifth Legion. As these proceedings were taking place, I heard a great clamor from the west of the city. I was soon informed by one of my guards that the noise I heard was from the two legions arriving from Gabaothsaul. Amidst this commotion, I was given my supper of mainly bread and water. Shortly thereafter, I said my prayers and then fell asleep on my mat.

I awoke in the early morning and lay on my mat thinking of many things. I thought of my youth spent right here in Jerusalem and the multitude of events I had witnessed during the years since I was a young child. Most memorable was the crucifixion and resurrection of our Lord and Savior Jesus Christ. Then my thoughts went to how my life had changed since the time I placed my trust in Jesus. There was my marriage, arranged by my father, to a woman from Jerusalem, and then the birth of our daughter, Sarah. I was sorry that I hadn't spent more time with my wife, Pricilla, but I was on several mission trips with Cleopas and Barnabas that took me a great distance from home and family for long periods of time. I hadn't known my daughter well either for she grew up without my being around. It wasn't until after she had married when she was fourteen that I got to know her, and it was then that she convinced her husband to accept Jesus on faith. It was also during this time that I ended my mission trips and stayed at home with Pricilla, for a great famine had come to the land and I was needed to help put food on our table. It was also during these last few years of Pricilla's life that we became a close and loving family.

Next, my thoughts went to Naomi and her relatives who had escaped the night before last. I prayed that they were safe and that their journey was peaceful.

These thoughts were interrupted when the guard brought me my breakfast and told me that the Twelfth and Fifteenth Legions would be arriving at Mount Scopus about mid-morning. He also informed me that after the arrival of the legions, I would be needed by the centurion for my language skills since some new prisoners had been taken during the night.

As I waited to be summoned by Aerius, I surveyed our camp. Though the legions had not yet arrived, I saw that our manipuli would be located on the southwestern edge of the great camp that would house the two legions. Directly to the south and west, I could see the walls of Jerusalem, and even on further to the south, I could distinguish the Temple that was built along the eastern wall. From this wall, the ground fell away from the city and down into the Kidron Valley before the ground rose again up to the heights of the plain on which I was standing. Directly south, I could easily see the Mount of Olives that was but a short distance away. This was the same place where my Lord and Savior Jesus had spent much of his time praying during his years of ministry. How I longed to see him again and to hear his voice. I got down on my knees and prayed for the people behind the walls of Jerusalem.

It wasn't long after my prayer that the Roman legions began their move from the west side of the city around the north wall to this, their camp on Mount Scopus, which was less than one thousand steps from the northeast corner of Jerusalem across the Kidron valley.

The procession was imposing, for it started with the blaring of the trumpets announcing the assembly of the troops, which I'm sure was heard throughout the region. Once the trumpets stopped, we could hear the drummers as they established the cadence for the march. We could not see the Romans for some time, however; only the beat of the drums told me that the troops were moving. Then the lead elements of the line emerged around the northwest corner of the city. Their route kept the troops out of the range of the archers positioned on top of the northern wall, and it also appeared to me as if every one of the citizens had climbed to the top of the city's walls and towers to view the spectacle of over thirty thousand troops as they marched in order along the north side of the city.

First came the auxiliaries. These units consisted of soldiers who had been sent to fortify the Roman armed forces. They were composed of non-Roman troops who were allied with Rome against Jerusalem. These soldiers came from the various kingdoms in the region.

Titus's army consisted of four legions plus these auxiliaries; there were the Fifth, Tenth, Twelfth and Fifteenth Legions. The Fifth Legion had early on received orders to advance through Emmaus and then on to Jerusalem to join up with Titus and the Twelfth and Fifteenth Legions already positioned near the western gate. The Tenth Legion was to come later in the day through Jericho and then on to the east side of the Kidron Valley to a place south of Scopus and there to establish their camp on the Mount of Olives.

That morning when the armies started moving with the commanders of the auxiliaries in the lead, there were following them the Fifth, Twelfth and Fifteenth Legions, all moving from the west side of Jerusalem on around the north end and concluding at the camp ground already laid out for them on Mount Scopus.

The line of march was led by the auxiliaries. Next came the engineers whose purpose was to prepare the roads and measure out the camps. Behind the engineers came the commanders' baggage, which was accompanied by enough armed soldiers to support and defend them. Titus himself came next along with a select body of men all mounted on black horses with beautiful coats reflecting the morning sun. His troop was followed by pike-men, who in turn were followed by the cavalry of the three legions. A short distance behind the legions rumbled the mighty engines of war, which in turn were followed by the tribunes and the leaders of the cohorts with their fighting men behind them. This, the main body of the army, marched in ranks of six men side-by-side, which seemed to me to be an endless parade. Following the foot soldiers were the trumpeters, who in turn were followed by the ensigns bearing the eagle and other designations of the units to be involved in the upcoming battle. At the very end of the line were the servants along with the baggage of all the troops who had proceeded them. As a final point, there were the mercenaries and those that guarded the rear of the army.

The procession went on and on, an endless line of fighting men and truly a spectacular army bent on the destruction of all of Jerusalem. This movement of troops took most of the morning, kicking up great clouds of dust that nearly obscured our view of Jerusalem. As soon as they arrived at Mount Scopus, they started the process of establishing their camp.

During the late morning, I, from my vantage point, could see that the vanguard of the Tenth Legion had arrived from Jericho and entered the Mount of Olives. Soon thereafter, the rest of the legion marched into this encampment. Once there, they dropped their weapons and packs and began the process of making the camp habitable. I could clearly make out the men on the Mount of Olives as they separated into different work parties and groups to go about the task of making the camp secure. From Mount Scopus, I was not only able to see the Tenth Legion on the Mount but the whole of the Kidron Valley to the south and then west to the wall of Jerusalem.

Many thoughts crossed my mind, and I paid little attention to the work the soldiers were doing. My mind wandered to many subjects, and I fell into a somewhat of a dazed trance as I considered the many events that had led me to this place.

THE FIRST BLOOD
IS DRAWN

I was abruptly awakened from my reverie by the shouts of a large group of men. At first I thought that the Romans on the Mount of Olives were celebrating some sort of victory. Soon though, I realized that the shouting came from the direction of the east wall of Jerusalem. As I raised my eyes to that place, I was shocked to see a number of Jews exiting one of the gates in the wall. On closer observation I saw that they were dressed in armor with shields, swords, darts and arrows clutched in their hands. They were streaming out of the gate and down across the Kidron Valley, headed toward the Roman work parties stationed at the Mount of Olives. I couldn't believe my eyes, for I instantly saw that they were attacking the Roman soldiers who had put aside their weapons in order to work on the encampment. They had been widely dispersed performing those duties necessary to set up their camp. As a result they were unable to gather together fast enough to form a solid defensive line from which to confront their enemies.

The Romans looked up at the charging Jews in disbelief and stood without turning and running for the safety of the camp. It seemed a long time before any of them realized that they were under attack. Then, as if they were one, they suddenly turned and ran for their weapons. For many, it was too late as the Jews were upon them. Those furthest from the onslaught hastily retreated from the enemy, trying desperately to

141

save their lives but more that half of them delayed too long. The Jews overran the position slaying a great number of Romans.

By this time the soldiers in our camp on Scopus became aware of the battle taking place in the valley of the Kidron. They donned their armor and prepared to go out and meet the enemy. First to move was Titus seated upon a magnificent black steed. He and twenty or thirty mounted troops sped out of camp to strike the Jews on their left flank. Soon to follow were other horsemen speeding down into the valley.

I watched this battle unfold right before my eyes as all of this took place just a little more than five hundred paces from where I stood.

Within minutes General Titus and his men charged down the hill into the side of the Jews attacking the men of the Tenth Legion who had been hard at work fortifying their camp. It appeared to me that the trained soldiers of the Tenth were confused over the disorganized way in which the Jewish soldiers attacked as they, the Romans, were used to a more orderly battle array.

The Jews seemed to be winning this skirmish by continuing to advance on the Tenth Legion, as more of their soldiers poured out of the city gate to join the apparent triumph. They became so focused on the Tenth that they were unaware of Titus and his now eighty or ninety horsemen galloping headlong into their own flank.

The troops of the Tenth Legion were in disarray and running up the hill to gather their weapons and establish a defensive line to put a stop to Jewish the assault. Many were struck down before they could turn and face their enemy. Not only were the Roman soldiers caught off guard, so were their officers. It was apparent to me that no one seemed to know what to do as there were no orders given. Finally, everyone turned and fled from the Jews. Had it not been for the attack on the flank by Titus and his men, the battle would have turned into a rout.

Once the Jews realized that they were being attacked on their left side, the intensity of their own thrust slackened as they turned to face the horsemen riding at full gallop through their midst. At this time, I saw Aerius and ten or fifteen other men on horseback leave the camp and rush down the hill to aid and support their general.

It wasn't long before the general was surrounded by the enemy, and I thought that he might have been overwhelmed by the Jews. As these thoughts entered my mind, I saw that Aerius and his men had reached the Jewish foot soldiers and driven straight through them to Titus' aide. This new onslaught by the Romans broke the ranks of the Jews who were trying to bring Titus and his men down.

Within a short time Titus was surrounded by his own cavalry protecting him from the Jews. The tide of the battle began to turn in the favor of the Romans, and the Jews retreated to the city walls. Titus and his men escaped from the middle of the mêlée. He continued to direct the other troops as they fought the Jews, who were losing heart and retiring towards the city gate through which they had come.

The men of the Tenth had had time to re-gather in a semblance of battle array and started to move forward on the retreating enemy. One of the horsemen with Titus rode from the general's side up the hill to the tribune, who was directing the Tenth's infantry. The tribune apparently told them to stop their attack, retire to their camp and continue fortifying it. Soon there was the sound of a trumpet playing recall, and the soldiers under the tribune's command turned and began trudging back to their camp.

A Jew on top of the wall who must have of been directing the battle waved a flag on a long staff in some sort of signal to the soldiers on the ground. The Jewish ground troops turned once again towards the retiring Romans and made another headlong dash towards them. At this same moment, the gates reopened and a great number of additional Jews poured out to join their comrades in pursuing the Tenth Legion.

This new threat put the Romans in disorder once again. Many threw down their weapons and ran away in fear of their lives. Again it was Titus who saved the day for his army. He and his hundred-plus horsemen turned around to attack the Jews on their left side and for a second time drove a deep wedge in their flank, scattering them and riding over those who tried to stand and fight. Each horseman used his sword, swinging it from side to side and slashing into the men on foot. Again the threat from the flank blunted the Jewish forward attack, and their strength waned as they turned to meet the cavalry attacking them.

I then looked to the camp of the Tenth Legion and saw that those who had broken and run in fear of their lives stop, turn around and go back to the weapons they had discarded and pick them up. Slowly they began to reform into skirmish lines and start down the hill to meet the onrushing Jews. Again it was Titus who single-handedly turned the tide of battle. I couldn't do anything but admire his courage, even though I had hoped the Jews would have been able to prevail over the Romans. This was not to be as it didn't take long for the Romans to form up and drive their enemy back behind the walls of Jerusalem.

I viewed the grounds where the battle had taken place and saw many inert bodies scattered around the landscape. In my youth I had walked many times up and down the Kidron Valley and had never thought that it would one day become a battleground. Now here before my eyes lay heaps of broken and lifeless shells, both Roman and Jews. It was truly a travesty.

It wasn't long after the Jews had retired behind the gates of the city that I saw the soldiers of the Tenth Legion return to their camp and start again in their efforts to fortify their position. I also noticed that the Roman medical personnel making the rounds of those who had fallen in battle, carrying the wounded away and stacking the dead in preparation for cremation on the fiery bier later in the evening.

It was at this time that Titus and his mounted troops returned to Scopus. From a distance, I could see that once the general dismounted he called for Aerius. I'm sure it was to thank him personally for once again coming to his aid. After that Aerius returned to the nearby stables and sent a soldier to get me and escort me to his tent.

With my hands tied behind my back, I was taken to Aerius. Once inside the tent the centurion told my escort to untie me and then to wait outside.

After the guard left, I said to Aerius, "I witnessed the battle and I was awed by the courage of Titus and of your own strength, skill and determination to serve your general." I went on to say, "I was saddened by the number of deaths and injuries to both Roman and Jews. It seems so senseless to me that a peaceful resolution cannot be reached. If only those bandits and criminals who have control of the city could be taken out and punished, none of this would be necessary."

Aerius scoffed at my thoughts. "The Jews, all of them, deserve to be punished. They think they're so much better than anyone else and that their God will save them from destruction. That misconception will lead us to victory. I've told you before that their God exists only in their imagination and that our power and might will bring them to their knees. But, I don't want to get into a philosophical discussion with you, for we have other business at hand. We have numerous captives that need to be interrogated, for which I will need your skills."

I was immediately put to work, interpreting for the interrogators who were questioning the Jewish prisoners. Many of these Jews were severely injured and in great pain, something the Romans took advantage of in forcing them to talk. I was sickened by their methods of hurting the prisoners in order to get them to tell all they knew. It was through their confessions that I learned how conditions in the city had deteriorated since I had last been there. Many of the prisoners were young men barely in their teens. They had been forced out of the city in order to attack the Romans under penalty of death if they refused. Many had been threatened by the gang leaders in charge of the city that their parents or siblings would be put to death if they refused to attack the Tenth Legion at the Mount of Olives. Then there were the Zealots, gang leaders and members of various rebel causes themselves. They were a haughty and arrogant bunch, out of touch with the reality of the situation and wouldn't believe that the Romans were intent on their destruction or that the walls of Jerusalem would ever be breached. It was so sad to me, for all I could see was death and destruction for all within the city's walls.

I also learned that most of the food supplies had been destroyed and many of the city's residents were on starvation diets. Even if the Romans didn't attack, the citizens would eventually die of starvation.

I worked with the centurion for the remaining portion of the day, interpreting all that these prisoners had to say. By the time it was dark I was exhausted and ready for sleep.

I was taken back to the centurion's prisoner's compound and given my meal. After eating, I lay on my mat, said my prayers and then tried to sleep. This didn't work, for my thoughts were of Jerusalem and the many innocent people caught in the middle of this tragedy.

THE SIEGE OF
JERUSALEM BEGINS

Throughout the ensuing days great preparations were underway fortifying the camps and reestablishing a sense of discipline throughout the legions. There were no requests for my skills, and I was left alone. There were no other prisoners in the holding compound to which I was assigned so there was little to do. Since the soldiers were busy with the camp, I had time to think, pray and catch up on sleep. Aerius and his men were detailed to continue their scouting, out and around the city, looking for the fatal weakness that would allow the Romans to break through the walls and into Jerusalem.

This was also an important time for the Jews, for the day of the Feast of Unleavened Bread had arrived, the time in Jewish history when the people had prepared for their escape from Egypt under the leadership of Moses. This was a special day of worship. It was also a day of praising God for His providence and intervention in setting His people free. I felt that many of the prayers that were being lifted up to Him were requests that He once again intervene in events and free the Jews from the army that was gathering outside the walls of their Holy City; also there would be prayers that the thugs and gangsters that controlled Jerusalem be dealt with in a harsh fashion and the city returned to the faithful citizens.

Much of my time was spent in my own worship to God and in prayers for those whom I had known over the last few days. There was Silas who had on faith accepted Jesus into his life and Naomi and her family, also making their way to Philadelphia. I continued praying for their safety and for their acceptance of Jesus as the true Messiah. It was during this time of meditation that I fell into a deep sleep.

It must have been some time later that I was awakened by the voices of a great multitude. These voices at first seemed to be part of my dream, for in my dream I was in a great valley with thousands of people who had been listening to the Lord Jesus speak to us about the greatness of God and welcoming us into the life eternal for our faithful service on earth. When he had finished the multitude stood as one and cheered in thanksgiving for the greatest of gifts, eternal life with God.

As I gained consciousness I realized that it had been just a dream, but then there were the voices and shouts of a large number of people. It didn't take long for me to realize that these voices came from the city. I stood and walked to the edge of my compound and stared over at the city. Many of the soldiers, too, stopped what they were doing and looked to Jerusalem, all wondering what it was that would cause such a boisterous reaction from the citizens inside the walls.

This sound continued for some time, and soon I was able to discern that these were cries of agony and not of joy. I hung my head for I realized that the sedition within was once again taking place. The civil war had not ended with the approach of the Romans but had just been put off for a brief period of time. Once again they were at each others throats. Even on this most holy of days, they were killing one another rather than uniting against a common enemy and in faith utilizing the power of God to prevail. How tragic it was. One of the Roman guards came over to me, the one who had thanked me for intervening for his friends who had allowed Naomi and her cousin's escape, and asked what it was that caused such a great outcry from the city. I told him that it was the various factions within the city fighting one another, in fact a continuation of the civil war.

This soldier looked at me in wide-eyed wonder. "How could this be? With our great army sitting at the very gates bent on their destruction, they are fighting over control of the city? How utterly stupid can they be?"

I shrugged my shoulders and said nothing, for there wasn't anything that I could add. The question remained, how mindless can they be? I returned to my mat and continued my prayers.

Late in the evening, after Aerius and his men returned from their scouting trip, I was summoned to his tent. "We have some more prisoners that we captured this evening," he told me before I was even inside. "They were caught trying to escape the city. We need you to interpret their words during our interrogation. So walk with me as we will go to the holding pen of Tribune Festus where they are being held."

He immediately started out in a fast walk, and I fell in step with him trying to match his pace stride-for-stride. As we walked, he talked of the great commotion going on in Jerusalem earlier in the day. "How is it," he asked, "that they could continue with their civil war? It's almost as if they are unaware of our presence outside the walls of the city they are trying to control. Don't they realize that even if and when they come together that they still can't prevent us from gaining control of Jerusalem? It only makes our task easier."

I mumbled my agreement and continued walking in silence. I, too, was curious as to what was happening and why they had not come together in order to fight the Romans who were determined to take control. If it meant the total sacking of Jerusalem, then so be it. The answer to my questions lay with the prisoners that we were going to interview within the next few minutes.

We arrived at a large tent and were quickly ushered inside. Aerius and I were taken to a narrow table behind which three officers sat along one side facing three prisoners who were on their knees with their hands tied behind their backs. They were dirty and disheveled, but appeared to be fairly well-to-do as their clothing looked to me to have been well tailored. All three appeared to be frightened. When they saw me they looked surprised, since they apparently thought that I was also a Jew but I was not bound and under guard.

I asked Aerius if it would be alright if I spoke with the prisoners for a minute or two in order to set them at ease and find out a little about them before the interrogation started.

Without a word to me, Aerius went to the one who was in charge and whispered into his ear. This officer listened intently and then slowly nodded his head.

Aerius walked over to me and said I could have just a short time. I approached them and kneeled on the floor in front of them and began.

"I am Caleb, son of Isaac. I, too, am a prisoner and my captors are using me to interpret your words for them. They have brought us together, for they want to know what is going on in the city and the reason for the uproar today. They also will want to know why you have tried to escape from Jerusalem."

The apparent leader of this group was a man younger than I was by eight or nine years. He answered in a low voice, "We all had family in Jerusalem; children, grandchildren and some of us still had our parents living with us. That all ended today."

I must have looked taken aback, for he said, "Yes, it is true. All three of us lost our families in just a short time late this morning. The priest, Eleasar, had promised that the gates to the Temple would be opened for all of the citizens and those visiting for the purpose of celebrating the Passover to come into the Temple and make their offerings to God.

"All of the people were excited by the news, for no matter what was happening outside the gates we still could go into the Temple and worship God and pray for the end of the sedition inside Jerusalem and for our release from the threat of the Roman army. All of this went well. The gates were opened early and the people entered into the Temple and made their sacrifices to the Lord.

"Unbeknownst to us, John, the rebel leader who controls most of the old city, the fortress, and some of the new city, had sent his men in robes that covered their armor and weapons on the pretext that they, too, were offering sacrifices to the Lord. When a large number of these men had positioned themselves around the court, they threw off their garments, drew their weapons and lashed out at all of the Zealots who were there to protect the people from just this kind of attack. These Zealots were so caught off guard that they quickly threw down their weapons and ran away, down into the subterranean tunnels and caverns under the Temple. Their actions left the innocent citizens placing their offerings on the altar open to attack by John's soldiers. These seditious bandits struck out at all within the courtyard. They killed and wounded hundreds, maybe even thousands of worshippers, and the floor ran red with their blood. When they had finished they made a truce, not with the upright citizens, but with the Zealots who had run away and hidden themselves. Suddenly instead of three tyrants, John, Simon and Eleasar, we now have two for Eleasar has joined with John against Simon. All of us here lost every member of our families. The number of dead and wounded was incredible, and it is a sight and sadness that none of us here before you will ever forget.

"The three of us came together and quickly left the Temple. Without stopping at our homes, we found our way out of Jerusalem and surrendered to the Romans."

"I believe what you have told me," I responded after a long pause, "for I am aware of the sedition taking place inside the walls. I will do what I can to intercede for you with your captors, but I cannot promise anything. I will pray for you."

I then went to Aerius and whispered all that they said into his ear. "I believe them, I added." I beseech that you let them go for they aren't a threat to you or to your army. They all have lost their wives and children today."

"Everyone has a sad story," he replied. "I'll see what I can do." He then went to the table where the three interrogators sat and spoke to them at some length. The prisoners sat silently where they were, each in a high state of apprehension, for the decision handed down from this court would determine their fate. As for me, I stood and silently prayed for these men.

At last Aerius left the table, and the three officers continued to whisper among themselves. After another few minutes, one of the officers turned to me and told me to ask the prisoners about where they lived in the city and to tell of all they knew about the defenses of Jerusalem.

I addressed the prisoners as a group, "They have asked that you tell them all you know about the defenses of the city. They need to know who is in control of the defenses and where the machines of war are that had been captured from Cestius."

These civilians then explained as best they could of what was taking place in Jerusalem.

They told in detail all that they knew of John of Giscala, of Simon of Giora and of Eleasar, where they were positioned in the city, and of the machines of war and where they thought they might be hidden in the Temple or somewhere nearby. These prisoners did not try to hide anything. I believe that it was their intent to turn over to the Romans a means whereby they could rid the city of these seditious rebels.

When the questioning was over, the interrogating officers called Aerius to their table and spoke to him in low voices. I strained to hear what it was that they were saying, but I was unable to make it out. Without much ado these officers stood and walked out of the tent. I continued to pray for these prisoners because the decision that the interrogators made was a decision between life and death.

Finally, Aerius came to me and said, "Tell these men that through the grace of the emperor of Rome that they will be set free. They will be escorted to the road that goes to Bethany and from there they are on their own. If they return, they will be sentenced to death."

I nodded to Aerius, said a silent prayer of thanksgiving and turned to the prisoners. "You have been honest in your answers to your captors, and they have seen that. And because of this you are to be set free.

I looked at the prisoners and then repeated what Aerius had said. I saw the look of relief on each man's face when as my words sank in.

The leader then asked, "What of our possessions in the city?"

"Do you really think that you could enter Jerusalem and gather what little you have left and then sneak out again without being captured? Don't be so naïve, sir," I answered. "You have just had your lives turned over to you. Rejoice in that." He hung his head as he realized how ridiculous his query had been.

"Where will we go and how will we be able to survive without food and water?" the third man asked.

"Listen closely to what I have to tell you," I said. "There is a small farm just off of the Bethany road about a half day's walk from the city's walls. In the rear of the farmhouse there is a little shed, and behind the shed is a well. There should be some skins in the shed with which you can fill with the water and maybe you can scavenge some food. Once you have rested and supplied yourselves with water, continue traveling east to Philadelphia. Once you get there I think it would be wise for you to look up my grandson, Abram. He is a tentmaker and one of the followers of The Way. They will help you to get started in a new life."

This man, Ezra, looked up at me in disbelief and asked, "Are you a believer in this Jesus as the Messiah?"

"Yes," I replied, "I saw him after he was raised from the dead. I talked with him."

"That cannot be true. You are not telling me the truth.

How can I rely on your word, for you believers of The Way have deluded the Jews for many years?"

"You can either believe me or not. I'm offering you and your friends a way to escape from the tyranny of the rabble that controls Jerusalem. You will also escape to safety, away from the wrath of the Romans. Take it or leave it. My advice to you is not to sit here and discuss philosophical or spiritual issues at this juncture in your life. What I have offered to you is freedom and the start of a new life. I sympathize with you over your recent losses of family and friends, but now is not the time to mourn. You must pull yourselves together and get on your way before the Romans change their minds."

Without any more being said the three men nodded their agreement. With my help, they stood on their feet, and a guard released the bindings. The second and third of the three shook my hand and in low voices thanked me. Ezra, on the other hand, nodded and said nothing. Aerius directed two of the guards to take them out of camp and to the Bethany road. I said goodbye to them and watched as they left the tent. It concerned me that in the midst of all of the turmoil of this day, this man Ezra wanted to argue beliefs with me. "Oh, you of little faith," I said to myself.

Shortly after these thoughts crossed my mind, Aerius summoned a guard and I was escorted back to the prisoner compound.

The next four days saw a tremendous effort on the part of the Roman legions as they prepared for the upcoming siege of Jerusalem. Once the encampments were secured, they began an enormous task of clearing the ground from the foot of the walls out to about one hundred paces. All trees and shrubs were cut down and hauled away. All of the ditches and trenches were filled in and the ground leveled, starting at the foot of Mount Scopus all along the northern wall to its westernmost reaches before turning south at the tower of Psephinus on south past the tower of Hippicus and ending at the northern end of the Serpent's pool.

This was a tremendous undertaking and the men of the legions and of the auxiliaries, as well as all of the servants, labored from before sunrise to well after sunset. Before sending these workers out, General Titus set up a guard of archers, horsemen and foot soldiers around the northern and western sides of the city. Their business was to discourage anyone on the walls above the workers or any of the enemy soldiers within the city from venturing forth in an attempt to attack the men clearing the ground in front of the wall. Once this defense force was established, the workers went out from camp and began clearing the land. This work they completed by the end of the fourth day.

During that fourth and final day of the clearing of the land, I had accompanied Aerius on a tour completely around the walls of Jerusalem. As I had spent a great deal of my life as a resident of the city, Aerius had asked that I join him as he looked for avenues through which the Romans could enter Jerusalem that would cause the least number of casualties to their troops. Shortly after sunrise, we mounted our horses along with five other horsemen and proceeded south down along the bottom of the Kidron Valley. Soon after, we passed the Mount of Olives, which now was the camp of the Tenth Legion. I couldn't help but to think that the Garden of Gethsemane, a place truly loved by the Lord Jesus, was once located here. And now instead of a place for solitude and prayer, it was nothing more than an encampment for an invading army.

Aerius interrupted my thoughts as he asked me about entrances through the narrow gates on this side of Jerusalem. I told him that I thought it would be difficult to launch an attack up from the Kidron Valley without sustaining numerous casualties due to the advantage the Jews had given the height of the walls. Aerius looked up from the valley we were in and agreed with my assessment.

"You, Caleb," he said "would have made a good soldier, for you seem to be aware of the strategic significance of this side of the city in relation to the high walls and the vulnerability of an attacking army."

"No," I said, "I just know how difficult it is to climb that hill in peacetime. I surely wouldn't want to try it in full armor with soldiers on those high battlements hurling rocks, darts and arrows at me."

Aerius chuckled at my remark and then asked, "Are you aware of any other hidden entrances around here?"

I had hoped that that question would never have been asked for my thoughts went immediately to the secret tunnel that Josephus and I had used when I entered the city just a few months before. After a short prayer and some more thought, I said, "There is a narrow tunnel near here that goes under the wall and into the city. No one can stand up in it, and it is a very long way to crawl from here to inside the city. There is very little air, and a large body of men could become trapped and suffocate."

"Show this to me, Caleb." He said sounding excited by the prospect of sneaking into the city unannounced.

We soon arrived at the spot where I thought that it was but it took some time for me to see the place as it had been dark when I had used it. We couldn't get too close to the wall, for there were Zealots on top who had been watching us as we rode along the path in the valley.

I pointed out the shrubs that covered the entranceway to the tunnel. "It's right over there behind the bushes. There's a large stone that covers the entrance and rolls away somewhat easily. From there you have to get down on all fours and literally crawl through on your hands and knees."

Aerius nodded, took out a hand-drawn map and made note of it. Just then I heard a swishing of the air. Suddenly some arrows hit the ground ten or twelve paces from where our horses stood. We all looked to the top of the tower at the southeast corner of the wall and saw four archers reload their bows in order to fire again at us.

Aerius looked up from his map at the Jews on the tower and then back down at his work and said as he finished making his notes, "They couldn't hit a horse if it were ten cubits in front of them."

Again the missiles were wide of their mark. Aerius raised his hand and brought it down, and we were on our way south. In a short while, we turned west into the Hinnom Valley, along the city's south wall.

We rode for what seemed a long time following this southern wall, stopping frequently as Aerius made notes. At the southwest corner we turned north and skirted west of the Serpent's Pool before coming to some soldiers of Tribune Festus's cohort marking out the camp for the Fifth Legion, which would soon be moving from Mount Scopus to this area just west and south of the Hippicus Tower.

Aerius ordered us to stop and dismount while he went to see the centurion in charge of the detail. I stood by my horse and gazed up at the gates that stood between the two towers extending high above the wall, wondering what was going on behind the great fortification. As I watched, a curious thing happened.

The gate at the base of the tower opened and a number of Jews in armor ran out. I don't know how many there were, but I would estimate at least two hundred. These men ran around the base of the wall in a disorganized fashion and yelled to those who stood on the walls above them to please let them back into the city. It appeared that the citizens of Jerusalem had at last cast out some of the seditious rebels, those scurrying around calling to their comrades to open the gate. Was the general public once again in control of Jerusalem and ready for the Romans to enter the city peacefully?

Those who had been cast out made brief threatening rushes at the Romans before turning around and running back to the gate and pleading with those inside to let them in. At this point the men on the upper portion of the wall cast darts, stones and arrows at the Jews who had been ejected out of the gate.

There were many Roman soldiers clearing the bushes and shrubs at the base of the wall who had witnessed this incident; they now rushed to their weapons. Without orders from their commanders and with the vision of victory over the Jews in their eyes, they rushed at the Jews that had been expelled from the city.

At this point in the western wall, there was an indentation in the wall itself. This indentation is bordered by three towers: Hippicus on the left or north; Phasael at the innermost point forming the apex of a triangle; and Mariame to the right or south. It was to this indentation that the Jews rushed when they saw that the Roman soldiers were coming at them with weapons drawn. As the Roman troops completely entered the indentation and closed in on these Jews who had huddled at the gate, more of their compatriots poured out of another hidden gate behind the Romans now totally inside the indentation and were able to cut off their retreat. The Jews on top of the wall now changed the aim of their missiles and directed them down on the entrapped troops. It appeared to me that a great slaughter was underway.

Many Jews and Romans fell, the killed and wounded alike. The Roman soldiers soon realized that the only salvation they had was to turn and to fight their way out through the Jewish soldiers who surrounded them. This they did, and within a short time and with the loss of many more soldiers, they fought their way out of the indentation and finally to the open ground. The Jews continued to chase the Romans for a time before withdrawing from the battle and retiring back to the gate. During this struggle, Aerius came and stood at my side, for I was holding the reins of his horse. I could see the disgust in his eyes. This disgust was aimed at his own countrymen, not at the Jews.

"How could they fall for a trick such as that?" he yelled to no one in particular. "They went forward without a commander or leader in sight." He then called for his men to mount up as he was ready to go in and join the fray, but by the time they were mounted the fighting had ended and all of the Jews had escaped inside the gates.

The Jews were jubilant over their triumph. They beat their shields with their spears as they yelled and danced in victory on top of the wall. Aerius could do nothing other than to continue on with our inspection. He had little to say as we continued north to the Psephinus tower, where we turned east towards Mount Scopus. Most of the clearing had been completed, and the land out from the wall to about one hundred paces was devoid of vegetation and trenches all of the way from the Serpent's Pool on the southwest portion of the city's western wall, north to the tower of Psephinus and then along the northern wall back to our starting point at Mount Scopus.

I later learned that General Titus had also witnessed this disorderly conduct by his soldiers and was furious with them for their lack of discipline and for not waiting for orders from their commanders. It was rumored that he was set to execute all of those soldiers who had gone into battle without orders. However, the other legions prevailed upon his goodwill and requested that he not carry out his orders of execution and, instead, solicit from the men their promise of obedience from this time forward.

So with this petition from the other legions, the order was rescinded and many of the men breathed a sigh of relief and re-pledged their allegiance to Titus.

Once the land around the base of the wall was cleared of the bushes, shrubs, trees and gardens, and the trenches filled and leveled, General Titus determined that he would move some of his legions in order to organize for his attack on the city. The Fifth Legion was to move around to the west side opposite and a little south of the gate of Hippicus and a little north of the Serpent's Pool. They were positioned far enough away from the wall in order to keep them out of range of the Jewish archers and dart throwers. Titus then moved the Twelfth and Fifteenth Legion from Scopus to the northwestern corner of Jerusalem, near what was called the Corner Gate by the tower of Psephinus. This placed them outside the western side of the wall that bordered Bezetha or the new city, a wall that had been started by King Herod Agrippa and finished later by his son. Finally the Tenth Legion remained in its camp on the Mount of Olives.

The walls to the south and east of Jerusalem dropped off into deep valleys, thus making them nearly impossible to attack. To the south lies the Valley of Hinnom, and bordering the eastern wall lies the Valley of the Kidron. Due to the height of the walls compounded by the drop-off from the base of those walls into the valleys, an attacking force would be unable to scale or even breach the defenses. All of the advantage would be to those who held the city. Thus the only practical attack could come from the north or west.

Again I was put in the detention pen. Not many guards were used for I had promised Aerius that I would not try to escape. Since that was my pledge, I didn't even give escape another thought. I was intrigued by the future and what would become of Jerusalem. I felt safe, or better said I felt my life would not be threatened, at least for a while as my skills as an interpreter were in demand.

I had also grown to respect Aerius. He was truly an enemy of the Jews, but as I came to know him better I found that he was a man of his word, a man I could trust as long as I was truthful and honest with him. I also wondered how I could witness my faith to Aerius without harming that friendship and trust.

JERUSALEM

Before I go on with my story, let me tell you a little about the city of Jerusalem. As you know, I grew up there, and I want you to know what it looked like to me before the great conflagration that took place at the hands of Titus and his Roman army.

I remember the city as a beautiful, clean place, with many markets, gardens, pools and fountains. A great many large and beautiful structures had been built over the years and particularly during the reign of Herod the Great. There was the sport Hippodrome, the Antonio Fortress, the many beautiful towers along the outer wall, and the tombs of Huldah, Absalom and David. There was Herod's Theater and his palace, and in particular there was the addition and expansion of the Temple and Temple Mount. The city could be said to rival Rome itself.

The most dominating feature of Jerusalem could be seen from almost anywhere you stood—the Temple, the dwelling place of God. The tabernacle itself was situated inside the walls of the Temple, which in turn was surrounded by a large marble floored court called the Court of the Gentiles. The Temple walls were situated in the center of this large court surrounding the Court of Israel, the Women's Court and the great sacrificial altar, which was directly in front of the tabernacle itself—a brilliant white marble structure supported with liberal amounts of beautiful acacia wood and covered with gold, silver and bronze. The tabernacle, surrounded by its expansive courts, stood atop Mount Moriah well above all other structures in the city and was unmatched in beauty and grace.

Outside the walls of Jerusalem were orchards, grassy parks, shade trees and gardens. As one approached from Jericho, which is to the northeast, the Temple Mount would suddenly come into sight from the overlook on the Mount of Olives. One's eyes were greeted with a rare and glistening treat—a shimmering city of gold.

A great number of trenches had been dug over the years to bring water to sustain these parks and gardens located outside the walls. There were also several large aqueducts that brought sufficient water to support the burgeoning population.

Jerusalem had been built on the south end of a ridge line that was bordered on the east by the Kidron Valley, which joined with two other deep valleys coupling with the Kidron just to the south of that ridgeline—the Hinnom and Tyropoeon valleys. The Kidron Valley ran in a general north to south direction east of the ridge upon which the city stood, while the Tyropoeon ran in a northwest to southeast direction just on the west side of the ridge. The Hinnom came out of the west-northwest and met the other two valleys at a place called the Well of Joab.

There were four distinct mounds bulging out of these ridges that rose up just to the west of the Kidron Valley and to the north of the Hinnom. It was upon these mounds that the city had been built. The first mound was called Acra. It was the first mound to the north of the Well of Joab and bordered the Kidron Valley. It was upon Acra that the ancient City of David had been built. In the beginning, this mound stood slightly higher than the mound to its north, the one called Mount Moriah upon which the Temple now stood. Because of Acra's superior height to Mount Moriah, much of Acra's top had been cut away in order that no building built upon it would be taller than the Temple.

This earth that was carved away was cast off into the Tyropoeon Valley, and it was here in the valley that the lower city was eventually situated.

The third mound, Mount Zion, was just on the west side of the Tyropoeon Valley, north of the Hinnom, and upon Zion stood the upper city. Finally there was another mound that bordered Moriah on the north and extended over the upper reaches of the Tyropoeon Valley and to the north end of the upper city; this mound was named Mount Bezetha. It was on Bezetha that the new city would grow.

Solomon, the son of David, built the first Temple upon Mount Moriah over a place called Ophel, which was a natural spring that brought a supply of sweet water up out of the ground to the city and more importantly to the Temple. Starting at a low level in the Kidron Valley, the very foundation of the eastern wall, that which protected the city and the Temple from an assault from the east, was built, and from that foundation rose the eastern wall, strong and impenetrable. This wall extended south along the ridgeline from the north-east corner of the Temple, on past the City of David, circled around the southern edge of the city above the Well of Joab, and then back to the north for a short way where it joined with the southwest corner of the Temple wall. In later years, the lower city would extend south of the Temple and to the west of the old City of David down into the Tyropoeon Valley that overlooked the Hinnom Valley. Solomon, the builder of the Temple, did not build a wall to the west and north of Jerusalem, the only protection being the wall around the Temple Mount itself and that around the City of David.

After Judea was conquered by Nebuchadnezzar and all of the Jews were carried off into captivity, the city lay in ruin for over sixty years. When the exiles were at last allowed to return, this by an edict from Cyrus the Great some six hundred years prior to my time, the walls were repaired. Over time a gradual expansion and rebuilding began to take place.

During the ensuing years, the city grew and spread to the west across the Tyropoeon Valley and onto Mount Zion. A slower expansion to the north in the new city took place as well. The Temple, built on Mount Moriah, continued to dominate the entire city to the south, east and west. However, the mound to the north, called Bezetha, had an ancient stronghold upon it called Baris, which eventually was incorporated into a larger more magnificent fortress. Baris had been restructured and integrated into what is now called Fortress Antonio by the late King Herod in honor of his Roman friend Mark Anthony. This citadel stood nearly as high as the Temple and thus blocked the view of those who had the misfortune to live directly north of Antonio, for they were unable to see the house built for God.

Jerusalem was entirely walled in by the time the Romans came to lay siege. The walls were built over time and were regularly expanded in order to protect the growing metropolis. As I have told you, the eastern wall had been built up from the Kidron Valley and was impregnable because of its strength and extreme height when viewed from the valley floor. This wall protected the Temple and the old city that was located directly south of the Temple.

Another wall was built that had its origin at the middle of the western cloister of the Temple Mount. It extended due west across the upper reaches of the Tyropoeon to the tower of Hippicus at the western edge of Jerusalem or just to the north of Herod's palace. From Hippicus, this wall then turned south bordering the western edge of the upper city on Mount Zion down to the gate of the Essens. There it turned northeast encircling the upper city around and above the lower city in the Tyropoeon Valley before joining with the original wall that protected the city of David at the southwestern corner of the Temple.

Another wall built in the years that followed originated from the gate near Hippicus called the Gennath Gate. The wall journeyed north for a short distance before turning east then north again, and then circled east to join with Fortress Antonio. This provided protection for the northern quarter of Jerusalem.

Next, there was a wall built along the Hinnom Valley from the southernmost part of the old City of David, south of the Pool of Siloam along the Tyropoeon Valley at the southern edge of the lower city. It then joined the wall that protected the upper city, thus giving that portion of Jerusalem a source of protection from an invading force.

Lastly there was a great wall built that enclosed the new city. This wall was started by Agrippa, son of Herod the Great, and finished by his son Agrippa II. It started at the Tower of Hippicus and ran due north to the Tower of Psephinus, situated at the northwest corner of the new city.

Here the wall turned east for a great distance all of the way to the corner tower overlooking the Kidron Valley, where it turned south along the Kidron and there connected with the original wall that protected the eastern flank of the Temple and the city.

Prior to the arrival of Titus and his armies, the city had been completely walled in. These walls had been built so well that they should have been able to withstand any attacking force. If it had not been for the sedition and civil war taking place within those walls of Jerusalem, the city might not have fallen.

Soon after the incident whereby the Jews tricked the Romans into battle, I was asked by Aerius to ride once again around the city with him. To my surprise, we were to join General Titus and others. This was to be another inspection of the walls and at the same time allow the commanders to determine exactly where it was that they would set up their camps and battering rams. We started from Mount Scopus and traveled west along the northern wall, which bordered the new city.

We rode two abreast with at least two hundred mounted troops in the column. Titus was in the lead, and Aerius and I brought up the rear. The Jews high on top of the walls looked down at us curiously, following along as we rode west. Our path kept us out of range of the Jewish weapons that they frequently brandished at us. There was another Jew who rode close to Titus in the procession and shouted to those on top of the wall in Aramaic. He implored them to surrender the city to the Romans and let the war end immediately, without resulting in the total destruction of Jerusalem. These pleas were met with jeers and obscene noises and gestures. Some of the Jews even threw their darts and javelins at this man and the one who rode close to him, for they had diverted from the safety of the column and approached to the very base of the wall bringing them within range of the enemy's weapons.

The Roman officer who rode with this Jew, a man called Nicanor, was struck by a dart and slumped in his saddle. The Jew who rode beside him quickly grabbed the reins of the injured man's horse and galloped back to the safety of the column. Nicanor's wound was not mortal but he lost a great deal of blood.

I later learned that this action by the men on the walls of Jerusalem had, in effect, sealed the fate of the city. Titus was enraged to the point he stopped all thoughts of appeasing the seditious Jews who were in control and continued, without further negotiations, to retake the city by force in the name of Rome.

Nicanor was taken back to the camp on Mount Scopus, and our column continued our scouting of the wall. It was soon confirmed that the attack would be directed at a position north of the midway point between the Psephinus and Hippicus towers, for there the wall had not been as well constructed because it had been hastily built at this point where it surrounded the new city.

It was also at this time new campsites for the various legions were determined. The Fifth would position themselves against the western wall just north of the Serpent's Pool, out of range of the Jewish weaponry. The Twelfth and Fifteenth Legions would set up camp on the northwestern corner of the wall near Psephinus. The Tenth, with their heavy machines, those weapons that would hurl stones, javelins, and darts, would continue to occupy the Mount of Olives on the eastern side of the Temple across the Kidron Valley.

Once our inspection was completed, the column made its way back to Scopus. I was once again put in detention and left to watch the activity as the various legions made their preparations to break camp. It was the day after the inspection trip that Aerius's manipuli pulled up stakes and we moved to what would be our new position near the Psephinus Tower. This time I was forced to walk as my mount was being used by one of the soldiers under Aerius's command so that he could run important communiqués between Aerius and Tribune Festus.

Once we arrived, the men under Aerius's command began the task of laying out the camp for the legions. The next day the auxiliaries and legions began to move in order to take up their new positions where they would begin to assault the walls of Jerusalem. The Fifth Legion was the first to leave camp shortly after daybreak. The men were quiet, and the only sounds heard were those of the marching soldiers as they moved in ranks of six abreast.

Soon after the Fifth had left, the Twelfth and Fifteenth started to move. Next came the auxiliaries. After the soldiers left, all that remained in the camp on Scopus were the noncombatants, the great engines of war that threw stones, darts and javelins, and their crews, who were skilled in their use. Finally in the late morning, these machines started to move towards their respective camps. It wasn't until after sunset that the Romans were finally in position.

I spent the next day watching the soldiers settling into their new camp and then beginning the business of retaking the city. Orders

169

from General Titus instructed the troops to burn all of the buildings in the suburbs located outside the walls. Further, the order to begin construction on breastworks was given. All of the lumber that had been cleared away from the base of the wall during the previous days was brought and placed in front of the three camps close enough to the wall so it could be used to build a barrier or bank to protect the troops and the engines of war. These barriers were placed in the cleared area near enough to the wall to allow the engines to hurl their missiles up and over it and into the city. Before this process got underway, archers and other troops were positioned in order to protect those building the banks from attacks by the Jews atop the wall and from those who dared to venture out of the gates.

In the late afternoon, I was once again summoned by Aerius to interpret for him what some new prisoners had to say. Two men had made their way through a hidden gate when others in the city were distracted in their work of preparation for the Roman attack. It had been late at night, and these men were eager to escape from what they saw as the total destruction of Jerusalem.

The men were both younger than our previous captives. I was suspicious of them, for it appeared to me that they might well have been Zealots. There was a certain arrogance in their attitude that belied their pretence of fear. I said nothing of these thoughts to Aerius, for I felt it would be better for me to talk with them first before I made a judgment as to their character.

The two prisoners were brought to the holding compound and forced to sit on the ground with their hands bound behind their backs. Two guards each with swords drawn stood just a short distance behind them.

Aerius, one of his deputies, and I stood directly in front. For the longest time Aerius glared at his captives without uttering a word. He stood with his feet spread apart and his left had on the hilt of his sword.

I'm sure the prisoners were wondering if he might just not draw the sword and run them through on the spot without saying a word.

"Caleb," he said finally, "ask them why they escaped and what it is that they expect from us."

I nodded to Aerius and then crouched down on my haunches and asked the apparent leader of the two. "The centurion wants to know who you are and why you have tried to escape the city."

"We are just honest and upright citizens of Jerusalem who have grown tired of the brigands who are running the city killing innocent citizens at will for no reason," this man answered without emotion.

"Let me tell you something. This Roman," I said pointing to Aerius, "will not tolerate lies and without a doubt you are doing just that. I know that you at one time belonged to the rabble that now rules Jerusalem. I know that you are Zealots and guilty of many crimes against its citizens." I had decided to take an aggressive tack against these two as I strongly felt that this man was lying. As I said these words, I looked into the eyes of the second man and saw a flash of fear. I knew I'd hit the nail on the head.

"No, no," the man replied. "You have it all wrong. We are innocent victims ourselves and have suffered at the hands of these men you accuse us of being."

I studied their faces for a minute and then became convinced that my judgment had been correct. I turned to Aerius. "These men are lying. They claim to be innocent citizens of Jerusalem, but my guess is that they are part of the crowd they call Zealots. It is my opinion that they may have a wealth of information about what is going on behind those walls," I said, gesturing towards the city.

"So now you are becoming an intelligence officer, Caleb," Aerius said with a scoff. "Do you want me to talk with Titus himself and have him grant you a commission as a Roman, or maybe even as a Roman officer?"

I shrugged and replied, "That isn't what I meant to convey to you. I want nothing more than to go home and not be responsible for judging these men, but I also feel that what I said is true and that they know a lot more than they claim. You don't need to worry about me challenging you for your position," I added with a laugh. "Let me see if I can find out any more information."

"Go ahead; I think you might be right. They may be concealing some things we'd like to know. You keep me informed and keep your questions on the subject of Jerusalem."

I nodded and then returned my attention to the two prisoners. "I too, am a prisoner here," I said. "I was captured last week and bear the scars of their whips. And, no doubt, they will not hesitate using them on you. They are looking for information that will allow them a quick way into the city without destroying it. What can you tell me about what is going on?"

"We know nothing," the leader said with a shrug and in an unconvincing tone. "We are just simple men who want to get away from the war."

"You're lying to me again," I replied. "If you want a taste of the cat o' nine tails then you will have it unless you are truthful with me." I looked at the other man who was much younger than the leader and asked, "Do you want to take the punishment, too? Are you letting this man speak your thoughts also?"

He, who had not said a word heretofore, shook his head and I could see the fear in his eyes. "I have done nothing," he nearly shouted. "I'll tell you what you want to know."

"That's better," I answered. "These people don't care what you did in the city or whether you are with John or with Simon. Their concern is information. What is going on? We heard about the joining together of Eleazar and John and that they control the Temple. What about Simon?"

The second man started to say something, but the leader shouted at him to be quiet.

I looked at the older man and told him it was in their best interests if they told all that they know. "I don't know why you decided to quit the city, but if you continue in these lies you will surely die before sunrise tomorrow. I am not here to aid the Romans. Like you, I'm a prisoner and must report to them what it is that you say. The reasons I'm advising you to talk are twofold. First, I don't want to see Jerusalem reduced to rubble, and secondly, I'm concerned about your lives. If they have the slightest inclination that you are not being truthful, they will kill you. Therefore, all that you need to tell them is what you have learned as to the deployments of their troops and the defenses they have at hand for repelling the attack."

The younger man looked at me and asked, "If we tell them these things, will they let us go?"

"I can't guarantee that," I answered. "But things will go better for you if you do. At this juncture in the siege, freedom may be hard for you to come by, but I think that I can assure you that you will live for a much longer time than you would if you continue to lie to the Romans."

I then looked up at Aerius and told him that I thought the men were ready to talk and that they would be truthful.

He thought a minute and then said, "Ask them about this man they call Simon. I want to know where he stays in the city and how many men he has who would be prepared to fight us to the end."

I then repeated the question to the two prisoners in Aramaic just as Aerius had asked it. The two men began to whisper between themselves, and I immediately put a stop to it. "I don't want you two talking except to me. If the centurion sees you talking, he will think that you are conjuring up another lie. So you," I said to the younger man, "what is it you know about Simon?"

The younger man answered. "We are not well acquainted with Simon, but we know that he rules over most of the upper and lower cities. He resides in the tower Phasaelus and from there directs his army and agents. An excess of ten thousand men have sworn their loyalty to him. There are also the Idumeans, nearly five thousand strong, who have also declared their allegiance to Simon."

I repeated his words to Aerius.

Aerius considered this for a moment and then asked, "What about John and Eleazar?"

I asked the younger man, but was answered by the older one whom I decided had resolved to cooperate.

"John has combined his strength with Eleazar and the Zealots. I don't know how many men were with John but it ranged in the vicinity of six thousand. Then with Eleazar came nearly two thousand, four hundred men.

"John and Eleazar hold the Temple, Fortress Antonio, the City of David and a small portion of the upper city. When John and Simon are not fighting amongst themselves, they attack and plunder the poor innocent citizens who have been caught in the middle of this madness.

My friend here and I have grown tired of the way things are going, and we wanted to escape the insanity. The food supplies are gone and starvation is rampant throughout the city. The state of things in Jerusalem makes it useless to try and stop the inevitable—the total destruction of not only the city but all of Judea."

Aerius listened intently to my interpretation of what had been said and then asked, "Query them about the machines of war that they took from Cestius a few years back. Where are they located and how many do they have?"

I repeated the question word-for-word in Aramaic and waited for a reply.

"Those machines are kept in the fortress," the younger man replied. "We were not allowed to go in and see them, but there are many."

"I have seen them," the older of the two continued. "There are fifteen or twenty of them. They have three large contraptions that can hurl massive stones for great distances and then there are five smaller stone throwers. The rest are machines that throw javelins and darts. They intend to keep the machines in Antonio until they determine where the Romans will attack and then wheel the machines into position once the attacking legions are positioned."

"I don't think that they are very well trained in their use," the younger man interjected, "for they are constantly asking us if we have ever had any experience with them."

"How do they plan to defend the wall? What instruments do they plan to use against us?" Aerius questioned, and I quickly interpreted in Aramaic.

"They have placed a large amount of heavy stones at the top of the wall. These will be used to bombard the attacking troops who venture too close. Archers, dart throwers and slings will be deployed against the attacks also," the younger man answered. "They will also try to burn the Roman machines and will use flaming arrows as well as attempt infantry attacks on the machines and the soldiers that man these instruments of war."

Aerius talked these things over with his deputy and then asked, "What about the new city? Are there many defenders there?"

After I asked the question in the men's own language, the older one responded. "I don't know how many are there as that will be under Simon's command. I feel they will meet any attack on the northern wall. However, if it is breached, those men will quickly retreat behind the second wall—the one that stretches north and west from Antonio out around the upper city to the tower Hippicus. This is the stronger wall and the main defense of Jerusalem."

This line of questioning continued on for sometime. There did not seem to me to be any further enlightenment. Finally, Aerius ordered the guards to take them away. Both men looked at me in apprehension as they were told to stand. I asked Aerius what was to become of them now that they had told him all they know.

He shrugged and said, "They will be held until the siege is over and then probably sold into slavery."

I reassured the men that they would not be killed but held until the city had been taken and then taken away with the other captives.

"What does that mean?" The older one asked.

"It means you will not die. It may mean that you will be sold as a slave or even that you will be set free," I responded. "So rejoice in that and be silent."

The men were then led away and taken to the general holding compound, and I was taken back to Aerius's camp.

THE BATTERING OF
THE FIRST WALL

After the various legions had taken up their positions and the breastworks were constructed, the engines of war were brought to the banks in order to begin the attack on Jerusalem. The final work involved placing shields of wood and metal around and over the top of the machines to protect their crews from the arrows and darts hurled at them from above by the archers and dart throwers stationed on the walkway behind the parapets at the top of the wall. Titus had also ordered the construction of three great wooden towers that were to stand at and above the banks. These towers, one at each of the three Roman camps, were to be between fifty-five and sixty cubits high. At the pinnacle of each of the towers were the archers, who would shower their arrows down upon the Jews protecting the city's wall. Once the towers were completed, they, too, would be shielded with iron plates to prevent the enemy from attacking them with flaming oil and arrows.

Since the cohort to whom Aerius belonged was a part of the Twelfth Legion, we were positioned just west and a little south of the Tower of Psephinus. From where I was, I could easily see the whole of the western wall as well as a good portion of the northern one—walls that protected the new city.

Finally when all of the meticulous preparations were complete, the great battering ram was brought to this location as it was decided that the initial attack would begin just south of Psephinus, where the wall was believed to be weakest.

This contraption was huge. It consisted of a giant frame made with two large vertical timbers that stood ten cubits high and nearly seven cubits apart. Joining these timbers was a heavy beam laid horizontally across the top. Over this beam strong ropes and a chain were slung and on this chain and ropes, below the crossbeam, hung a huge log that was at least two cubits in diameter and nearly twenty cubits long. On one end of this log, the end that would strike the stone of the wall, was an iron cap shaped to look like the head of a charging ram. The log was held by the ropes from the overhead beam and perfectly balanced so that it could swing fore and aft without toppling the whole apparatus. Handholds had been placed on the log that would allow its crew to pull it back and then to push it forward with great force.

Positioning this battering ram took a great deal of effort as the Jews constantly bombarded with rocks and stones the crew trying to situate it in a strategic location. They even shot arrows, threw their darts and dropped flaming oils in their attempt to thwart the ram from being positioned close to the wall for the full momentum of the swinging log to strike with its most devastating power. Roman archers shot their arrows at the defenders on the wall trying to drive them away. As the battering ram was heavy and clumsy, it took nearly all day to position it. Finally as the sun set on our third day in the new camp just west of the northwest corner of the new city, the ram was ready. During that night, the crew placed a shield of skins and metal plates over the ram as protection from the Jews high above on top of the wall.

Early the next morning, before the sun was up, there was the loud blare of numerous trumpets as the trumpeters played a call to arms, which could be heard throughout the region. Shortly after, there was a loud and low resonate thump that reverberated throughout the city as the battering ram was brought into play against the western wall of Jerusalem. Before the ram struck a second time, there was the indescribable sound of the numerous machines of war releasing their first volleys of deadly missiles up and over the walls, into the new city. Further to the south, near the Serpent's Pool, the other legions also began their attack on their portion of the wall just outside the upper city that sat on top of Mount Zion.

Soon there was a loud outcry from the citizens of Jerusalem as they screamed in terror at the initial assault by the Romans. I could only conjure up pictures in my mind as to the horror the citizens were enduring. Volley after volley was let loose into the city. Stones weighing in excess of the weight of two grown men were hurled up over the wall and would then fall upon the hapless citizens and buildings below.

The battering rams continued to beat against the solid stone of the wall, and with each blow I could feel the ground beneath my feet reverberate as small chunks of the rock and mortar began to crumble and fall to the ground.

I later learned that within the walls of Jerusalem, the people were experiencing a living hell as the huge stones thrown by the Roman siege machines fell from the sky and landed on buildings and unfortunate victims who were in the wrong place at the wrong time. A great fear enveloped all of the citizens, for there appeared to be nothing in their immediate future except death and destruction. Those who tried to escape and were captured by the rebels had their throats slit along with the other members of their households. We also learned that John and Simon stopped their warring on one another and came to an accord, which allowed their armed militias to come together and man the walls in order to meet the threat of the Romans.

Soon after the start of the ramming of the walls and before the break of dawn, a large number of Jews sprang from an obscure gate near the Hippicus tower. These men, though not skilled in the art of war, made up for their lack of skill through their zeal. They came out with torches and flaming arrows and attacked the great battering ram with the intention of setting it and the other engines of war on fire. Their archers high atop the wall shot their arrows at the Roman soldiers, who were trying to defend the machines from such an attack.

This flow of battle began to overwhelm the Roman attackers, and the Jews tore down the hurdles and other protective cover on the machines and set them on fire. A great slaughter was taking place, and the Jews did not seem to care for their own lives; they fought to the death in a most frightful manner. The Romans, not used to fighting this kind of enemy, gave ground and began to retreat from their machines behind their breastwork.

Titus soon joined the battle and led a large cavalry charge into the right flank of the Jews. This onslaught did little to stop the Jews in their forward progress. The battle seemed to grow as more Romans joined the fray. There also seemed to be an endless flow of Jewish men pouring out of the gate at Hippicus.

As the Jews advanced, I could see that the fires were beginning to catch hold on the machines. I almost concluded that the Jews would win this first encounter. The dead and wounded littered the landscape, and the ground turned red from the spilled blood.

It was at this point that a large contingent of infantry, auxiliaries from Alexander, came forward at double time and joined in the skirmish. Their skill in war was no match for the Jews, and they soon stopped the advance and quickly forced a reversal in the flow of the battle.

Not only were they able to force the enemy from the machines, they expertly extinguished the fires that would have destroyed them. One last push by the Jews brought the fight to a standstill as the antagonists fought tooth and nail toe to toe. It was here that General Titus made another cavalry charge into the right flank of the Jews, and that was sufficient to turn the tide.

Soon the Jews were backing away and returning to the gate. Finally the gate was closed and barred, leaving a small number of their men to face the Romans. They quickly surrendered, and the battle was finished at least for the moment. The only danger remained from the arrows and darts that were thrown from high above on the wall. As the Roman soldiers returned to their banks, they helped the wounded and took many of them with them.

At noon of that same day when the sun was high above, General Titus ordered that one of the Jewish prisoners be crucified. This was to take place immediately on a slight rise of ground outside the walls just north of the camp of the Twelfth and Fifteenth Legions in full view of the residents of Jerusalem.

I believe that it was his intent to intimidate the enemy into surrender. It didn't work.

That night as I lay on my mat trying to sleep I heard a tremendous sound, like thunder but different. This incredible roar continued much longer than thunder, and amidst this noise I heard the cries of many men. My first thoughts were that the Jews had once again come from the city to attack the Romans. I believe this same feeling permeated the men in our camp as the soldiers around the compound rushed to their arms, ready to fight off any intruders. I heard many calls from one to another for the password of the day in order to determine if the other was a friend or an enemy.

There seemed to be a great deal of fear in the men. The night was black as pitch, for there was no moon and most of the fires had been extinguished, which made it difficult to determine whether others nearby were friend or foe. I did not feel this fear as my status as a prisoner would keep me somewhat immune to any fighting that might take place.

After what seemed to be an interminable amount of time, the thunder ceased with a loud crash. But the cries of injured men continued. I was baffled as to the cause of this uproar. It was different than the sounds of battle that I'd heard earlier in the day but it was definitely a man-caused blast.

It was later, after the sun had risen, that we were able to discern exactly what had happened. The great wooden tower being constructed by the soldiers of the Twelfth and Fifteenth Legions had fallen at the darkest time of the night. It was suspected that the ground on which it had been built was unstable and caused one side to sink into the soft sand and thus crash to the ground. The wooden tower had been completed at dusk. The soldiers were positioning some of their engines of war on the top. Other troops were climbing the tower in support of an early morning catapult assault on the wall of Jerusalem. The added weight of these men and the heavy stones that were to be hurled into the city was more than the tower could stand; it was this weight along with the movement of the men that brought about its destruction. The number of killed and injured was great and brought on a feeling of despair among the soldiers.

The Jews when they saw at early light what had caused the great thunderous sound danced in jubilation over the incident and felt that their Lord and God had brought about this calamity. This was their sign that with God's help they would defeat the Romans.

This feeling of elation on the part of the Jews and the feeling of despair on the part of the Romans were short lived. Titus and his generals were soon out riding amongst the troops encouraging them to continue with their work on ramming the walls. Once the killed and injured had been removed from the wreckage of the tower, Titus ordered his engineers to rebuild it. Before the day was finished, the tower had been re-erected to one third of its previous height and within two days it stood thirty cubits higher than the original. The new structure was considerably more robust and stood on firmer ground. So within the span of two days from the calamity the archers, dart hurlers and the lighter machines were once again atop the resurrected tower showering their deadly missiles down onto the Jewish defenders on the wall.

On and on the battering of the wall went, relentless and seemingly without an end. It kept everyone awake, for every few moments the heavy ram would hit the solid stone of the wall and the concussion would reverberate throughout the metropolis. I felt for the citizens inside Jerusalem, for their fears could only continue to grow. With each tremendous thud of the Nicor (a name given the ram by the Jews for it was felt that nothing could defeat it), I imagined their anxiety grew. The soldiers seemed to be under stress, too; for they knew that when the wall finally gave way, they would have to jump into the breach and face the enemy.

Over these days the need for my services dwindled, and I was left quite alone. Occasionally a prisoner would be brought in for interrogation and then taken away—to where I did not know and didn't want to know. I feared that they would be put to death by the men of the Fifteenth Legion. These captives were warriors from inside the city captured as a result of daily sorties that they, the Jews, made against the Romans. Their purpose was always to attack and destroy the machines. For not only did the ram and its crew continue with its work, the other machines were also at work constantly hurling stones, darts and javelins up and over the wall into the city. This action of the machines was not only taking place from the camp of the Twelfth and Fifteenth Legions on the northwest wall of the new city, but also from the southwest against the upper city. Here the Fifth Legion used another battering ram and other machines of war. On the east side, from the Mount of Olives where only the heavy catapult machines of the Tenth Legion were stationed, they too hurled their own huge missiles over the wall into the City of David and the lower city.

At first the great stones that were thrown over the wall were white, the color of the natural stone found in the general vicinity. It wasn't long before the Jews placed a watchman on the wall where the machines were located, and whenever a stone was launched he would call out that a stone was on its way. I surmised that this was to warn the citizens within the walls to take cover. It was at this same time the Romans started blackening the stones with the carbon of their camp fires, making them more difficult to see in the evening and nighttime.

Along our portion of the wall, on the northwest side, the Jewish defenders were growing weary of the day-in, day-out bombardment. They lessened their attacks on the machines, for they were unable to burn the catapults and battering rams since they were too well defended. Also the great towers of wood built at Titus's direction constantly bombarded the Jews who worked along the top of the wall. These Roman towers were protected in large part by sheets of iron and numerous soldiers. Because of the height of the towers, the Jews were unable to retaliate against their enemy. It was at this point that the Jews started their retreat to the inner wall, for they found it impossible to properly defend themselves against the Romans positioned high up in the towers. The constant pelting they underwent from the darts and arrows eventually caused them to abandon this position in favor of the relative safety of the second wall.

Thus it was on the fifteenth day of the siege that a breach was made at a point not too far from where I was held prisoner. This breach was not large, but it did lead into the new city, Bezetha. The top portion of the wall had begun to crumble the night before. However, it wasn't until midmorning that the lower stones began to give way. Finally, they fell more into the city and onto the fissure created by the battering ram. Not much debris fell outside the wall or onto the ram or its crew.

Soon after, the first elements of the infantry climbed over the debris in the fissure and set up a defensive perimeter so other soldiers could move forward, clear the debris and widen the fracture in the first wall. Once the soldiers had entered through the fissure, they moved quickly to the nearest gates and opened them so the entire Twelfth Legion could now enter the new city. They found few enemy defenders, for as soon as the wall had begun to crumble the Jews had scurried behind the second wall, the one that extended first north from Fortress Antonio and then in a semi-circle around to the west before joining with the Hippicus Tower.

Once inside Bezetha, the Romans found that this part of the city was still in ruins following the destruction it had suffered at the hands of Cestius some four years earlier. They also found many bodies of citizens who had either been murdered by the scoundrels and rabble who had taken control sometime before the siege began, or of those citizens who had succumbed to starvation. No matter how they died, it was a gruesome sight. Titus now had control of the whole of the new city, from the western wall, through which they'd gained entry, to the eastern wall that bordered the Kidron Valley and all north of the Temple and Fortress Antonio.

Shortly after the breach and the Romans had entered through the gates, I was summoned by Aerius. There were several prisoners taken and it was up to his team to interrogate them. As I walked through the gate and into Bezetha, I was repulsed by the sight that greeted my eyes. Nearly all of the buildings and houses had been destroyed, and those that still stood showed signs of the terrific battle that had taken place both recently and four years earlier. That which had not been burned to the ground had been battered into rubble by the great machines of war. The streets were littered with broken walls and stones, and there were many bodies strewn about.

I was sickened by what I saw--bodies scattered about, wrecked and destroyed homes and small buildings. What was particularly repugnant was the thought that most of the dead had been executed by Jews, not by the Romans. The optio who had summoned me from my holding compound hurried me to the place where Aerius and the new prisoners were. The stench of death filled the air, and I felt weak and nauseous.

"Caleb, you're finally here," Aerius said without preamble. "I need for you to interpret what these poor wretches have to say." He motioned to five women and children who had their hands bound behind their backs and were kneeling on the ground in front of him.

"What is it you want me to say to them?" I asked, for they looked totally emaciated and bewildered. "I don't believe that they can give you much information for I'm sure that the rebels who hold the city would just as soon see them dead as to tell them of their plans."

"Just translate what I ask and then give me their answers," he said gruffly. "I'll determine whether their answers are pertinent or not."

"At least give them something to eat," I asked. "Then maybe they'll be more willing to tell you what it is that you want to know."

"It is better to keep them hungry," Aerius replied. "Promise them that we will give them food when we are satisfied with their answers to our questions."

I nodded to Aerius and then I kneeled down near the older woman who looked to me as the one who would be most likely be able to tell me what Aerius wanted to know. "The Romans have some questions that they need to ask you. If you are truthful in your answers they will then feed you and the children," I said in Aramaic.

The woman shrugged and motioned that she did not understand. I asked her if she understood the language of the Romans and again she shrugged. Next I asked in Greek. With this her eyes brightened and she nodded.

I looked up at Aerius and told him that I thought that they were Greeks, probably here for the Passover celebration. He considered this for a moment and then said, "We'll question them anyway. Ask her why she didn't escape into the city with the others."

After I put the question to her in her native language, she told me with tears in her eyes. "They wouldn't let us enter. Because we are of Greek origin and we were unable to help them defeat the Romans, they forced us to stay here. They said there was not enough food in the city, and then they ran off and left us to the mercy of your army."

I repeated what she had said to Aerius, and I, too, fell silent. Aerius considered these things for a moment and then said, "Ask her which gate the Jews entered when they left her."

After repeating the question in Greek, she nodded towards Antonio Fortress and said, "They entered the Damascus Gate, over there just north of the fortress. They have their machines that throw rocks and darts up there in the fortress readying them for your attack. At least that is what they said to one another before they left us."

"What were they like? I mean what was their frame of mind when they knew that the Romans would enter the wall today?" I asked.

"They were very angry and tired, for they hadn't slept for a long time, and they were disappointed that the wall hadn't held longer. They always felt that God would somehow come to assist them and save them from destruction. When the great tower that the Romans built fell to the ground, they felt that God at last had come to their aid. However, not long after that, the tower was rebuilt and filled with soldiers driving the soldiers away from defending the top of the wall.

"They were very discouraged and started their retreat behind the other wall to the south."

I repeated these things to Aerius and awaited his answer. He talked these things over with two other officers, I suppose trying to decide their next move. As they discussed these things amongst themselves, I asked the woman, "Are you Greek by birth and a citizen there?"

Her answer surprised me. "My mother was Greek, but my father was a Roman. I was born and raised in Athens and I only speak Greek for that is the only language used in my home, but because of my father I am a Roman citizen."

"How about these others with you? Are they Roman citizens also?" I asked.

"Yes," was her simple and only reply.

I looked to Aerius and waited for him to complete his conversation with the other officers. When he had finished I told him, "These people, even though they are of Jewish faith, are citizens of Rome."

He looked at me for a full minute with a quizzical look on his face and then finally asked, "What do you mean?"

"Just that. Her father was a Roman even though she was brought up in Athens. These others who are with her are members of her family and also Roman citizens. Because of their nationality the bandits in control have treated them shabbily."

"Well," Aerius said thoughtfully, "I guess we'll feed them and then set them free so that they can journey home once we are satisfied that what she says is true. Tell her that she has given us a good account of conditions in the city and that we will send them to Caesarea under the protection of our supply caravan. There they can get on a ship to take them home."

"Sir," I replied, "you have a good heart. I will relay the news to her and to her family." With that I turned to face the woman and repeated what Aerius said word for word. As I spoke a smile broke out on her face and I could detect that she felt as if a heavy burden had been lifted from her.

She told me that their trial in Jerusalem over the past months had been one of tremendous strain, for many times she'd felt that they all would be murdered either by the rabble who controlled Jerusalem or by the Romans. She grabbed my hand kissing it in thanksgiving. I pulled away and said that it was nothing that I did and that she was fortunate to have been captured by Aerius.

"You still have a hard journey ahead of you," I added, "so eat up while you can and regain your strength. May God go with you."

After I had finished talking with her Aerius told one of the guards to take the family out of the new city, feed them and get them on a pack train for Caesarea where their citizenship could be substantiated.

I watched as they were led away and prayed that God would be with them and keep them safe on their long journey.

This ended the first phase of the siege on Jerusalem. General Titus gave his troops a day of rest before he gave the order to move the camps in preparation for the second phase of the attack. During this time, I was confined to the prisoner compound where I, too, rested and meditated about all that was taking place here in the city of my birth.

THE SECOND WALL

Soon after this incident with the prisoners and our day of rest, General Titus ordered the troops of both the Twelfth and Fifteenth Legions to move from their current encampment outside the walls of Jerusalem into the new city. Their new camp was to be near the wall that bordered the northern side of the Antonio Fortress at a place called the camp of the Assyrians. This position, though, was to be far enough away from the wall to keep the soldiers out of range of the darts and arrows of the Jews who manned and defended the fortress.

It wasn't yet two days since gaining entry into Bezetha that the siege continued. The Nicor or battering ram was brought and put to the wall just north of the fortress. Late in the evening of the sixteenth day of the siege about two-days after entering the new city, the battering began anew. This time though, the Jews began mounting more frequent and vicious attacks against the Roman legions. The rebels in the city were coming to the realization that their position was desperate.

As time passed, Aerius granted me greater freedom. I was no longer confined to a holding compound or for that matter always under the watchful eye of a guard. This was simply because I had no other place to go. When the legions entered the new city and set up their camp, Aerius's manipuli was outside the Damascus Gate north and west of the Antonio Fortress. This gave me a great view of the battering ram and the other machines of war. It was here on the machines that the

191

Jews focused their attacks on the legions. They wanted to destroy the machines.

What the Jewish soldiers lacked in tactical skills, they made up for with their zeal. Frequently they sallied forth from their gates in an undisciplined fashion, charging the battering ram and other machines of war that had been brought up to hurl their deadly missiles over the wall. There were frequent clashes around and near these huge machines as the Jews seemed intent on disabling them in one form or another, or better yet, burning them to the ground.

The Romans defended their war machines in an orderly fashion and normally beat off the attackers preventing them from inflicting serious damage.

Much blood was spilled over these frequent battles, and most of the wounded and dead were Jews since they were not skillful enough to defeat the Roman defensive line. The soldiers on neither side could not sleep well, each waiting for the dawn when the fighting would be renewed. The soldiers slept in their armor with their weapons at the ready position. In the open field, the disciplined troops of Rome were unbeatable. However, when they attacked the walls, the Jews from their superior height were the ones to prevail.

Each side sent forth courageous men who proved themselves in battle. These men would distinguish themselves for their audacious skill in confronting their foe, each with the thought of inspiring their comrades and impressing their commanders. The Jews, out of the fear and dread they had of Simon, would recklessly throw themselves into the fray knowing full well that it would be better to die in the cause than find themselves being brought before their leaders because they had exhibited cowardice in the face of the enemy. On the Roman side soldiers and officers alike were willing to prove their valor before their leaders in order to be noticed, maybe even by Titus himself, who seemed to be everywhere on the field of battle. These soldiers of Rome were used to winning in war and were determined to defeat the city's defenders in as short of a time as possible.

One such Roman was a man by the name of Longinus. He was a large man who stood well over four cubits and weighed nearly one and one-half times my weight. During one confrontation between the two armies, he ran from the ranks of his own position facing lines of Jewish soldiers, who had come out of the gates of the city for an attack. He quickly covered the ground between the opposing forces and ran straight into the Jews who opposed him. Midway across the open land, he pulled his great sword from its scabbard and brandished it over his head as he charged into the first line of Jewish troops. The Jews were throwing their darts at him, but they all fell short or bounced harmlessly off his shield. He continued running and soon made contact with the enemy. Two soldiers immediately fell mortally wounded to the ground as others tried to back away from this ferocious onslaught. After recovering from the initial shock of this attack, the Jews tried to surround him, but Longinus killed another man who was trying to get in behind the Roman. After his courageous rush into the midst of the enemy troops, Longinus withdrew to the position between the two lines and turned, shouting insults to his enemies. He stood his ground, daring any man to come out and oppose him. Both armies held their positions leaving Longinus alone in no-man's-land between the two lines of troops. Finally, a Jewish soldier rushed from his own line charging out to engage the Roman in battle. The two men with swords drawn met, the Jew slashing his sword down upon Longinus's shield. Longinus slashed quickly with his own weapon, hitting the Jewish soldiers breastplate and sending him whirling backwards for a step or two. The two men glared at each other and slowly circled looking for the weakness of his adversary. Bit by bit, they turned in a tight circle facing each other as the soldiers on either side cheered them on. A quick slash by one man was skillfully parried by the other, and the sound of the swords striking the other could be heard above the cheering soldiers.

I watched, fascinated by this event, as the two men struck at one another looking for a flaw that would lead one to an ultimate victory over the other. Neither line moved as all of the combatants stood transfixed by the battle unfolding before their eyes. I knew that this would eventually lead to one of the men's death, but I was unable to look away.

They continued to circle, and the clang of sword on shield and sword against sword rang out over the sound of the cheering troops. I do not know how much time passed, but the battle seemed to go on and on. Finally, Longinus lunged towards the Jewish soldier, who struck down with his sword. The Roman took the blow on his shield, which he held above his head, and then brought that shield down and thrust it into the other man's body, pushing him backwards with such force that the Jew lost his footing and fell to the ground, landing on his back. Longinus then quickly thrust his sword through his opponent's chest, killing him on the spot. Not satisfied with the victory the Roman then took his sword and with one mighty downward swing, cut off the man's head. He lifted it by the hair with his left hand and held it high in the air. The men in the Jewish line fell back in horror and retreated back to the gate and into the city.

I was sickened by the display as the Roman soldiers cheered loudly before the city's walls. As they retired back to their camp, they shouted insults at their enemy. The remainder of the day saw little offensive activity on the part of the Jews. One of their bold and valiant soldiers had been decisively defeated by a Roman.

The next day, though, the Jews renewed their attempts to put an end to the Roman siege. Starting at daybreak, literally thousands poured out of the gate and rushed the great machines of war. A terrific battle ensued, and many soldiers on both sides fell wounded or dead on the battle ground. The sound of the fighting was deafening as the soldiers fought tooth and nail to defend or to destroy the great machines of war. The sounds of sword upon sword or sword upon shield could be heard above the cries and shouts of the men. I saw General Titus upon his mount, along with other cavalry troops, attacking the flank of the Jewish soldiers. It was a terrible and desperate battle as the lines surged fore and aft from the advances each side made in order to defeat their enemy.

Aerius and his men always seemed to be in the forefront of the battle since their mission was to provide protection for the machines of war. I saw some of them fall either to the darts of the Jews or under the sword of an advisory, but more frequently I saw Aerius's soldiers slay and wound many more of their foe. I prayed frequently to God that this awful business would come to a quick end, and most of all I prayed that the city of Jerusalem and its Temple be spared from destruction. However, in my heart of hearts, I knew that in some way God's anger was being dealt out due to their lack of faith of the leaders, John and Simon; that God's chosen people were being punished for the lack of faith of the rebels who controlled the city. Once again the Jewish religious leaders had chosen to turn their backs on God, and instead of worshipping Him they were devoting their lives and worship to false gods or no gods at all.

At the end of each day of fighting Aerius would come back to camp and begin preparations for the next day's battle. He always seemed excited about the fight and anxious for the next day to arrive. It wasn't long after we had entered into the new city that he would come late in the evening to talk with me. I came to realize that even though he had spent his entire adult life in the army, he was a bright and perceptive person. He was an intellect in his own right and constantly trying to expand his horizons. Because I was reared in a different culture, he came to me to search for my views on these cataclysmic events. He questioned me at length on my spiritual views and values, thus giving me an opportunity to witness my faith to him.

We were not able to establish a common ground as our views on things were vastly different. He rejected all that I told him about the Jews being God's chosen people. I told him that they, a large number of Jews, had rejected their God and had suffered because of it. I spoke of Abraham, the first to be chosen by God. I then told him of Moses, who many years later brought the Israelites out of their bondage in Egypt here to the chosen land of Israel. Then I told him of David, the king who made Israel a great and powerful nation, and of his son Solomon, who built the great Temple right here in Jerusalem. Finally, I told him about the prophets of old sent by God to warn the Israelites to change their ways and turn back in faith to their God or else suffer the consequences. I told him of the destruction of Judea and Jerusalem some six hundred years prior—that this earlier destruction and deportation of the Israelites had been foretold by those prophets many years before it had come to pass. I told him of the Babylonians under Nebuchadnezzar, who entered Israel and destroyed the city and the land. The Babylonians had then carried off the people into captivity throughout the known world. I also told him of the return of the Jews after sixty-five years in exile and the eventual rebuilding of Israel. However, after all that had happened to them, they had continued to disobey their God and turn their hearts to worldly things.

"Finally," I said late in the night of our second week of our discussions, "God sent His only son, God incarnate in man, to the Jews. This happened some seventy years ago and this, the Messiah, lived right here in Judea. He was conceived by God in a virgin named Mary and was born in Bethlehem. My father witnessed the announcement of this event when he was a young man. This man, called Jesus, grew to manhood in Nazareth before announcing his purpose, which was to proclaim our God as a God of love. He called on all to repent of their sinful ways, turn their hearts towards God and obey His law and His words.

"Many Jews again rejected the very Savior they had been waiting for and handed him over to you, the Romans. He was taken out of the city to a point very near to where we are right now, and they crucified him."

"Then if he died upon that cross," Aerius interrupted, "that would prove that he was not your so-called Messiah." He smiled at this observation for he felt that he had proved his case, thus trapping me with my own words. "Dead men can do nothing except in name only, and the world continues to move on without them. Look at the great Julius Caesar and even of Anthony and all the other great ones who have passed on; they can do nothing for they are no longer among us. What they did do and the words that they spoke may have some effect, particularly on those who had seen and heard them; but their influence wanes as time moves forward. So this Son of God whom you talk about, this Messiah has passed on, and his words remain only with those of you who saw and heard him.

Soon you'll be gone, and the memory of him will be lost in history." Aerius then leaned back against the wall of the burnedout house we were in with a smug look on his face, daring me to challenge his argument.

"In almost all instances, your argument is sound," I answered. "However, in this case I know you to be wrong. You see, this man was truly the Son of God. This man called Jesus did die upon that cross, for I was there and witnessed his death. I saw him taken down from the cross and carried to his tomb and prepared for burial before a great stone was rolled across the entrance. Even the Jews called upon Pilate to place guards at the grave's entrance to prevent his followers from coming in the night and stealing his body. So there he lay in death for the remainder of Friday, all day Saturday and on into Sunday."

Aerius continued to grin in his smug way sure that he had me trapped.

"Then a miraculous thing happened," I continued. "At daybreak on Sunday several women who had been followers went to the tomb and were astounded to see that the great stone had been rolled away and that Jesus was gone."

Aerius's grin began to fade as I continued.

"They entered the tomb and found two men dressed in brilliant white robes. The women were frightened and bowed before them, but one said to them, 'Why do you look for the living among the dead? The one you look for is not here, He is risen! Remember how he told you that he must be delivered into the hands of sinful men, crucified and on the third day be raised again?'

"The women then remembered his words, left the tomb and rushed to tell the other followers what they had seen. The other followers did not believe them, for they, like you, felt that once one dies that's the end. Two of Jesus' followers, Peter and John, did go to the tomb, and they, too, saw that it was empty and wondered about the event."

Aerius interrupted, "An empty tomb does not prove that a man who has died has regained his life."

"That is not the end of the story," I continued. "For you see, a friend and I met and talked with him, with this Jesus, that evening as we were walking from Jerusalem to our home in Emmaus. This very man whom I watched die on the cross came alongside us on the road and spoke to us. Later he appeared to the other followers, and in all, over four hundred people were eye witnesses to his life after his death. He still bore the scars of the nails that were driven into his hands and feet. Finally, after forty days before many other witnesses he ascended into heaven."

"You are saying crazy things, Caleb," Aerius said somewhat doubtfully. "This cannot be. A man cannot die and then regain life. He was taken down from the cross too soon—he had to still be alive. I don't have time to listen to your gibberish!" With that said, Aerius got up and left my little shelter and went back to his tent.

After he was gone, I said my evening prayers thanking God for the opportunity to witness my faith to a man who had never before given much thought to spiritual things.

At daybreak the next day, the fighting resumed. The Jewish soldiers poured out of the gate in another attack on the battering ram and the other war machines. At first they were successful in setting the timber on one of the machines on fire. This fire was quickly extinguished by its crew and some of the nearby Roman infantry. As the fire was being put out and before the full weight of the Roman soldiers could drive the attackers away, these Jewish aggressors set another machine on fire and slaughtered its crew. More Roman troops came forward, and after a terrific battle drove the Jews back to the gate, through which they disappeared into the city.

There were some Jewish soldiers who remained outside the gate and pleaded for their lives. In return, they promised to provide the Romans with important information about capturing Jerusalem. This proved to be nothing but a ruse as it was their intent to slow the Roman assault on the city. They called to Titus and asked for his aid and friendship so that Jerusalem would be spared further injury. Titus, in hopes of reaching a peaceful solution, replied that he would prefer to negotiate a peace, for he, too, did not want to see the siege continue. This parley between the Roman leaders and the Jews continued for a full day until it was discovered by Titus that the enemy was buying time for Simon and John to continue the work of building up their defenses. It was when some negotiators went forth to talk with the Jewish soldiers that they came under attack from the men they were talking with and from other soldiers on the walled tower above the battering ram.

Infuriated by this subterfuge on the part of his enemies, Titus ordered a redoubling of the effort to topple the Jewish tower overlooking the battering ram. So in answer to this threat to the large ram battering at the wall, another smaller ram was brought forth and positioned to attack the stone in the tower the Jews were using to sustain their attack on the larger. Soon the tower began to shake and tremble under the tremendous pounding of two rams, the small one working on the tower itself and the large one battering the wall adjacent to the tower. During that night, the tower collapsed into a heap of rubble and its wooden foundation and inner structure were set on fire. As the tower was not an intricate part of the wall, no entry was gained. The rams were repositioned and started their battering on another and weaker portion of the wall.

Finally, in the early morning of the fifth day after taking the first wall, a breach was made in the second wall. This opening was not very wide and instead of continuing the battering to widen the breach, General Titus sent forth over a thousand of his choice troops to the opening to establish a defensive perimeter inside the gap. Aerius and his men were the lead team into the city.

At this point in the wall the entry into Jerusalem was at a place called the Market for Cloth. Here the streets were narrow and lined with low one and two-story buildings, an excellent place for the Jews to defend, for many men could be hidden in the dark recesses of the structures and alley ways.

It was my impression that General Titus still had in mind the taking of the city without it enduring further damage. It was for this reason that he did not insist on a widening of the breach. It should have been apparent to the enemy that they could not stop the Roman advance and that surrender would be preferable to the death they would suffer if the fighting continued.

There was a hush in the sounds of battle after the breach had been made. The Nicor was stopped, and the other war machines went silent. The only sound was that of the men entering through the breach and forming up in their defensive stance. Not one Jewish soldier was to be seen, and the silence continued. I could hear some of the men whisper to one another, probably questioning the eerie hush that had settled over the battlefield.

Once the defensive perimeter had been established the lead elements started to send reconnaissance parties up and down the nearby streets. In the dim light, I could make out what I thought to be Aerius and a few of his men start down one of the nearby alleys. I had to stand outside the breach out of the way of the other soldiers, who also were trying to peer inside the small opening in the wall. I, of course, because of my status as a noncombatant, was required to stand far to the rear, behind the troops. However, I had been able to climb atop a burned-out house near the wall opening, and therefore, I could see over the men and on into the city.

The silence continued only to be broken by the occasional shout of a soldier as he yelled to his commander that all was clear. The men inside and outside the wall began to relax, and of course their thought had to be that the Jews had gone back behind the third wall leaving this area to the Romans, just as they had done for Bezetha when the first wall was breached.

As the scouting parties returned with their reports that no one had been found and as the defensive line began to relax, a sudden and thunderous sound resonated up and down the streets. It was a massive force of shouting Jewish soldiers, beating their swords on their shields, rushing towards the breach from a place far inside the city. These troops, countless in number, poured out of the streets and buildings, soon overwhelming the meager defensive perimeter that the Romans had earlier established. Then, out of the upper gates, another throng of Jewish soldiers charged at the Romans outside the breach on the second wall.

The fighting that ensued was fierce and bloody. The sounds of the battle intensified as more and more troops became engaged in this life-and-death struggle. Those Roman soldiers caught inside the wall were being quickly overwhelmed as the breach was too small for them to escape in a rapid and orderly fashion. General Festus, the commander closest to the breach on the outside, deployed the full weight of his command against the Jews on his side of the wall and drove them back to the upper gates. At the same time, General Titus ordered his archers to enter the breach in order to use their weapons to protect the men inside the wall as they started to withdraw in a more orderly fashion. As soon as the archers entered through the opening, they established positions at the upper ends of the streets that led to the breach. They shot their missiles at the enemy in rapid succession, driving them back away from the Roman soldiers who were trying to escape through the gap in the wall.

Aerius appeared in the midst of the Jews, swinging his mighty sword and cutting a path through the enemy so that he and his men could escape back to the wall from deep within the city. Slowly the weight of the Roman discipline was able to overwhelm the chaotic fanaticism of the Jewish troops and push them back, away from the breach in the wall that allowed the Romans to retreat. They brought with them as many of the dead and wounded as they could. Soon they were back outside the wall, somewhat bewildered by all that had just taken place.

The scene inside the city was one of sorrow to my eyes as I saw many of the dead and wounded that littered the streets of Jerusalem. A place where as a child I had spent much of my time with my parents shopping for cloth and other items in this once prosperous market place was now a place strewn with broken and maimed bodies.

That night Aerius once again sought me out and came to talk with me late in the evening. He told me that he and his men had been surrounded by the Jewish soldiers and nearly overwhelmed in their attempt to escape back to the wall. Three of his men had been killed outright, and for the first time in his life he felt that his life might also come to an end. "I'd been in tight situations before," he related, "but never had I felt that I would be struck down as I felt today. Some strange power seemed to be with me and helped me and the others escape.

"Ever since then I have been thinking about what you talked about the other evening when you told me about this man, this God incarnate you called Jesus. Could his power be the one that brought me and my men to safety?"

I looked at him a long time before replying, trying to formulate words that would help him understand. "Terrible things happen to us, Aerius," I started. "These things happen because of man's evil and wrongful thoughts and deeds. This fighting isn't brought on us because of God's desire to see us kill one another. Rather, we bring it on ourselves. In this instance many of these Jews have turned their backs on God, and this war that seems to be leading to the destruction of Jerusalem may be the result of His anger towards them for their rejection of His son Jesus. However, do not forget that it is His desire that we love one another and that we glorify Him in all that we do. The big stumbling block here is the result of His greatest gift that He has given to us—the gift of choice. We, not God, decide what it is that we want to believe or not to believe.

"He could easily command us to follow and praise Him in all that we do. If that were to be the case, we would be no less than His slaves, not our own masters. As a result of this gift, we choose to either believe or to not believe in Him or in His Son Jesus.

"Because you have heard the words and because you have decided to consider them, maybe He has chosen to put His arms of protection around you and give you guidance and strength as you make up your mind about the choices you have before you."

"Does this mean that if I choose to accept this Jesus on faith, that all of my troubles will go away?" Aerius asked. "That I will not die in the fighting and be under His protection?"

"I wish it were that easy," I replied. "But that's not what it means at all. Things could get worse for you during your lifetime. What it does mean is that you will reside in paradise with Him, with God, once you die. It means that you will have eternal life and dwell in the house of the Lord forever.

"So as you consider these things and as you continue on, God is giving you a chance to accept His invitation to believe in Jesus on faith and attain eternal life."

"And if I refuse, then do I just die and continue to descend to the underworld, and cross over the Styx, never to know peace and serenity again? Am I never going to be able to think or to see the beauty of the earth once more?" Aerius wondered.

"I can't answer that for you," I replied. "I do know that those who do not accept Jesus or those who reject Him are eternally separated from God. Does that mean oblivion or lack of sensual function, or does it mean existing in another realm with senses, such as in hell, I cannot say. As for me, I accept what I've seen and what I've told you as being the truth of God. I, therefore, will cross over at the time of my death and be with my Lord forever.

"From the time I first accepted Jesus, my life has changed. It hasn't gotten easier, and my situation now as a prisoner has not brought me greater ease. However, I must admit it has given me greater peace of mind. I am more able to cope with any situation now than I would have been before my faith acceptance. Most importantly I know what the future holds."

"I am a soldier," Aerius said, "I cannot change my ways. If I accept this, this invitation, then I no longer can properly do my duty. Your Jesus would condemn me."

"I don't think that's the case at all, Aerius. I think you can continue on in your chosen profession but act in a way that will honor God. For example, your war here and now is to fight the evil that has taken hold of Jerusalem. Simon and John are far removed from God and doing a great harm to the people they have entrapped in the city. As I see it, you Romans are here in order to set these people free from the horrors that have been brought down upon them by these brigands who have seized control."

"Let me think these things over, Caleb," Aerius said quietly. "It's getting late and I must be ready for tomorrow."

Aerius stood, nodded to me and left my shelter. I stared after him before my eyes returned to the small fire that was burning in front of me. I quickly said my prayers, particularly for Aerius. Then my prayer went out for Naomi and her family and finally for my grandson and all of the other believers back in Philadelphia.

The next day the fighting resumed at daybreak. The Jews came out of the upper gates, attacking the crews of the machines of war. The Roman infantry quickly came to the aid of their comrades at the machines and soon drove the Jewish soldiers back to the gate, which they squeezed through and bolted shut.

Soon after that event, the Romans set to work widening the breach in the wall. The Jews on the other side were ready for this action and quickly fell upon the Romans with their darts and arrows. It was also evident that the Jews were becoming more expert in the use of their own weapons of war, for they were now throwing their stones and darts with greater accuracy.

The fighting continued throughout the day as the Romans entered the breach only to be met by a barricade of Jewish infantry battling tooth and nail to prevent their enemy from coming through the crumbled portion of the wall. There were more and more frequent clashes of the lines of opposing infantry, and during the second day it was evident that the Roman foot soldier, due to his training, was superior in this type of combat. This did not stop the Jewish soldiers from putting up a stout, fanatical defense.

It was during the late evening of the second day of trying to regain entry through the second wall that I was summoned to Aerius's tent. The soldier who escorted me said little other than I was to report to Aerius immediately, so we walked in silence from my shelter to the centurion's quarters. Upon entering, I found Aerius and two other officers standing over a man kneeling on the floor of the tent; he had been wounded. To me, he appeared to be in great pain and was mumbling in Aramaic that he didn't understand what his questioners wanted. He was dressed in a uniform that I took to be of an Idumean officer.

Aerius looked up at me and said that he needed information about the Jewish deployment on the other side of the wall and that I was to find out as much as I could from this man.

I knelt down beside the man and said, "My name is Caleb. Like you I'm a prisoner, and it is my work to interpret your words to the Romans." I felt that identifying myself as a prisoner would help him speak a little more freely with me.

"You appear to be an Idumean officer. Were you under Simon's command?"

"Yes," he replied. "I led a troop of soldiers whose objective was to defend the breach in the wall at all costs. This has been done successfully up until this time. We are getting weaker, though, since all of us are beginning to suffer from the effects of the lack of food." With that said the man fell silent, his head dropped and he stared down at the ground.

I looked up at Aerius and told him word for word what the man had said.

Aerius thought for a moment and said to the other officers, "What else is there to ask? They are starving and getting weaker by the day."

One retorted with, "Ask them how much food they have left."

Without waiting for Aerius, I put that very question to the Idumean.

He thought a moment and then replied, "The fighting men have been taking food from the civilians, which will be sufficient food for another month, though even that is not adequate to sustain our strength properly. On the other hand, as a result of our taking supplies from the citizens, those poor people are slowly starving to death. John and Simon do not want the soldiers to suffer from a lack of nourishment and have therefore given orders to plunder food from non-essential citizens who aren't involved in the fighting. In addition, any citizen or visitor who says that we should capitulate to the Romans, no matter his status, is executed on the spot and all of his food and water confiscated and distributed among the fighting men. There is to be absolutely no talk of surrender by anyone inside the city on penalty of death.

"As a result of the Romans being expelled from the new breach in this wall, the insurrectionists are satisfied that victory is theirs, that the God of the Jews will give them enough sustenance to drive the Romans out of Jerusalem and out of all of Judea."

"Do you truly believe this yourself?" I asked.

"I did until my capture this morning. Now I have been made aware of the strength of this army and the countless troops that the Romans have at their disposal."

I again relayed this information to Aerius and his fellow officers. They talked this over for awhile before asking me to get more information from the prisoner. There was little he could add to what we already had at hand. After another round of questioning, the prisoner was taken back to the holding compound and I was escorted back to my shelter.

For another day, the Romans persisted in their attack on the second wall. Finally in the early evening of the third day after they had first broken through the wall, they entered the breach for the second time and regained possession of that portion of the city, this time for good. The Jews retreated behind the third and final wall. The Romans now had possession of all of the new city and the upper third of the Tyropoeon Valley and all that part of Jerusalem that extended north from the Temple wall due west to the three towers of Hippicus, Mariame, and Phasael. It was at this point that General Titus decided to relax the siege and allow his soldiers a few days of rest and recuperation.

THE ASSAULT ON
FORTRESS ANTONIO

The next evening after the Romans had secured that portion of the city north of the final wall that protected the Temple and the fortress, Aerius came to my shelter for a late evening chat. I hadn't seen much of him for several days since he was always in the forefront of the battle, facing those dangers a soldier at war takes on as a daily task.

He was in high spirits for he'd learned that the army was to be paid the next day. This was a special event, as it had been some time since their last payday. Also with the relaxation of the siege, he and all of the Romans were in a festive mood.

"We have come to the point where the city will be ours in a short time," he exclaimed shortly after seating himself on the ground near my small open fire. "We have a few days in which to get our pay and then rest before the final push into Jerusalem. I know General Titus has given us this time off in order for the Jews to reconsider their position and in all probability surrender before the battle begins again. They have to be aware of our power and that if they continue to resist they, and their precious city, will be utterly destroyed. They can't but help to see that their position is hopeless."

"I hope you are right," I answered. "But I think that you have to consider that they may have a completely different mindset. All of the prisoners whom you have interrogated have emphasized that any citizen caught even talking about surrender would be summarily executed. That doesn't sound like a stand that will be changed. These evil doers who are in control of the city have committed such dastardly crimes that they are not going to give up without a fight; they'll fight until the death. I guess I mean not only their own deaths but the demise of everyone inside the walls."

"If that is what they want, then we will be glad to oblige them in that wish," Aerius smirked in response. "What we want is what we get; no one can stop us in our quest."

I let the subject drop there for I knew that he was right. The Jews would either have to surrender or die. I knew in my heart that they would not surrender. We then went on to discuss other, rather mundane subjects before Aerius got up, stretched and bid me good night. I watched him leave before turning to my prayers and then rolling up in my blankets for another fitful night of sleep.

Early the next morning the blaring trumpets quickly brought me to full wakefulness. Shortly after the trumpets sounded, I heard the voices and shouts of many men as the Romans, dressed in their armor and finest ceremonial dress uniforms, began to form up on the parade ground in the center of the old camp outside the first wall. The order of march then started at the tower of Phasael and proceeded south to the Serpent's Pool, then along the Hinnom Valley to the Kidron Valley where the parade turned north to the Mount of Olives and the camp of the Tenth Legion, which lay directly across the valley from the Golden Gate that led from the Temple.

Here they received their allotment before continuing north around the city and back to where they had started. This parade continued on for nearly four days. It seemed that all of those residing in Jerusalem watched this vast army as it marched around the city of Jerusalem. Every space on top of the wall was crowded with onlookers. Even the tops of the houses and buildings that were high enough to view the line of march were packed with spectators watching the Romans and probably wondering why the city leaders would not relent and surrender.

On the fifth day, once the army had received their benefits and there was no sign of surrender from the Jews, General Titus ordered that the siege would continue. The Twelfth and Fifteenth Legions began building protective banks before the fortress wall of Antonio, and the Fifth Legion began building an embankment near the Monument to John. It was during this time of construction of the banks that Simon's men and their allies, the Idumeans, made frequent sorties against the Romans of the Fifth Legion. At the same time John and the Zealots attacked the Romans building the banks before the fortress. These clashes were frequent and violent. Because the Jews held the higher ground, they attained a great deal of success in these attacks. They were also gaining a great deal of skill in the use of the captured machines of war.

The Romans would not be deterred in their building efforts, though, and were able to continue the construction despite these repeated attacks.

One morning a Jewish man, a man who'd once been a high priest in the Temple, now under the protection of Titus, set out on his horse along with a Roman escort of five mounted troops. They rode slowly around the outer walls as this priest exhorted the rabble in control of the city to give up Jerusalem to the Romans.

"You cannot hold them at bay, and they will enter the city," he shouted. "If you keep up your resistance, the city will be destroyed along with all who live in it. For the sake of Jerusalem and all of the innocent victims trapped behind the walls, bring an end to this terrible conflict. Save yourselves and allow those non-combatants inside the walls to come out and be fed and to taste freedom. The Romans do not want to interfere with our beliefs nor do they want to destroy the

Temple. They will allow us to retain our possessions. Throw down your arms and open the gates so that we may live and give glory to our God in peace." He and his entourage of Roman guards continued to ride around the walls pleading for the rebel leadership to give up and to save the city from destruction.

This plea was met with disdain by the rabble that held Jerusalem. They shouted out their scorn and contempt in no uncertain terms, and in many instances hurled darts and rocks at this man. He continued all day calling out to the citizens to rebel against this rabble and to save the city, all to no avail.

In the meantime the Roman soldiers continued to increase the height of their embankments. Once this construction was completed, they then brought their machines of war to the banks where the crews readied them for the time they would be ordered to commence the attack.

In the middle of the night of the fifth day after taking the second wall, I was awakened by one of the soldiers who told me that Aerius had need of my skills to interrogate some new prisoners. I struggled to my feet, and without a word we walked to the place where the new internees were held. As usual, I found them on their knees with their hands bound behind their backs, Aerius standing over them glaring menacingly.

These men, four in total, were not soldiers, and I soon discovered they were just citizens of Jerusalem caught up in the evil doings of the rabble. Their emaciated appearance told me what they'd been through. None of them had eaten in many days.

"There are many more like these," Aerius said. "They're coming out of Jerusalem in large numbers. We assume that they heard their countryman exhorting them to surrender as he rode around the walls today. Find out what you can and tell me what it is they have to say."

I nodded to Aerius, and then as was my custom knelt on the ground in front of the men. "Why have you left the city and come over to the Romans?" I asked the group in general.

"Our families are gone," the first one answered. "My two children died last week, and then my wife died last night, all taken by starvation. These others," the man motioned to the three men with him, "who are friends of mine have suffered similar fates. The soldiers have forced their way into our homes and have taken all of our food for themselves leaving us nothing. Even for those who have no food, the rebels still break down their doors and ransack their homes leaving it in shambles. If they believe you are hiding something, even though you have nothing, they will slit your throat and leave you to rot on the floor."

"Why have you waited so long before trying to escape and come over to the Romans?" I asked.

"We were fearful at first for what the Romans would do to us. Then the soldiers threatened to kill us if we even talked of giving up to them. Finally, each of us has been burdened by a family member who would have been unable to make the escape—an elderly parent, a young child or an infirm family member. If we escaped and left this person behind, they would be slain by the soldiers. We finally came to the conclusion that we could not be treated in a more despicable manner by the Romans than how we have been treated by our own Jewish leaders. Those who are wealthy have been treated in a cruel manner also. For if they close their doors to eat what morsels they have been able to gather, then their doors are broken down and whatever they have will be taken out of their very mouths. The Romans will not treat us this way. Besides it would be better to be sold into slavery than to die." After saying these things the man hung his head.

I looked at the others, and they nodded their heads in agreement confirming what first man said was true.

I looked up at Aerius and told him what I had been told. "The conditions in Jerusalem," I added, "seem to be worsening. These people are starving and have fled the city now that those who had been unable to escape are no longer around to hold them back."

Aerius acknowledged me with a nod of his head and continued to study the men on the ground. He turned to the other officer who was with him and told him to be sure that these men were given something to eat and then put in the holding pen.

"And you think that we Romans are the cruel ones, don't you Caleb?" he said to me in a cryptic and sarcastic tone. "I see the cruelty emanating from the city of your own God.

I see His anger being meted out on His own people." He stopped speaking for a moment, seemingly lost in thought, before continuing. "This confirms what you told me, that they, the Jews, have refused to be obedient to Him and He's venting His anger upon His own people. What a shame that this all had to come to pass."

I didn't know how to answer him, for I knew that what he said was close to the truth, that the Jewish leadership had brought this on themselves. "You are right; the Jews cannot blame the Romans. I have seen the humanity in General Titus. I believe that he would restore the city and the people's possessions to them if only they would repent and open the gates. But because of their stubbornness, the city and the Temple will be destroyed."

As the prisoners were being led away I asked Aerius, "What is to become of these people who are successfully escaping from the city?"

"As far as I know," Aerius replied, "they are being given some food and told to leave, to go away from the city and not to interfere with our work. I don't think that that type of amnesty will last long. Soon all will be sentenced to slavery or death."

I gulped at those words and a feeling of despair overcame my whole being.

Aerius continued, "That is the sentence for those who think they can stand in the way of the Empire. Rome will prevail over all people for all time. If any nation dares to stand in our way, we will destroy them. The general's good will is coming to an end. Once we breach this third wall, all within will be either killed or captured, and the prisoners will be sold into slavery."

There wasn't much more for me to say. I nodded to Aerius and started back to my shelter. The guard who had summoned me earlier accompanied me along the way. Once inside my little abode I knelt down and said my prayers, pleading with God that He save the city from destruction.

I soon learned in the days that followed that many of the inhabitants escaping from the city had sold their most valuable possessions for next to nothing. The money, or coin, that they had or obtained from the sale of their possessions was ingested whole in order to be hidden in their bodies. They would then leave the city only to be captured by the Romans and set free. At the first opportunity and where they thought they would not be observed, they would then defecate and reclaim the gold coin they had previously swallowed. Their reasoning for this was that anyone in Jerusalem caught with valuable possessions would have them taken by the rebel soldiers and in many instances have their throats slit.

This stealthy way of smuggling their wealth out of the city did not go unnoticed by some of the Assyrian soldiers who were part of the Roman auxiliary forces. It didn't take long for these rogue soldiers to realize that by capturing the escaping Jews and murdering these poor victims, they could then disembowel and take the gold coin for themselves. The war had degenerated into an unholy crusade.

We also discovered that during the night many Jews would make their way out of Jerusalem, either through tunnels, hidden gates or by ropes over the wall, gather whatever edible plants they could find, and then reenter the city to share with others or to eat them for themselves that which had been gathered.

Many of these were the soldiers who were also in need of food, as even the Jewish soldiers were short on supplies. General Titus ordered his men to look for these who came out at night and to take them captive. Soon the Romans were bringing in great numbers each night. Many of these prisoners fought with the Romans and tried to escape back into the city. The number of captives grew and soon many of the soldiers of the legions were doing little other than guarding prisoners. Some of these captives, old men, women and children, were at first set free as I have told you. However, this amnesty was soon ended and all captives were interned. As their numbers grew, many more of the soldiers had to be taken from their duties and pressed into service as guards.

This proved to be intolerable for the General. It was thus decided to put the men prisoners to death, by crucifixion. The women and children were held in enclosures and would later be sold into slavery. It wasn't long before the ground was covered with crosses, and this was only within twenty-one days since the taking of the second wall.

I later learned that the Jews would take city dwellers to the top of the wall and force them to look out upon the hundreds of crosses upon which were nailed men suffering slow and agonizing deaths. John and Simon both used this as a deterrent for those who had thoughts of escaping over to the Romans.

The work on the banks before Antonio and the monument of John continued unabated day and night. Within seventeen days the banks were completed. There were four defensive embankments built in total. The first was put up by the Fifth Legion along the north wall of

Antonio Fortress. Then to the west some two hundred cubits, another embankment was built, this one by the Twelfth Legion. A third bank was constructed by the Tenth Legion along the western wall of the fortress, and next to it, before the high priest's monument, the fourth and last embankment went up about two hundred-twenty cubits to the south. This was erected by the Fifteenth Legion.

General Titus brought up all of the machines of war and positioned them behind the banks. Next the great battering ram was brought into position on the sixteenth day of April. At the same time Aerius's manipuli was repositioned close to the Fifth Legion behind the embankment before the walls of Antonio, and my little shelter was positioned further north of the embankment, out of harm's way.

On the night of the sixteenth, Aerius came for short time to discuss and maybe even to debate our philosophical views as we so often did. He was buoyant, for now the preparations were complete. The last wall would be brought down soon, or so he thought, and this great battle was in its last stages. The city would be in Roman hands in a matter of days.

"Just wait and see the punishment that your so-called God will bring upon His people," he bragged. "Their stubbornness and their lack of faith will be dealt with through the hands of the Roman Empire."

"I sadly agree with you in part," I concurred. "However," I added, "God often holds little surprises that could or could not affect the outcome. For example, you expect the city to fall within days, but I think it'll take longer. I just hope and pray that the bloodshed will end and the land can return to peace. The great number of crucifixions and the number of people who have had their hands cut off and sent back to the city has sickened me. The brutality of it all is something I hope I'll never have to witness again."

"Even I who have fought in many wars have come to similar conclusions," Aerius said. "I enjoy the challenge, the physical confrontation, but I do not enjoy watching so many innocents die. I don't mind striking down an enemy soldier or, if he is better than me, being struck down. I do not like the slaughter of women and children. But, that's war. Maybe our talks have softened me and my thinking. Maybe I have been in too many wars, and I'm growing weary of this lifestyle." He went quiet for a minute, and then looked up and said, "Well, I must be off, for the final push into Jerusalem will begin at daybreak." He bid me a goodnight and walked to his tent.

I watched him go, noting a sadness in him that I'd not seen before. I said a prayer for his safety and for his soul, and then rolled up in my blankets and was soon in a fitful sleep.

I was awakened during the night by a dreadful noise—a noise that was not only thunderous in sound, but one that shook the ground upon which I slept. At first I thought that I was dreaming and had been in the middle of a giant earthquake. However as I slowly came to my senses, I realized that the sound was real.

I jumped to my feet and ran to a small rise just north of my shelter in order to survey the entire campsite of the Romans. From that vantage point I could see that it was early in the morning, for the eastern sky was light though the sun had not yet peeked over the horizon. I looked to the fortress and the embankment the Fifth Legion had built and saw little of it, for there was a great cloud of smoke and dust rising into the sky from the bank itself. As I watched, I saw some flames coming from the base of the smoke. These flames were small at first, but as they burned they grew in size as more air fed them. Soon all of the wood that had been used in their construction was consumed by a great conflagration.

I stood and watched for a long time, unable to discern what was happening. As the sun finally rose up over the horizon, I could see more of what was taking place. After careful study, I was able to determine that a large portion of the defensive bank put up by the Romans had collapsed into a large fissure in the ground.

Many of the Roman soldiers who at first tried to put out the fire gave up for the flames and heat were too intense, and it appeared to me that there was nothing left to save. They stood and watched in abject dismay.

I, too, was mesmerized by the sight, but was quickly brought out of my reverie by the sound of many voices. I looked up to the wall of the fortress and saw many Jews standing on the top yelling and cheering as the banks burned. Soon out from a nearby set of gates, which the enemy had opened during the tumult, poured many Jewish soldiers in full armor. They rushed at the Romans, who were not ready for this assault.

A great battle began to unfold before my eyes. The Jews, though not as skilled in battle as the Romans, overwhelmed the out-numbered defensive force quickly due to the ferocity and intensity of their assault. Soon the Jews were attacking the machines of war in an attempt to burn them to the ground.

It took awhile for the Roman troops to re-gather their composure and begin to fight back. Troops from the Twelfth Legion rushed to aid the Fifth's soldiers caught in the deadly trap as they were now nearly surrounded by the Jews. Many men fell that day, for the battle was ferocious and the fury of the Jews was hard to deny. Some of the machines were set on fire, but the fires were quickly extinguished by the Roman auxiliaries. After a long and arduous fight, the Jews began an orderly retreat back into the city via the gates where they had emerged.

The fire at the embankment continued to burn throughout the day, and it was difficult for me to determine its origin. I stood watching the Romans as they slowly gained control of the fire and began to put it out, covering it with shovelfuls of dirt and buckets of water. As I watched the proceedings during the late afternoon, I was once again summoned to Aerius's tent.

As I walked with the trooper who had come for me I asked him, "What was it that started the banks to burn?"

"I don't know," was his answer. "It seems that the ground under the banks gave way and all above fell into an opening, and before we knew it the fires started burning. I was over with the Twelfth Legion's camp when it all started, so it still is a mystery to me. The centurion has some prisoners who he wants to interrogate, and maybe they can shed some light on what has taken place."

I said nothing, and we walked the rest of the distance in silence. When we arrived at the camp, Aerius, as was his usual style, was standing over the prisoners who were on their knees and bound in the customary manner. All three of them were soldiers and were still wearing their armor. Not one of the three appeared to be out of his teens, and they looked as if they hadn't eaten in a number of days. Be that as it may, they were contemptuous towards their captors and did not seem to be in fear of their future. I'm sure they knew that they would soon die.

"Caleb," Aerius called out as I approached. "We need to see if these fellows have had anything to do with the collapse of the banks and with the great fire that followed this morning. So you know what to do," he directed without further preamble.

I squatted down in front of the men and said in Aramaic, "I'm here as an interpreter, and I, too, am a prisoner of the Romans. They are mystified by the great upheaval of their banks this morning, and they would like to know if you can enlighten them on the subject."

One of the men said in an arrogant manner, "We have worked the same number of days that the Romans have. As they constructed their banks, we have been digging a tunnel under the wall and subsequently out and under their banks to plan this big surprise for them."

The second of the three continued. "Once the tunnel was complete, we filled the part under the banks with burnable materials soaked in pitch, bitumen and lamp oil."

The third man went on to explain. "Last night two men lit all that material and then came back through the tunnel. Afterward we all climbed to the top of the wall and waited to see what would happen."

"Yes," continued the first, "we shored up the ceiling with timbers and waited for them to burn and finally collapse. What a beautiful sight to see that dirt and material from the banks fall into the crater and finally burst into flames! Our only regret was that more Romans did not die."

"We planned this morning's attack," the second man added, "to coincide with the confusion caused by the cave-in and fires. It went much better than anyone had hoped. God is still with us, and we shall prevail."

"Interesting story," I said. "However, the war for you is over. You are now in the hands of your sworn enemy. So be hopeful that they will treat you in a kindly manner." I hesitated a minute and then asked, "Is there anything else that you want to say about today's events? Remember that what you say may be important toward your future. You have seen the crucifixions from the wall, and I don't think you would like to end your life in that manner. I think that if you would be less arrogant in your conduct and plead to their sense of mercy that you might not die but live."

One of the men quickly said, "I don't want to die. I'm only sixteen. I have many years ahead of me."

"Then don't brag to the Romans on your success in undermining the banks and be truly repentant of the fact that you've been forced by your leaders to go into battle," I admonished. This thought of encouraging these young men to lie and thus force me to lie to Aerius in turn went against my better judgment.

"We were not forced to fight," the third man said. "We want to remain free from the iron hand of Rome."

"That's up to you," I replied, "but if I were you I'd not let them know that, unless you are ready to give up your lives here and now. You have a decision to make. Do you want me to tell your captors that you fought willingly or that you were forced into battle?" I felt for these young men, and I wanted to do what I could to help them add years to their lives rather than to give them up here and now because of bravado, and personal ego. As I said this type of encouragement to the young men went against my conviction that I shouldn't lie or encourage others to lie. On the other hand if they didn't they would surely be put to death by their captors. I wanted to see these young men live. I therefore felt that God would understand my reasons for encouraging them to not brag of their success.

The three young men looked at each other, nodded a quick agreement, and then the older one said to me, "We've decided that we want you to tell them that we were forced into battle."

"Good choice," I answered. "I think I know how hard it is for you to say that, but you'll probably live for a longer time now that you've decided to go along with the story that you were forced into battle." I looked up to Aerius and told him everything that the young men had said, and I emphasized that they were forced to fight for the rabble that controlled the city on threat of death for themselves and for their families. Aerius accepted this without comment and then ordered the guards to take them to holding. I did not like how I felt for lying, but

I did feel that a higher purpose was served by adding years to the lives of these very young soldiers.

That was the last I saw of the three young men, and I'm not sure of their fate but Aerius did indicate that they'd probably be sold as slaves. I continued to pray for them in the days that followed, asking God to spare them, and that He also forgive me for my not being truthful with Aerius. Since that time I have felt that my prayers were answered, though the young men may have been enslaved I feel that they survived with their lives.

Two days later I again accompanied Aerius and some of his men over to the banks of the Tenth and Fifteenth Legions in order to interrogate some newly captured prisoners. There were five of us in total—four on mounts and me, of course, on foot walking beside Aerius's beautiful coal-black steed. It was a fine day, and the sun was high in the sky. The temperature was comfortable, and it felt good to get away from my little shelter and to stretch my legs.

These banks were located over on the west side of the third wall near the pool called Amygdalon. As we approached the fortification from the north, we could see that the Fifteenth Legion had brought their machines up to the banks and they had been engaged in battering the wall. From our vantage point, which was on the high ground, we had a panoramic view of the banks and of the machines as they continued their relentless pounding of the city. All of these contraptions of war had been covered with skins and pieces of iron in order to protect the soldiers who operated them from the arrows and darts hurled by the Jewish defenders standing on top of the fortification.

As we started down from the rise in the ground towards the banks, I saw three men, Jews I presumed, run from the gates towards the banks. They each were wearing body armor and each carried a shield on his right arm and a torch in his left hand. They held these torches high and waved them to and fro as if signaling the Romans working the machines on the banks. The soldiers stopped their work and, as if frozen in place, watched the three men approach without thought of defending themselves. At this juncture, the banks were lightly defended, and all of the Romans were transfixed by the fact that only three men would dare attack them. In no time the three reached the banks and easily climbed over them, and then went on through to the Roman soldiers at the machines. They put their torches to the machines setting two afire immediately, and then all three turned to attack the battering ram. By this time the Romans realized what was happening and started to hurl their darts and stones at the three Jews, none of which hit a target for the Jews used their shields to ward off the missiles.

Aerius had stopped to observe the event and at first was unable to grasp the whole of the situation. When it became clear what the enemy was doing, he ordered me to stay where I was and for his three men to follow him. They each spurred their steeds and were off in a blink of an eye. Since the banks were lightly guarded, the Jewish attackers seemed to be having a great deal of success in their endeavors. As Aerius and his men sped down the rise, I heard the sound of many men yelling at the top of their voices. I looked towards the nearest gate and saw a large number of Jewish soldiers pouring through them and toward the banks. Aerius and his men reached the banks first and soon disappeared from my view. The Jewish soldiers also rushed to the banks and were met by a small number of archers, who rapidly fired their arrows into the mass of men trying to mount the embankment. Soon and without regard for their losses, the Jewish troops mounted the banks and rapidly overwhelmed the remaining Romans, who were trying to retreat back to their camp.

A great hand-to-hand battle ensued. Those Romans who had retreated, and yes, even those who had run in fear of their lives, began to re-gather their courage and start to move against their enemy.

The Jews were successful in igniting some more of the machines with their torches and before the smoke and dust became to thick to see, I realized that the three men who had started it all were able to escape back to the wall. Soon the dust and smoke obliterated my view of the fighting, but by the sound of it, it must have been a terrific struggle.

General Titus and a number of his select troops had left the camp earlier in the morning on an inspection trip of Fort Antonio. It was when this great battle had been going on for nearly forty-five minutes that I saw him coming towards the banks from the northeast. Soon he and his fifty cavalry troops were at full gallop headed towards the right flank of the Jews. Without regard for his own life or limb, he and his men charged into the Jewish soldiers. These Jewish troops quickly swung to their right to face the onslaught of the mounted troops of Rome. Many of the Romans, once they realized that their general had become engaged in this great conflict, took courage; particularly those who had run or retreated, and then turned back to face their enemy.

The power of the mounted troops soon overwhelmed the Jews, and they began a slow retreat back to the gate through which they had come. They did not panic, though, and withdrew in a very organized fashion, holding back the weight of the advancing Romans. As quickly as it had begun, the combat ended, and the Jewish soldiers entered the city and closed the gates, leaving a battlefield littered with a great number of wounded and dead.

I finally left my vantage point up on that rise of ground and went down to the field of combat to lend aid to those who had fallen and still were alive. I could see that the Roman banks had been severely scarred as a result of the fighting. Much of the wood that held the earth in place was still burning, and many of the war machines had suffered similar fates. Small groups of Romans were doing their best to put out the flames and save the breastworks from total destruction by the flames.

The Romans in their anger had killed and mutilated the Jewish soldiers left on the field, and there was little that I could do to save or comfort them.

In the days that followed, General Titus, after consultation with his area commanders, ordered that a siege wall be built entirely around Jerusalem. The purpose of the wall was to prevent any supplies, particularly foodstuffs, from going into the city. The general had tired of the war, and his purpose was to tighten his grip on Jerusalem and thus weaken it further through starvation. The soldiers under his command were also growing weary of the fight. Their hatred of the Jews became more open and pronounced with each passing day. With the hatred and with their eagerness for the battle to end, they built the siege wall, one that would completely encircle the city, in the miraculous time of just three days. This wall started from the camp of the Fifth Legion outside the Antonio Fortress and extended to the Kidron Valley and thence to the Mount of Olives. From there it went south to the Hinnom Valley, where it turned west to the monument of the high priest and over to the mount on which Pompey had camped many years earlier. It then rounded the northern edge of Jerusalem and Herod's monument where it rejoined Titus's camp, thus encompassing all Jerusalem. Once the wall was completed, there were thirteen watch towers positioned on the siege wall, approximately one every two thousand paces, manned day and night. In addition, there were to be constant mounted patrols riding around the outer perimeter of the siege wall. The net result was that no one would be able to enter or to leave the city.

Conditions in the city deteriorated rapidly. Through the captured prisoners whom we interrogated, we learned that starvation was taking its toll upon the residents. Entire families were succumbing to the ravages of the siege. Worst of all, bodies began to pile up in the city streets, becoming a breeding ground for virulent diseases as they slowly decayed, thus leading to another toll being taken on the population by pestilence. Many of those sent to clear away the bodies of the dead died in their efforts. A formal burial was out of the question.

There was an ever-growing hatred exhibited by the Romans towards the Jews. It wasn't uncommon for them to display to their enemies atop the wall the bountiful amount of food and drink they had in their possession.

One day in April, Aerius's manipuli and I accompanied General Titus and his tribunes as they rode around the city to inspect the siege wall. Again I was able to ride, a means of locomotion I much preferred to walking. As we rounded the southwest corner and traveled down the Hinnom Valley where it joined with the Tyropoeon and Kidron valleys, we came upon a large number of decaying bodies of the citizens who had died and been collected and thrown over the wall into these valleys. The whole troop stopped and viewed the carnage in silence.

There were so many bodies—men, women and children—in various stages of decomposition that we were unable to count them. The stench was so great that we were forced to cover our faces with kerchiefs so we could continue on without vomiting.

After a time, I heard the general cry out, "Oh God of the Jews, this disaster is not of my making! Bring these people to their senses and let this carnage end."

This sight of so many dead was another of my first encounters with the horrendous realities of war. Till the day that I take my last breath I will never forget that sight. These were not the bodies of soldiers but of civilians who happened to be in the wrong place at the wrong time.

As we continued on around the city that day, I said little more as I was too choked up to carry on a conversation. I prayed to God to please stop this war. But then I had to finish my prayer with the words of my Lord and Savior, Jesus, "Let your will, not mine, be done."

THE ROMANS
SECURE THEIR HOLD
ON ANTONIO

Conditions in the city continued to worsen. There were still a great number of citizens who tried to escape the persecution of the rebels and bandits under John and Simon, for their authoritarian rule was being taken to the extreme.

We learned, from those escaping, that the priest Mathias, who had originally asked Simon to come into the city in order to help them depose John and his Zealots, was murdered by the very man whom he had invited into Jerusalem. Simon not only had Mathias murdered, but before doing so, made him watch as three of his sons were killed by soldiers before they did him in. Simon proved to be more ruthless than John. Terrible barbaric practices were continuing even though the end was near. A wholesale slaughter was underway. Many of the Jews continued to escape from Jerusalem in order to get away from the reckless and brutal leadership of the bandits in control. Their thinking, I'm sure, was that it couldn't be worse to be in the hands of the Romans. This wasn't the case in most instances. Many of those who did come out were bloated from starvation and immediately sat down to eat in excess once in the hands of their captors. Many died as a result, for their bodies could not adjust to this sudden abundance. Other escapees could not even enjoy their first meal, for once captured, they were run through by the Arabians or Syrians attached to the Roman forces, and then their bodies were disemboweled as these foreign troops searched for swallowed gold and jewels. It had been learned that many of the Jews escaping from the city used this means to smuggle their wealth from their homes. I even heard it said that in one night, nearly two thousand Jews who had escaped were killed for this very purpose.

General Titus, upon hearing of these tragic events, wanted to issue a warning that anyone caught in this barbaric and murderous act would immediately be put to death. It appeared, though, that if these orders were carried out he would lose a large part of his army, since a great number of his own soldiers had been caught taking part. The only answer was to resume the attack, distract the men from their greed for riches, and finish with the issue at hand. Take Jerusalem!

The order came on the fifth day of May for the rebuilding of the banks, particularly those around the Antonio Tower, which had been undermined and then burned. There were no longer any trees left in the vicinity. All of the woods and trees in the parks surrounding Jerusalem had been cut down by the Romans and used for the building of the original banks. And as those banks had been in large part burned, the soldiers now had to cut trees and bring them in from a distance, nearly a full days travel, in order to rebuild the banks in front of Antonio. These new defensive positions were completed within twenty-one days and were considerably higher and stronger than the originals.

My once beautiful city of Jerusalem looked barren and in ruins, as if it now stood in the middle of a large wasteland. Not only was the hallowed ground around Jerusalem laid waste, but the sacred objects inside the Temple itself had been desecrated by the bandit John. The golden dishes and vases he had melted down into bars, and all the other utensils he ordered removed from the inner sanctuary. All of the bread, wines and oils used by the priests for the sacrifices were taken and distributed to his soldiers. A greater sacrilege could not have been carried out by a heathen enemy, yet it was done by Jews themselves. There seemed to be no end to the horrible acts committed by the seditious leaders who controlled Jerusalem.

It was also evident that countless lives had been lost, not only to the battle raging in and around the city but as a result of starvation. I heard it said that more than one hundred thousand had died. The count was of those bodies that had been taken out of the city and dumped in the Well of Joab. No one knew how many corpses remained inside the walls. Prisoners that we interrogated reported that many of the large houses had been filled with bodies and then sealed in order to prevent the spread of disease.

Once the banks had been completed for a second time, the Romans set up a stronger security around them in order to prevent the Jews from coming out to burn them as they had before. All of the soldiers were on edge and watchful, for they did not want a repeat of what had happened before.

On the fifteenth of June, just as the Romans were positioning their engines of war, the Jews mounted a new attack on the banks in front of Fortress Antonio. Those Zealots under John ventured out of the gates with torches determined to set the banks on fire. The Romans were ready for them and quickly formed up in ranks and easily repelled the attack. The Jews ran forward uttering loud shouts and directly into the first line of Roman lances, resulting in a great number being pierced and then falling, wounded or dead, to the ground. The Jews up on the wall threw their darts and stones down upon the banks but the Romans held. Many of the machines were brought into action by the Roman soldiers, and they were able to throw their deadly darts and stones at the Jews near the gates. In short order, the skirmish was over, and within a short time the Jews withdrew from their attack and re-entered the fortress.

After the battleground was cleared the battering rams were brought to the wall. As they were being positioned, the soldiers were subjected to a heavy bombardment of rocks and darts hurled down from the fortress.

This day ended with a terrible slaughter of the Jews. Their attack had not been as determined or as tenacious as previous attempts, and it was evident to me that the effects of the siege and starvation was taking their toll on the defenders of Jerusalem.

Late in the afternoon, the rams were in position and started pounding the solid stone that made up the wall. The sound reverberated throughout the area and the wall shook and vibrated, but held. High above the rams and on the walkway atop the wall, the Jews pelted their darts and rocks at the Romans driving the machines. They in turn covered themselves with their shields and continued with their work.

From my vantage point, I could see some of the soldiers working at the large stones in the base of the wall near the rams. It appeared to me that they were trying to dislodge some of those enormous stones that made up the foundation upon which the wall rested. This event took place near where the tunnel, dug by John's men in his attack on the Roman banks, had been positioned. These Romans were also being pelted from the top of the wall, but they too were using their shields and pieces of iron to protect themselves from the various projectiles being cast down on them. As the sun was setting, I saw that three of the great stones had been dislodged and that they were working feverously on a fourth.

After the dinner when all was dark and relatively quiet, Aerius stopped by for a talk. He'd been busy with the war, and I had not seen him for a number of days. He told me of the things that had been happening and of his confidence that the fortress would soon be in the hands of the Romans. Once that took place, the attack on the Temple would begin.

Even though I had expected this, I was saddened to learn that the Temple would soon be involved with the fighting and in all probability be destroyed. As we were talking, we heard a tremendous dull thud and thumping that shook the ground upon which we were sitting. After, came the cries of men in desperate pain.

We both jumped to our feet trying to figure out what had caused the tremendous crash. Then Aerius said, "I think I know what that was! I'm sure that the wall gave way at the spot where our engineers had undermined it. It was over their tunnel, and if I'm not mistaken, the wall collapsed into that chasm. You, Caleb, stay here and don't get in the way; I'm going to the wall to survey the damage." He left at a run and disappeared into the blackness of the night. I had hoped to talk with him some more about his beliefs, but that would have to come at another time.

There were few fires around the camp, and the moon and stars were covered by clouds and the dust kicked up by the crash. I wasn't able to see much from my shelter and determined that I would have to wait until early the next morning before I could survey the damage. The cries of what I thought to be the dying and wounded men soon quieted, and all was silent for the rest of the night. I was unable to sleep much that night, though, as I constantly wondered about what had happened.

As the day began to break and the sky grew ever brighter in the east, I could soon discern the fortress that was no more than four hundred cubits from my position. At first I could just see its outline against the overcast sky and then with each passing moment more details soon became clear. I saw a great rift in the wall to the east southeast of my shelter. Aerius had been correct; the wall had indeed collapsed into the tunnel the Zealots had dug.

The Romans had immediately moved their infantry up to the breach during the night, but they did not enter for there was another wall behind the one that had just collapsed. The Jewish Zealots had hastily built this second wall in hopes of trapping the Romans and holding them off from their attempt to enter the fortress. The Jews were now on top of both walls throwing their darts and rocks at the Romans, who were seeking shelter under their shields and behind some of the large stones that had been part of the broken-through wall. The battle seemed to halt, and for some time a standoff prevailed, for the Roman soldiers knew that the first of their own to attack the breach would surely die.

After a time the soldiers withdrew out of range of the dart and javelin throwers. It wasn't long after this that General Titus stepped forward to address his troops.

The General seemed to me to have a high standing among his men. I believe they respected him not only for his leadership capabilities, but also for the fact that he showed no fear in stepping up and confronting his enemies face-to-face. He declared to his men that they were unconquerable and that if a man were to die that it was better to die in battle against his enemies for the sake of Rome. He went on to say that he would greatly honor the first man to climb the wall and confront the Jews. If that man should live through the ordeal, he would then honor his bravery and give him a command of many.

Once the general had concluded his talk, one man stepped forward, a Syrian by birth, a man called Sabinus. He was of slight build and not one you'd consider to be a bold and courageous man, yet he declared to Titus that he would mount the wall and confront the enemy.

He quickly donned his armor and picked up his shield in his left hand, drew his sword with his right and raced for the fissure in the wall; soon eleven others followed his lead. The Jews atop the wall bombarded Sabinus and those following him with darts and stones. Sabinus, though wounded several times and holding his shield over his head for protection, continued to climb to the top. Some of those who followed him fell under the missiles thrown at them, while the others continued to follow Sabinus to the top.

Once he reached the top the Jews began to retreat, for the first three that opposed him were struck down by his sword. The Jews, believing that the whole army was following Sabinus, quickened their retreat. However, they soon discerned that Sabinus was now alone, for the other eleven had fallen either dead or wounded. With this revelation, the Jews turned from their retreat and began attacking the Syrian. They soon overwhelmed him and then killed him on the spot. Once this was done, they threw his body down onto the rubble below.

The soldiers of Rome quickly retrieved his remains and that which remained of the other eleven who had initially followed Sabinus and took them back to their camp for cremation. I cannot, to this day understand why these men volunteered to undertake the task of climbing out of the fissure and up to the top of the fortress, other than to prove to the son of Caesar their courage.

Again a stalemate prevailed. This all happened on the eighteenth day of June.

It was an additional two days before another attempt was made at taking the wall. It was shortly after dark that a group of fifteen Roman soldiers crept across the opening between their banks and the wall of Antonio. The first two men quietly slit the throats of the two Jewish guards who were there to protect the fissure caused by the collapse of the stones into the tunnel. Once that was done, they swiftly climbed to the top over the rubble and broken stones. Once their position was solidified, the bugler with them put his horn to his lips and blew the loud and long tune that signaled a Roman charge. This so frightened the Jews that they picked up whatever was at hand and started running for the narrow ramp that led from Antonio to the floor of the Temple Mount with the fifteen Romans hot on their heals.

Halfway down this ramp, which was bordered on each side with four-cubit-high walls, the Jews overcame their initial fright and turned to meet the Roman soldiers charging after them. Here a great battle ensued, for at the sound of the trumpet Roman soldiers poured over their banks and up to the top of the wall to join their comrades. This ramp, which joined fortress Antonio with the Temple, was not much more than ten cubits wide. Darts, arrows and rocks could not be used due to the intermixing of the soldiers from both sides, and the battle degenerated to nothing more than hand-to-hand combat utilizing sword and shield. A great noise arose as the men in the rear yelled to encourage those in front of them to fight harder.

These men in the forefront could not retreat as their own men behind them continued to push them forward. Many fell that day, and those that survived walked upon those who had fallen. The battle lasted what seemed to be a very long time, and the carnage continued well into late morning. The Romans had the hope of taking the Temple in their minds as the Jews fought to save their most sacred building. More and more Jews came up from the city to join in on the battle and to cheer on those who held the ramp. As the Roman camps were widely dispersed around the city, their number on the ramp was considerably fewer than the number of Jews. They were forced to give ground as their enemy continued to disregard their own losses and push their way back up the ramp towards the fortress.

This fierce battle didn't end at noon or afternoon, but continued on through the night and well into the next morning. The number of dead and wounded continued to clog the ramp. Around midmorning the Romans were forced to relinquish their hold on the ramp. However, the Jews were unable to reenter the fortress, for as soon as they left the relative safety and protection the ramp offered, they would be taken down by the arrows of the Roman archers.

At the battle's end, the Jews could claim that the Temple Mount had been saved. But the Romans had control of Fortress Antonio and the tower, Baris. Another step to the taking of Jerusalem had been accomplished.

ON TO THE TEMPLE MOUNT

Throughout the day, small groups of soldiers from both sides continued to skirmish at the top of the ramp that led from the fortress to the Temple. Late in the afternoon, one Roman centurion who had been at General Titus's side during the battle became enraged when a Jewish soldier ran a Roman through with his sword and added insult to injury by slitting his victim's throat. This man, Julian, jumped from the tower of Antonio onto the walkway and ran to the ramp. He drew his sword, and before the Jewish soldier realized what was happening and could raise his sword in his own defense, the centurion ran him through.

Julian didn't stop there. He continued on down the ramp swinging his potent sword, striking down the enemy as he rushed towards the Temple courts. His aggressive action put the other Jews on the ramp in flight as they rushed pell-mell towards the apparent safety of the Temple. Julian continued after them, and the moment he stepped off of the ramp onto the polished floor of the outer court, the Court of the Gentiles, he slipped and fell to his back with a tremendous crash as his armor and shield slammed onto the floor. This stopped the Jewish flight. When these soldiers turned and saw that the Roman was alone they headed back to the fallen centurion.

Julian was unable to regain his feet before they were upon him, and from his prone position he tried to fend off his attackers. He protected himself as best he could with his armor and shield as the Jews surrounded him, thrusting their swords at his body. He took many wounds on his limbs but his armor protected him from taking a fatal blow. Before his comrades could rush to his aid, one of the Jews thrust his sword deep into his body at the shoulder rending him helpless. Another enemy then slit his throat, and Julian died on the spot. The Jews quickly turned and ran to the safety of the Temple walls, as Roman soldiers came to retrieve Julian's body and take him back to the ramp. Here the Romans stayed, and now the ramp was in their control, too. The bravery of this lone centurion added another piece of the city to the Roman conquest.

General Titus was greatly moved by the bravery of his friend and mourned his loss. He eulogized his death, pointing out to his soldiers his tremendous courage—a courage that all soldiers fighting for Rome should emulate whenever they enter battle against the enemies of the Empire.

The next day General Titus ordered the men to begin widening the breach and dig at the foundations of the Antonio tower. He needed a wider opening in order to bring his army forward for the final assault upon the Temple. He also ordered that his personal interpreter, the Jewish priest I spoke of earlier, to go out and again offer the tyrants John and Simon an opportunity to save the city and its Temple from destruction by opening the gates and peacefully allowing the Romans to enter. If that were not satisfactory, then John and Simon would be allowed to assemble their armies and march out of Jerusalem to an open field and fight their battle without inflicting further damage on the city.

This second day of July was a very important day for the Jews since it was the first time and in accord with the prediction of the great profit Daniel some six hundred years earlier, that the Daily Sacrifice failed to be offered to God. This interpreter rode close enough to the wall so that he could be heard but far enough away to remain out of range of the darts and arrows of the Jewish defenders. He was quick to point out to those who stood upon the wall that he, as well as General Titus, was aware that the sacrifice was no longer being offered.

"The Romans do not wish to destroy our Temple," he shouted. "They do not wish to interfere with our customs and our religious worship. So throw open the gates and let them in, for if you do not, our city will be destroyed, and I fear that the Temple will be burnt to the ground. Open the city, and you and all of the citizens will be provided with food and you will be given animals for the sacrifices so that they may begin again and that we may praise our God in peace."

There was silence from those on top of the walls as well as from the Roman soldiers. I had a feeling that a great sadness prevailed over both sides of the lines—the Jews wishing that the fighting was finished and that they could return to their worship, the Romans not wanting to destroy the Temple.

After a short pause, the seditious leader, John, responded by casting aspersions upon the interpreter before adding. "The holy Temple, God's dwelling place here on earth, is not in jeopardy. It is you and your Roman army that face total annihilation, for our God is on our side and will strike you down before you set one foot on this holy ground."

The interpreter, speaking in Aramaic, answered in a sarcastic tone, "Am I to understand that you have kept God's holy covenant? That you have kept the Temple clean from all impure things? That you have continued the sacrifices without interruption?

"You despicable man, who has held all of Jerusalem as your hostage and raped and pillaged without giving a thought to the living God, expect that He will miraculously come to your aid and defeat this large army that He has assembled to bring about your own downfall? Oh you foolish man, do you not know that He will not withhold His wrath much longer before He brings about His justice?

"However, I say to you, John, that if you repent and change your ways and ask God's forgiveness, I am sure that He would forgive you. The Romans would also pardon your treasons committed against them and the citizens of Jerusalem.

"Do not let that which has been foretold by the ancient prophets come to pass. For it was written, that when a governor of this state shall begin to slaughter his own people that God will bring forth the fire and ruin upon all of Israel. In this case, that mechanism of our destruction is this Roman army. Repent of your wicked ways, throw open the gates, and bring this conflict to a swift and just end."

At the conclusion of this last appeal to John and also to Simon, the interpreter returned to the camp of General Titus. There were some catcalls and sarcastic remarks from John and his men about the speech, but on the whole a silence prevailed over the entire battlefield. I believed then and I still do to this day that many of the citizens of Jerusalem truly understood that if nothing was done and soon they, the Temple and the city would be defeated and burned to the ground. As an affirmation of that belief, there were many defections to the Roman side. Most of those who came over during the remainder of the day and on into the night were high priests and their families as well as many of the nobles and their kin.

Theses defectors were greeted warmly and treated well by General Titus. He sent them to the small village of Gophna, a short distance away, with the promise that when the fighting had ended they would have their possessions restored. In answer to those who had defected, John told the people that the Romans had killed them all once they had been captured. When Titus got wind of this lie, he sent for these people and brought them back from Gophna in order to parade them around the wall of Jerusalem so that the citizens still within the walls could see for themselves that the prisoners had been well treated. Even these prisoners pleaded with the seditious to open the gates and thus put an end to the fighting.

As in previous days when the citizens of Jerusalem saw that these defectors had truly been well treated, many more made an effort to escape. Some were successful, but those who were caught in the act by the soldiers of the seditious leaders were executed on the spot.

Once again Titus with his interpreter went forth to offer John and Simon forgiveness and an honorable peace if they would open the gates and let the Romans enter. "We do not want to destroy your Temple nor your city," the interpreter implored. "But if you do not concede to our demands then we will take the city by force of arms."

The seditious did not respond to this request and even yelled their insults at the general. For some unknown reason they were determined to fight on, and I believe they felt that God Himself would step forward and come to their aid and destroy the army before it entered the Temple.

I thought to the contrary. God's wrath was spoken by His son, Jesus, who stated that the God of the Jews would not allow their contempt to continue, and that the Temple would be destroyed and not one stone would be left on top of another when this terrific struggle was finished.

Titus was unable to bring the whole of his army against the Jews as they were scattered by legions around the city. Further, the opening in the wall of Fortress Antonio was too narrow to allow the whole army to assemble quickly and then proceed over to the ramp that led down to the Temple Mount. Therefore Titus had each centurion of the Tenth and Fifteenth Legions choose the best thirty fighting men from their one hundred and give them over to an attack force assembled for the taking of the Temple. Two nights after the last appeal to the seditious leaders and after the midnight, these handpicked men from each of the

243

legions quietly descended the ramp leading from the fortress down to the main floor of the Temple Mount.

The Temple Mount was attached to the fortress along its north wall. The Temple itself was located in the center of the mount and was in turn surrounded by a large court called the Court of the Gentiles. Around the outer perimeter of this court was a covered porch supported by ten-cubit tall marble columns that extended from the floor of the court to the roof. The covering over the porch was held in place by great wooden beams that supported a walkway on top of the roof, which also surrounded the entire perimeter of the Court of the Gentiles.

The Temple Mount was over five hundred paces long going north to south and then nearly three hundred and fifty paces deep on the east to west sides. The Temple sat in the middle of the Court of Gentiles with the main entrance facing to the east toward the Mount of Olives. Even though the Temple was on the floor of the mount surrounded by the Court of Gentiles, there was another wall that separated the inner courts and Temple itself from the open area of the court.

As it was dark I was unable to discern the action as it took place, but I do know that the noise of the battle was deafening. It wasn't until early daylight that I was able to make out any of the action. Only through the word of Aerius was I able to understand what had taken place, for he had come to visit with me the following night. It was after the dinnertime and sometime after the sun had set that he entered my little campsite near the outer wall of the Fortress of Antonio. He looked tired, but even that did not dampen his enthusiasm for the battle that had taken place earlier in the day. Before we could talk of loftier things, he started describing the events which had taken place.

"We had high hopes of finding the Jews asleep. We tried to enter the columns leading from the ramp out onto the Court of the Gentiles and from there onto the walls of the Temple. This planned surprise did not work because their guards were awake and waiting for us to attack.

"The Jews seemed to know our plans and were ready even when the first soldier stepped off of the ramp onto the marble floor of the outer court. With loud shouts they were upon us with a great clamor. Quickly a vast battle ensued, which resulted in hand-to-hand conflict between our soldiers and the soldiers of John's army. Other Jewish soldiers awakened by the shouts and cries of the battle poured out of the Temple gates and into the fray. The noise and darkness were so great that the men could not distinguish one another by the language or sight. The Jews were even attacking their own men as those rushing out of the Temple swung their swords at whomsoever was in front of them. We quickly formed our skirmish lines. The front line of pike men, kneeling with their shields held in front of them and their pikes anchored on the floor, were ready for the first onslaught of Jews. Many of these soldiers unable to see in the darkness were immediately skewered. Those running from the Temple to join the fight pushed their own men that were in front of them into our defensive line. Our line held against the initial assault and fell back only a few steps. Then our infantry stepped in front of the pike men with swords drawn and shields held high to fend off the enemy. This great battle continued for the rest of the night and on into the morning. I have to give credit to the Jews, for they fought valiantly and did not fall back a step to our attack. In the dark and as a result of their lack of organization, they killed many of their own men, for those pouring out of the Temple in the dark struck down any man who was in front of them whether they were Romans or Jews. I was in the center of the infantry with my hundred men. We were better able to distinguish friend against foe because all of us had the same watchword that could be used as a form of identification. As the men in front grew weary of the fighting, they would fall back, and the men behind would step forward and take their place.

"We knew that General Titus and his staff stood in the Antonio Tower cheering us on in our endeavors to take the Temple. Once the sun began its climb above the horizon, we were better able to assess our positions. This also provided the Jews with the same advantage, and their soldiers began to form up in skirmish ranks and attack us in a more organized fashion. So, on the Temple Mount two great armies fought tooth and nail for the Temple. If we could but take it the war would end soon. The Jews are now as determined to defend the Temple, as it represented to them their very faith. Neither side gave any ground as the battle raged on. The battle continued after the sun rose above the horizon. We all became weary; my arms felt as if I were holding large stones instead of my sword and shield. All of us were exhausted, and as if by mutual agreement the battle ended and we returned to our original positions. The floor of the Temple Mount was littered with the bodies of the dead and wounded."

Aerius hung his head a minute as though lost in thought before he added, "I have to give credit to the Jews for they fought fiercely today, and their faith in their God seems strong. It may take longer to defeat them than I had originally thought."

I nodded my agreement with his assessment and added, "The scoundrels in control of the city lack faith. However, those who have taken up arms, those who are not in league with John or Simon, still believe in the one God, the One they believe who still dwells in the Temple." I paused a moment then asked, "How is it with your faith, Aerius?"

He glared at me and without a word rose to his feet and started back to his tent. Speaking over his shoulder, he said, "I am tired, Caleb. I must get some sleep." And he was gone from my sight.

During the ensuing days, the Romans continued widening the opening in the wall of Fortress Antonio, removing stone from upon stone. Within a short time this gap was quite large, allowing them to secure both the narrow ramp that led from the court up to the fortress and two thirds of the northern end of the porch on that court. Once this task was finished they placed more troops on this northern perimeter of the court under the porch roof that protected them from the arrows and other missiles hurled at them by the Jews positioned on top of the walls that surrounded the Temple. In order for these soldiers to be safe from a Jewish frontal infantry attack, they began to build new banks on the floor of the court between the porch and the walls surrounding the outer Court of Israel that opened onto the Temple itself. The construction of the banks took several days as much of the material had to be brought in from over a great distance. The land that surrounds Jerusalem had been literally stripped of all its trees in order to build the banks used for the earlier fighting.

As the Romans continued to erect their banks, the Jews continued their attacks trying to delay the inevitable—the capture of the sacred Temple. They made frequent sorties against the workers who were building the fortifications as well as against the Romans who were hauling the materials for them. At other times they would steal the Roman horses that were grazing outside the walls. This, I suppose, was to use them for their food. General Titus became very upset with those soldiers caught leaving their animals unattended. Those who then lost those horses that were in their care would in turn lose their lives.

On the morning of the third day after the initial battle for the Court of Gentiles, a short time before sunrise, a large force of Jewish soldiers slipped out of the city, crossed the Kidron Valley and ascended the hill towards the Mount of Olives en route for the Tenth Legion's camp. I believe that it was their intent to catch the Romans off their guard and gain control of this strategic position. This was not to be. The guards detected the sound of the approaching enemy and sounded the alarm.

Another pitched battle took place. The Romans holding the higher ground had the advantage and were able to hold the Jews at bay. The enemies made repeated attempts to break through the Roman defenses, but were constantly driven back by the superior fighting skills of the soldiers of Rome. The Jews took heavy losses but continued with the attack, throwing themselves on the lances of the pike men in hopes that those who followed would be able to overwhelm the Romans. However, the Roman lines held.

Just before the sun peeked over the horizon, one final attempt was made by the Jews to break through the Tenth Legion's defenses. As before the challenge was repelled. When this final attempt failed, the Jews broke and began running back to the city with a number of the Tenth's cavalry in hot pursuit. A centurion in charge of the horsemen by the name of Pedanius led the charge against the enemy, who were at the time running pell-mell toward the city's gate from which they had come. Pedanius was a large powerfully-built man standing a little taller than me and an excellent horseman.

His powerful steed soon caught up with the stragglers of the Jewish army retreating towards the gate. Pedanius, without slowing, leaned way down out of the saddle of his horse and caught the first soldier he came upon running to the city. He grabbed this man by the ankle of his right foot, hoisted him up off of the ground and held him high by the ankle in his powerful left hand. No matter how hard this victim struggled, he could not shake himself free from the strong grasp of his captor.

Pedonius then took his captive to General Titus, who rewarded his centurion for his great skill and strength and ordered that the hapless Jew be put to death for being part of the attack against the Tenth Legion.

Time was growing short for the Jews of Jerusalem as the days seemed to fly by. At the time, the Romans continued with the construction of their banks on the floor of the Court of Gentiles. Before the banks were completed, we were already into the first week of July. The Jews were fighting out of desperation, for I am sure that at that time their food supplies, or what were left of them, were rapidly dwindling down to nothing. Their frequent attacks were reckless, and many of their soldiers gave their bodies up to the Romans in headlong assaults against the banks. I truly believe that many of them threw their lives away in order to put an end to the misery they had been suffering during the long months of this siege.

After their final assault on the Tenth Legion on the Mount of Olives, the Jews concentrated their attacks on the banks the Romans were building north of the Temple on the Court of the Gentiles. On the second of July the northeastern cloister, the columned barrier that separated the Court of Gentiles from the Fortress of Antonio and that was still in their control, was set on fire probably at the order of John or Simon. They then allowed the roof, which was constructed of wood, burn all along that corner from the Temple Mount and around the eastern perimeter to about eighteen cubits east of the fortress's southern wall. This allowed the Jews to see the Romans better if they dared to sneak under the roof in order to attack their flank from the eastern edge of the court.

In the days that followed, the attacks continued, with the Jews constantly expending their energies to overturn the banks that the Romans were building. The Romans were ever on their guard to prevent the Jewish soldiers from breaching these defensive positions. The deaths and injuries were great on both sides, but the Jews, because of the desperate straits they were in, lost a greater number of men.

My service, as an interpreter to the Romans, left me well apprised of the war. I was encamped near the fighting, and from my vantage point in the fortress I was able to view the daily battles. When called upon by Aerius to interview the captured prisoners, I heard many tales of woe. They told stories of wounded prisoners who were dying from infection and gangrene. As there was little fresh water or bandages, many of the injured went to the extreme of having their limbs, hands, feet, arms or legs amputated before serious infections could develop, in order that they would not die of these terrible afflictions that were brought on by disease and decay.

With the beginning of each day, I would start my prayers with a petition to God to bring this terrible conflict to an end and that He would imbue the rebel leaders with the wisdom to give up and open the city to the Romans. This was not God's plan, for the war continued and many combatants on both sides died. Both the Roman and Jewish soldiers fought as if they had a desire for the fighting to continue. From the Roman standpoint, it was a desire to capture the city and an ever-growing hatred for the Jews and their fanaticism. For the Jews, it was a struggle for their very existence. I feel that they knew that they would be enslaved if they were defeated, and to them death was preferable to captivity. I felt deeply for the Jews for I was born one, and I desired to see them a free and proud people again. However, without the destruction of the seditious leaders, that was not going to happen.

There was a Jew by the name of Jonathan who came forth early one morning after the sun had risen and challenged the Romans to a one-on-one contest to the death. Jonathan was not a very big man and was of appalling appearance. His face was badly scarred with pox, probably from a childhood disease, and his hair was long and scraggly. His clothes were torn and ill fitting. He stood out before the Roman banks, calling upon them to send out a soldier to fight him man-to-man. When no one stepped forth, he cursed them, called them cowards, and profaned the name of the emperor and all of those who claimed to be of Roman birth. Next he accused all who fought with the Romans to be terrible cowards and unworthy of any respect.

This tirade by Jonathan went on and on. I knew that the soldiers of Rome didn't want to go out against him for it would gain them nothing. However as the name calling became more specific and degrading, one of the horse soldiers attached to the Fifth Legion leaped out from behind the protection of the banks and ran out to face this despicable character. In his rush to meet this adversary, carrying his shield in his left hand and his sword with his right, he slipped on the marble floor of the Court of Gentiles and fell onto his back. Before he could regain his feet, Jonathan was upon him and slit his throat.

As the soldier lay dead on the floor of the court, Jonathan exalted his prowess by jumping on the body of his victim and continuing to shout insults at the soldiers behind the banks. As this contemptible character was prancing about in his moment of triumph, an archer atop the banks drew an arrow on his bow and with careful aim let it fly, piercing Jonathan through the heart. He clutched his chest and then fell dead upon the body of the Roman he'd killed just minutes earlier. The fortunes of war always seem to lead to death.

At this point in the battle for the Temple Mount, the Romans controlled the northern portion of the Court of the Gentiles, from the wall of Fortress Antonio to their banks that were located just outside and parallel along the northern wall that surrounded the inner courts, the Women's Court, the Court of Israel and the Temple itself. The remaining part of the Court of the Gentiles, that which was located south of the Roman banks along the western, southern and eastern porches and of course the Temple walls and all inside of them, remained in the hands of the Jews.

It was at this time that General Titus ordered his troops to continue building their defensive banks against this northern wall that protected the Temple. This was done in anticipation of bringing the battering ram against this final structure that stood in the way of taking control of the Temple itself. The construction of the banks turned out to be a slow process since the Romans had to bring materials even farther out from the city than before. Further, the Romans were on their guard against vicious attacks upon their construction crews throughout the days and nights by the Jews. This stalemate lasted for four days involving light fighting as each side tried to solidify their positions.

On the fifth day of July, conditions of the stalemate changed. The Romans were nearly finished with the building of the banks and were preparing to bring their machines of war out onto the Court of the Gentiles. The Jews had not stood quietly by as the construction proceeded. They had devised a strategy whereby they could draw the Romans into a trap.

As I've told you, there was a raised portico that surrounded the entire Temple Mount. This structure stood quite high above the floor of the Court of the Gentiles. There was a walkway atop the portico that had been used by the Romans in the early days of the century whereby troops stood on this raised causeway in order to keep peace among the Jews during their celebrations. The Roman soldiers would come down the ramp from Fortress Antonio onto this walkway and stand above the crowds that filled the Temple Mount during these festivals.

At this particular juncture in the siege, the Romans controlled only the northern part of the portico and a short distance along the western part of the mount. The rest of the Temple Mount, its walkway including Solomon's Porch, and along the east side of the mount were in the hands of the Jewish defenders.

Late in the evening before the sun set, the Jews started withdrawing their troops from the upper walkway of the porch all along the western wall. The Jews, slowly and under the protection of additional soldiers who had come from the safety of the walls that surrounded the Temple, began to move away from the walkway, across the Court of the Gentiles and on into the gate that led into the Court of Israel and the Temple.

A large number of Roman troops who witnessed this withdrawal and without orders from their commanders rushed from the security of the banks and immediately went to the upper walkway to claim it in the name of Rome.

Unbeknownst to the Romans, this was a well planned trap. For below the floor of the walkway, which was supported on top of tall stone pillars by great wooden beams, the Jews had placed pitch, bitumen and other flammable materials between the beams. Once a great number of Romans were on the walkway, an individual came out from hiding and set the materials beneath the platform on fire.

The blaze took hold rapidly, and great flames soon shot up from beneath the structure, engulfing the hapless soldiers. As the fires grew and continued to consume the supports for the walkway, many of the soldiers began to jump off of the burning timber and down into the lower city where they perished from their injuries. Others tried to jump from the walkway onto the floor of the Court of the Gentiles. Here they were immediately set upon by the Jews who held this part of the court. Those who were not seriously injured from the jump tried to fight off the Jews. They were soon overpowered and slain as were those who had sustained injuries jumping that great a distance dressed in their armor and holding swords and shields.

This battle continued to rage as the fires consumed the wood and all of the Romans who had rushed out without orders to take this western portion of the Court of the Gentiles. The walkway and timbers of the portico soon collapsed and fell to the floor. A large number of Roman soldiers now lay dead on that floor or below the western wall down in the lower city. The soldiers who did not rush out with their comrades were unable to lend support to those who perished. The Jews had not only cut off the path of retreat to those who climbed the ladders to the upper walkway, but had established a defensive line of soldiers who had re-emerged from the Temple, preventing the Romans still behind the banks from coming out.

These events continued to inspire the rabble to persist in their struggle against Rome. Each little victory that they were able to achieve seemed to convince them that the Lord at last had come to their aid.

As their confidence grew from this event, they devised a plan to burn more of the walkway. More than two hundred cubits of the portico had burned during this latest battle resulting in the death of over one hundred of the Empire's soldiers. The Jews then went around from under Solomon's Porch on the east to the walkway along the northern wall and set that portion on fire which had not already been burned and which bordered the fortress. This was done in hopes that it would prevent the Romans from bringing materials from there out to the embankment they were still building along the wall that separated the Court of the Gentiles from the Court of Israel, which in turn surrounded the Temple itself. This incendiary act was committed during the darkest part of the night and proved to be highly successful. However, all of the Jews who had undertaken this endeavor were either captured or slain.

Those who were captured were first interrogated and then most of them were executed. However, some, who it was confirmed had been compelled to fight by the rogue John, were imprisoned. Those who were interrogated by Aerius and whose tales I interpreted told of the gruesome conditions that persisted in the Temple and that portion of the city which was still in Jewish control. Almost all of the food supply was gone and most of the water was badly contaminated. The weaker citizens, mainly the maimed and elderly, had died, and there were constant battles among those who remained over whatever food that could be scrounged up. All of the cats and dogs had been slaughtered and eaten, and any rodent that was caught was swiftly cooked and consumed. There were consistent reports of cannibalism. One report that was particularly disturbing was that of a women who had eaten her own child. Oh, the depths of depravity to which some of God's chosen people had fallen.

The fighting continued both day and night, interrupted only when the combatants became so weary they would, by what seemed to be mutual agreement, retire to their respective camps to rest before sallying forth and beginning the process all over again. Day after day and night after night, they would come forth and meet out on the Court of the Gentiles, fighting tooth and nail in order to slay their adversary and thus protect the Temple or for the Romans to protect the embankments they were building ever closer to the walls that surrounded the inner courts and the Temple.

Each day the Romans would take control of a little more of the court. Early on they won control of the northwest corner from their banks back to the portion of court that bordered the fortress. From there they were able to extend their control all along the northern cloister up and to nearly 60 cubits from the eastern wall—that portion which the Jews had burned at the beginning of the battle. Next, the Romans were able to gain control of the entire western section of the Court of Gentiles, from the wall around the Temple out to and including the porch, its columns and roof. From there they extended their holdings to include the southern wall and much of the southwestern cloister up to about thirty or fifty cubits short of the inner wall surrounding the Temple and its courts. Each time that the Romans were able to seize a new segment of the Court of Gentiles from the Jews, their engineers would immediately start constructing the protective banks until the embankment surrounded nearly three sides of the Temple.

By the twenty-third day of July, all of the Court of the Gentiles was in the hands of the Romans. The banks had been completed, and the great battering rams had finally been brought forward in order to begin breaking through the wall that separated the Court of the Gentiles from the Court of Israel and the other inner and most sacred courts, the tabernacle itself and the altars used for burning the sacrifices. This wall extended from the eastern end of the Temple Mount, out and around the inner courts, the Temple and back to the eastern wall. The whole of this part of the Temple Mount was now surrounded by Roman troops on all three sides as they stood in Court of the Gentiles readying for the final assault. Inside these walls that only the devout Jew could enter waited the enemies of Rome, who were prepared to give their lives for the defense of their beloved shrine.

Early in the morning of the twenty-fourth, the order was given for the rams to commence their work of breaking through the wall. The Roman machines battered at the dense stone for six days to no avail, for these walls had been so well constructed that not a boulder budged or broke loose. The stones that made up the wall were huge and so well fitted to each of its neighbors that nothing like a mere battering ram was able to shake them or even move them in the slightest. As the assault team worked with the rams, another team tried to undermine the gate on the north side. Even though the outer stones around the outside were removed, the gate remained in place, held in position by the inner stones. The Romans failed to break through and gain entrance to the inner sanctum.

During the battering and work on the gate, the Jews harassed the Romans with their darts, arrows and rocks. They also mounted frequent attacks from secret or hidden gates within or below the wall, wreaking havoc with the teams trying to breach the wall and gates.

After failing in the attempt to bring down the wall and penetrate the gate, the Romans brought forth a large force with ladders that would allow them to climb to the top of the fortification and break into the Temple from above.

The Jews watched patiently as the Romans crossed the Court of the Gentiles and then placed their ladders against the walls. Once done, the infantry mounted the ladders and began to climb to the top, three to five men at a time on the ladders. As the Romans climbed, the defenders brought forth long forked end timbers that were caught on the top rung of the ladders and then they pushed the ladders away from the wall and over backwards causing considerable death and injury to the attacking force. Those that were particularly close to the top fell a great distance to their deaths.

Against other Romans who mounted the ladders, large caldrons of flaming oil were poured down, consuming the ladders and killing more of the attackers. Other Jews would run and catch the top of the ladder and jump from the wall, carrying the Romans and themselves to their deaths on the hard floor below.

This was a terrific struggle, and many on both sides lost their lives. The Jews were willing to die in defense of their sacred Temple and poured every ounce of their being into its defense. The Romans, being unable to breach the wall, began to retire back to their original positions, leaving the floor of the court littered with the bodies of the wounded and the dead. During this retreat, the Jews were able to gain possession of the ladders and of the battering rams, which they destroyed and then burned. They also came into possession of a few of the other machines of war and set these afire as well. Worst of all, they then killed the wounded Romans around base of the wall before retiring back inside the Temple walls. This was a great slaughter for both sides, and at the end of the daylong battle, both sides retained the same positions they had held just the day before.

I am able to tell you of these things as I had been allowed to enter the fortress and was therefore able to view the battle from atop of one of its walls that faced the Court of the Gentiles.

Once the Roman soldiers retired back to their own lines, General Titus gave orders for a select team of men to set fire to the northern gate. This was to take place at the darkest part of the night. As we waited for the fires to be set, I was summoned by Aerius, for my skills as an interpreter were once again in demand. Many enemy troops who were trying to escape had been captured during the recent battle. Again we heard the same story of the depredation the citizens of Jerusalem were suffering. Most of these escapees reported that they had been forced to fight the Romans through the strongarm tactics of the rogues Simon and John. They all stated that if they had not fought, they or their loved ones would have been killed. However, now that those dear to them had either starved to death or been assassinated, there was no longer any reason for them to remain in the city. Further, because of the amnesty offered by Titus to those who crossed over the line, they had chosen to defect and get out of what was to them the ultimate destruction of Jerusalem and their own deaths.

Shortly after the middle of the night, I saw a small fire begin around the northern gate. It then apparently went out for I was unable to see any light emanating from that spot after five or ten minutes. My thoughts were that the fire went out on its on accord or that those sent to start the fire were caught and the Jews extinguished the flame. I then went to my mat, said my prayers and fell fast asleep.

I was awakened in the early predawn light by shouts from some Roman sentries in the Antonio Tower.

"Fire," they yelled. "The gate is on fire!"

I jumped up from my bed and raced to a window that overlooked the northern wall of the Temple. There before me in the predawn light, I could see smoke billowing up from the bottom of the gate and drifting high above the wall. Soon I was also able to discern some flames along the bottom, which quickly took hold and began leaping up towards the top.

As I watched, the blaze seemed to gather momentum with each passing second and rapidly the entire gate was engulfed. Apparently, the wood beneath the gold and silver gilt that adorned the gate had smoldered for a long time before the flames took hold.

The whole of the armies, both Jews and Romans, were mesmerized by the fire, as no one from the Jewish side took any steps to extinguish the flames. All day long the gates burned, for the wood in them was extremely thick. Late in the afternoon the wooden walkway on the Jewish side and near the top of the wall caught fire, and it, too, started to burn.

I learned later through Aerius that as the flames consumed the gate and the adjoining walkway, General Titus had gathered all of his commanders for a meeting in order to determine the next course of action that they should follow. His second-in-command, the commander of the entire army, each commander of each legion and each of the prefects in charge of the different districts of Israel and Syria were all in attendance. The big question before the group was: should they destroy the Temple or let it remain standing? If it were to remain unscathed, it would always be a rallying point for the Jews, even after the war. On the other hand, it was a magnificent structure that would be shameful to destroy. After a long debate, General Titus decided that it would be best to preserve the Temple, and therefore ordered that the structure not be burned. He then directed his commanders to form a special team of men to go out and extinguish the flames that were consuming the north gate and the adjoining cloisters.

These fires burning around the Temple walls were of great concern for the Jews who had found refuge inside the walls and inside the Holy House itself. They found that the Roman noose was ever tightening, and I'm sure felt that the day of their defeat must be near unless their God would deliver them from the hands of their oppressors. That was beginning to seem unlikely.

Soon after the Roman conclave had terminated, a new prisoner was brought before General Titus. This man was recognized as a deputy to Simon himself and was well known for his heavy-handed treatment of the Jews inside Jerusalem. His name was Ananus. He was feared by most of the Jews because he had been responsible for the torture and death of many of his own people.

As Titus's interpreter was on an errand for the general, I was summoned by Aerius and brought before Titus himself to do the interpreting for this man. When I entered the room in Fortress Antonio, Ananus was sitting on the floor facing General Titus and four members his staff. Aerius led me to a place in front of the prisoner and introduced me to the general as an interpreter who spoke Latin, Aramaic and Greek. I had never been this close to the general before, and I was impressed by his regal bearing. There was no doubt in my mind that he was the one in charge. He was shorter than I had imagined, for I had only seen him at a distance. He had the typical Roman nose and dark, almost pitch black hair that curled slightly from his forehead around and a little above the ears to the back of his head. He was clean shaven and spoke in a soft yet commanding voice. Though he was just a shade shorter than I, he was broad shouldered and powerfully built, giving him the appearance of a much larger man. He was dressed in a white tunic over which he wore bronze armor and attached to that body armor at the shoulders was a red cape. The general nodded to me after my introduction and motioned for me to interpret his words to the prisoner. I bowed slightly before the general and then went down on my knees in front of the prisoner ready to put the questions to him in his native tongue, Aramaic.

From the outset, it was apparent to me as well as to the general and his staff that this man was contemptuous of the Romans. Further I was able to discern that he had given himself up as he knew the Jews were beaten, and he didn't want to be slaughtered with those who continued to fight. He then spoke of the amnesty offered to all Jews who came over to the Romans.

At the mention of this, I could see that the general was highly agitated by this request. "Why should I not have you put to death for the dastardly deeds you have committed upon your own people?" Titus asked.

I then interpreted the question in Aramaic to Ananus. He thought for a moment and I could see for the first time doubt enter his mind. I didn't think that he was aware of the fact that the Romans knew of the oppressive actions he'd committed against his own people.

"But sir," he replied, "I have done nothing other than try to convince our leaders that it would be fruitless for us not to surrender to the power of Rome. My attitude from the beginning has been to let you into the city and surrender control to you, so that we might go on with our lives, praising and worshiping our God."

It was easy for me to see that he was lying as he quickly regained his confidence. I interpreted his words exactly as he spoke them without comment.

"I have heard it said," Titus continued, "that you have become very wealthy by confiscating all of the wealth of your victims and that you have stashed that wealth away in a vault below the city in order to come back after the war and retrieve it." The general then motioned for me to interpret his words to Ananus.

When I had finished repeating the general's word Ananus was struck dumb for a short time, like a child caught in a lie to his parents. Finally, he replied. "Oh great and powerful, you have been misinformed. I have not profited by this conflict; to the contrary, I have lost everything."

"I know that you came to Jerusalem from Galilee and brought nothing with you so you have lost nothing. I also know of the cruelties you have committed on your own people, unspeakable atrocities. I therefore condemn you to death."

I looked at Ananus as I repeated these words to him and saw for the first time fear fill his whole being and again he was struck dumb. I looked back at the general and noticed that one of his commanders was whispering in his ear. After the man had spoken to the general, Titus put the elbow of his right arm on his left arm that he held across his lower chest and twisted his lip with his right hand as he thought. Then he spoke slowly and deliberately. "Tell Ananus that because I had promised amnesty to all who crossed over to us from the Jewish side I will spare him his life. I will not be called a liar. However, that is all I will do, for it is my opinion that he should die, but because of my promise he will live the rest of his life as a prisoner of Rome." He then looked to his guards and said, "Take him and give him fifteen lashes and then throw him in the stockade."

When I had interpreted these words to Ananus his face lit up, but when he realized that he would be in prison for life and that he was to suffer a beating with the infamous Roman whip, he threw his hands to his face and wept.

Titus and his commanders turned and left as guards came forward and lifted the prisoner to his feet and dragged him away. As I sat on my knees looking after him I felt a tug on my arm. Aerius had come forward to help me to my feet and lead me back to my shelter.

As we walked that short distance, Aerius said, "I have been chosen by the general himself to lead a select cohort to go and put the fires out. It truly is an honor. The reason is that Titus does not want to be seen as the man who caused this great tabernacle to be destroyed. It is therefore our duty to keep the fires from reaching the wood that is within the Holy House itself."

"But wouldn't that give the Jews a rallying point?" I protested. "Isn't this a sign to them that they cannot be defeated and that their God is still protecting them?"

"That's the general's decision. I will only carry out his orders," Aerius replied as he dropped me off at my shelter and then continued on his way to command the cohort that would try to put out the fires.

As he walked away, I suddenly realized that it was I who was defending the destruction of the Temple by my questions to Aerius. I concluded, in my own mind, that my hatred for the tyrants Simon and John had led me to the conclusion that the Temple should be destroyed because of the way that all of the Jewish leadership had turned their backs on God. "Cannot man stop questioning the truth about their creator and accept on faith what He has given them?" I said to myself as I went to my knees in prayer to ask for forgiveness for wishing that His Holy Tabernacle be destroyed.

The special manipuli led by Aerius had great difficulty in quenching the fires. They were able to subdue the flames to some extent but couldn't put them out entirely since much of the burning and smoldering of the heavy wood was taking place inside the Temple walls, especially near the northern gate. The Jews were in a disturbed state and did little to prevent the Romans from trying to extinguish those flames in and around the gate for to let the gate burn would allow the Romans to enter that much sooner. At the same time the Jewish soldiers worked at putting the fires out inside the walls, but their hearts weren't into the task. It was difficult to stop the burning as water from the Gihon Spring was in short supply. So much of the wood under the stone of the cloisters and the metal of the gates continued to smolder on into the night and the next day. There was a constant pale of smoke that hung over the Temple and as I learned later that the smoke could be seen from great distances from areas around Jerusalem. Those who saw it from far off viewed it as the end of greatness for God's chosen people and the end of Israel itself.

Once Aerius and his men withdrew from the walls that surrounded the Temple in the late afternoon, other Roman soldiers set out from the banks and encircled three sides of the Temple to keep the Jews closed in behind its walls. The Court of the Gentiles was solidly in Roman control around three sides—the north, the west and the south. It was these three sides that the soldiers guarded. Each man was heavily armored and each carried a large shield and broad sword.

Early in the morning some time before sunrise, I heard a loud and continued uproar in the court. I rushed to the wall of the fortress and peered out through a window onto the Court of the Gentiles. There in the moonlight, I could discern a great number of Jews pouring out of an eastern gate in a determined effort to drive the Romans from the court. The Roman squadrons soon came together to meet this threat by forming a solid line shoulder to shoulder with their shields held in front of them in one hand and their drawn swords in the other. It presented the Jews with a formidable wall, and many of them fell wounded or dead in front of the shields. Soon their number began to overwhelm the Romans, and they began to fall back in an organized fashion while maintaining their shields as a defense and preventing their adversaries from overrunning them. Slowly they fell back to the west and along the north side of the court. The soldiers who were guarding the south side quickly came to their aid and helped to bolster the sagging line. The Jewish soldiers rapidly outnumbered the defenders, and I felt that soon the Romans might be overwhelmed. It was at this time, though, I heard the sharp thunder of horses as a troop of cavalry galloped down a ramp from the Fortress of Antonio and out onto the Court of Gentiles. The pounding hooves of the horses could be heard above the other sounds of the battle. Without hesitation the horsemen drove their steeds into the flank of the Jewish soldiers. The horsemen had their swords drawn and quickly dispatched those Jews who were unfortunate enough to be unable to move out of the way of the charging cavalry.

Quickly the tide of battle changed as the Jewish attackers ran back towards the gate. As the lines separated with the withdrawal of the Jews and the Romans withdrew back from the skirmish lines, the sounds of battle diminished. However, when the Jews saw that they were not being pursued and instead the Romans were also falling back from the fight, they stopped, hesitated a moment, and then charged yet another time into the Roman force. The fervor of the battle increased as the Jews rushed the Romans. The sound of swords clanging against one another, the clash of shields parrying swords, and the dull sound of thrown rocks finding a target once again filled the air. The horsemen, who had retired back to the ramp, turned their animals around and charged back into the Jewish flank. This time the Jews held their ground, and the battle continued unabated for another period of time shorter than the first encounter.

Many men were wounded or struck down onto the cold, hard, marble floor of the Court of the Gentiles, never to rise again. Finally as the sun rose above the horizon, both sides, tiring from the encounter, began to withdraw back to their lines to lick their wounds. Before the morning sun peered over the eastern wall the battle was over. The medics from both sides began to carefully clear the floor of their own dead and wounded, and by the middle of the morning it appeared as if nothing had transpired at all.

When the battle was over, I felt a great wave of fatigue overwhelm me. I returned to my mat in order to get some sleep, but to no avail. Many thoughts raced through my mind. What of the future? Were the Jews to be totally annihilated or carried off into captivity? Was the Promised Land no longer to be theirs? What of my own future? Would I ever be a free man again? Would I be allowed to leave and go back to Philadelphia once the war was finished as I had been promised?

There were so many unanswered questions. My thoughts then went back to the events that had transpired since the time of the crucifixion of Jesus—my marriage and my work as a missionary. I hadn't thought of my family for a long time. I lay down on my mat very depressed and I wished for those days that have gone by, especially my wish was for the company of my wife and daughter.

PRICILLA AND SARA

My apprenticeship as a tentmaker under the tutelage of my uncle drew to a close nearly three years after starting. It was at this time in my training that my father and mother traveled to my uncle's house in Emmaus. I hadn't seen them for nearly eight months since the earlier part of the year, during Passover, when I'd traveled to Jerusalem to spend that time of celebration with them. When my parents arrived in Emmaus, we had a festive reunion and spent several days catching up on the news of the events taking place in Jerusalem. My father was as relaxed and outgoing as I had ever known him to be. He seemed happy with the way things in his life were going, and his only serious concern was over the conditions with the Pharisees and the troubling way they were leading the faithful.

The Messiah had been crucified less than two years earlier, and now the Jewish leaders had began to persecute those who believed in Him. Their vehement hatred of Jesus led them to commit many crimes against the believers. Many were arrested and imprisoned for short periods of time and many were ostracized from Jewish society. It was soon after the first year following His death that the heaviest hand of persecution fell upon the followers of Jesus. A Pharisee, by the name of Saul, began rounding up believers and putting them in jail. His strong-armed tactics brought fear into the hearts of the believers, and, as a result, we, the faithful, began to meet in secret.

Whenever my father and my uncle got together, it was usually a good time as they would reminisce over the days of their youth; that is, when they weren't speaking of the Jewish leadership and their heavy-handed methods. I had never known that my father was not always a stern and somewhat harsh disciplinarian, at least not until I heard them talk of the trouble they got into as young boys; it was enlightening.

When my parents were readying themselves for their return to Jerusalem, my father pulled me aside and told me that he had accepted the fact that Jesus was the true Messiah and that he and my mother had become followers of The Way.

I was delighted by this conversion and felt relieved by his acceptance of Jesus, for it gave me a warm feeling to know that we were now of the same thinking. We discussed his acceptance at some length. He said it was the scriptures of old that had led him to believe that Jesus of Nazareth was the promised Messiah who the prophets had written about so many years earlier. For the first time, we had a deep and philosophical dialogue, one that made me feel his equal rather than an errant son.

After a moment of silence, I said, "Uncle has not yet declared Jesus as the Chosen One. My friend Cleopas and I have many times told him of the work of Jesus, and he just keeps putting off a decision. Each time that Cleopas returned from one of his visits with Jesus and his followers, he would tell me and Uncle of the miracles or of the things that Jesus said. Uncle always listened to what was said and even asked questions, but he never made a commitment. I want so much for him to see the truth. I pray daily for him to declare his faith and acknowledge the same truth you and mother have accepted. It seems to be so difficult for him to change from the old ways."

"My brother has always had a stubborn streak in him," my father said. "However your mother and I have talked about this with him, and I believe that he is nearly ready to declare his faith in Jesus. He told me that you and your friend had talked often of Jesus and the miracles that you saw him perform, but that he found it difficult to change. Your uncle may have a wonderful sense of humor and he has enjoyed talking with you and Cleopas about Jesus, but he is finding it difficult to change his ways. Give him time, Caleb, and I think you will see him as a follower sooner than you think."

My father fell silent for a moment. When he started talking again, he dropped the next piece of news on me. "Your mother and I have struck up a friendship with another believer and his wife who have become close friends of ours. This man is devout, and he, like me, was trained in the ways of the Lord. We have spent many days together studying the scriptures of the prophets of old, and each of us, independent of the other, has come to the same conclusion that Jesus was truly the Son of God and the One who came to deliver His people Israel from their sinful ways.

"How wonderful it is, Caleb, that we are now one, you and I, in our thinking."

"Oh father," I exclaimed, "you don't know how long I've prayed for this. Mother too?"

"Yes, your mother, too," he answered. "But the good news I haven't told you about yet is that my new friend, Simeon, has a daughter." Father paused a moment and gave me a loving look before he continued. "Simeon and I have arranged for you and her to be married."

I was dumbfounded at the news. All I could utter was, "Married? Me?"

"Yes, you are at the age that you should take a wife, and we feel that the two of you will be a match made in heaven. You and Pricilla will be married next month," he continued. "I have talked to your uncle, and he is pleased with the way you have learned the business and feels that you are ready to start out on your own in Jerusalem."

I gulped and felt a little faint. I couldn't think of a thing to say except to repeat the words I had just said. "Married, me?"

"I have met her, Caleb, and I can tell you that she is five years younger than your twenty-two years and that she is a believer."

"Married?" I repeated again and then asked, "Is...is she pretty?"

"Yes, she is pretty," my mother said as she came up behind me. "She is a lovely girl, and I'm sure you will quickly fall in love with her."

"She has a fine mind and is quite outspoken about her faith," my father added.

After my parents left that day, time seemed to fly by.

There were so many things that had to be done. A place for us to live, for me to work and the materials for the business had to be purchased. It was an endless chain of details that needed to be worked out, all before the upcoming wedding.

Parting with my uncle was difficult, for we had grown very close over those years that I had spent with him. Out of generosity, he gave me many of the tools and materials I would need for my own business. However, the really good news was that his son, now fourteen, was old enough to start learning the trade and thus would fill the void when I left to start work in Jerusalem.

The time for the wedding arrived, and the marriage was a grand affair. I did see Priscilla a few days before the wedding. We got along well, though we both were somewhat shy and conversation did not come easily at first. This had been a chance meeting, and as soon as we realized that we were the ones matched for each other by our fathers for the upcoming wedding, we quickly said our goodbyes. I had been immediately taken by her beauty. She was tall for a woman and slender with long black hair that fell to her waist. She had dark piercing eyes, high cheekbones and olive skin. Her lips were full and red, and she possessed white and well-formed teeth. I was immediately smitten by her charm, dreamed of her often and became impatient for the wedding. I felt especially blessed, for I didn't feel worthy of one so beautiful. Because of my height, nearly four cubits, and somewhat awkward ways and plain appearance, I just didn't feel worthy of such a wife.

The wedding was a large affair, for many of our relatives came to Jerusalem for the big event. Even my cousin Timothy and his wife, now with three children, traveled along with my aunt and uncle down from Cana for the ceremony. My other uncle and aunt from Emmaus were also there and proudly paid for the feast and took over the job of finding places for all of the out of town guests to stay. It was a grand event, but it all ended too quickly. Before we knew it, we were alone in our own place, and I was busily involved in setting up my trade. Soon though, both Pricilla and I adjusted to a whole new way of life. Not only were we man and wife, but best friends.

We immediately devoted our lives to the development of our faith and reached out to those who did not believe, to other believers and to all who were in need. We were even fortunate enough to either meet or to see and listen to those apostles of Jesus who had known him well. These men had been changed. Instead of being merely followers, they had become powerful leaders of the faith. They said that after our Lord had ascended into heaven, a power came to them that was called the Spirit of the Lord. It was through this spirit that they were able to better understand what it was that Jesus had taught during his life when he was still with us. This Spirit had also interpreted the words of the prophets as they applied to his coming.

We met most of all in secret, in homes of the believers, for our greatest fear was of the Jewish leaders, who on nothing more than a whim might have us arrested. Even in view of the threat from the Jews, many new converts came to join us by accepting the faith. The numbers of our following grew rapidly. It wasn't long before the Pharisees grew more purposeful in their persecutions. One in particular comes to mind, a man I mentioned before, named Saul of Tarsus. He was passionate in his resolve to completely obliterate our faith. He said publicly and vehemently that "…this viper's nest of followers of the so-called Messiah Jesus must be eliminated."

We all feared him for his zealousness, which led him to extreme measures to search us out and to dissuade us from our faith. He felt that we would destroy the purity of Judaism. These were troubling times for the believers. It was this same Saul who had held the cloaks of the men who had thrown the stones and rocks that led to the death of a wonderful man, a disciple named Stephen. I came to fear this Saul, and though it was not right with our faith, I hated him for what he was doing to the fellowship of believers in Jerusalem.

Saul was an educated Pharisee with a quick mind and a sharp tongue. I felt that it would not be long before he attained the position of high priest of the Temple. It was his zeal for power and authority that drove him to travel to Damascus to persecute the believers there. With a bodyguard of other Jews and even some Roman soldiers, they left one hot morning by horseback for the long journey. During the last day of their trip, when they were just a short distance from Damascus, Saul was struck by a vision that only he was able to view. His traveling companions saw only a bright, intense light. I later learned that Saul had had a personal confrontation with our risen Lord, Jesus of Nazareth. The other members of his entourage saw nothing but heard sounds and voices that made little sense to them. The result of this confrontation was that Saul was left blind and had to be led into the city.

He was taken to a house of a believer, and there spent several days trying to recover from the event. Another believer in Damascus also had had a vision at the same time as Saul's and was told to go to the house in which Saul was staying and to bless him in the name of our risen Lord. This he did, and Saul's vision returned along with a strong and unshakable faith in the Savior.

Saul's mindset changed immediately, and he miraculously became a believer in the divinity of Jesus. So convinced was he of this that he straightway began preaching powerfully trying to convince the Jews that Jesus was truly the Messiah and that he truly was the Holy One who had come to save them from their sinful and wicked ways.

Most of the followers of The Way doubted this astounding conversion and still feared Saul. The Jewish leadership of Damascus, to the contrary, realized that he had changed and began to fear that he might pollute the minds of the other Jews and convince them to follow Jesus. As a result, the great persecutor, Saul, became the persecuted, and he had to go into hiding, into a home of one of the believers.

Only through the quick action of another believer, a great evangelist named Ananias, was Saul able to escape from Damascus. Late one night Ananias and some friends lowered Saul in a basket through a window in the wall of the city to the ground outside the gate and from there took him back to Jerusalem.

There he was introduced to the apostles and other disciples of Jesus. Many still were not convinced of his sincerity and remained doubtful of Saul's motives. I was one of these. However, another great disciple, a man called Barnabas, stood before the leaders and defended Saul as a true convert to the faith. It wasn't until much later that I was convinced of Saul's true faith in Jesus as the Messiah.

I heard Saul speak on more than one occasion, and his words were always an inspiration. However, my doubt and that of many others forced Saul to return to his native home in Tarsus, where he remained for nearly eight years.

During these turbulent times, I was reunited with my friend Cleopas. He had been active in preaching the word to the Jews and the Samaritans in the north, trying to convince them of their need to repent of their sins and commit themselves to Jesus as the Messiah.

Shortly after Saul left Jerusalem for Tarsus, Cleopas returned to the city to tell the other disciples of his success in bringing new converts to the faith. We had a wonderful reunion, and he spent nearly a week in our home. Pricilla was taken by his love for the Lord, and we both enjoyed listening to his stories of his work. While he was with us, he introduced me to a man from Cypress, whose name had originally been Joseph but now he went by Barnabas, the one I just told you about.

He was a wonderful person with the love of the Lord in his heart. He was a man of medium height and what I'd call rotund in stature, with thick black curly hair and beard. He was always laughing, and the moment he entered a room filled with people, you could hear his laughter above all the noise of the others. He had an infectious personality, and everyone crowded around him to hear him tell humorous stories of his mission trips. He was a great encourager, and after talking with him I always came away with a new feeling of hope and confidence.

After spending a week with us, Cleopas set out on another mission trip that took him further north and east into lands outside Judea. I was sorry to see him go, and he had encouraged me to join him. I wanted to go but knew in my heart that I needed to stay in Jerusalem for Pricilla's sake and for the sake of my business, which was going well but needed my constant attention. There was also much to be done in uniting the members of The Way as our number of believers continued to grow, despite the persecution from the Jewish religious leaders.

It was during this time that we learned that Pricilla was pregnant. I was elated over the prospect that I would at last have a son, for I was sure that the child would be a boy. I fanaticized over his future and thought of the great things he would do in the name of the Lord. On the other hand, Pricilla thought that the child would be a girl. This only added confusion to my dreams. For what events could a woman accomplish in this man's world? Then I remembered that it was a woman who had brought the Lord Jesus into the world, so maybe there were things a daughter could accomplish. Secretly, though, I still hoped that the child would be a boy.

During the last trimester of Pricilla's pregnancy, she began to experience some difficulties and once nearly lost the child. I was devastated and fervently prayed to God that the gender of the baby didn't matter as long as he, or she, was born hale and hearty and that Pricilla would regain her health. The midwife who attended to her was fearful that we might lose both the mother and child and demanded that Pricilla spend the last three months in a very limited and a reduced stress role in her household capacity. At last the fateful day arrived, and Pricilla gave birth to our daughter, Sara. During the birthing process I waited in the room next to where Pricilla was and as I heard her cries I feared the worst. The delivery was long and arduous, and I wept openly as I prayed for all to be well. I have never felt such anguish as I did then, and I hope I never will have to feel that way again. Finally, after what seemed to be a long day, maybe even days, I heard the cry of a baby. Soon the midwife came into the room where I was waiting and announced that I had a new baby girl. I rushed to Pricilla and saw in her arms the most beautiful sight I had ever beheld, my daughter Sara.

Pricilla was weak and unable to attend to the baby for the longest time. It was nearly six months before she regained her strength, and for that matter she now seemed more susceptible to colds and other ailments that were flying around. Even though her physical condition was weakened, her will to serve was not, and it wasn't long before she was back at her work of serving the other believers.

It was on Sara's first birthday that I was summoned by Barnabas. He told me that he needed me to work out in the mission field with my friend Cleopas. Apparently Cleopas had been severely injured by some Jews in Antioch. I was to travel there to help him as he recovered and also to lend aid to him as he tried to establish a fellowship of believers in that great city. I was reluctant to leave my work and my family; however, Pricilla was insistent that I proceed to Antioch. My work had prospered, and I had hired an able assistant who was a believer. He, too, encouraged me to go for he would run the business and he and his wife would look after my family.

I was unable to come up with any more arguments against leaving Jerusalem and though at first I was reluctant, I along with five other believers started out towards Antioch early one morning in March. We made the trip in ten days. When we arrived we proceeded directly to the house in which Cleopas was staying.

We found him in good spirits and nearly healed from the wounds he had suffered at the hands of the Antioch Jews. He had been stoned but fortunately suffered no broken bones, only cuts and bruises. The faithful had rescued him before more severe injuries had been inflicted.

The six of us quickly went to work establishing a fellowship of believers in Jesus the Christ in the great city of Antioch. We spent many months trying to get things organized and bring a semblance of order to the members. We had both Jew and Gentile believers, yet they failed to get along with one another. The Jewish believers felt that all believers, Gentile and Jew alike, should adhere to Jewish rituals, the principal stumbling block being the ritual of circumcision. The Jewish men felt that the Gentile convert should also be circumcised and observe the other ritualistic patterns they had spent a lifetime following.

Cleopas was a great evangelist and found success in preaching the truth about Jesus and bringing people to believe in him. However, he was not an organizer and was at a loss as to what to do to bring order to the chaos that was raining all around us. I, too, began to become frustrated with the results, as I was unable to bring the differing factions to an accord. After eight months of trying to establish a unified church, the other men who had traveled from Jerusalem with me felt that it would be appropriate if Cleopas and I would move on and work on establishing new fellowships in other cities and towns, for they were aware of our discouragement. They would stay awhile longer and try to bring agreement among the two factions and to grow the church.

After much prayer and careful consideration, Cleopas and I, with the others' blessing, started to journey south towards Jerusalem. Cleopas was greatly relieved to be once again on the road to speak and witness his faith to non-believers, for this was his calling. He was particularly glad to be out of the day-to-day administrative and peacemaking details of establishing the fellowship. On the other hand, I felt great disappointment over the fact that I was unable to resolve the issues that were at hand but I was delighted to be on my way home. I believed that I, too, was a lot like Cleopas and called to speak and witness to believers and non-believers alike rather than to try my hand at resolving conflict between factions or to administer the organization. No matter, this left me with a strong sense of failure in my first missionary endeavor.

We spent several months wending our way back to Jerusalem, meeting with moderate success in bringing people to accept Jesus as the Messiah. When I finally returned home, my daughter had turned eighteen months old and there I stayed with her and Pricilla for over a year.

Barnabas had welcomed us home with open arms and great words of encouragement for he felt our mission was a vast success. Even though divisions still existed and it would be some time before resolution to the differences would be resolved, our work had furthered the cause of Jesus. "For you must remember," he cautioned us, "that the fellowship's leadership here in Jerusalem must decide how this issue about rituals will be handled."

Time passed quickly. My daughter reached age five as I worked my trade in and around Jerusalem. I sometimes traveled throughout Judea and neighboring areas, spreading the good news about the coming of the Savior. I frequently went out with Cleopas, and during one of these times I became reacquainted with David and Martha, whom I had met earlier during my encounter with John the Baptist. Martha and Priscilla soon became good friends, and when David and I made several trips together into Judea, they lent support to one another during those times we were out doing mission work. I was never home as much as I should have been, and I'm sorry that I didn't spend more time with my daughter and wife; however, Priscilla was busy with the work of the believers in Jerusalem and tending to the details of rearing our daughter. It was an exciting time, for there were many converts to the faith and many new fellowshipa to be started and staffed with pastors.

When Sarah was seven, I once again set out on a long mission trip to Antioch, this time with Barnabas. He had received word that many of the issues between the Jewish believers and those converts among the Gentiles had not been rectified. Our mission was to bring resolution to the issues and therefore strengthen the Church. It was a long and arduous trip as the weather was against us. The wind blew constantly and the cold temperatures slowed our pace to a crawl. There were ten of us in the caravan, and one obstacle after another seemed to confront us. It took us over two weeks to make the trek, and we were all relieved when we finally arrived inside the protective gates of Antioch.

Once there we realized that the situation with the Church was chaotic to say the least. Our problems seemed to multiply as we were immediately confronted by the two factions that would not get along with one another under any circumstances. We spent several months trying to resolve the issues that divided the people and to bring peace in the name of the Lord.

Finally Barnabas threw up his hands in disgust and blurted out to the leadership of the Antioch fellowship that he was leaving the next day to travel to Tarsus and get the only man he knew who could bring resolution to these issues. "I'm going to get the man known to you as Saul, now called Paul, and bring him here to talk to you and to bring you all back to Jesus the Christ.

"He is the only man I know who can find a way to resolve these differences that have divided us into two distinct groups. We need unity in this congregation so that we may continue to grow and to spread the good news throughout the world."

Barnabas stomped out of the room, with me following close behind. Once we were out of hearing range of the others, I asked, "Are you really going to bring Saul into this situation? Can we trust him?"

"Caleb," Barnabas responded, "I know you don't trust him, but I do. I know him to be an honorable man who had a true meeting with Jesus in a vision on his way to Damascus several years ago. He is a man truly committed to the cause of proclaiming the good news of Jesus' divinity to the entire world. He is the only man who can bring a resolution to the division between the Jewish converts and the Gentiles. It is because he was trained as a high priest and because of his commitment to telling the whole world of Jesus' life, death and resurrection that he must now step forward and lead us to spreading the good news throughout the world.

"Caleb, you have a young child at home in Jerusalem," Barnabas continued. "I want you to return and take care of your family and continue to work with the believers there in order to help them grow. My job, on the other hand, is to stay here and work with Paul to straighten out the issues and then continue on as a missionary.

"So go on to Jerusalem, my friend, and do your work there to bring more believers to Christ. I will get Paul and bring him here to resolve the differences, and then we will continue on to other cities and countries to spread the word that Jesus is the Lord and Savior to the entire world."

I felt a longing deep within me to return home and was relieved that Barnabas was letting me off of the hook, so to speak. I therefore accepted his advice and started my return trip home the next day. I traveled a short distance with Barnabas and left him and the two others who traveled with him at a turn in the road as he set out for Tarsus and my traveling companions, and I continued on south to Jerusalem.

Once I arrived home I stayed in and around Jerusalem without leaving the country for a number of years. There was a great deal of work to be done in strengthening the body of believers and taking care of all of the members.

I also spent more time with my family and grew closer to them. I particularly enjoyed watching my daughter grow into a strong believer herself. At the age of fourteen, Sarah was married to another believer and moved in with her new husband, who was working as a tentmaker with me.

The next year a great famine struck all of Judea and Jerusalem, and our work for the fellowship was enlarged as we tried to feed those who had no food. Those were difficult years as many citizens of the country perished from starvation. We, through the help of the now strong congregation in Antioch, were able to survive, as Barnabas and Paul brought aid to Jerusalem from the membership of those believers. That was the last time that I saw Barnabas, and I will always remember him for his strength and wonderful nature of loving all men. I was also able to see that Paul was an unequaled missionary for spreading the word of Jesus Christ.

My friend Cleopas also came to Jerusalem that same year before he started on another great missionary trip that eventually took him into the city of Rome itself. I never saw him after that visit but received word that even though he was persecuted by the Romans, he was still able to start new congregations of believers and to spread the word of Jesus Christ among the pagans of Rome. I did hear that shortly before the Jewish war with Rome had started that he had died, from what I don't know.

In and around the sixty-sixth year after the birth of Jesus, both Barnabas and Paul had been martyred for the cause of Jesus the Messiah. There were few of the original apostles still alive. I, too, now, am one of the few men that actually saw the Messiah who still lives and breathes. Soon, there will be no witnesses left, and all who believe must come to Jesus on faith. Praise God for His empowering grace.

In the year following the famine that engulfed Jerusalem and all of Judea and as the rains at last began to fall, my beloved Pricilla fell ill with the influenza that ravaged the country. She passed on to her reward, that of everlasting life in the arms of a loving and gracious God. I was devastated! The loss was nearly more than I could bear. If it hadn't been for the loving care that I received from my daughter, her husband and their now two-year-old son, I, too, might have succumbed in my grief.

THE BURNING OF
THE TEMPLE

I spent a number of mornings and afternoons thinking of the past, my family in particular. The skirmish I had witnessed on the Court of Gentiles brought all of the memories to the forefront of my mind. Soon after the battle ended, the sun rose above the horizon and the temperature soared. The weather had been hot, the skies had been clear, and there seemed to be no relief in sight. Sleep for me was difficult, particularly in the room that I occupied in Fortress Antonio. The air was so warm and still that sleep had eluded me. As a matter of fact, I hadn't slept well for some time, for I was concerned over the future and particularly what was to become of the nation of Israel, for it was the land of my birth, a fact in which I took great pleasure. Another concern was my own future. Was I going to be released and allowed to return to Philadelphia? Would I see my grandson again? Would I be able to meet up with Naomi? She had been on my mind ever since she and her family escaped. Aerius had promised that I would be free to go the moment the hostilities ended, but what would happen if he were seriously injured or killed? I gave up trying to sleep and got up to my knees in prayer as I petitioned God to bring a quick end to the fighting.

During the middle of the afternoon when the heat of the day was at it highest intensity, sleep was impossible. I left my quarters and went to the top of the pathway on the wall of the fortress in hopes of catching a cooling breeze. As I stared down on the floor of the Court of Gentiles, I wondered what would happen next in this strange battle that was apparently drawing to a conclusion.

I looked at the banks that were spaced around the wall of the Temple. All looked quiet and relatively peaceful—that is, until I heard the command of a Roman soldier. I looked directly down and saw the manipuli led by Aerius file out on the ramp from Fortress Antonio, down onto the court and to the north gate of the Temple in a another effort to quench the smoldering wood that had continued to emit an ever-larger column of smoke. The soldiers were well armed and surrounded other soldiers who carried skins, which I assumed were filled with water. They ran at double time across the court to the north gate and quickly threw the water from the containers onto the lower portion of the gate. Great clouds of steam billowed and boiled upward, obscuring my view of the soldiers.

The steam quickly dissipated, and the soldiers retreated back to the fortress to refill their containers with more water.

Soon the manipuli was again crossing the floor of the court with fresh water to throw on the still smoldering wood. When they were halfway between the fortress and the northern gate, a large number of Jewish soldiers emerged from the northeast corner of the Temple. They were yelling at the top of their voices and running pell-mell towards the Roman firefighters. Aerius, too, saw the threat and ordered his men to prepare for the onslaught. Those who carried the water dropped their containers, drew their swords and fell in behind the soldiers who carried the shields.

There was a great crash as the two opposing forces met on the Court of Gentiles in front of the smoldering north gate. Though outnumbered two to one, the Romans held their own by holding close ranks and using their shields, effectively fending off the attackers. Soon they started pushing the Jews backward by brute force. Another cohort from the fortress entered the court and rushed the enemy on their right flank, pushing them even closer to the still smoldering north gate.

The Jews were no match for the Romans, and they seemed to lack the necessary strength to resist as a result of the severe starvation of all of the citizens of Jerusalem. The rush on their right flank had surprised many of the Jews, and they were pushed back hard against the gate—so hard that the gate sagged under the weight of the retreating soldiers.

I could hear the screams of pain from those who touched the hot smoldering wood and red hot silver and bronze that adorned the front of the gate. The Jews continued to back up under the pressure of the Roman soldiers, and more and more men began to pile up onto the blocked entrance. Suddenly the hinges on the left side gave way, and the gate fell open just enough for the Jews to enter the opening and escape into the inner court, the Court of Israel.

Dumbfounded at what had happened, the Romans stopped their attack. Before they could regain their senses the Jews had escaped back into the court and then into the security of the Holy House itself.

The Romans soon overcame their initial shock and one by one squeezed through the opening and reformed their defensive line on the other side of the wall. There they were hidden from my view. I rushed from my window and out to the walkway that led down to the ramp.

One of Aerius' soldiers, seeing me running, asked, "Where are you going in such a hurry? Are the Jews attacking?"

"No," I replied. "The north gate to the Temple has given way, and your men are entering onto the inner court."

This soldier said nothing to me in reply and took off yelling, "The Temple gate is open! The Temple gate is open!" The other men began gathering around him as he tried to explain what had happened.

I continued to run out onto the Court of Gentiles, to the first embankment just north of the gate. The Roman guards, who had been there, had picked up their armor, shields and swords and had run to the gate and squeezed through into the Court of Israel. I soon found myself alone at the embankment. All was chaos on the floor as more and more soldiers streamed out through the wall of the fortress, an opening that had been widened by the Roman engineers in anticipation of an attack on the Temple by all participating legions the next day.

I soon heard a great noise coming from inside the gate. I rushed to it and stood just outside trying to peer into the Court of Israel to see what was happening. Some Roman soldiers were feverishly working on the gate to open it further to allow more of the comrades to enter. Others were in hand-to-hand combat with the Jewish soldiers who had come out of the tabernacle and Solomon's Porch, which extended along the eastern edge of the Temple Mount.

More and more Romans were coming to the gate, and after a great effort the large, heavy doors swung open from the right hinges before the left side collapsed to the floor with a resounding crash. When this happened the Roman soldiers poured into the Court of Israel and quickly overwhelmed the Jews who were trying desperately to prevent the Roman advance. The fighting was bloody, and the inner court was already strewn with countless bodies. I finally ventured inside the wall and crouched a little east of where the north gate had once stood, hiding myself behind a stone bench that had been placed against the wall. I watched as the fierce fighting continued and the dead and wounded began to pile up, one on top of another. I was terrified by what I saw, yet I couldn't take my eyes off of the scene.

From my vantage point I could see the Temple, which faced east, off to my right. There in front of the Temple entrance stood the sacrificial altar raised above the floor of the Court of Israel. The main entrance to the Temple remained hidden from my view but this entrance was a place where no man, except for the priests, was supposed to enter. I'm sure many of the Jewish soldiers had sought refuge there in violation of the law, and they apparently were rushing out of the tabernacle in order to join in on the great battle.

The sounds of the fighting were deafening as I heard the clash of metal upon metal sword and shield. There were the loud cries of the wounded and dying as they fell under their enemy's weapons. It was a ghastly sight and one I'll never be able to shut out of my mind's eye.

I began to fear for myself. If I were seen by a Roman who did not know me, I, too, might be struck down—such was the hatred the soldiers felt for the Jews. Even though I was a follower of Christ, I was dressed in civilian garb and because I was descended from Jewish parentage, I, too, could be a target of that hatred. As the fighting gravitated away from the east gate toward the altar and to the front of the Holy House, I slowly crept away to a safer hiding place under some of the burnt timbers of the upper walkway that had fallen to the floor at the base of the wall off to the left of the gate. Here I was able to hide in the rubble without being detected but at the same time to view the unfolding battle clearly.

I was amazed to find a great number of civilians of Jerusalem on the floor of the inner court. Sadly, these citizens were being cut down in large numbers by the Romans. It didn't matter their age or their gender, they were the enemy and were run through or had their throats cut. I later learned that many of the citizens had come to the Temple Mount a few days before as a result of a premonition of yet another false prophet. He had urged all citizens to go to the Temple, for he had a vision that God would work a wonderful miracle that would defeat the Romans in one mighty stroke. This prophecy was false, as untrue as was the prophet. Needless to say many lost their lives that day for believing this man and venturing out into the combat zone.

As I watched the battle unfold, my attention was drawn to a small group of Roman soldiers approaching the north side of the tabernacle.

Their were no Jews there, but they seemed to be walking away from the fighting taking place on the raised sacrificial altar in front of the Temple. At first I wondered if they were running from the battle, but then one of them picked up a smoldering board that had fallen from the burning walled cloister above them. He blew on this wooden board until it burst into flames. When it burned with great intensity, he ran over to the wall of the tabernacle and motioned for his compatriots to join him. Once there he positioned himself under a window, which I believed led to one of the many rooms that surrounded The Holy dwelling of God himself, the Holy of Holies. Another soldier then boosted him up so that he could stand on the shoulders of the burliest member of the group. Once atop this man's shoulders, he touched his blazing board to a curtain that was billowing in the breeze. Immediately the curtain burst into flames, soon consuming other objects in the room. The men, after igniting the curtain, helped the culprit down and rushed back to the battle in front of the sanctuary.

I turned my attention back to the fighting and was appalled by the atrocities that I witnessed. The so-called disciplined troops of Roman were on a rampage, killing anyone who got in their way—women, children, enemy soldiers and even the elderly. The floor of the inner court in front of the sacrificial altar and on up to the tabernacle itself was littered with bodies. Even the ramp that led up to the altar was piled with the dead and dying. Where some of the court floor was still not hidden by bodies, it was covered with the blood of the hapless victims.

Out of the corner of my eye, I saw a brief flash that drew my attention back to the window where I had seen the Romans ignite the curtain. At first, smoke was coming out of the opening and soon another tongue of flame leaped out into the clear air. The tabernacle was on fire! I watched, hoping the flames would soon die out. This was not to be, for almost immediately the flames continued to grow, leaping out of the window unabated. Instead of slowly extinguishing for lack of fuels, the flames grew in intensity. I watched, hypnotized, as the growing flames leaped from the window halfway up the side of the tabernacle. Soon another window further to the east started to emit smoke. It wasn't long before flames started to lick out at the outside wall of another room. There was no question in my mind that the Holy House of God was on fire.

I watched paralyzed, unable to do a thing to help save the Temple. I soon heard an increased sound I thought to be from the participants of the battle. However, as I watched, I realized that this sound came from the mouths of the Jews all around the Temple and from those out in the rest of the city as they came to the realization that their Holy of Holies was burning. The moans of pain continued to grow as many stopped their fighting to stare at the tabernacle that now had great billows of smoke rising high above it.

Soon there was a great clamor at the north gate, not far from where I was hidden. Onto the floor of the inner court rushed none other than Titus himself, followed by his entourage of staff officers and the commanders of his legions. It had not been his intent to attack the inner courts and the tabernacle itself until the following morning. Further he had declared that the tabernacle should be left standing and not be destroyed by fire or by any other means. He quickly shouted at the top of his voice for his commanders to order their troops to stop the fires, but this was all to no avail. The troops did not hear them, or if they did, they did not pay attention to the orders.

Soon Titus and those with him cleared a way to the doors of the tabernacle and entered. I learned later that they were truly astounded at what they saw, for the fires had not yet spread into the main sanctuary. The beauty of this house of God was unequaled in the entire world. Much of the interior was adorned in gold and silver with beautiful wood carvings throughout. All who saw the inside were deeply impressed, and Titus once again went outside to try to force his soldiers to stop their fighting and work together to quench the fires before the entire structure was consumed.

I saw Titus and his entourage come out of the main doors, and he shouted in a loud voice and gave signals with his arms. Those with him also shouted in chorus, trying to gain the attention of the troops. The soldiers did not hear them nor did they see them, for their hearts and minds were set on their hatred for the Jews and on looting all that was precious within the walls of the Temple. Titus then ordered the staff officers around him to use their swords to beat his own soldiers into obeying his command and turn their attention to putting an end to the fires. All of these efforts fell on deaf ears, for the soldiers were so enraged that nothing could stop them from their mindset of destruction and plunder. Even as Titus worked to turn the soldiers' attention to his commands, they were running in and out of the tabernacle setting more parts of it afire.

By this time, there were fewer Jews still able to give battle. Many who could still fight retreated back to the east, under Solomon's Porch, which, too, was burning. They held off as many of the Romans as they could while a number of them escaped down into the tunnels under the floor of the Temple Mount. The Romans did not follow the escapees but instead turned their attention to finishing off the enemies who were putting up resistance in and around the tabernacle. At the same time, many other Romans continued to search for valuables inside the structure.

The Jews had stored much of their wealth in the rooms that surrounded the Holy of Holies. Even though many of these rooms were burning, the Roman soldiers broke down the locked doors that barred entrance to these rooms and ran in to steal the loot hidden inside. As they worked feverishly to pillage the treasury of the Jews, the Temple fires continued to burn and to grow. Sections of the wooden roof that had caught fire began to collapse and crash to the floor far below. I could see flames now towering high above the structure itself. There arose such a clamor of noise that it was difficult for me to even distinguish my own thoughts. The shouts from the victorious Romans were deafening as more and more soldiers from the various legions made their way out onto the Temple Mount. I also heard loud moans and plaintive cries from the wounded and dying victims on the Temple Mount. But even more distinct were the cries of the Jews who remained in the still undefeated parts of the city to the west of the Temple.

The burning parts of the structure became so hot that it melted the bronze, silver and gold that adorned the whole of the tabernacle. This molten metal then flowed down into the cracks between the stone that supported much of the building. It was here that I saw many of the soldiers use their swords and large iron bars to pry the stones apart in order to retrieve the now cooled precious metal that had flowed into the cracks.

As the fires joined into one great conflagration, General Titus and his retinue of officers left the front of the Temple and retired to the north gate near where I was hidden. Here they looked back on the great fire that was not only consuming the tabernacle but all of the wood and combustible materials in and around it, including Solomon's Porch. The heat of the fire was nearly unbearable. Some of the smoldering boards around me burst into flames, forcing me to get out of the danger of being burned alive. As I crawled out from under the debris, I was captured by one of the centurions who was with Titus.

He grabbed me from the rear and threw his arm around my neck, nearly lifting me off of my feet and gagging me. He pulled his sword from his belt and prepared to run me through. I was able to shout out, "General!" before the man's grip tightened.

Titus turned to face me and demanded, "Whom have you caught there, Liberalus?"

"Another Jew trying to escape," was the reply and with this the soldier eased his hold around my throat.

"It is I, Caleb, sir. I was the one that interpreted the prisoner's words for you yesterday," I gasped.

"You belong to Aerius, don't you?" the general asked.

"Yes sir," I responded. "I saw the tabernacle burning and got caught up in this fighting. I was afraid to return to my shelter for fear of my life."

Titus looked at me for a moment and then told the centurion, "Release him; he's not going to try and run. Where is Aerius?"

When no immediate answer came a call went throughout those surrounding Titus, "Find Aerius and bring him to the General."

Soon I heard a call from not too far off, "I'm here, General."

"Come and take custody of your charge. I don't want this man or any of our interpreters in the midst of this battle," Titus admonished. "They are in danger from our own troops as well from the seditious rabble that started this war."

"Yes, sir," Aerius replied as he brusquely yanked me by the arm and pulled me aside. "I'll see to it. He'll never enter the battle zone again, sir."

Aerius didn't take me back to the compound but told me to stand with him near the outer ring of officers that surrounded Titus and his staff. I believe the incident was soon forgotten, as the general turned his attention back to the chaos that was taking place within the walls of the Temple. I heard Titus say to those around him somewhat wistfully,

"I didn't want this to happen. I wanted to save this beautiful structure from destruction."

We watched, all of us, soldiers, officers, and Titus alike, as the flames continued to grow. Smoke began to billow out of the front doorway of the Holy House itself, for I'm sure one of the soldiers had lit a torch to all of the other combustible materials inside such as curtains and wooden adornments. The anger of the Romans towards the Jews was a hatred that no officer could restrain. Their desire for the treasure and other loot within the Temple drove them to defiance and even disobedience of their commanders. I believe even Titus realized at this point that he would have to wait until this anger played itself out before he could regain command of his troops.

After viewing the proceedings for a long time, the general turned and walked back across the Court of the Gentiles and into the Tower of Antonio. Aerius gripped my arm and led me back to the shelter of the fortress, to that part which hadn't been torn down in order to allow the legions to enter the Temple Mount. He did not utter a word—that is, until we were out of hearing range of the general and his staff.

"What on earth were you doing there?" he growled. "You could have been killed, either by your own people or by ours. You pull one more stunt like that and I'll throw you into the stockade for the remainder of your days. You may never get back home unless you listen to me and obey my commands."

"I'm sorry, but I got caught up in the moment. I couldn't believe that the tabernacle would ever burn. It represents the Jewish faith and with its demise, I feel that this could be the end of Israel."

"But I thought you claimed to be a follower of this man Jesus and that you were no longer a Jew," Aerius argued. "Therefore the fall of the Temple was not important for your faith, and your other disciples will continue on, not needing the trappings and symbols used by the Jews."

"In part you are right, Aerius. We can continue on, but the foundation of our faith in Jesus is that he himself was born and lived as a Jew. True, it was the Jewish leadership that demanded his death on the cross, but that did not make him any less a Jew. For he said that he'd come not to change the law but to fulfill it by providing a new covenant between God and the Jews. He also offered this covenant to all people, not only the Jews, but to the Gentiles also.

"It was the Jewish leaders who perverted the law and changed it, thus causing the Lord God to send His Son Jesus in order for the Jews to see the true light of His Kingdom. Even then, even as he lived among us, many rejected Jesus and his teachings. So, the burning of the tabernacle, God's own dwelling here on earth, has been condemned to destruction—a symbol, as I see it, of God's anger with His chosen people.

"I just guess it's the sight of the actual destruction taking place that has drawn me to view its demise. Maybe I was drawn by something within me that could not believe that it would ever be destroyed. Maybe I felt deep down that God would, in some miraculous way, step in and turn around these events and save His people and His tabernacle." With that said I hung my head and said nothing further.

"You are not to disobey my orders again," Aerius responded in a softer tone. "I've grown fond of you, Caleb, and I would not want to loose you needlessly. With whom would I talk about these earth-changing events that have taken place over the past few years? None of the men in my manipuli have the education or worldly views that you have, and I would, in all probability, turn back to my old sinful ways."

I looked at Aerius before answering, and the thought crossed my mind that maybe he had listened carefully to me after all—that what I had said about the Lord might have made an impact upon his life. I said a brief prayer to that effect before stating, "I will stay away, sir. I too, appreciate our friendship and would not want to cause a rift between

294

us. I was just carried away by the moment and didn't think before I went charging out towards the Temple. You have my word on it."

Aerius nodded and left without another word. I went to the nearby window of the fortress and watched as the Temple continued to burn fiercely, emitting great clouds of smoke and tongues of fire that leaped high into the air.

It was then that I realized that it was the tenth day of July. It was on this exact same day 639 years earlier that the Temple had first been burned as a result of an invasion by the Babylon king, Nebuchadnezzar, who had come to carry off the captives, the chosen people of God who lived in Judea, and take them to Babylon. This sudden realization was a shock to me, deeply distressing my soul. For once again the Israelites were to be scattered throughout the known world.

It was another two days before the fires died down and left smoldering piles of rubble strewn about the floor of the once magnificent Temple. The whole of the Temple Mount resembled little more than a pile of rubble. For as the fires continued to smolder and consume all of the wood and timber in the structure, the marble stones in the walls would crack and shatter due to the tremendous heat and would then tumble down on the floor below. A few of the walls still stood tall, like huge skeletons representing all that was left of the once great nation of Israel.

Countless bodies were strewn about in a haphazard way as thousands upon thousands had died during the rampage of the Roman soldiers. Not only had they killed every Jew in sight, but they let them lie where they had fallen. I even witnessed many of the soldiers as they used great iron pry bars to separate the stones of the tabernacle in order to get at the gold and silver that had melted during the firestorm and flowed between the cracks of the remaining marble and granite slabs. It was at this time that the words of my Lord and Savior Jesus came to mind of the lesson he had taught his disciples on that day as they left the Temple many years before.

"These magnificent buildings will be so completely demolished that not one stone will be left on top of another," he had said. And as predicted, the greed of the Romans was such that they were literally tearing the tabernacle and all adjoining structures apart, stone by stone. All of the wood that had been used in the structures was burned. This included the walkways at the top of the walls that surrounded not only the Temple but the Court of Gentiles. As these wooden structures were consumed by the fires, many of the walls that they were adjoined to also tumbled down in different places, leaving large gaps.

Another prophesy made by the Son of Man, Jesus, came to mind as I viewed the innumerable bodies that littered the whole of the Temple Mount: "And when you see Jerusalem surrounded by armies, then you will know that the time of its destruction has arrived. Those will be the days of God's vengeance, and the prophetic words of the scriptures will be fulfilled. How terrible it will be for pregnant women and for mothers nursing their babies. For there will be great distress in the land and wrath upon this people. They will be brutally killed by the sword or sent away as captives to all the nations of the world. And Jerusalem will be conquered and trampled down by the Gentiles."

After the fires burned themselves out and as the soldiers finished gathering all of the loot that they could, a semblance of order began to return to the Roman army. The officers at all levels once again established their authority over their men and the marching drill and practice with arms began to instill the appearance of discipline back into the ranks. Not many of the disobedient soldiers were punished, and those that were only received light extra duty sentencing. I believe that it was felt that too many men gave way to their hatreds and lusts, so if all were severely punished, there would be little left of the army to fight the battles that remained. For the old City of David, the lower city and the upper city on Mount Zion had yet to be taken.

When the fires died down to nothing more than smoking embers, those who had been taken prisoner were charged with the task of disposing of the bodies of the thousands who had been slain during the great struggle. Next, the prisoners were put to work clearing large sections of the Temple Mount in order for the Romans to set up their camps, displaying to the remaining Jews that they had indeed taken control of Jerusalem. The bodies were taken and placed in an open area of the new city, just to the north and west of the Temple Mount, and there they were unceremoniously burned in a great funeral pyre. The reason, I believe, behind this move was to prevent disease from festering and spreading as the result of decay.

After the situation had settled down and the Temple Mount had been cleared of the rubble and of course of the bodies, Titus assembled his troops on the large Court of the Gentiles just in front of what remained of the Temple. Many of the walls that had surrounded it had fallen and been carried away. The only recognizable portion that remained standing was a portion of the eastern wall, its gate and the southern wall with its gate still intact.

With his troops assembled before him all along the eastern part of the Temple Mount, atop the ruins of that great altar, stood Titus and behind him was the shell of the once great and revered tabernacle—now little more than a pile of rubble.

It was from this place that he addressed his men. "We've come a long way since we first marched from Caesarea through Judea and thence to Jerusalem. We still have more battles before us, but we can take pride that the Temple Mount once revered by the Jews as their most holy place is now in our hands." Titus paused a moment before continuing, "We must take the rest of the city, and I, again, will offer the rebels the opportunity to accept amnesty before we renew our attacks. If they accept the offer, our work here will be at an end. If not, we will lay waste to the whole city, for no one can stop the Roman army, the most powerful force upon the face of the earth."

This brought a loud and sustained cheer from the soldiers as they yelled at the top of their voices and raised their swords high into the air. "We will pause just a few more days, and then we will continue with our fight for the city," he said after the cheers of his army quieted down. "I will give the citizens just one warning before the full weight of Roman arms falls upon them. If they do not concede to our demands then the whole of Jerusalem will be devastated by fire and death."

Once Titus said this, a hush fell over the assembled troops and the soldiers bowed down, not only to Titus, but to their battle flags and ensigns. This to me was a sign that the only gods that they saluted and prayed to were their gods of war. When they stood after their prayer to their false gods, a tribune stood and shouted, "Hail to the son of Caesar!" This brought a loud and sustained cheer from all of the Roman troops.

After the fires died out and the embers cooled, it was discovered that many Jews had hidden themselves in different and secret places on the perimeter of the tabernacle. Some had found refuge in hidden rooms that were not destroyed by the flames while others had hidden in tunnels beneath the floor of the sanctuary. Still others had found ways to hide themselves in the upper reaches of the structure, beneath the eves of the roof of attached outbuildings. As time progressed their thirst and hunger forced them to reveal themselves to the Romans. It was amazing to me that they survived the holocaust, for the fires had been horrendous and destructive. Needless to say, many more perished than survived.

One group of men that came out of hiding after the fires had died down to little more than smoldering embers were Temple priests who presented themselves to General Titus and begged him to not put them to death.

"You are the priests of this Temple?" He asked through his interpreter.

"Yes," the oldest of the group replied. "It has been our duty to perform the sacraments before our God and to guide the people in their faith."

"You have failed in your duties!" Titus declared. "If you had been diligent and faithful to your God then your Temple would not be lying here in ruins. You, who have been charged with the duty to protect this sacred structure have allowed brigands and criminals to overrun that which is holy to you and then to defile the God you have pledged to serve. Because of your failures, you do not deserve to live. I sentence you to death."

With that the men hung their heads and wept bitterly, for they would not only lose all of that they held dear but they would also die in shame. Titus then ordered that all of his troops be put to the task of tearing all of the structures on the Temple Mount down in order to find the hiding places where others had sought refuge, a furthering of the fulfillment of the prophetic sayings of my Lord Jesus.

WAR ON THE CITY
CONTINUES

Two days later after the soldiers cleared the debris of what remained of the Temple and scavenged all of the valuables, including the sacred utensils used for the sacrifice of animals, the menorah and the gold and silver cups and plates, the Romans started their preparations for the taking the unconquered parts of the city. These included the old City of David south of the Temple Mount, the lower city in the Tyropoeon Valley and the upper city that stood on Mount Zion. Before the orders were given to begin the burning of the City of David and that which lay in the Tyropoeon Valley, John and Simon sent an emissary to Titus requesting a conference. The general, feeling that this could mean surrender on their part, agreed to hear their petition.

It was decided by Titus that he and his army would stand on the western side of the Temple Mount while the two leaders of the Jews would position themselves near Herod's palace on the east side of the upper city, near Herod's bridge that joined this part of the city with the Temple Mount. It was further directed that an impartial interpreter be appointed and positioned at the midpoint of the bridge in order to interpret what the two sides had to say to one another. That interpreter was to be me.

The next day General Titus, dressed in his finest battle regalia and surrounded by his tribunes, prefects, staff officers and all of his soldiers, stood at the western side of the Temple Mount just above the market place of the lower city, or better stated, at the terminus of the bridge that lay between the upper city and the Temple Mount. The two Jewish leaders John and Simon and the remaining Jewish population of Jerusalem stood at the western end of that bridge prepared to present their terms to the Romans. I was the one selected by Titus to interpret the words shouted out by one side to the other. I had been chosen for this task since it was felt that I would be impartial and present the words from each side without bias. It was also a sign to the Jews that through the use of an interpreter, the Romans were the conquerors and they, the Jews, were the vanquished.

Before sending me out on that bridge where I could speak his words to John and Simon, the general admonished his troops to withhold their anger and not discharge their darts or arrows at the enemy. He then turned to me and nodded, indicating that I was to proceed out on to the overpass to the appointed place and interpret his words in Aramaic to the Jews.

I walked to the middle of the bridge filled with a great deal of apprehension in my heart, for I did not know how the words of the general would be accepted by John and Simon and I definitely didn't know what demands they would make of Titus. When I reached my position on the bridge, I turned to face Titus so that I could hear what he had to say. Once I did that, the crowd on both sides fell silent. The sun stood directly overhead, and there was no wind—not even a breeze. I thought to myself that if I closed my eyes I could imagine that I was standing alone in the desert with no one around me. It was that quiet.

Titus paused and did not say a word for a seemingly long time before he began. He stood up straight with his shoulders squared and his feet spread a little more than a cubit apart with his hands on his hips.

"I hope you, John and Simon, are satisfied by the terrible misery you have brought to this great city," he shouted.

I quickly turned and repeated these words in Aramaic to the Jews before turning back to face the general, a process I followed throughout his discourse, interpreting sentence by sentence.

"Since the beginning you have grossly underestimated the power of Rome," he continued, "while overestimating your own strength and might. Through your madness and brutal attempt to defeat Rome, you have brought destruction and desolation upon your city, your people and your Temple. Ever since the time of Pompey, you have been rebelling against us. You have depended upon your own resources to defeat Rome, and you have not understood that there is no nation on earth that has the power to triumph over our armies. Before you are only four Roman Legions, and you have been unable to prevail against them or even hold us at bay. No nation near or far will come to your assistance, and none could bring enough men and arms to defeat Rome even if they did choose to side with your cause. Do you think that you as a people are physically stronger than we are? Do you even think that your military adeptness is greater than our own? Do not be so foolish to even think that you can stand against Rome. Even the Germans are our servants. The Britons have succumbed to Rome, and they are surrounded by what they considered greater walls than these— an endless expanse of water—while the militaristic Carthaginians have been conquered and now submit to our authority.

"It is the kindness and patience of Rome that has brought you to this rebellion. We are the ones who allowed you to possess this land and have allowed you to have your own kings to rule over you. Most importantly, we have allowed you to maintain your lands through the laws of your forefathers and to continue to remain faithful to your God. We have permitted you to collect tribute that is donated to this God of yours without interfering or taking this offering from you. Your wealth has grown without our intrusion on these collections. Because of our generosity, you have become wealthier than us. Then, in answer to our kindness, you have taking this wealth and used it to make war against us and our benevolence.

"True that during the reign of the ruthless and self-indulgent Nero, you did have cause for alarm over your future, yet you did nothing but lay still waiting for another time to rebel. It was at the time that my father came into your country with the intention to do nothing more than to admonish you over your indiscretions against Cestius that you chose to attack us. Had my father come with the intent to destroy you, he would have come directly to Jerusalem and laid waste to this capitol in the very beginning. As an alternative, he went into Galilee attacking lesser cities, thus giving you time to repent of your misdeeds against the Empire. Instead of repentance, you took this as a sign of weakness, and because of the internal dissensions within Rome after the death of Nero, you chose to further your insubordinate behavior by escalating your attacks against us and against your own king.

"When my father Vespasian was made emperor you once again increased your violence against us, your benefactors. You alone out of all the domains under the rule of the Empire made war against us while all other states sent their emissaries congratulating our ascension to the imperial throne. You alone showed yourselves to be our enemies. You even went so far as to invite neighboring countries to join you in your fight against us, yet none would unite with you. You built new walls around Jerusalem as your seditious acts increased. Then, to add to your injury, you started fighting amongst yourselves. We know that all of your food supplies are gone, destroyed in your own civil war.

"As our forces approached the city we heard that your citizens wanted peace. In this I rejoiced, as it had not been my desire to go to war with you. I offered you my right hand in friendship, but you refused my offer. After each major engagement I again offered you sanctuary and life, but each time you rejected our goodwill and the war continued. We accepted those citizens who escaped and came to us seeking immunity from the fighting. We then set them free to travel away from the war. Only those who wanted to continue with the fighting were severely punished. Still you, John and Simon, cast aside our benevolence and continued to seek our ruin.

"I unwillingly set my machines of war against your walls; I withheld my troops from slaughtering your people; and after every victory I came to you as if we had been defeated beseeching you to end this genocide. I withheld attacking this Temple, which now stands in ruin upon this mount. Yet you sought refuge in it against your own laws, and you were the instrument that set it on fire. You and some of your soldiers escaped to the upper city as your very own people fell beneath the might of my army. Now in your cowardice, do you seek my right hand of friendship? Oh, you miserable creatures! What is it you want from me now that your people are dead? Now that your Temple lies in ruin? Now that your city is in our power?

"As I do not want this carnage to continue, I will grant you your lives if you throw down your arms and deliver yourselves and your soldiers to me here and now. I will preserve what is left and punish lightly those responsible for this unfortunate event. The rest will be preserved for my own use."

When I had finished these words of Titus to the Jews, both sides fell silent for another passage of time. I held my breath, for I hoped that the response from John and Simon would be one of acquiescence for the generous terms offered to them by the general.

Simon then stepped forward and made the reply to the conditions spelled out by Titus. I had never seen Simon before, and I was surprised by his size. I judged that he stood a little taller than me and weighed quite a bit more than I weigh, yet he appeared slim and athletic. I thought to myself that this man surely did not suffer from the famine to which the rest of the city had been subjected. I further wondered how many had died in order for him to eat. Simon had a full beard that had been trimmed close to his face, making him appear younger than I had thought he actually was. His voice was deep and loud, resonating out over the vast arena of the city. He was easily heard as he stood at the end of the bridge dressed in his finest armor, shouting his reply to Titus.

"We," he began, "will not be able to accept your generous offer." My heart sank as I repeated these words to the general. "We have sworn never to acquiesce to Roman arms. I therefore beseech you to give us leave to proceed through the wall with our families and go into the desert leaving the city to you. In that event, you will have your victory, and we will be able to retire from this fight without giving ourselves up to you as we have sworn never to do. We will leave immediately, and your victory will then be assured today." As I interpreted these words to Titus, I thought, *How smug and prideful these men were to think that they could declare terms to the Roman army.*

"Caleb," the general shouted out to me in what I felt was a bewildered tone, "Tell these scoundrels that they are never to petition me again, nor are they to approach me even as deserters to their cause." His tone told me that their demand had been flatly rejected. "Tell them that this fight isn't over until the whole of the city lies in ruins at my feet and that no one will be spared. All who do not die will become captives of the Roman Empire and enslaved for the remainder of their days. Tell them that they'd better be prepared to find an escape if they value their lives, for the war will continue from this moment forward and all captives will be treated in accordance to the laws of war."

When I had completed what the general had dictated, I waited for a few moments for a reply. But instead of answering, Simon turned his back on me and the Romans and reentered the upper city gate, which was rapidly shut and latched. I then made my way back to the Temple Mount and stood in front of the general. He thanked me for my services, and I went to stand beside Aerius, who was not far from his general in a crowd of other officers.

Titus then turned to his officers and men and shouted loudly in order to be heard by all, "We will burn and plunder the city beginning at sunrise tomorrow morning. Sharpen your swords, prepare your darts and arrows, and start moving the machines to the western wall of the upper city."

A loud shout came from the throats of the Roman soldiers as they returned to their camps to prepare for the final assault.

As we walked back to camp, Aerius said, "You did a good job, Caleb. I think the general appreciates the work that you have done for him. Though I could not distinguish all of the words you said, I do know that it was a literal interpretation as you spoke to those criminals Simon and John and in turn your interpretation as to what they said to us."

"I tried to be as exact as possible," I responded. "Don't forget that I hold these men, Simon and John, responsible for all that has taken place over the past year. If it hadn't been for their greed and thirst for blood this never would have happened. God is forgiving, but they have tried His patience to the extreme. His anger is being taken out on all of the Jews, not only for what they have done here but also for what they did nearly forty years ago when they rejected His son Jesus. I am filled with grief for the victims, but I'm not surprised that it has come to this."

"You are truly convinced about this Jesus not only being man but also being God, aren't you, Caleb? I've wondered about your conviction. You have nearly convinced me that what you have said is true—that is until today. I see that you truly believe and that it would be impossible for me to change your thinking."

"I'm surprised that you haven't seen that before. I have always tried to be truthful with you, Aerius. I'd like to think that we are friends, and I would never say anything to you that would mislead or deceive you. My purpose is to lead you to the truth, and that truth is that this man Jesus is truly the Son of God. He came to earth to show all of the people that He loves them and wants a relationship with them."

We then walked the rest of the way to the camp in silence. I could tell that Aerius was seriously considering the things I had said and in his own way was trying to accept them in his heart. I didn't want to push too hard for I didn't want him to turn away. The decision was his and his alone.

Early the next morning just before sunrise, I saw a number of Roman soldiers leaving the Temple Mount. Each one carried a torch as they hurried along the western border and then departed through the southern or Huldah gate, thence down the stairs, marching quick time past the Huldah monument and then into the old city, the City of David just to the south of the Temple area. There they took their torches and began to set fire first to the repository of the archives, to the council house and to Ophlas, all located atop Acra. Soon the fires gained momentum and spread to neighboring structures, including the streets and houses as far as the palace of Queen Helena. As the fires continued to burn, they spread across Acra, and soon they burned down off of the hill and into the lower city situated in the Tyropoeon Valley. Many of the houses that contained the bodies of the thousands who had succumbed to the famine also burned. It was a horrific sight and smell that both saddened and sickened me.

As the old city burned, some men and women, relatives of the man called King Izates, escaped from under the watchful eyes of Simon and John and sought sanctuary with the Romans. They asked that Titus allow them to enter under his protection, for they had finally come to realize the foolishness of their stand with Simon and his crowd.

An angry Titus received them without sentencing them to death. However, they were put into his custody and I believe remain his prisoners to this day. I further believe that they were taken by Titus back to Rome and marched through the city streets as hostages along with other trophies from his victory over Jerusalem.

The fires in the old City of David took hold and clouds of smoke filled the air and traveled skyward to be seen from great distances. The fires continued to spread down the southern slopes of the Tyropoeon Valley and consumed more of the houses and other structures of the poorer sections of the lower city near the pool of Siloam, and then continued on towards the palace of Queen Helena.

After the sun had been up awhile, I saw other troops of soldiers pour out of the western Coponius Gate, march through the lower city near Herod's bridge and move toward Mount Zion, the walled-in citadel of the scoundrels that still resisted Rome's powerful legions. The Romans marched up to the royal palace of Herod and fought their way through the eastern gate before it had been latched and tightly sealed. It wasn't long before they entered the outer court. I heard loud shouts and sounds of battle in and around Herod's palace as a great battle ensued.

It wasn't until that evening that I learned what had taken place. Aerius came to visit me after dinner and talked of the events of the day. Aerius looked tired and worn out as he sat cross-legged on the ground across from me. It was late and not too long after he'd finished his duties caring for his men. The fire that separated us was little more than a few glowing embers, since I had decided to let it burn itself out after I'd cooked my own meal over it. I could see that Aerius was burdened by the things he'd witnessed that day, so I said nothing more than a quick greeting. He placed his elbows on his thighs and his chin in his hands, staring into the glowing embers.

After a few minutes of silence, he began to speak in a soft voice telling me of the events of the day. "We walked a short way across the bridge that leads to the upper city before we let ourselves down into the streets a short distance away from the wall that surrounds Zion and Herod's Palace. Once on the streets, we rushed toward the gate that opens onto the outer court, and we were fortunate enough to be able to force our way through that gate and onto the court." Aerius again fell silent as he stared into the fire.

"What I saw, Caleb, was something I wasn't ready for. I've seen great brutality over my years as a soldier but I've never been witness to a people that brutally kill their own women and children with no remorse at all." Again he stared into the embers of the dying fire.

"What happened?" I asked. "Did Simon and John slaughter the innocent women and children?"

"As we entered the court these people, the women, children, the old and infirmed were in the court and throughout the rest of the palace. I assume they'd sought refuge there, for it is a formidable fortress. Unfortunately, they had left the gate through which we entered not properly sealed. We immediately started to round up these civilians as our prisoners. Our intent was not to kill them.

"As we began to surround them and get them to their feet in order to lead them out of the palace, the Jews under Simon and John suddenly broke into the courtyard. There must have been two or three hundred men. My command consisted of only one hundred and fifty soldiers, and I called for them to retreat without the prisoners to the gate through which we had entered. And you know, as the Jewish soldiers entered they paid little attention to us but instead set out against their own helpless people bludgeoning them with there swords and axes. They then went through their garments searching for loot and food. The blood flowed, and the whole of the court became slick with it. Still they kept on killing innocent women and children who had no means of defense. Soon a large contingent started after me and my men, and we defended ourselves as we quickly exited through the gate. The last two soldiers were taken prisoners before they were able to squeeze out the door.

"I don't know who those soldiers were, for they had been assigned to me just before we left the mount to attack the palace. After we were out, I formed my men into a skirmish line around the gate in order to attack the rebels if they dared to leave through the gate to reenter the lower city. The Jews then bolted the gate shut, and we heard a lot of yelling and screaming from the dying and wounded. Apparently John and his men continued the slaughter of the innocent civilians still in the court of the palace.

"We waited outside the gate for a very long time, hoping the Jews would come out and engage us in battle. The noise inside the gates continued, for how long I dare not guess, before it began to subside. Then at the middle of the afternoon, it grew quiet, and soon we heard the bolt to the gate being drawn back. It opened quickly, and before we knew it one of the captured soldiers was brought out into the street escorted by a group of Jewish soldiers. They made preparations to behead him in view of all. I was ready to give the order for my men to attack, when this soldier seized a lax moment on the part of his captors and ran from them straight for my skirmish line with his hands still bound behind his back. Seeing that their plan had been thwarted, the Jews quickly reentered the gate, closed it, and bolted it shut again.

"With the gate bolted shut, I knew that it was impossible for us to gain entry with the small force I had. I decided it was time for us to go back to the Temple Mount and return this soldier to his commander. On our way back, he told us that the other soldier had had his throat slit and his body dragged through the streets of the upper city in an act of avenging themselves for their defeat at our hands. They then wanted to make an example of this soldier we had just rescued and literally dragged him outside the gate in order to cut off his head in front of the whole Roman army. This soldier knew that they were nervous about my command being just a short distance away, and as they were distracted by that fact, he saw an opening when the executioner was drawing his sword, rolled away from him and stood and ran to us.

"I heard later this afternoon that Titus was not happy over the fact that soldier had allowed himself to be captured. The general therefore deemed him to be unworthy of being a Roman soldier and had him stripped of his arms and ejected out of the legion. A sentence, for a professional soldier, that is worse than death itself."

"Thrown out of the army?" I asked in dismay. "I would think that his escape would be worthy of a promotion."

"Capture means surrender and is an unthinkable act on the part of a Roman soldier," Aerius concluded before he fell silent staring into the embers of my dying fire.

I knew that Aerius felt guilty about the fate of this man and wished he could in some small way redeem him back into the army, but this was impossible. So to change the subject I asked, "You're telling me those criminals are still killing their own? How can they do that after the carnage that has taken place over the past few months?"

"They're your people, Caleb," he answered. "You tell me."

"I can't claim them," I said. "These are not actions I was taught, even as a Jewish child. Most especially after I accepted Jesus as my savior, we all have been taught to respect human life. All life is precious to our God. I do not understand these unsavory deeds, for they go against the commandments. God must be weeping over the loss of His people. Not so much over the deaths as over the loss of their faith in Him. He wants a relationship with His people, and instead His Law has been cast aside as we have allowed unfaithful men rule over us." I paused after this outburst, and I, too, looked at the dying embers as I shook my head in disbelief.

After a moment of silence I looked at my friend and asked, "How is it with your faith, Aerius? Have you been able to see that after all of this mass mayhem and murder, war is not the way it's meant to be for man? That there are better things we can do with our God-given skills? That we were not created with the intent to destroy but to build up?"

"Caleb, don't you see that that is what Rome is all about?" Aerius responded. "That is exactly what we're doing. We are bringing the Jews back under the protection of the Empire. When we are through here, we will begin to build it back up and make Jerusalem a strong and vibrant city once again."

"I'm sorry, Aerius, but I do not see it that way. Rome gets its way only through war and destruction and by forcing its will upon the subjugated peoples. Do you call this an improvement?" I said motioning with my arms towards the destroyed Temple and the burning city. "Thousands upon tens of thousands have died here in the last six months. Is that improvement?"

"Caleb, this has been brought about by your own people. I witnessed these brigands slitting the throats of women and children today as they searched for food and plunder among the weak and frail. It was a nightmare. This is not the way our armies work. We fight a legitimate war against other armies. And after we defeat them we bring them under the protection of the Empire and educate them in the ways of the civilized Roman world. This is what leaves them better off and more prosperous. "He fell silent and picked up a small branch and threw it into the embers of the fire.

"I see that we do not agree," I said. "Perhaps someday we will come to an accord. It is my belief that men should be free to believe as they want, not forced to conform to another's authority. But that is a delicate subject, one that must be handled carefully."

"You want me to believe in your God, Caleb. Isn't that your purpose? To force your views on me so that I will become like you?"

"My purpose," I explained, "is not to force my views upon you. Rather my purpose is to convince you through reason of my faith. My intention is for you to make your own decision about accepting Jesus and the Lord God. I would never try to force you to believe, for that would not bring the kind of change that God wants. You would only go through the motions, and your actions would lead to nothing. God wants us to accept Him on faith; that is, believing in what cannot be seen and touched. That's what I'm trying to do. I would not try, even if it were within my power, to force my will and beliefs upon you."

"You're a different kind of man, Caleb," Aerius said after a moment. "You sure challenge me. When I think I've figured you out, you come up with something new. I do wish I had your faith, for you seem to be at peace, even with this genocide that surrounds us." He paused another minute and then bid me goodnight. "I will see you in the morning. I think you will be free to return to your family soon. I hope that pleases you." He struggled to his feet and started to walk away.

"It does please me Aerius, have a good sleep."

Early the next day soldiers from the Tenth Legion began to form up on the Temple Mount in rank and file. They were heavily armed and ready to do battle.

The tribune in charge of the legion addressed his men. "We will move into the lower city, wipe out all who are still there and burn it to the ground. Centurions, you have your orders, so proceed to your assigned positions and get this final operation underway. Tomorrow the war machines will be positioned against the western wall of Zion and the battering for the final offensive will begin. Dismissed!"

The soldiers broke up into various elements and rushed from the Temple Mount and down into the lower city. Many of the soldiers picked up torches and lit them from a large fire that had been burning near the western cloister of the Court of Gentiles. I watched mesmerized by the actions of the troops as they filtered down into the streets and set fire to various buildings and houses along the northern edge, parts of the city that had not burned the day before. In some of the areas I could not see the troops, but I could keep track of their movements through the streets by the sight of the flames and smoke from fires they set as they raced westward through the streets of the lower city.

Any Jews still in the lower city were quickly dispatched by the soldiers, for there were no civilians left, only the rogue soldiers who were in league with Simon or John. These seemed to think they had time to continue with their looting, and most were surprised by the presence of the Romans and were not ready to do battle. They were quickly killed and left where they had fallen.

Shortly after noon, the soldiers were at the base of the wall that enclosed the upper city. They weren't able to attack it without their machines, for it was too formidable for them to tear down and too high for them to attempt to scale. They stopped and formed a defensive line and awaited orders from their commander-in-chief.

The rebels behind the walls continued with their dispassionate killing of the civilians who were enclosed behind the fortifications with them. Anyone who dared try to escape and was caught in the attempt was quickly murdered and left on the street. Any individual other than a soldier loyal to John or Simon was seized and searched and, if found with food or precious metals or jewels, had their throats cut and their valuables confiscated. It was a continuation of the blood bath as the rebels didn't seem to realize that they had lost the war. Their greed for valuables drove them to these new depths of depravity as if no war had taken place.

They held a misconceived conviction that when and if the Romans breached the final wall and thence the upper city, they would make good their escape by hiding in the tunnels and subterranean rooms that proliferated under Jerusalem. The Jews that remained in the upper city and elsewhere had concluded that any death would be better than death by starvation. This gave them the will to attack the Roman troops with suicidal zeal or a devil-may-care attitude. It therefore impeded the advance of the Romans as they worked to bring all of their machines of war against the western wall of Zion.

This led Titus to the decision that because of the height and strength of the wall and the unyielding attitude of the Jewish defenders, he needed to build banks against the portion of the wall that surrounded the west side of the palace. This was done by his four legions. Another embankment was to be constructed by the auxiliary armies against the eastern wall of the upper city, Zion, near Herod's Bridge and the wall that protected the Xystus or market place.

So on the eighth of August the work began. As I have told you, the land for great distances around had been stripped of all the trees for the previous banks built early on in the siege. It therefore became necessary to bring in new logs and material from over a greater distance than before.

During this interval not a great deal of fighting took place except for a number of skirmishes initiated by the Jews in an attempt to delay the inevitable. Starvation was at work now against the entire population, for even the Jewish soldiers didn't have the stamina to foray out against the Romans in force. Once they left the limited safety of the gate in their attack, they were easily slaughtered or turned back by Titus's troops.

It was at this time that the Idumeans, who had been allied with the Jews, decided they'd had enough. In order to withdraw from the battle, their commanders sent five emissaries out to Titus to ask if he would accept their surrender.

Titus met with the men and, though angered that they had come to this decision so late in the battle, agreed to accept the surrender. I believe that he hoped that this would break the back of the Jewish resistance and that the war would once and for all be over as a result of the withdrawal of the Idumean forces.

These five emissaries made their way back to the gate through which they had come during the darkest time of the night. To their surprise and dismay they were met by Simon and John, who'd heard of the attempt to surrender. Without saying a word each of the men was run through by Jewish swords. The five emissaries and all who had accompanied them were killed and immediately dragged to the gate and thrown out, left to rot in the street. Once the brigands were assured that the men were dead, Simon ordered his soldiers to locate each of the Idumean commanders and put them in prison.

Now without their leaders, the Idumeans began to desert to the Romans. Many were caught by Simon's men and slain. However, many more were able to leave undetected and make their way through the gates or over the wall and surrender to the waiting Romans.

Titus accepted these men under the terms worked out with the now slain emissaries. He was of the hope that if the Idumeans did in fact surrender then maybe the seditious leaders, Simon and John, would end the war. He was tiring of the conflict and therefore went back on his order to kill all who escaped. The number of Idumeans and Jews who chose to escape grew in number day by day. Not only did individuals come but entire families. Commanders were put in charge of these now prisoners in order to differentiate those who needed to be set free, sold into slavery or needed to be punished. The war was nearing its end and becoming more administrative in nature than actual fighting. Thousands were set free, but a greater number were sold into slavery.

So many, in fact, that the price each prisoner brought was only half the price they would have brought during normal times.

During this time one of the priests escaped from the upper city and was brought before the general. The soldiers that escorted him fully expected that he would be put to death as were other priests who had been captured in the days since the Temple had been destroyed. This priest, though, offered to give to Titus implements from the Temple if he would spare him his life.

"What could be so valuable to me that would cause me to change my mind and grant you life instead of the death you deserve for failing to properly serve your God?" Titus asked of the man.

"I will be able to show and deliver to you a great deal of the solid gold utensils used by the priests in our work in the Temple," he responded. "These utensils are hand-crafted and beautifully adorned with precious stones and jewels, lending to them great value. I had hidden these things long ago, and only I know where they are. For my life I offer these valuables to you."

"Show me these implements, and I will then determine if they are worth your life," Titus responded.

So the priest led Titus and several soldiers assigned as guards to a secret vault located below the floor of the court of Israel where the prized possessions were kept. All of those who viewed the booty were awed by its beauty and value.

After seeing and feeling this loot, Titus accepted the offer and the priest called Jesus, son of Thebuthus, delivered as claimed two of the holy candlesticks, various basins, and implements used for the sacrifice. He also brought a great amount of silver, gold and numerous priestly garments inlaid with jewels and precious metals. This priest was then set free and allowed to travel away from Jerusalem along with his family.

Within a period of eighteen days, the Roman soldiers were able to bring in the necessary materials for the banks and to construct them next to the western wall of the upper city. After the construction was complete, on the twenty-third of August, the battering rams were bought forward and the final phase of the war commenced. For three days these huge machines pounded the wall in relentless fashion continuously, both day and night. At the end of the second day, my head ached from the sound of the machines smashing the wall rapidly and consistently for the rumble of one strike would barely stop resonating before the ram would strike again. I was unable to sleep well at night for the rhythm of the ram against the stone in the wall was disruptive to my thoughts and sense of sleep.

It was just before sunrise on the third day of the battering that the western wall began to crumble under the relentless pounding. I was in a fitful sleep at the time, when the first huge stone fell away with a resounding crash. I heard the cheers of the soldiers as they realized that at last they could enter this portion of the city and engage in the final battle of the war.

I quickly leaped from my mat near the western wall of the Temple Mount and climbed to the top of the cloister in order to see this final advance against the stubborn Jewish defense, but without success for it was still too dark. Even after the sun had peeked over the eastern horizon, I was unable to see through the pillars of smoke and flame that still burned in the lower city to that portion of the wall that had fallen. It was not until late morning that I was able to distinguish new and large fires burning in the upper city. These had been started by the Romans, and thus I was able to discern their progression from the break in the wall over near the Serpent's Pool on the southwest side and then northward towards Herod's Palace.

Aerius gave me an update later that night. He told me of the proceedings, for he'd viewed the events from somewhere near the Serpent's Pool and also after he had entered the breech in the wall.

He said that the break came suddenly and quite unexpectedly, for the engineers had originally felt it would take a week before they would be successful in the endeavor.

"Part of the reason for success," he said, "was that the Jews did nothing to harass our men working the rams. In addition, we used not only the large ram but two others that are slightly smaller, and when the three machines worked together in close proximity the wall vibrated to such an extent that it began to crack and crumble early on before giving in and falling.

"Once the fissure opened," he continued, "our foot soldiers quickly entered the breech and established a defensive perimeter awaiting an assault from the Jews. Many of the enemy, when they realized that our soldiers had entered into their last bastion of defense, threw down their arms and ran away. Others attacked our men, but the Jews were quickly defeated and pushed back towards Herod's palace. It was another horrific blood bath, Caleb. Many died at the hands of our troops. It seemed like they wanted to die. They came forward to meet us but put up little defense and were then quickly run through."

"It sounds to me as if they, too, had taken the pledge never to surrender to you Romans and thus chose to die at your hands rather than to be captured, killed or sold into slavery," I sighed.

"Yes, that must be the reason," Aerius answered. "As we fanned out from the breech in the wall and traveled up the streets towards the palace, we encountered many enemy troops, but they didn't have much fight left in them and they seemed to be surrendering their lives to our swords. The streets ran red with their blood.

"Over the ensuing time more and more of our troops entered the upper city and began to set fires throughout the area. Many entered the private homes of the citizens and found nothing but the bodies of the families—those who had succumbed to starvation. It was an eerie sight, one so disgusting that we left the dwellings without even attempting to loot the houses. Instead we burned them.

"I also heard this evening that a large number of the Jews had rushed out of a southern gate and run to the siege wall just south of the Hinnom Valley. They had tried to break through in order to escape, but they were easily cut down by the Roman soldiers who stand guard for that purpose.

"We approached Herod's palace about midmorning and had little trouble entering and taking control of that position. We encountered no resistance from the great number of citizens who had sought shelter there. Once we had broken through the gates to the courtyard, they gave up peacefully. I think they were glad that the war, for them, was finally over. Our next objectives were the three towers Hippicus, Phasael and Mariame. We felt that it was here that the rogues John and Simon were holed up, for our intelligence told us that since the Temple burned they had spent the most recent days in one of the towers.

"We knew these were formidable structures and would not budge under the impact of our war machines. I didn't want to see troops sent up into these fortifications, for I feared we would lose many men in trying to take them by force. The question remained, 'How long would it take to starve them out?' However, when we finally arrived we found them to be deserted. The rabble had left them and run away.

"We continued to clear the streets and alleys of all resistance. The Jewish soldiers did not give up and continued to fall under our swords. They were determined not to be taken prisoner and preferred to die. Most were in such poor health due to starvation that they easily fell to our weapons.

"Now, Caleb, that is why I have come to see you this evening. We have not caught these seditious leaders of the Jews, and we feel that they have escaped underground. We know that there are numerous tunnels and rooms below the streets of Jerusalem. I need you to come with me in order that we may interrogate the prisoners who will have the information we need. This is so we can start the search tomorrow."

"I'm available," I said. "I'm still your prisoner and will do the best I can to help you find those who have escaped. I know a little about the subterranean structures, and I think you will need to be careful for it could be a dangerous operation."

"Why do you think that?" Aerius responded. "We just need to go down in force and dig them out."

"There are numerous branches off of the main tunnels. Even Solomon's stables are located somewhere down there. Many secret passageways and doors cannot be easily seen, and there are some areas where you could become trapped without a way out. So, be careful. I have only once been down there and that was when I was a child. I can't remember much about it except that it was dark, and, because it was like a maze, difficult to find one's way around. I also remember that children would occasionally wander down there and become lost for days. There were even stories that some died before they were ever found."

"More the reason that we need to interrogate the prisoners," Aerius said thoughtfully. "I hadn't thought that the tunnels would have been that extensive. Let me report this to my tribune and get his thoughts on how we should approach this hunt. We can't let Simon and John escape. They must be punished. I know that the general would like to take them back to Rome in chains before they are executed.

"Meet me at the Temple Mount in the morning at sunrise, and we will begin the interrogation. All of the prisoners are being taken there and held until we can determine their fate."

"I'll see you in the morning then," I answered. Aerius got to his feet and walked away from my fire.

I shivered as I thought of the horrible task that lay before the Romans and the Jews. The subterranean passages under Jerusalem were to me a scary place. I remembered the time that my father had taken me down into the tunnels and how scared I was with only his torch burning, casting great shadows on the walls. I felt that everything was closing in on me, that I couldn't breathe, and that we would die there and never be found. Fortunately, our stay below the city streets was not a long one. When we finally climbed back up out of that terrible place and once again set our feet on the top of the Temple Mount and breathed in the fresh air, I swore then and there that I would never enter those tunnels again.

The next day I awoke with a start as I heard the drums from one of the Roman units beating out a rhythmic cadence; slow and deliberate was the beat. I then came to full awareness and realized that the drums were playing as they accompanied victims being led out of the city gates for execution. All Jewish officers who had fought with and for John and Simon were being summarily executed for their role in opposing Rome.

I didn't want to view this event. I shut my eyes and prayed that all of this madness would go away and that I would be able to leave and go back to my family in Philadelphia. I thought of my grandson Abram and wished desperately that I was there working with the leaders and all of the followers. Then my mind went to Naomi, and I longed to see her and to know if she were well. I wondered if she had truly accepted Jesus on faith and had come to know him. "If only I could leave, then all would be well," I said to myself. However, another thought crossed my mind, "How would my being there have any effect on events taking place in Philadelphia? Oh, what a dilemma life is." Then I knew that the only control I had on the situation was through prayer, so before eating and going to join Aerius and the interrogations, I got on my knees and prayed fervently for those I wanted to be with at home. Soon a feeling of comfort and peace engulfed me. I felt that my prayer was heard and, most importantly, answered.

As I walked to the place where I was to meet Aerius, I came to the ultimate realization that this war had changed my life forever. There were images in my mind that I knew would never leave me—the violent deaths of so many, the piles of human remains in the houses, streets and valleys, and the numerous innocent victims caught up in war for being at the wrong place at the wrong time. It was all so sordid that an overpowering sorrow filed me and brought tears to my eyes. If I could only leave and return to my home. However, the reality of the situation was the imagery of all I had witnessed would follow me wherever I would go. This nightmare would end, but the images of death and destruction would live on. Just as those much cherished memories of my wife and my daughter had stayed with me long after their deaths.

Shortly after sunrise, Aerius gathered his manipuli on the Temple Mount and began giving instructions. I was too far away to hear all of his words, but I was able to grasp the gist of what he said. He was telling them that they were going down into the tunnels and caverns under the city to search out and capture or destroy those Jews who sought refuge there.

When I arrived where the soldiers were standing, Aerius gave the order for the men to stand at ease. He came to me and said, "There has been a change in the plans, Caleb. We won't interrogate prisoners until later as we have been ordered to go into the underground and search out the rebels. So go back to your shelter and wait for my return, and stay out of the way."

"I will," I replied as Aerius turned on his heal, brought his manipuli back to attention, and ordered them to march towards an entrance to the underground tunnels.

I shuddered as the thought of going down below the streets into the darkness and, to me, the scary underworld of Jerusalem. In my mind I conjured up all sorts of frightening scenarios, each ending in my rapid demise. I then asked God to take these thoughts from me, which I then followed with a prayer for Aerius's safety as he and his men entered the tunnel that led below the Temple Mount.

Large portions of Jerusalem were still burning, and great numbers of prisoners were being brought to the holding compound on top of the Temple Mount. It was here that their fate was decided. If they had been innocent victims of the leadership, that scum that brought on the war, they were released and sent on their way. If, instead, they'd joined the forces that opposed Rome, then their fate led either to death, imprisonment, or slavery. I watched as the endless parade of prisoners was marched up to the tribunal of Roman officers who decided the fate of the prisoners. Some were directed to the right, some to the left of the officers who were holding court. Those who went to the right were taken into custody for further review, while those that went left were taken to a holding compound in the central courtyard of Fortress Antonio. The majority of those sent to the fortress were women and children. I surmised that they had been declared innocent and would eventually be set free.

I was filled with a sense of overwhelming sadness as I watched these proceedings from my window of the fortress, a point seventeen cubits above the Court of Gentiles. I was too far away to hear any of the words said by the judging officers as to the sentence of the court on these poor souls.

Around noon, I turned from the window and went to my mat on the floor of the room where I stayed. I lay down with the hope of sleeping but soon realized that I would be unable to do so. The weather was stifling with the temperature nearly overwhelming my ability to think. Any breeze that came my way only brought the smell of smoke and the attendant ash from the fires that were still burning throughout the city.

It was an uncomfortable situation, and I went to my knees praying to God that He would send relief; a change from the heaviness that filled my heart over the suffering of the people of Jerusalem. How I wished and prayed that I could escape and return to my new life in Philadelphia.

"Anything, Lord, to take my mind away from this death and destruction that I have witnessed over the past six months," I declared aloud in my anguish.

It was not too long from that declaration that I realized a change was coming, but not the one I had prayed for—that of returning to my home.

SAVING AERIUS

Ever since the Romans had captured the fortress, Aerius had assigned one of the small rooms as my holding cell. I quickly convinced him that I didn't need a guard and that I could be trusted and would stay wherever he wanted me without prompting. His trust grew over time, and I was soon allowed to roam about the structure without supervision. I knew that escape was impossible, and I also had a somewhat morbid curiosity as to the ultimate outcome of the war; this interest is what kept me in Jerusalem. Trying to escape had never been much of a goal on my part.

That feeling was in the process of changing. Now that the fighting had ended for the most part, I was beginning to feel restless about my future. The desire to leave was an ever-growing notion in my mind.

The smoke from the fires had filled the room in which I was staying. Therefore, to get away from its choking presence, I left my place of confinement and walked down onto the Court of the Gentiles, staying close to the wall of the fortress and keeping my distance from the prisoners and the tribunal taking place at the southwest corner. I surely didn't want to get mixed up with that group. Fortunately for me, my appearance was more that of a Roman citizen than that of a Jew. Aerius had insisted that I get rid of the beard and trim my hair in the Roman style so that the Roman soldiers wouldn't mistake me for one of the Jewish prisoners.

"If you are going to be walking around here without a guard then you must not draw the attention of our troops, who might mistake you for an enemy," he stated emphatically.

He had his orderly give me Roman garments and ordered me to put them on before he had one of his men come into my room and cut my hair and shave off my beard. The new garments were clean and in good repair. My old clothes were getting threadbare and had developed a number of holes in them as well as being filthy. I had always tried to keep my beard trimmed close to my face but it was nearly impossible to keep my once dark red hair from getting long and unkempt. So the shave, haircut and new garments made me feel better. I even had enough water to take a long delayed bath.

Aerius then allowed me to move about the fortress without guard if I adhered to certain stipulations as to where and when I would roam. The newfound freedom felt great, but it still didn't get me any closer to my friends and grandson in Philadelphia.

I walked a short distance along the western edge of the Court of Gentiles until I came upon a break in the cloister where I could stand on the edge overlooking the city—which was in ruins. Some of the fires in the upper city were blazing brightly, and smoke filled the air. In the lower city, all that remained were the still smoldering ruins of the myriad homes and shops of the once proud owners. Devastation surrounded me, and I could still hear the citizens as they cried and moaned over the death and destruction still confronting them. It was a sight and sound that brought tears to my eyes.

As I stood and contemplated the scene, I heard the yelling of some soldiers behind me as they emerged up the stairs and onto the floor of the Temple Mount. As they weren't too far from me, I recognized them as some of the soldiers in Aerius's manipuli. They were led by Aerius's second in command, a deputy that I had become friendly with ever since I interceded for his friends, sparing them the severe discipline that would have definitely been meted out the night Naomi had escaped.

"Longius," I shouted. "What's happening, and where is Aerius?"

He looked at me with a sadness that reached deep within my soul, for I could tell that something terrible had happened. "We came under attack by the Jews in the tunnels, and Aerius was struck down by an arrow shot by one of those scum," he replied. "There were many men in the band, and we were unable to retrieve him. I think he's still alive as I saw him crawl into one of the side tunnels that lay between us and the Jews."

"I need to go and find him," I shouted out before I could even consider a proper response. "Tell me where he is."

"It's too dangerous down there for you, Caleb. Even our soldiers won't go down into the tunnels again unless we go in with overwhelming force," Longius replied.

"It might be easier for me to go alone," I countered. "They might take me for one of their own if I dress properly."

"I don't deny your courage, but I know you to be somewhat strong minded. If you give us some time, I'm sure the tribune will give us a large contingent of troops to contend with the rebels. Just be patient, Caleb."

"Tell me where he is, Longius, and just don't let anyone know where I'm going. I'm sure his wounds need attention. You know that if the Zealots find him, they will do unspeakable things to him. He doesn't have the time it will take for a new force to be assembled and sent down to search for him. Where is this side tunnel where you saw him escape?"

He then started describing the position where they had encountered the rebels. "Go down these stairs," he said pointing to stairs located on the very southwest corner of the Temple Mount. "Enter the tunnel through that little building to the left. There once was a large stone covering the entrance, but that has been rolled to the right revealing another stairway that leads down into the underworld of Jerusalem.

"You'll need a lantern, for it is dark as pitch down there. At the bottom of the stairs you'll find a path or tunnel that leads north straight under the Temple Mount. Soon you'll arrive at the place they call Solomon's Stable. Cross that large room and directly across is an entrance into another tunnel. Don't take the one you'll see to your left or the one that will be on your immediate right. Go straight across the room, enter that tunnel, and continue on for about four hundred steps. There you'll find a smaller room. In this one you'll take the tunnel on your immediate right and from there proceed for three hundred and sixty steps. That is where we encountered the rebels. About another twenty steps further on should put you at the entrance of the tunnel into which Aerius crawled."

I repeated his instructions and it helped that many years ago I had been in Solomon's Stable so the picture was somewhat clear to me.

He continued, "One of the men in our group used chalk to draw a line on the wall, so follow that marker. Every one hundred paces he drew a large circle with an 'X' in it to help find the way in and back."

"Good luck, Caleb. I hope we'll be able to come to your assistance later in the day. Take plenty of oil for your lamp, for it is a labyrinth down there."

He then turned and departed to go and report to the tribune. I quickly rushed up to my room, changed into my old clothes and tried to take on the appearance of a Jew. My beard was not long but it had been nearly a week since I had had the shave. I rubbed some dirt on my hands and face and tried to appear as if I hadn't been clean for several months. I then finished my disguise by putting a wrap over my head. Next, I grabbed a storm lantern and some extra wicks, a smoldering cord with which to light the lantern, and finally a large skin of water and as much oil for the lantern that I could carry.

Within fifteen minutes, I was on my way down the steps that led to the building concealing the entrance into the tunnels that would put me under the Temple Mount. It was here that it struck me as to how stupid this whole quest of mine was. I had many years before sworn that I would never again go down into the caverns beneath Jerusalem, and guess what? I was on my way, and fear and claustrophobia gripped my very soul.

Once I reached the opening that led down some steps, I hesitated and briefly looked back, back to what might be my last glance at the brightness of daylight. I then turned and faced an unknown future, said a little prayer that God's grace would continue to cover me. I kneeled down and blew hard on the smoldering cord in order to ignite the wick of my lantern. As I got to my feet summoning all of my courage, I hastened down the fifteen steps that put me into the entrance of the tunnel. The air was rancid and had a moldy smell. Instead of it being cooler, it felt as if the temperature were higher.

I walked slowly at first as my eyes adjusted to the dim light that my lantern emitted. With this lantern light, my body threw strange and frightening shadows on the walls and floor of the tunnel. These strange shapes only heightened my apprehension and caused me to jump frequently for I felt that someone else was with me. As I continued along I began to adjust to the low light and the somewhat strange shapes my shadow threw on the walls of the tunnel. I frequently turned to check over my shoulder to be certain that I was alone.

I walked for what seemed to be a long time, constantly wondering if I were on the right path. It seemed to me that I should be approaching the place called Solomon's Stable. I hadn't been able to make out the chalk line on the wall that Longius had said his man had put there. As I continued to walk my fears continued to grow. Had I somehow taken the wrong entrance? Had I missed the stable all together?

Just as my fears were reaching their peak and I was beginning to contemplate returning to the mouth of the tunnel, I saw through the dim light my lantern threw that I was approaching a large underground room.

I stepped inside the room and stopped for a moment holding my lantern high over my head to get a better view. Suddenly I heard a demanding voice from behind me. "Who are you? What are you doing here?"

I froze out of fear not knowing what to do or say. I knew that this was a Jew for he spoke Aramaic. I then choked out, "I'm escaping from the Romans and looking for refuge here."

"You're a Jew, a citizen of Jerusalem?"

"Yes," I answered timidly. I knew that what I said was very close to the truth.

"Turn around and face us," another voice commanded.

I slowly turned while still holding the lantern over my head and faced three men, all of whom were much younger than me. They were very lean and somewhat emaciated as they stood in their armor with their weapons drawn and pointed menacingly at me. These young men were shorter than I, and each sported long and somewhat scraggly beards that indicated to me that they were still in their teens. The thought crossed my mind that I was glad I was wearing a loose fitting robe without a belt around my waist, for even though I was slender in stature they would have easily seen that I had not been starving. My week's growth of beard also hid the full, round appearance in my face.

"What are you doing here?" the taller of the three and to my left demanded another time.

Again I repeated, "I'm trying to stay free and not fall into the hands of the Roman despots. They've murdered my son who fought for Jewish freedom, and I know as soon as they learn that I was his father, I, too, will be killed or sold as a slave. Is it safe here?" I asked this hoping to turn the questioning around, refocusing on their plight and not my own. As always I felt guilty about lying but I felt that God would forgive me, for this was a matter of life and death, mine and Aerius, and by telling the truth to these criminals both of us would surely die.

"We are safe for the time being," the middle one answered. His answer was in a softer voice, so I felt that they believed my story. "We did run into some Roman soldiers this morning but chased them away. They'll be sending a larger force down here soon, and we were preparing to rejoin our other comrades who are in a secret location that I don't think the Romans will ever find somewhere near Hezekiah's Tunnel. We'll take you there, for we Jews must stick together and continue to fight the Romans.

"We have a large stash of gold and jewels from the people of Jerusalem hidden away and with that we'll raise an army to continue our fight for freedom. We even have been able to steal food and other supplies out of the Romans' own kitchen. So follow us. We'll take you to our leader and then on to the hiding place. Once the Romans relax their vigilance, we can once again go above ground into the daylight."

"Oh, I feel as if I have been saved by God to have fallen into your hands," I declared loudly and with a deep sigh.

"Don't thank God, for He has done nothing to save us. You can thank your lucky stars that you fell into our hands. You should realize by now that there is no God," the third man admonished.

I let the comment drop, for to get into a religious argument at this time was not a bright idea. "I will take your advice," I answered. "Go on and lead the way."

"Your lantern is better than ours so you lead the way, and we'll follow giving you instructions on where to turn as we move along," the apparent leader of the group commanded.

"Very good. In which direction do I start?"

"Take that tunnel off to your left and walk about six hundred paces. From there we'll take a smaller passageway that leads down to another room. That's where our comrades are."

"Good," I replied and started off in the direction indicated. Few words were said as I led the way. I tried to memorize all that I saw for at some point I had to get away from these fellows and in so doing find my way back to Solomon's Stable. Like the man had said, I counted the steps as best I could, but it was difficult for the men following me were asking me questions.

"Where were you during the siege?" the one directly behind me asked.

"I was in the lower city taking care of my parents, just trying to keep them alive until it was over. You see they were incapable of taking care of themselves as both were invalids." This was a story one of the captured citizens had told us during one of the interrogations that I interpreted for Aerius. I felt that this would be a sufficient answer as to why I was not involved in frontline fighting.

It seemed to satisfy their curiosity and nothing more was asked of my personal life. We soon arrived at the smaller passageway that started down for an untold number of steps. At the bottom, the passageway became narrower and lower. I had to stoop in order not to bump my head, and we continued to walk in single file. I felt more and more that the walls were closing in on me, and I had to concentrate on counting my steps in order to take my mind off of my claustrophobia.

As we kept on walking, the man bringing up the rear of our little procession asked the others, "What are you going to do with all of the loot we have stashed away?"

"I'm going to buy a large house with stables and stock it with the finest horses in the land," one of the others replied.

"Keep quiet," the apparent leader admonished. "We have other business to attend to. The Romans are still in control, and none of us will escape for some time yet. Don't start spending your plunder until we are free."

That little exchange told me a lot about the men. They had no intention of using the money to build a new army. These were the brigands that killed and stole from the innocent citizens of Jerusalem. It was good that I had answered their questions as I had, for they must have felt that I was poor and had nothing which they could take. I continued to walk in front them not knowing what would come about with this detour. My purpose had been to rescue Aerius, and here I was walking into a den of thieves and criminals. I wasn't positive that one of them wouldn't stab me in the back and leave me to rot in the tunnels below Jerusalem.

The passage took a sharp turn to the left, and I could see a light, forty or fifty paces ahead of me. At last there was something besides the monotony of the enclosed walkway, but where would it lead me?

The perceived leader of our little group said, "This is our headquarters, at least for the time being. We have been able to find some comfort here, and our hope is that the Romans won't come and find us."

"How many of you are there?" I asked.

"More than one hundred," the man directly behind me answered.

We reached a room filled with men mostly dressed in various garments that resembled the military outfits Simon's men had worn during the recent fighting. *Scum of the scum*, I thought. How am I going to get away from these people with my life? As this thought crossed my mind, I broke out in a cold sweat, and my sense of guilt was greater than before because of the lies I had to tell.

No one seemed to notice our arrival, and for that I was thankful. I didn't need to be recognized for if I were I'd probably die. The leader stood by my side, and in the dim light of numerous lanterns I could see that he was probably in his mid to late thirties. His traveling companions were much younger, probably in their late teens or early twenties. As for those others in the large room, they were of various ages. I carefully examined the perimeter and noticed that there were three or four different entrances to this expanded space. Where they led to or from was a mystery to me.

The leader who had brought me into this den of thieves said, "I want to introduce you to my commander. We could use someone like you to help us steal food from the Romans. When they see young Jews up in the city, they stop us and usually arrest us. Someone of your age would in all probability go unnoticed. Yes, you can be a great asset to our cause."

I just nodded at the comment and followed him as he approached another man about the same age as he. The leader then whispered in his commander's ear as I stood and watched and prayed that I could soon be free of these people.

The commander just stared at me as the other whispered in his ear. When he was finished the leader summoned me with a gesture of his hand. I didn't like the look of the commander, and as I approached I kept my back to the tunnel through which we had entered the room. I felt I might need a quick escape.

"You look familiar to me," the commander said. "Where have I seen you before? What is your name?"

"Silas," I responded not wanting to divulge my real name. This constant lying seemed to be coming easier. It bothered me a great deal for in doing so I felt that my nervousness might lead others to see through my lies.

"That doesn't sound familiar, but I'll remember where I've seen you before. Are you sure we haven't met prior to this?"

"No."

"I believe we have. Just give me a little time to think it over." The commander proudly stated., "I never forget a face."

I began to sweat profusely since I realized that he might remember seeing me as the Roman interpreter. If he put it all together my life would be in jeopardy.

Much to my relief there was a stirring of the men on the opposite side of the room and then a loud roar that led to cheering. I tried to see what had caused such an uproar, but I was unable to determine what it had been that brought on such an excited response among the men.

It was then that the man who had brought me to this room said, "The general has arrived—General Simon."

I gulped as I thought of the great hatred that I felt for this criminal who had brought on the terrible destruction to my beloved Jerusalem. I stepped back a pace or two making my way towards the entrance to the tunnel, for I felt that it was time for me to leave. The commander might remember where he'd seen me, and while all of the commotion was overtaking the crowd I thought that I'd better make a run for my life.

Just as the cheering hit its peak, I turned and hurriedly made my way to the entrance of the tunnel. As I ducked into the passageway I heard the commander shout to the one next to him, "That man's name is Caleb. He's the one who interpreted the words from Titus on the bridge. Where is he? Bring him to me!"

I ran as fast I could back up the passageway and quickly reached the turn that would lead me back to Solomon's Stable. I could hear a great deal of commotion from the room where the murderous Jews were hiding out, and it wasn't long before I heard them gather their weapons and start after me. My lamp and oil were a hindrance to my running but I didn't dare throw them away for then I'd never find my way out of the tunnels under Jerusalem. I put the storm shield over the lantern in order to conceal its light and kept on running. I heard the voices of the men behind me, but I couldn't tell how far away they were.

Before I knew it I was at the entrance to Solomon's Stable. I lifted the storm shield in order to find my way to the passage that Longius had described. I quickly discerned the opening through which I'd come and looked straight across the room for the passage that Aerius had taken before he was wounded.

I ran across to the tunnel entrance and stopped for a moment to listen for those who were pursuing me. It appeared that they were still far down into the other tunnel, so I decided to continue my search for Aerius. I found what I believed to be the right entrance of the tunnel and then searched for the chalk mark. It wasn't long before I saw a faint white line and determined that I had found the right entrance. Here I replaced the storm shield on my lantern and continued on in the blackness of the tunnel. Longius had told me to walk four hundred paces and at the end of which I would enter another small room, so I slowed to a walk and started counting my steps in the dark. I didn't dare let the light of my lantern shine, for the rabble chasing me might be able to find me. I felt my way along the wall and occasionally stumbled over debris on the path, but I held firm to the count of the paces I took.

At three hundred paces, I stopped, held my breath and listened carefully for any sound of my pursuers. I could distinctly hear them for the sound carried well up and down the tunnel's stone walls. They apparently were in the stable and must have stopped there as they tried to figure out which of the three tunnels I had taken. After this short pause I continued forward. When I'd counted four hundred and ten paces I entered the small room I had been told about. Again I stopped as indecision washed over me. If I dared to shine my light it might be seen by my pursuers. However, without the light I might take the wrong entrance. I decided that the best thing would be not to use the light at all. Instead I stepped to my right and felt my way with my back to the wall. After four short steps to the right I found the void of the entrance that I thought was the one Longius had mentioned. Into this new tunnel I walked the three hundred and sixty paces and then the additional twenty or so to find the tunnel entrance that Aerius had crawled into to escape his attackers.

I stopped and listened. I could still hear the indistinguishable sounds made by my pursuers off in the distance, If only they would break up into smaller search parties then I felt that I could escape and find Aerius. I didn't like the thought of ten or twelve men coming en mass after me. Two or even three would be easier for me to evade.

Because Solomon's Stable had three or more branches, I felt that the rabble would find it necessary to search each of the tunnels. The only way to do that quickly would be to break up into smaller search parties; at least that was my hope and prayer.

As I continued my search I didn't find the alcove. I went another ten paces and still nothing. Then I remembered that Longius had not said what side of the tunnel Aerius was on when he slipped away from the Jewish attackers and I'd assumed that it would be on the left. I then crossed over to the right side of the tunnel. With my back to that wall I felt my way back towards my starting point, and that is where I finally found the opening.

I entered this opening and groped my way along the passage. I quietly called to my centurion, "Aerius, are you here? It is I, Caleb." There was no response. I continued along the wall for another fifty paces and then called out again, but louder this time. "Aerius, it is Caleb, can you hear me?" I didn't want to shine my light for I felt that the Jewish rebels might be close. I took another ten paces and came to the end of the passage. It led nowhere for the ceiling had collapsed and blocked the tunnel.

I sat on one of the large stones that had rolled onto the floor and tried to figure out what to do. I was frightened and felt closed in almost as if I were going to suffocate. I was coming to the conclusion that I needed to get out into the sun again before my fears got the best of me. The darkness made me feel as if I had been placed in a grave, and that if I didn't get out I would surely die.

It was at this point I heard the voice of one of the Jewish pursuers, in the outer tunnel. "You two look in this tunnel, and we'll go ahead and search the next entrance.

I could see light from their torches approaching my dead-end tunnel, the one in which I was searching for the centurion. I quickly ducked behind the stone on which I had been sitting, hoping against hope that I wouldn't be discovered. I blew out the still burning flame in my lantern, for even with the storm shield in place a small amount of light escaped from the lantern. I then prayed fervently for God's intervention in my life and in my situation.

From my hiding place, I saw two men enter and proceed down the path toward me. I prayed hard to God that I wouldn't be discovered. They walked slowly inspecting every inch of the alcove.

When they were within six or seven cubits of my hiding place, the first one stopped looked hard towards where I was, then crept forward a step or two and then shouted, "I see you, hiding behind that stone. Come out so I can skewer you like you deserve, you traitor Caleb. You deserve to die for helping the Romans." The two men then advanced towards me rapidly cutting off any avenue of escape.

I slowly rose to my feet and stepped out in front of the rock behind which I had been hiding. "Get it done with, you scum," I growled. "Add another innocent victim to your trophy list."

They both had their swords drawn and pointed at my chest. I took a deep breath and closed my eyes, prepared to meet my end at this very moment. I no longer felt fear and said a brief prayer that I would finally meet the Lord Jesus face to face and live eternally at His side. I then opened my eyes and looked into the eyes of the Jew closest to me ready for his thrust. But it didn't come, instead his eyes opened wide in disbelief. Then a look of pain crossed his face. He dropped his sword, and it clanged loudly to the floor before he dropped to his knees and fell on his face on the floor of the tunnel. His companion looked at the fallen comrade and then looked at me just before the same series of expressions crossed his face followed by his collapse over the body of his dead companion.

Their still burning torches lay on the floor next to their bodies.

I stared in disbelief at the two dead men and then lifted my eyes. There in front of me stood my friend, the one I had come to save, Aerius.

"Aerius, where did you come from?"

341

Aerius did not answer at first but leaned against the wall of the tunnel and grimaced in pain. It was then I saw the arrow lodged in his shoulder. I stepped over the two dead bodies, put my arm around him and helped him sink to the floor in a sitting position with his back to the wall. I could see that he'd lost a lot of blood.

Once Aerius caught his breath and the intense pain from the physical effort of striking down the two enemy soldiers had eased, he said, "I didn't see you come in the tunnel as I must've passed out. Your call awakened me, and I was about ready to respond when I heard the enemy come down the passageway. I thought I'd better see what would transpire before answering you, and I'm glad I did. I don't have the strength or the will to carry your body out of these tunnels," he said with a grunt that I believed to have been meant as a laugh.

"Here I came all this way to save you and as usual you turned the tables on me and saved me. You were God's answer to my prayer; thank you."

"Well, I'm not God, a far throw from it, but you are my friend and I couldn't let you die that way. Now you'll have to help me get out of this damnable place. There are many more Jews down here than I'd ever imagined, and now they will be looking for the two of us with increased vigor." He tried to get to his feet. I quickly went to help him as I could see that he was in excruciating pain.

The dropped torches were beginning to die out, so I used a burning ember to re-ignite my lantern. I helped Aerius to his feet so that he could lean against the wall of the tunnel. "We'll have to walk in the dark," I told him as I helped him put his good arm over my shoulder, "or we will be discovered by the rabble that roams in these dungeons below the city."

He grunted a reply as we made our way to the main tunnel that would lead us back towards the stable area. Just before we reached the junction, I heard more Jews coming back down the passageway. I stopped Aerius and pushed him back against the wall. We took a few more steps back hoping that they would pass us.

The one in front said, "I sent Simon and Jacob down this tunnel; you and I will go onto the next one on the right. He can't get away, for this passage leads straight into the Fortress of Antonio, right into the hands of the Romans. I don't think that this Caleb would be down here if he was still on the side of Rome." They continued discussing my situation as they strode on by the entrance and down the path to the next tunnel.

It was then I knew how we would get out. We would follow the tunnel until we came to the fortress. I again put Aerius's good arm over my shoulder and stepped out into the main tunnel. Just then the light of the torches of the two men who had walked by disappeared as they turned into the next tunnel joining ours.

"We have to hurry so we can get by the next entrance in case their route terminates in a dead end," I whispered to Aerius. He groaned as we started walking forward to what I hoped would eventually lead us to the fortress.

We said little as we continued on past the tunnel entrance that the two Jews had taken. I looked down into the blackness of that opening and could see a glimmer of light from their torches as they proceeded deep within the bowels of the passageway. I could tell that Aerius was weakening as he put more of his weight on me and began to take smaller steps. The going was difficult as I dared not use the light from my lantern and the path was strewn with debris that had fallen from the walls and ceiling of the cave. Aerius didn't utter a sound, but I could tell that he was laboring under the duress and strain of walking. It wasn't too much longer that we approached an alcove or enlargement of the passageway. I had been feeling my way along the wall with my free hand as we had walked, and I soon discerned that we had reached a widening in the tunnel or maybe even a junction with another entrance. I stopped and took Aerius's arm from around my shoulder and had him lean against the wall.

"Wait here," I told him, "while I see if I can find a place for us to rest." I used both hands trying to determine the extent of the alcove or if indeed we had reached a junction with another tunnel. It proved to be a small room, and to my relief I determined that it had a little antechamber in which we could stop for a short while. I also felt that in that little side chamber we could safely, but briefly, let our light shine.

I groped my way around the rest of the alcove past the continuation of our tunnel and then back to where I had left Aerius. I found him in a heap on the floor, for he'd passed out from the exertion and loss of blood. I lifted him as best I could and carried and dragged him to the antechamber. There I laid him down on the floor, went out of the room and looked both ways up and down the tunnel we had traveled to be certain no one was coming. I did not see or hear any sign of the Jews. It was black as pitch. I rushed back to Aerius's side and, concealing the light emitted by my lantern as best I could, I lifted the storm shield. Aerius looked drawn and deadly pale.

I removed his armor and then tugged at the arrow, which didn't budge. I then broke off the feathered end as close to his body as I could. I decided that I would try to push it on through his shoulder and out the other side. I took a deep breathe and pushed it hard and rapidly. It moved and continued its path to the other side fairly easily. I thought that it had almost gone completely through him on its original momentum off the bow. Aerius let out a loud groan as the arrow moved and he opened his eyes. I reached behind him and could feel that the point was out and free of his shoulder. I then rolled him over on his good side, and after some effort I was able to pull it out of the wound. Aerius moaned again.

I bound the wound as best I could with some rags I had had the presence of mind to bring with me for just such a purpose. Aerius was unconscious by this time. I put the storm shield back on the lantern and decided to rest as Aerius slept. I was totally worn out. Playing surgeon to an injured soldier was not part of my calling, and it had taken a great deal of concentration and effort to remove the offending arrow. I also was concerned about any internal damage the projectile had caused as it passed through his body, for it had gone under the shoulder armor between it and the breastplate, a placement that might cause severe internal bleeding. Of course, I was also afraid that he might develop an infection from the wound. I had to get him out of this underground world and up into the fresh air as soon as I possibly could. He needed to be under the care of a physician or surgeon. I felt that before we made the final push up to the fortress, I would rest a few minutes myself.

It wasn't long before I, too, fell asleep for an unknown amount of time. What finally awakened me was the sound of some voices off in the distance. It was the Jewish rabble still searching for me. I felt panic building in my very soul and didn't know what to do. I had slept in a sitting position on a rock with my back to the wall. I started to rise to a standing position when I felt a hand on my shoulder holding me down.

"Be quiet, don't make a sound. Maybe they will walk on by this tunnel." It was Aerius. He had regained consciousness and was standing at my side. He pulled me to my feet, and we walked to the entryway to the small room we were in. "Stay close to the wall, Caleb," Aerius admonished. "They will have to enter this room to see us. Take my sword, and if they do find us, cut them down. I'm too weak to endure battle."

I stared into the darkness not knowing what to say. I couldn't kill anyone, not now. My faith told me quite the opposite; I was to befriend my enemy. I had done enough with my lies, I could do no more. Just then the three Jewish men entered the alcove and held their torches high above their heads so the light would shine into every nook and cranny of the room. As quickly as they entered, they left, and continued on up the tunnel in the opposite direction we would be traveling.

I breathed a sigh of relief and thanked God that we had not been discovered. I then whispered to Aerius, "We must get on our way. I have to get you to the surgeon so that he may care for your wound and get you onto the road of recovery."

"You'll have to help me," he responded, "I don't have a lot of strength left." I again had him throw his good arm over my shoulder and we started on our way out of the room and into the main tunnel that I hoped would take us up and into the fortress. Our progress was slow and I knew that my companion was laboring under the strain of his wounds, but he didn't complain. We stopped frequently and few words were passed between us.

After what seemed like an endless walk we finally came to some stone stairs that led upward into what I thought would be Antonio Fortress. The climb was steep and included many steps, more than a hundred. Aerius had little strength left and kept placing more of his weight on my shoulders. I half carried and half dragged him up the stairs. At the top was a door covered with dust and spider webs. I pushed against it, and it didn't budge. I then sat Aerius on the top step and pushed harder against the door—nothing. My hopes for escape began to fade. I knew I couldn't go back down those steps, return to the stable, and make our way to the original entrance I had used to enter this underground world since it was filled with the scum of the earth who were out to kill me.

I stood up and summoning all of my strength. I ran as hard as I could from the top of the stairs and hit the door with all of my force with my left shoulder. The pain from the blow against the wood of the door was excruciating, but I felt it give, just a little. My pleasure of feeling the door move overcame the soreness in my left shoulder. I again went to the top of the steps and ran full force against the offending barrier and hit it with my right shoulder. It gave a little more. After the fourth attempt it opened enough so I was able to squeeze through. A great deal of debris had fallen against the door, which had prevented it from opening. I cleared most of the rocks and stones away, and the door, or what was left of it, swung open.

We were at the bottom of yet another staircase. At the top was another closed door, but I could see some light emitting through a crack underneath the door. I had no idea what time of day or even what day it was for that matter. All I knew was that it was daylight and that the end of this terrible journey into the bowels of Jerusalem was drawing to a close.

I checked on Aerius and found that he'd passed out, so I left him and deftly climbed the second staircase. This second door was also locked shut, but it led to a room with a window, which I could see through a large knothole in the wood. I wasn't sure if we were at the fortress or somewhere else. I was completely disoriented as to my location.

I tried pushing against this door and found that it gave a little under my pressure. I looked down the stairs and could not see anything in the blackness behind me. I whispered loudly, "Aerius I'll be right back. I'm going to check and see what I find on the other side of this door."

There was no response and I felt that he was still out cold. Then with all of my might I pushed on the door, and it came crashing down. I found myself in a little room with another door opposite the one I had entered, which led to the portico along the western wall of the fortress. I walked down this short corridor to the main courtyard and was suddenly surrounded by numerous Romans, who were as shocked as I at my sudden appearance in their midst.

I was quickly surrounded by soldiers with swords drawn pointing menacingly at me. "I am Caleb," I shouted, "I have an injured Roman centurion that I've brought up from the underground tunnels below the Temple. He is seriously injured and needs your help."

"Who is the centurion you have?" one of the men asked.

"His name is Aerius. He's been wounded with an arrow. He needs immediate attention," I yelled. "Please believe me. I was the one who did the interpreting for Titus out on the bridge when he put forth the demands to Simon and John the other day."

An officer who had been there with the group came over, looked at me closely and then announced, "This is who he says he is. I recognize him. Where is Aerius?"

"I will show you, follow me," I said as I turned and headed back down the corridor to the little room. I crossed to the door that led down the staircase and quickly went down the steps to Aerius's side.

A number of soldiers had followed me, and soon we were all there looking down on the prone Aerius who was still unconscious.

"It is his right shoulder and he's lost a great deal of blood. Be careful with him," I admonished.

They lifted him to his feet and carefully carried him up the stairs, through the room, down the portico and out into the court of the fortress, which was at the time used as the hospital for all of the injured and sick Roman troops. They laid him down, and one of the soldiers ran to fetch the surgeon.

By this time I was exhausted. I fell to the ground on my knees and prayed ever so fervently that Aerius be spared. I then rolled off of my knees into a sitting position. No one said a word to me, and I watched as the surgeon approached from across the courtyard. He went immediately to Aerius's side and carefully examined his injuries. He then ordered that those soldiers near him to use a nearby litter and transport him to the surgery located on the far end of the courtyard. The men carefully lifted him onto a cape and then onto the litter before they lifted him and carried him to the surgery. As the litter bearers reached the far side of the courtyard, none other than General Titus appeared before the group who had assisted me with Aerius. After interviewing these men, he then went to the surgeon and some of the other men who had helped bring him up from the tunnels into the court and asked about the event that had brought Aerius here.

I noticed that one of them pointed in my direction, and I hoped they were telling the truth about what had happened. I didn't need to be taken back into custody. I lowered my eyes and stared at the ground wishing ever so fervently that I could return to my grandson in Philadelphia. When I looked up, I saw the general approaching me with a group of his officers. I swallowed hard and prayed that what they had to tell me would be good news.

As the general approached I struggled to my feet, and then he was there right in front of me. I bowed slightly and remained silent. "It is my understanding that you went down into the tunnels below the Temple to retrieve one of my officers, is that correct?" he demanded.

"Yes sir," I answered. "I knew that he had been wounded and cut off from his men. He commanded them to return for reinforcements before returning to retrieve him. When I heard what had happened I decided to go look for him as I felt that my being a civilian would probably go unnoticed by the rebels, as I, too, was once a citizen of Jerusalem. This I was able to do."

"Why would you, a Jew, go to the aid of a Roman officer?" he asked.

"Sir, Aerius is my friend. I despise what this rebel scum has allowed to happen to my beautiful home of Jerusalem. I know that you, sir, have given them every opportunity to surrender and save the city, but yet they have refused your generous offers. The result is that I dislike these men who have brought on this devastation as much as you and your army do." I didn't go on to tell the general that my hope was to bring Aerius to Christ or that I was a believer myself. I then fell silent and waited for his response.

"I'm impressed with your courage, Caleb," he replied, "misguided though it may be. We would have sent reinforcements down to retrieve him if you'd just waited."

"I was afraid for Aerius's life. I felt that he might be captured or worse bleed to death if help didn't get to him in a timely fashion. I know that it was foolish of me, but I felt that waiting another morning or afternoon might be a matter of life and death."

The general considered this for a moment and then responded, "You brought him up alive, and for that we thank you."

"There is another matter, sir, that I would like to bring to your attention," I said.

"What is that, are you looking for a reward?" he answered somewhat sarcastically.

"Oh, no sir, it's that I saw that brigand Simon down in the tunnels."

"You saw him?" he demanded. "He's still alive?"

"Yes sir. He was in one of the large rooms under the Temple, he and a formidable group of his followers. They have been coming up at night and stealing food from your own stores. They seem to know the underground tunnels well, and I think they plan to stay down there until your army moves out. At which time, they plan to come up from the tunnels and escape into the countryside. They have great treasures stored away that they plan to squander on themselves when this is all said and done."

"This is important news you have brought me," the general replied thoughtfully. "Can you give us an accurate location in order for my troops to go and find them and destroy them once and for all?"

"I can. Let me speak with the one who will lead the expedition, and I'll give him the specifics. I, too, want to see these men brought to justice."

"I seem to have misread your motives, Caleb. I thank you for the life of one of my centurions and also for the valuable information concerning the location of the enemy soldiers. Is there anything that you want? For you have been a valuable asset to us and our quest to reestablish control of the city."

"Sir, there is only one thing that I desire," I replied, "and that is to return to my home, to my family and to my friends in the city of Philadelphia. I wish for nothing more."

"Then that wish will be granted. You are free to return whenever you want. We will supply you with a horse and the necessary food and water to sustain you for the journey. Is there nothing else?"

"No, sir," I replied, "I will stay around long enough to see how Aerius is and then when that is determined, I will leave. Thank you for my freedom."

The general said nothing else and turned on his heel and walked away. As he walked he talked to one of his officers, and I heard him mention my name and nothing else. I hoped that he was giving instructions concerning my departure.

I went to my cell in Fortress Antonio, and washed up and changed into some clean clothes. My next stop was the infirmary to check on

Aerius. On my way there I discovered to my amazement that I had been in the tunnels below the city for only a little more than a day and night. It felt as if I'd been down there for a lifetime. I determined then and there that I would never enter another tunnel or cave for the remainder of my years on this earth.

At the infirmary I found that the surgeon was working on Aerius and that I could visit with him later in the afternoon. Since it was lunch time I went to the kitchen. Here I ran into Longius.

"You made it back, Caleb," he shouted to me when he spied me at one of the long tables used to serve the officers. "I was concerned over your safety and, of course, for Aerius. The news is that you found him and brought him up alive. Congratulations on a job well done."

"Thank you," I replied. "It was a difficult journey fraught with dangers as I did encounter the Jewish rabble. I was only able to escape as a result of Aerius's appearing out of nowhere and saving me from ending up on the pointed end of a Jewish sword."

"That's not unusual, Aerius always the warrior, will never go down without a fight. As a matter of fact the tribune has not sent down a force yet to sweep that place clean of the rebels."

"You mean that if I hadn't gone on my own, Aerius would still be there?" I asked incredulously.

"Keep this to yourself, but the tribune is a weak man. He has no military training and is indecisive in all that he does. He comes from a well-to-do family in Rome and is here only to enhance his own image as a warrior. He had been elected to the Senate and volunteered to serve in order to augment that appearance. We do not admire him," Longius whispered in a low voice. "Without your help, Aerius in all probability would be dead."

I just shook my head and thanked the Lord that He had protected me during my adventure.

"I further understand that you have found the hiding place of the rebels below the city," he continued in his normal voice.

"Yes," I answered. "They seem to know the tunnel system well and took me to one of their principle hideouts."

"They took you there?" Longius asked with raised eyebrows.

By this time we had been served our rations. As we ate, I explained to him exactly what had happened to me, finding Aerius and our adventurous journey up through the tunnels and into the fortress.

"That's quite a story, Caleb," Longius said when I'd finished. "You have become a strong asset for Rome."

"That's not the point," I responded. "I'm not here to aid Rome in her conquest of Jerusalem. I came here to aid the believers of The Way to escape this calamity. Now that the fighting is nearly over I would like to see these evil men, brought to justice. Even though I feel that the Jewish people have not been faithful to their God, It is John and Simon who have been the ring leaders that have brought on the destruction of Jerusalem. God has only used Rome to punish these people for turning their backs on Him, but that's another story and we won't debate that issue now."

"You're still talking about your God, aren't you Caleb? Don't you know after all of this time that there are only the Roman gods? They are the ones that give us our strength and it is only through them that we are victorious. It's as simple as that."

"Ahh, Longius, you have yet to see the light. I hope some day you will be able to come to the realization before you die that there is but one God, that His Son lived right here in Jerusalem thirty-five years ago, and that by accepting Him on faith right here and now you will have eternal life."

"I don't have the time to debate the issue with you, Caleb, for I am to take you to the man who will lead our expedition into the tunnels and round up this Jewish rabble; besides Aerius warned me that you would try and convert me to your faith," he added with a chuckle. "Come finish up, and I'll take you to the one who will lead the attack. You can give us the means of finding those rats that dwell under the city."

I briefed the officers who were to lead the expedition on all I could recall of the time I had spent in the tunnel system. I drew a map of the rooms and alcoves and of the blocked tunnel in which I had found Aerius. I also gave them the number of steps I had taken in the different tunnels, at least the best I could remember.

The officers thanked me and went to their men to make preparation for their encounter. I then left that group of men and felt relieved that they hadn't asked me to lead the way. I'd had enough of the subterranean city and wanted nothing more to do with it. My next goal was to go to the infirmary and visit Aerius.

Before I went to see Aerius, I watched as the troops who were to take part in the search for the Jewish remnant below the city form up and move to the tunnel entrance. I prayed for the safety of all and further beseeched that God end all of the killing and let peace return to this Promised Land. Once they disappeared down the steps and into the structure that housed the entrance to the tunnel, I proceeded on to the infirmary.

I wandered around the large courtyard that held all of the wounded soldiers. I was somewhat surprised by the large number who were bedridden. I knew that many were sent back to Caesarea on a regular basis, but those unable to travel were left here and treated by the army's surgeon. This must have been a huge task. I supposed that many who were seriously wounded and unable to travel were left here to die. As I wandered through the medical center, I was approached by one of the medical attendants.

"What are you doing here?" he demanded.

"My name is Caleb," I replied. "I brought the injured centurion called Aerius here earlier in the day. I have come to see how he is."

"I've heard of you," he answered. "You're the Jew to whom the general has granted amnesty for saving the soldier from the hands of the enemy."

"It was a little more involved than that," I said, "but you could say that was the case. How is Aerius doing, and how serious are his wounds?"

"You'll have to see the surgeon; he's over on the far side of the court tending to the centurion now."

"Thank you," I answered and headed in the direction the attendant had pointed out. The surgeon was an older man close to my own age. He was short, rotund, and quite bald. He wore a white toga with a gold belt around his imposing belly.

He had a serious look as he finished dressing the wound in Aerius's shoulder.

I startled him when I approached and introduced myself. "Sir, my name is Caleb, and I've come to see how the centurion is doing."

The surgeon stood up from the prone soldier and looked at me quizzically for a moment. "Oh, you're the one who brought him up from the tunnels below the city. I'm not used to seeing civilians in this area of the fortress."

"I'm sorry, sir, I didn't mean to trouble you. However, Aerius is a friend and I was concerned about his condition."

The surgeon looked down on his patient, and then said with a sigh, "He's not responding well. The arrow did some internal damage, and we are now waiting to see what will happen. Are you the one that removed the arrow from his shoulder?"

"Yes," I answered. "I've never done anything like that before, but I felt that at the time it was the best thing to do. He was bleeding profusely, and as soon as I removed the offending missile the bleeding stopped or slowed."

"That was the right thing to do," the surgeon said. "I think there may have been something on the point of the arrow, for there are signs of a serious infection beginning to set in."

"Will I be able to speak with him?" I asked.

"He's asleep now, but you can stay here with him if you choose and speak with him when he awakes."

I sat down on the floor next to Aerius's litter and waited for him to come around to consciousness. I was utterly worn out, and it wasn't long before I was dozing as I sat with my back against a nearby wall It wasn't too long before Aerius began to stir. When he became conscious of his surroundings, he seemed confused. I went to him and put my hand on his good shoulder. He looked up at me, and at the other litters around him. He winced from the pain in his shoulder as he tried to sit up.

"You'd better not try to sit or get up," I said. "You've lost a lot of blood, and I would imagine you are very weak."

Still he struggled to partially sit by placing the elbow of his good arm under him.

"Where am I?" he asked as he looked all around viewing the numerous wounded on other litters placed nearby.

"You're in the infirmary at Fortress Antonio," I told him. "When we came up from the tunnels below the city we ended up in one of the rooms in the fortress. They then brought you here to the infirmary."

"What day is it, Caleb? How long have I been here?" he asked with a puzzled look on his face.

"You've been here for a good part of a day. It's been just two days since you and your men entered the tunnel, and about a day and a half since you were struck by the enemy's arrow. Don't concern yourself with those things, though, for here you are safe and you can recuperate from your wound."

Aerius lay back on the litter, and I could tell that he was trying to reconstruct the events that had led him here. After a few moments of silence, he finally said, "It's all coming back to me now. You were the one that brought me here. I remember you being attacked by those Jews in the tunnel. I also remember running them through. I seem to be forever watching after you." Aerius chuckled before he started a violent cough that resulted in him spitting up some blood.

When the cough subsided, I said, "You always are watching out for me. I would probably be dead now if it weren't for your watchful eye."

Aerius quickly changed the subject. "How am I? What does the surgeon have to say?"

"He says you lost a lot of blood and may have an infection in the wound. You'll be down for some time. They're trying to treat you the best that they can. Even Titus was concerned about you."

"The general came to see me? Why would he be concerned about me?" he muttered. "I'm just a lowly centurion."

"You saved his life once, Aerius, don't you remember?"

"I guess I did, but that was so long ago. I didn't think he'd remember."

"He did, Aerius. He saw you right after we came up into the fortress, and then he came and talked to me. I told him how you saved my life, too. I wouldn't be surprised if there were a promotion in all of this for you. As a matter of fact, there will be a ceremony tomorrow where he will reward the troops with their share of the plunder for their part in conquering the city."

When I finished talking I saw that Aerius had passed out again. I was very concerned for him. He seemed so weak, which was so unlike him. I got up and went to the surgeon, who was working on another soldier. I told him that I had spoken to Aerius and that he seemed to me to be terribly weak.

The surgeon just looked at me and said that he'd lost a lot of blood. Only time would tell whether he would recover or not. "I'm concerned about the infection deep inside the wound. We will care for him as best we can; only the gods know whether he will live."

I nodded and left the infirmary, returned to my cell, fell across my mat, and went sound to sleep. In my subsequent dream, I heard an insistent voice that urged me to remain at Aerius's side. My impression was that his injury was worse than what had been determined by the surgeon. Further, I felt that the possibility of eminent death of my friend was real.

I awoke in a cold sweat and quickly returned to the infirmary. On my way I prayed that my thoughts and impressions were wrong and that

God would heal my friend. When I arrived I found the surgeon and an orderly attending to Aerius, who was awake but looking extremely pale.

As I approached, the surgeon stood and came to my side. "Your centurion is not well. I think that the arrow penetrated the upper portion of his heart and there is continued internal bleeding. He seems to be slipping away."

I felt a cold chill sweep over me and then asked if it were all right if I talked to the patient.

"He needs rest," the surgeon said, "but I suppose it won't hurt to talk for a short time." He and his orderly started to walk away, but before he was too far, he turned and said, "The general is very interested in this man; he has asked of his condition on several different occasions. Don't put too much stress on him."

I assured the surgeon that I wouldn't and then sat next to the litter.

Aerius opened his eyes, "Is that you, Caleb?

"Yes," I responded. "I wanted to check on you and see how you were doing."

"I heard what the surgeon said. He thinks I'm not going to make it. The way I feel now I'm not so sure myself."

"You'll be all right. It'll take a lot more than a Jewish arrow to finish you off," I joked. "You're too tough and stubborn to die."

"I hope you're right, Caleb. I've been thinking about those things you and I have discussed over the past few months. Those things about your God and this man you call Jesus who came as the Messiah. How could I ever become a follower of his? I haven't led a good and sin-free life. I've killed many men and have felt good about my ability to survive at the cost of another's life. Your God would have nothing to do with me even if I did accept Him. I've committed too many sinful deeds in my past."

I studied Aerius for a while before answering. I wasn't sure if he were being honest with me or if he were making fun of my beliefs. Finally, I ventured, "It doesn't work that way, Aerius. It doesn't matter when you accept Jesus on faith. However, once you do accept him with a repentant heart and sincerely believe that he is the Son of God, that's all that is necessary."

"You mean that as I lie here on my deathbed, all I have to do is accept who he said he is and I can live forever?"

"With sincerity and repentance and a true feeling that he is who he claimed to be, you can attain eternal life. It has to be honest and genuine from the heart. Without that, it won't work. The words are meaningless unless the heart is behind the words."

"I've lived a pretty tough life; I have killed and maimed other people. I've even cheated and pushed my way to the top of the heap, not caring who is in the way. I've done immoral things and enjoyed it without giving a second thought about those I've hurt. And you're telling me that this will all be forgiven if I just ask for his mercy by saying these few words?"

"I tell you the truth, Aerius, that this is a fact. As long as you are truly repentant in your heart for those things you have done in the past, and try to live in a way that is upright and faithful to the cause of goodness and righteousness in the eyes of God, your past will be forgiven and you will start anew as far as He is concerned."

"You have lived a good life, Caleb. Any man can see that who has been around you for some time. However, you are telling me that I can be as clean and as good as you by just accepting Jesus and asking his forgiveness for all of those sins I committed in the past. That you and I could be equal in the eyes of God."

"That's exactly right. Jesus once told a story that addresses this issue and gives you an idea of what this means. He said, 'Once there was a landowner who had a vineyard whose grapes were ready for harvest. The year had been a good year and the vines were burdened and needed to be picked. This landowner went to the nearby town in the early morning and contracted with a number of men offering them so many deneri for a day's work. The men went to the vineyard and began to pick the grapes. At noon, the landowner saw that there was still a great deal of work to be done and that he needed more workers, so he again went into town and hired another group of men for the same number of deneri and they too went to work.

"Before dinner time, he once again concluded that more people were needed to harvest the crop, and for the third time he went to town and hired more workers for the same pay and set them to work picking the grapes. Finally, one last time, before sunset, he determined that an additional number of workers were needed, and he hired more men to help with the harvest.

"When the crop had been gathered and finally brought in from the vineyard shortly after dark, he called the workers together and paid them. When those who were hired earlier in the day discovered that they were paid the same as those that had been hired much later, they complained to the landowner that he'd been unfair to them. The landowner replied to those people that it was he which owned the land and he therefore had the right to determine the pay of the workers that harvested his crop.' So you can see, Aerius, God is the landowner just as He is the creator of all things, He has the right to determine who gets paid or, in our case, who gets salvation. This is His gift to those who believe. The time of day that we are 'hired' does not matter, and the pay is still the same. It is our true belief and unwavering faith that we have in Jesus that earns us this salvation. That he is the one that can set our lives straight and that when we believe in him as the true Son of God and accept him on faith with a repentant heart, we, too, through God's loving grace, can receive eternal life."

Aerius was silent for a short while as he thought these things over. I could tell that he was getting weaker, and his breathing was becoming shallow. The bandages over his wound were turning crimson, and I felt that he didn't have much time left.

"Even though I'm dying, will he accept my confession of faith?" he finally asked. "After all of our talks, Caleb," he continued in a whisper, "I believe that you have found that which is right. I hadn't been able to bring myself to believe you; however, I do now. I know that you're right and that the right and proper thing for me is to accept your words and accept Jesus as the Messiah. I renounce my life as I lived it, and if I had known these things before, much would have changed.

"I do believe and accept Jesus and ask forgiveness for all of those sins I have committed in my life." He paused and closed his eyes. He was having trouble breathing.

"Aerius," I called out, "don't die now." There was no response, his eyes were closed and the breathing was barely detectable. I got up and ran to the surgeon. "He's not breathing well!" I told him. "Come and help him."

By the time we got back to Aerius, he was dead. The surgeon closed the centurion's eyes and looked at him for a long moment. "He lived longer than he should have, for the wound was serious and would have killed most men on the spot. You did all you could to save him and for that you should be commended. I don't know many of the soldiers here who would have had the courage you showed when you went out after him under the city. Take heart, for I will tell the general of your loyalty."

"I don't need you to do that. My reward has already been given to me by Titus; my freedom. My true sorrow is the death of this man, for he was my friend."

The surgeon just shook his head for I don't think he could believe that I, a citizen of Jerusalem, would have a Roman friend. He motioned for the orderly and in silence they began to prepare the body for cremation.

I said my last goodbye to my friend and with a heavy heart went back to my room. I was sad for the loss, but on the other hand, I was joyous over the fact that Aerius had accepted Jesus and would dwell in the House of the Lord forever. I would meet up with him again!

RETURN TO PHILADELPHIA

Late that evening accompanied by a special honor guard, Aerius was cremated The general himself spoke on his behalf, extolling him as great soldier of the empire, an example that all soldiers should strive to emulate. When this ceremony was completed, some of the soldiers in Aerius's manipuli came to me and thanked me for what I'd done in going down into the tunnels to retrieve their leader whom they admired and yes, I'd say loved. I was touched by their expressions of loyalty to him and maybe a little surprised, for he had been a tough taskmaster; however, I believe that his decisions and the discipline he meted out was fair, and they knew that.

After the ceremony I returned to my cell and immediately fell into a long and deep sleep. On arising the next day, I found that Titus had ordered all of his troops to assemble on the Temple Mount. His intent was to inform the men of how the clean up or concluding action in Jerusalem was to proceed.

Once the men had gathered by legion and auxiliary, Titus stood before the troops and extolled their courage and the might of the Roman Empire. "It is because of you, your courage and valor, and yes, because of your devotion to Rome that we once again are victorious over our enemies. No nation on earth will ever be able to stand against our power and might.

"Therefore," he continued, "because of your commitment and sacrifice in the face of a devious and deceitful enemy, all of you will share in the riches and plunder of a conquered Jerusalem. The auxiliary units who fought with zeal and dedication to Rome will be relieved and begin their journey home until they are once again needed. The soldiers of the Twelfth Legion will be the vanguard of our victory into Rome. They will take the booty and prisoners and proceed to Caesarea to board the awaiting ships for the trip home. I will accompany the Fifteenth Legion, which will follow the Twelfth in one week, to Alexandra, where we too will board ships bound for Rome. The Tenth Legion will remain here in Jerusalem as a deterrent to anyone who might think about taking possession of this city once again. The remaining troops will continue the work of subduing all of Judea before they return to Antioch.

"Before we depart we will take a week to tear every stone on this Temple Mount down and cast it into the valleys that surround us. There is to be no stone left standing in its original place. It is also decreed that all of the walls that surround this city will be torn down and cast aside, except for a portion of the western wall. This will be left so that any who have the notion that they can defeat Rome will be able to determine that no physical obstruction will stand in the way of our armies. The walls of Jerusalem were the most formidable ever built by man. The remaining portion of the city will be burnt to the ground. We will leave standing only the three towers, Mariame, Phasael, Hippicus and that portion of the western wall I mentioned. We will leave no reason for the Jews ever to want to return and rebuild this city. By my decree as the son of our great emperor Vespasian, Jerusalem will be left uninhabitable."

Following that statement a great roar arose from the throats of the assembled troops, "Hail to Vespasian, hail to Titus and all hail to Rome!"

I had heard enough, for Jesus' prophecy would now be carried out. I did not want to stay in the city another day and determined that I would leave immediately. When the ceremony was over, I sought out Longius and told him of my decision to start home.

"I will be sorry to see you go, Caleb," he said to me. "You have become a favorite of the men of our manipuli. However, I understand why you want to leave, and I think it better that you do. Many Jews are being slaughtered still by our soldiers without regard for whether they worked with the bandits John and Simon or not. I have been told that the general has promised you provisions and a horse for your trip home. In addition, I will send two of my soldiers with you for one full days journey as a means of protection. Once they leave you, be careful and be wary of any Roman troops you may see along the way, for there is a great deal of hatred against your people and they may not respect what you have done for Rome. I will have your horse and guards waiting for you outside the western gate of the fort in a short time. The destruction of the city has begun and soon men will move in here to burn and tear down the fortress. I will meet you at the gate, Caleb."

"I will be there as soon as I gather my things," I replied.

I ran to my little cubicle to collect my meager belongings. One of these items was a belt knife Aerius had given me, an item I would now cherish and keep with me always as I remembered my friend whom I now knew I would see again when we meet in the afterlife.

True to his word, Longius and the two guards were waiting when I stepped out of the western gate. The animal didn't look strong and to my surprise it was a donkey. I sighed and decided it was more than I had when I came into the city, for I had last entered on foot. I threw my bag of belongings over the saddle and climbed aboard. Off we went through the streets along the second wall towards the Gennath Gate near the tower of Hippicus.

As we approached the gate from the city side, Longius spotted the general not too far from our street. He leaned towards me and whispered, "The general is inspecting the destruction of the northern portion of western wall, which started this afternoon."

Before I could answer, one of the officers near Titus spurred his horse and sped towards us. I saw the color drain from Longius's face for he, I'm sure, feared that he'd done something to displease his commander. Longius and the two soldiers who were to accompany me saluted the tribune smartly by bringing their right arms across their chests and sitting at attention saying nothing. At this point I was beginning to feel uneasy for the thought crossed my mind that General Titus may have rescinded my order for release. I said a quick prayer that this was not the case.

The tribune pulled up close to Longius, leaned forward in the saddle and whispered into his ear. When finished, he spurred his horse forward and sped back over to where Titus and his other officers stood, leaving Longius in the middle of a salute. He watched as the high ranking officer returned to Titus's side, looked at me and then back to his commander. Finally Longius said, "Caleb, the general wants me to give you my horse."

I gasped and said, "But isn't that the one that belonged to Aerius?"

"Yes," he replied. "He didn't think it appropriate that you should leave the city on an ass after all that you have done to help the Romans secure Jerusalem. Caleb, if it were anyone but you I'd be irate, but your kindness and support makes the giving up of this magnificent steed more palatable."

"Thank you," I stammered, "I know how much Aerius thought of this animal. I just trust that it doesn't grieve you too deeply to have to give it up. Is there another horse that you would rather I have?"

"In answer to your question, yes; however, I don't think that that would be acceptable. It's all right, Caleb. I already own a fine steed and to relinquish Aerius's horse to you does not trouble me too greatly. I thank you for the thought."

"I'm grateful, Longius, and I hope our paths cross again but under more pleasant circumstances. God bless you." With that said I transferred my sack of belongings and the saddlebag of provisions to the horse and with difficulty mounted the horse Storm. By this time Longius was walking the donkey back to the makeshift stable. I looked over at the general, who was watching to insure that his order was being carried out. I raised my hand in thanks. He nodded his farewell and turned his attention back to the wall.

I dug my heels into the flanks of the horse and proceeded through the gate with my escort where we immediately turned south and continued on around the Serpent's Pool down to the Hinnom Valley where we turned east. We continued along the valley that paralleled the south wall and on down to the Well of Joab. I was deeply moved by the scenes of disaster that I saw. Many of the buildings no longer could be seen for they had been destroyed, and pillars of smoke and even flames could be seen leaping into the sky. The smell of smoke and decaying flesh filled the air. It was in the Well of Joab that so many of the bodies of the citizens had been dumped, and the sight was sickening. We skirted around the mass grave and continued on to the east. Once we were a short distance from the southeast corner of Jerusalem, I stopped to take a last look at what had once been a magnificent city—one that, in its time, had rivaled Rome in beauty, but which now lay in ruins. The Temple ruins were barely visible above the walls. Smoke and fire filled the air along with sounds of the Roman soldiers tearing apart all those buildings that still stood.

"Caleb, we need to keep moving," one of my escorts shouted at me.

"Yes, yes you're right," I replied. I turned back in my saddle, never to look upon Jerusalem again. I could feel tears streaming down my face as I thought of the terrible end that had befallen my place of birth, my lifelong home.

We continued along the road that led to Bethany and soon approached the farm of Silas. I could see that the house had been burnt but that the stable still stood. It looked a little bedraggled though, and one portion of the roof had collapsed. I suggested to my escort that we spend the night here, for there was a supply of water and a place to sleep under a roof. It was getting late, and the sun would set within short time.

My escort agreed with my recommendation, and we went to the stable. There we found that the hay mow was still intact and that there was still a supply of hay with which we could feed the animals and use as our bedding for the night.

The two soldiers who were with me agreed that they should alternate standing guard through the night just in case any marauders might try to steal our supplies and horses. After eating a cold and meager meal, I wandered around the property for a short while. I discovered that the well still had good sweet water, and to my joy, I found that the supplies that had been hidden in the shed had been taken and that the flooring had been carefully replaced. To me this could only mean that Naomi and her family had been here before they set off to Philadelphia. At least that was my hope. With that confirmation in my mind, I returned to the stable and slept soundly throughout the night.

At daybreak I was awakened by the soldiers who were escorting me, and we were soon on our way after replenishing our supply of water. The escort traveled with me throughout the day, and we then spent the night under the stars.

The next day, early in the morning twilight before the sun was above the horizon, they bid me farewell, as it was time for them to return to Jerusalem.

"Be careful of the Jews and even of the Romans. The Jews will rob you of all you have and then kill you. They will be especially interested in your horse," the leader said after they had mounted their steeds. "But I also caution you to be careful of Roman soldiers, for they will not know that you have been sent forth by General Titus himself. They may take you for a thief and just as soon kill you as to take you prisoner. Good luck on your journey."

"Thanks for the warning; I will be careful. I pray that God be with you," I responded.

The two soldiers spurred their horses and turned back towards the city at a slow trot. I suddenly felt all alone. The warnings had frightened me, and before I started I scanned the countryside around me. The only people I saw were the two escorts who were now some distance away. I further decided that it would be wise if I traveled at night. This was not only an issue of my safety but it was the prudent thing to do as the August daytime temperatures were sometimes unbearable. I thought of this fact as this particular day seemed to be starting off as a real scorcher, unlike the preceding days when the temperature had been rather moderate. I mounted Storm and determined to travel just long enough before the sun got too high in the sky. Then I would seek out a daytime hiding place for me and my horse.

I didn't see a soul during that early morning. It wasn't too long before the sun began to burn with an intensity that made it nearly intolerable to continue. It was shortly before high noon that I found a hiding place down in an arroyo. There were some rocks and tall scrub bushes that I used for hiding and as a shield against the heat of the sun. I fed some hay to Storm and gave him a little water. I, too, had a drink, and then settled down and tried to sleep until the sun got low in the sky. I wasn't successful as many of the images of the fighting that had taken place over the past six months flashed through my mind, keeping me awake. I also thought of the poor innocent victims of Jerusalem, those who had been loyal to God and faithful to the covenant. Their suffering was not of their own doing and it disturbed me that even though they had not accepted the messiah they had remained firm in their beliefs and faithful to one god. The only answer was that despicable men had brought on this calamity, not God. It was the free and wrong choice of men like Simon and John.

Finally the sun began to settle towards the horizon in the west. I drank some more water, gave some to the horse, and saddled him before loading my provisions over his back. I next climbed up into the saddle, and we started out on our journey again. The air was still quite warm, and we moved slowly through the barren and deserted land. Shortly after the sun set, I realized that we were just a short distance north of the place where I had buried my friend Josephus. I turned south and soon came across the now dry stream bed where my other friends and I had stayed during Josephus's last time on earth. I dismounted and led Storm along the path for a short distance until I came upon the grave. So much had happened since that time that I felt as if this event had taken place years ago, but in reality it had been only eight months since those tumultuous times. I knelt down and said a short prayer, imploring God to look favorably on this lost soul, knowing full well that his choice left him eternally separated from Yahweh.

After spending no more than a short time there, I remounted and continued on at a little faster pace as the air had turned cooler. Storm and I trudged on throughout the night. The air, of course, was cooler than the daytime temperature, but it was still warm. I dismounted several times to give water to the horse and have some myself. I had to be stingy with it as our supply was limited and we needed enough to reach our destination. I also walked a great deal of the time as I didn't think it right to overburden the horse in this hot weather.

I don't know how far we traveled but near dawn as the horizon to the east was beginning to brighten, I remounted Storm and continued on at a slow pace. We both were tired, but I knew it wouldn't be long before we reached our next a hiding place. We came upon another dry streambed and followed it for a while. As we continued we entered a canyon that had been carved out of the rock by the stream many eons ago; a small canyon that I had used on my previous trips as I traveled between Philadelphia to Jerusalem. I decided that I would spend the day on the other side of the canyon as there was a large open plain just beyond and on the east end of the canyon there were numerous hiding places where we could spend the day time before we crossed the open ground after sunset. As we approached the end of the canyon I could see that the sun had breached the eastern horizon and the light was beginning to fill the darkest corners of the canyon. I was intent on finding a hiding place.

As we squeezed through the narrowest part of the canyon before it entered the plain, I was startled and frightened when a man jumped in front of my path and grabbed the reins of my horse. He was dressed in dingy, dirty clothes that had large tears and holes in them. He had a drawn sword and he pointed it at me in a threatening manner. "Your horse for your life," he yelled.

Storm reared up on his hind legs nearly unseating me. I looked over my shoulder. There were three other men standing behind me, all with spears pointed towards me and swords sheathed on their belts. They, too, were ragged and emaciated in appearance. I quickly concluded they were some of the soldiers who had been followers of John or Simon and had managed to escape from the city.

"Your horse for your life!" the man holding the reins of Storm shouted again.

I knew that I must do something, or I would be dead within minutes. Without saying a word I dug the heals of my sandals into Storm's flanks and yelled at him to move. He again reared high, kicking the man holding the reins in the chest knocking him down. We then charged over the fallen man and galloped forward onto the plain at full speed as I leaned forward with my arms around the animal's neck. We both were frightened, and Storm was at full gallop in an instant. Just after we leaped over the one the man trying to block our way I saw a spear fly by our right side, thrown by one of the men who had come up behind us.

We were quickly out of their range, and I detected no more thrown objects tossed in our direction. After a terrifying high-speed gallop, I stopped Storm and dismounted. Looking back, I could not detect the men who had tried to waylay our progress. Apparently they had decided not to pursue me. Both Storm and I were breathing hard. Before continuing on I took the time to give us both a drink of our precious water. Then I began walking, leading Storm by the reins. We had traveled through the remainder of the night. I knew that the horse was tired and I elected to walk awhile to let Storm rest. I determined that I didn't want to run into those thugs again, so we walked on even though the sun had come up and the temperature was climbing. My thoughts were to get as far away from them as I could. It was in the late morning when the sun was nearing its zenith that the heat became too much for either of us to continue. I located an east facing outcrop of rock and situated us in its shadow.

I fed Storm and gave him some more water. I decided I could forgo a drink though I did wet a small rag and moistened my lips and tongue. The water had to last us another two days, and it was getting precariously low. The heat was nearly unbearable, and I slept very little. In the late afternoon, I finally did fall into a light sleep for a short time only to be awakened by a bad dream. I had the notion that those men who had tried to take my horse were nearby. I jumped to my feet, looked around and saw nothing, but the feeling from the dream was so strong that without eating or drinking any water, I mounted Strom and lit out to the east. After traveling for a short time, I stopped and looked back to the outcrop of rock where we'd taken shelter earlier in the day. There to my surprise I could see the figures of three men. I said a silent prayer thanking God for awakening me in time to once again escape capture and even escape with my life.

It wasn't long after that the sun set in the west that the air cooled, giving me new hope and strength that I would reach my destination. Around midnight, I stopped for a time to rest and feed my precious animal and myself. The night was clear, and the air had a definite chill to it, which seemed to invigorate both of us. After eating and drinking a small portion of water, we continued on. My thoughts went to those men pursuing me. Jews by birth and probably brought up in the ways of faith, how was it that they turned their backs to God and sunk to the low level of thievery and murder? The choices made by men can lead to self destruction was my conclusion.

Early the next morning before sunrise we came upon an old well that I had visited during my previous trips. There had always been a small amount of water here, and I felt it would be a good place to spend the day, though I was ever vigilant and on the alert for any of my pursuers. There wasn't much water to be had, and it took some digging to reach it but I found enough to satisfy our thirst. I slept better that day, but each time I awakened I looked to the west to be sure the men weren't still out there.

At nightfall, I filled my water skin, took a long drink, and gave a drink to Storm before climbing aboard and starting out. That night's trip was uneventful, and for the first time since leaving Jerusalem we were able to luxuriate in water, for we were now only a half days ride from Philadelphia and my water skin was still half full.

I wanted to enter the city early in the morning so after a meal in which I finished my provisions, I slept until well after midnight. Very early in the morning, we started on the final leg. I found it hard to contain my excitement as we approached Philadelphia. It had been over eight months since I had last left my home and I was anxious to see my friends, my grandson Abram, and, of course, to meet up again with Naomi, if only she were still there. Shortly before the sun came up and from the distance, I could see a few lights come on as the citizens awakened for another day of work.

As I at last entered the gates of the city, I was giddy with joy and anticipation. As it was still early and the sun hung low over the eastern horizon, I met few people in the streets. Things seemed to be the same. The local merchants were just beginning to put their wares out for the early shoppers like they always had for years. I decided that I would go directly to my, or maybe I should say my grandson's, place of business for he would also be opening the shutters and preparing for another day.

I proceeded down the main street of Philadelphia, and at the third intersection I turned right and continued down that street for about forty paces. There we stopped, for I was in front of our little business. The awning had been lifted, and I could see Abram at the back of the shop gathering some of the materials that would be placed in front for potential customers to examine before buying.

I dismounted Storm and stood in the street in front of the store and waited to see if Abram would recognize me. I watched as he gathered a large amount of materials in his arms and turned around to carry them out to the street where he would arrange them in order of the different materials used in making tents. The pile of wares that he carried in his arms towered over his head, and he had difficulty trying to navigate around the furniture as he brought his load to the street.

"Wouldn't it be easier sir," I said, "if you made two or three trips instead of trying to do it all in one?"

"Oh, I've found that one works well for me," he answered with a slight note of irritation in his voice.

"Well I don't think your grandfather would approve of your methods," I answered trying hard not to laugh out loud.

"What do you know of my—" he started to answer as he turned to see, around his load, who this person was who would dare question how he ran his business. When he caught sight of me, he stopped dead in his tracks and stared at me for a long time before he dropped his load to the ground. Slowly recognition began to sink in. He whispered at first, "Papa?" Then he shouted, "Papa is that really you?"

"Yes, it is my boy," I responded. "It really is me, I've come home to stay!"

Abram dropped all that he carried in his arms and threw his arms around me in a hug that nearly squeezed the breath out of me. I was at last home, my journey ended.

REUNION

"Papa, what—? Where—? How—?" Abram stuttered, trying to take in the fact that I was standing there, right in front of him.

"Slow down, Abram," I chuckled, "I'll tell you in due time about all that has transpired over the last eight months. In the meantime, I wish you'd release your grip before you crush my ribs. Would you then get me some water for my horse, for he and I are both thirsty?"

"Oh, Papa, I'm sorry. Your sudden appearance is such a shock. I'd nearly given you up for dead. The others will be so happy to see you!" he nearly shouted as he released his arms from around me and backed away. "Are you all right? Well and whole?"

"I will answer your questions in due time, but for now I'm hungry and could eat a horse," I responded with a yawn. "I would also like to go inside, sit down and rest for a while, for I've been through quite an ordeal."

"Papa," Abram said somewhat hesitantly as he looked down at the ground. "I have some news that I need to tell you first." He stopped speaking for a moment and slowly drew a circle in the dust of the ground with his right sandal, seemingly lost in thought.

"Is something wrong that I should know about?" I asked anxiously. "Did someone die? What is it?"

"I got married two months ago," he stammered. "Married! But you're just a boy," I answered. "How old are you now?"

"I turned nineteen four months ago. I've taken on the duties of an adult and I've kept our business going," he argued with the strength of his conviction.

"That you have," I relinquished. "You have done a marvelous job I'm sure. I didn't mean to jump down your throat, but to me you'll always be a child. Who is your new bride? Is she someone I would know?"

"I believe you've met her, Papa. She is the cousin of Naomi. I believe that you saw her in the Roman camp just before they escaped and traveled here. She, too, is nineteen and just a wonderful woman."

"Naomi is here?" I asked. "Halleluiah! She and her family did come to Philadelphia, and they are staying here? I've prayed that that was the case; I can't wait to meet up with them again. Abram, it's such a shock to think you are now grown up and married. To think that you are married to Naomi's niece. Call her here so that I may meet her and congratulate her."

"Yes they are all here, and they are so thankful to you and to God for their escape and the ability to start a new life. There are others too, who have come because of you. Silas and some other citizens of Jerusalem have also come; all are thankful to have escaped the horrors of the war. Now come inside and let me reintroduce you to Sara. She, too, will be as excited as I am at your return. Oh, and the most important news is that all of them, including Naomi, have accepted Jesus as their Savior. They are believers and followers of The Way."

"Praise God," I shouted, "I must see all who have come to join the congregation, and most certainly I must see Naomi as soon as possible."

We entered the house that was in the back of the shop where Abram and I had made our tents, and there I was reintroduced to Sara. She was so excited to see me again that she threw her arms around my neck as if I were a long lost friend. I congratulated her on her marriage to my grandson, and then, unable to hide my excitement, I asked her, "What about your aunt, Naomi, Is she well and happy?"

"She speaks of you every day. We received occasional word that you were still alive, but that you were a prisoner of the Romans. We have prayed for you and that you would soon return to us, and now our prayers are answered."

"I thank you for those prayers, and God has been gracious to me."

"Abram, make your papa comfortable, and I will go and fetch Naomi." She flew through the door and up the street. I must admit that my heart seemed to skip a beat.

Abram fixed me something to drink, and I sat on a cushion and made myself comfortable. As he scurried around the room straightening things he told me all about the believers in Philadelphia and how it had grown over the time that I had been gone.

"Some of those who were interrogated by you and the Romans have come here to get away from the war. Not a small number of those have committed their lives to the Lord Jesus as the true Messiah. Some, of course, have retained their old beliefs. However, this is how we knew that you were still well and not rotting in some Roman dungeon. Even those who did not confess their faith to Jesus stopped by and told us of you and how thankful they were for your advice."

"I tried to tell all of the prisoners the Romans released," I said in answer, "that I thought they could find peace here in Philadelphia. And of course I told them they should come here to you, for you and the other believers would help them establish a new life. Our purpose as faithful followers, of course, is our witness to Jesus as the Christ, but it is also to offer help to those who do not believe, to find justice. I know that you did offer that help and encouragement. Your mother and father would be so proud of you, just as I am."

I looked out the door, and I could see that Sara was returning and walking swiftly. Beside her was none other than Naomi. When they entered through the door, I heard Naomi say to Sara, "Now what is so important that I must stop all that I was doing and come immediately home with you and see—" She never did finish her sentence for at that instance her eyes adjusted to the low light inside the house and she saw me.

We looked at each other for a moment, and then she ran to me and embraced me. I had never been a demonstrative person, and I was at a loss at what I should do. Then my emotion overcame my reserve, and I threw my arms around her and lifted her while kissing her on both cheeks. I then set her down. She released me, stood back a step, and looked me over closely.

"You need some good home-cooked food, Caleb. You look awfully thin," she finally said. "I've looked forward to this day for a long time when we could get to know one another without being captives of the Romans."

"There is so much for me to tell you—all of you," I said indicating Abram and Sara who stood mute as they watched our greeting. This embarrassed me, for I felt no different than a love struck youth. I was at a loss for words. I think Naomi was, too.

Finally Abram declared, "I'm closing our shop for today. I will go out and gather all of the members so that we may meet and share our meal in community tonight. Then, Papa, you can tell us about all that you have seen over the last eight months. I'm sure it will be quite a story."

"Yes, I do have a story to tell. It still saddens me as I think back on the terrible things I've witnessed. But let me say that there were also good things that came of my adventure, some of which are right here. You, Abram, and your new wife Sara, and then my meeting up with Naomi again. And by what has been said, the number of new converts to The Way is very gratifying, particularly those who had escaped from Jerusalem."

"You also said something about, Silas," I continued. "He's here? Are you telling me that he confirmed his acceptance of Jesus as his Lord and Savior?"

"Yes, he's here and a more devoted follower you will not find," Abram answered. "He's brought many who have been outcasts to us. What a godly man he is."

"Silas, a godly man? I never would've believed it. Praise the Lord for His acts of redemption."

"Come and walk with me," Naomi said as she led the way to the door. "Let's leave the youngsters alone to get to their business of gathering all of the people for tonight's meeting." Turning to Abram and Sara, she said, "I will feed Caleb as he and I have much to talk about."

I followed Naomi's lead and walked with her still somewhat dazed by all that had transpired over the time since I arrived. "Please take care of the horse for me, Abram. His name is Storm, and yes, he's part of the story I have to tell you."

We walked a short distance in silence as we both were a little embarrassed at being alone together for the first time. "It seems strange," I began, "that we've never been out from the watchful eyes of others since we first met. It's something that's going to take a little getting used to on my part. In addition, it's stranger still that I am walking peacefully along without worrying about my future or wondering when the next attack will come.

"I've thought a lot about you, Naomi. I frequently wondered and prayed that you and your family safely made your escape and came here. I was so pleased when Abram told me that you had indeed made it here to Philadelphia and surprised when he said he was married to your niece."

"You should be proud of your grandson," she responded. "He can be a very convincing speaker. It wasn't long after we arrived that we accepted the Lord Jesus on faith and became participating members of The Way. It's been so fulfilling, and most importantly all of our prayers for you have been answered."

We fell silent again and walked without saying a word the short distance to where she and her sister lived. I drank in all of the sights and sounds around me. People were strolling through the merchant stalls buying the supplies that were needed for the day. Most all seemed content and well fed, not the emaciated ghosts that had inhabited the streets of Jerusalem.

"What are you smiling about, Caleb?" Naomi asked.

"I feel that I'm walking in a dreamland," I answered. "To see all of these people happy and content with their lives; it's in such contrast to what I've seen over the last eight months. It's like a beautiful dream, a dream I frequently had during the final days of the war. That dream had been for Jerusalem and one that will now never come true; but here in Philadelphia it's not a dream—rather, it's a reality."

We reached the door of Naomi's house, and inside I was greeted enthusiastically by her family.

That evening the whole congregation gathered in a large outdoor amphitheater and after a short service I began telling my story. This I did for the next three nights, for there was much to tell.

I soon returned to my labor with Abram and enjoyed putting my hands to work. I also continued my work of evangelizing the truth, and our numbers continued to grow. Most importantly within the following three weeks of my return to Philadelphia, Naomi and I were married.

EPILOGUE

I never learned the truth about what happened to the two tyrants, John and Simon. I believe that John was killed by the Romans shortly before Titus left for Rome. It was also rumored that Simon was captured and taken by the general as a trophy of war and then executed for his role in bringing about the destruction of the once beautiful city of Jerusalem.

Soon after mopping up the remnants of the Jewish defenders, the Roman armies were on the move headed for Rome and eventually a large spectacle and celebration highlighting the plunder and captives that they brought back with them after their defeat of Jerusalem. Once the Jews were paraded through the streets of Rome, they were forced to labor as slaves for the Republic. The young men were immediately put to work building the great coliseum in the center of Rome. It was here, after its construction, that many of the Jews, as well as many believers of The Way, were eventually sacrificed in various games of warfare or other forms of idolatrous worship. This all was done for the amusement and entertainment of the Roman citizens. The barbarity of these useless human sacrifices still brings my blood to a boil.

Many of the other prisoners were sent to Egypt and put to work as slave laborers in the mines located in that land. Those that were not strong enough to work or to travel were summarily executed, for they were of no value to the conquerors.

Even though they had conquered Judea, the Roman occupation forces were under continued attack by those Jews who had escaped Jerusalem or others who were still free and roaming the countryside. Zealots, Essenes and other rebels, or whatever cause they professed to support, continued to harass the Romans, particularly their small patrols that tried to keep the population under tight rein. It was not an organized effort to regain control of Judea but to punish the Romans where they could. Even though the Romans sent out large cavalry and infantry forces to confront these rebels, they met with little success. As quickly as the Romans approached a band of rebels, these freedom fighters would swiftly withdraw to the safety of the fortress called Masada, located at the very southern end of Judea. This impregnable fortress had been built by Herod the Great before the turn of the current century. The situation became untenable and at the same time damaging to the Roman image as conquers of the nation of Israel. Therefore in the second year after Jerusalem fell, General Titus ordered his commander of the Tenth Legion, Flavius Silva, to lay siege to that last Jewish stronghold and to destroy it and its population.

This endeavor became a large undertaking, for the fortress sat atop a mountain accessible only by a narrow twisting path. Its position and the narrow path made a frontal assault on the fortress an impossible task.

The supply of water and food for the defenders was sufficient for a long siege, and there was little they had to do in their own defense but to wait until the Romans climbed the path and tried to batter open the gates. This, the Romans, or any army for that matter, were unable to do. Whenever the Romans did in fact try to attack the fortress in mass, the rebels stood atop the walls and hurled arrows, darts and rocks at them until they retreated. On the other hand, the Romans who were encamped at the base of the mountain had to bring their water and food from far away Ein Gedi. This situation could result in a stalemate that could possibly last a few years or longer unless another stratagem was developed.

In response to the stalemate, Flavius Silva came up with an ambitious plan. First, he had his troops build a siege wall completely around the base of the mountain and set strategic base camps around that wall to prevent any of the citizens in the fortress from either leaving or entering the Masada Fortress. Once this was accomplished, he set to work building a ramp that started at the base of the mountain and extended up the western slope to the only gate that led to the entrance to the fortress. It was a masterful plan and entailed months of labor on the part of the troops and Jewish prisoners taken from Jerusalem. The slope of the ramp was such that his battering rams could then attack and break through the main gate.

There were nearly one thousand Jews, men, women and children, locked behind the gates of the great fortress. They watched with interest as the laborers worked on the ramp around the clock, day after day, week after week, and month after month. When it became clear to the inhabitants of Masada that the ramp was going to succeed, they struck on a plan of their own. The thousand inhabitants at Masada gathered in groups by families, and the night before the Romans began their attack on the main gate they all committed suicide.

When the Romans finally broke through the entrance leading into the fortress they did not find any of the inhabitants alive. Though the victory was clearly to the Romans, there must have been a terrible letdown to the fighting man's spirit when he discovered that all of the work in building the siege wall and the ramp led to nothing.

With the capture of Masada, the Jewish wars came to an end and effectively the Jews were left without a homeland and scattered throughout the known world. Jerusalem, even though it had been utterly destroyed, was declared off-limits to the Jews. This was done so that descendants would not try to rebuild the city or the Temple. They were allowed to enter only once a year and only on special occasions. With the fall of Masada, the Jewish nation ceased to exist.

Naomi and I enjoyed a wonderful marriage that lasted nearly twenty-two years until her death just three short years ago. Our church continued to grow, and we have been able to spread the Good News to a multitude of new believers who have come to accept Jesus as the Christ on faith. It has been truly a blessing to watch the growth in numbers and to also watch my grandson, Abram, grow in faith and become a powerful preacher of the Word. He has led many missions out and around all of the lands that surround the Mediterranean. The work of his son, my great grandson, Joshua, has continued to bring in many new members to the Church. The work of spreading the Love of God to the unbelievers goes on to all of the lands of the known world.

My reason for standing before you at this time is to continue that work and to tell you the Good News and to also tell you that I believe that I am the last of those who personally witnessed our Lord and Savior Jesus Christ when he was with us as the incarnate Son of God. After I am gone, all will have to come to him on faith for there will no longer be eye witnesses to stand before you and tell you of the miracles and wonders he did as he walked the earth. I will soon be joining him and those of my family who have gone on before me, but as long as I have breath within me I will continue to preach the Good News.

Accept what I say as the truth, for I have personally seen all I've related to you with my own eyes. I have witnessed God incarnate in the body and spirit of Jesus Christ. He still lives and sits at the right hand of the one and only God. It is incumbent on you to make that decision while you still live and breathe here on earth, for once you cross to the other side you will not be able to make that choice and you will be condemned to eternal separation from God. Accept now, and thus be granted eternal salvation at the feet of your Lord and Savior.

www.ingramcontent.com/pod-product-compliance
Lightning Source LLC
Chambersburg PA
CBHW020523110726
47899CB00004B/1224